MW01518055

The Scarlett Divide

A. N. Jones

ISBN: 9798873891368

All characters and events in this book are a work of fiction.
Any resemblance to events (real or otherwise) or persons (living or deceased) is unintentional and purely coincidental.

For everyone who believes in a better tomorrow - this is for you.

1

Tired. The word didn't begin to describe how she felt while getting their group ready to make their escape from Dolus. Although if she felt the way she did then undoubtedly the others fared no better. Possibly even worse. Agent Scarlett Wintyrs moved her gaze over those she had come to refer to as her team. Although a couple could still prove to be wildcards, her gut said to trust them. As her eyes moved over each of them in turn - Damon, Zaliki, Feiyan and William - understanding dawned that she would do anything for any of them. Most especially William.

They had had only one night together since their first face to face meeting but,, as far as romantic encounters went, that one was easily the best of her life. Though one which never should have happened. He was her Spymaster. And she was sworn to protect him. With her life if necessary. Scarlett's eyes lingered on the handsome Texan while he leaned against a wall. The fact he continued to valiantly fight against whatever drug their nemesis exposed him to did not go unnoticed. If only they could have analyzed that white powder but the Centurian Agency was compromised. They had no way of knowing who, if any, of the staff remained loyal to William. Mario Vargas did an excellent job of sowing doubt in each of their minds.

Mario Vargas, a Spymaster (though Scarlett was loathe to admit he held the title), proved to be not only the man who once saved her life but also quite possibly the most cunning foe she'd ever faced. In fact, before she encountered him here, she always referred to him as her knight in shining armour. Little had she known, though, that even back then he'd been manipulating events in order to have them unfold in his favour.

What troubled her most was how easily Vargas managed to fool her back then. Despite the fact she had still been relatively new at her job at the time, Scarlett prided herself on being an excellent judge of character. When it came to Mario, however, her instincts steered her in the completely wrong direction. At least now she knew the truth. And, for the moment anyway, they were free of him. Only until his men liberated him from his restraints and the perfectly positioned explosives but Scarlett was comfortable in saying that his freedom would be quite awhile in coming.

For now they needed to continue focusing on getting out of Dolus and into the crowds of people to have even the smallest chance of remaining hidden for a bit while they regrouped. On the plus side, Damon and Zaliki managed to destroy the gems from the Ruby and Sapphire Caress so other Centurian Agency assets remained safely anonymous. Even if they no longer maintained loyalty to William, Scarlett felt better knowing their identities stayed safe.

"Are there any locks on the exit door we need to be concerned about?" Feiyan, former mentor of Scarlett's now turned undercover agent, inquired. The woman single-handedly taught Wintyrs not only everything she knew but also things that normally couldn't be taught. Such as how to see what lies underneath a person's outer facade. Scarlett had been such an excellent pupil that Feiyan thought she could go outside the normal training regime. Which helped further shape the younger woman into the agent she was today. One of, if not the, best agents the Centurian Agency ever had join their ranks.

"One. But no worries. We can get through without a problem." Damon Raynott replied.

A man of mystery, Damon faked his own death after discovering the agency they worked for was trying to kill him. The only way out he'd been able to come up with was actually 'dying'. Which unfortunately led him to joining the black market in order to survive while also using the moniker of 'Tengu' so he wouldn't be discovered. Not only had he managed to build himself up as a well-known black market dealer along with amassing, what amounted to be, an amazing stash of wealth - he also became feared by many as no one knew who this 'Tengu' was.

"Let's just get going then, shall we? I really don't want to be here when his men discover how you lot booby-trapped their boss." Zaliki requested, glancing over her shoulder to view where they'd come from to ensure they weren't yet being followed.

If there was one member of their little team Scarlett was intrigued with almost as much as she was with William, it would be Zaliki. Originally introduced to her by Damon, they'd believed her to be no more than a guardian who looked after one of the stash houses for agents from any agency. Then came the discovery that she was actually a field agent herself. And a damned good one. After helping them out of a tight jam, she'd agreed to leave her own agency to join theirs. A promise that gave Scarlett and William one more person they felt they could trust.

"Agreed." William seconded what Zaliki said.

Scarlett noted the man who now laid claim to her heart was slurring his speech a little more. They couldn't risk any further delays which might prove troublesome - perhaps even deadly - for him. Getting out into the crowds was one thing. Where they would go from there was another matter entirely, she realized.

"Where will we go?" Scarlett asked into the group while leading them to the rear door of Dolus, the exclusive members'-only club Damon and William jointly owned.

"Grand Cayman Island is large but it's still an island." Damon spoke up again, knowing William wasn't up for a long explanation at the moment. "Vargas knows my alias now which pretty much eliminates us using any of my three houses here."

"I don't suppose you have a place under another pseudonym, do you?" Wintyrs glanced over at him as they arrived at the door.

"You know I always have one backup plan - at the very least." He shot her a grin. "He won't even suspect it."

"You used your real name didn't you."

"But of course. No one would ever suspect I'd be foolish enough to use the name I gave the Centurian Agency. I mean if you think about it, doing something like that is incredibly stupid."

"It's incredibly... something... that's for sure." Her mind couldn't quite believe what her ears heard. No one in their field, in their right mind, would use their true name to purchase property. However she had to admit - it'd be extremely unlikely Vargas would consider looking for any kind of real estate owned by Damon Raynott. "Please don't tell me it's another mansion masquerading as a beach house..."

"Oh, no, nothing so extravagant. Michael Malley is the one with the money - not Damon Raynott."

"So just a mansion then?"

"Very funny, Wintyrs." Damon shook his head while unlocking the door. "How's William doing? Think he can walk on his own?"

Scarlett turned her eyes from Raynott and back to their Spymaster. It didn't take a doctor to see he was going downhill - and fast. "Maybe for the moment but I don't think that's going to last long."

Blowing out a breath, Damon nodded slowly. "Alright. You four stay put. Let me see if I can get us a ride. Might not be a hovercar but I think anything is better than nothing. I'll be right back."

Wrapping one of William's arms around her shoulders, Scarlett did her best to support him. When his coordination stabilized she peered over to his other side then smiled when she saw Zaliki there mimicking her her movements. Balancing him between them, Scarlett and Zaliki helped William through the door into the parking lot while Feiyan walked backwards behind them in order to guard their rear.

"I can walk." William protested. "On my own." He clarified when he noted the disbelieving looks on the women's faces. "What? I swear I can."

"Yeah and I'm the sugar plum fairy. I'm calling bull on that one, William." Feiyan said over her shoulder.

"She's right." Scarlett stated softly. "You're shaking with the effort of just standing there let alone putting one foot in front of the other."

"But I…"

"If you do this on your own then we'll be moving even slower and the chances of us being caught rise exponentially." Zaliki felt inclined to point out.

Hating having to be dependent on anyone merely to walk, William grumbled a few incoherent words under his breath then nodded his assent. Sadly, as soon as they supported him in earnest, he discovered they were right. Letting them lead him along also afforded him the opportunity to think more about the drug Vargas used against him. The original design had obviously been to knock him out so he could be secreted away somewhere. Yet there seemed to be more to it than meets the eye. Almost like it was being reactivated with the more he tried to do after initially waking from the effects. He couldn't recall coming across a drug like it. Not during his tenure as Spymaster nor during his time in the field.

"What is taking Damon so long…" Feiyan wondered then raised an eyebrow as a fancy six-seater hovercar painted a lovely deep shade of red came to a stop directly in front of them the doors raising to allow admittance.

"C'mon, you four. Time's a-wasting." Damon called to them from behind the steering yoke. When they didn't immediately climb inside, he wanted to applaud. Only when the women heard his voice did they join him.

Scarlett climbed in first, into the back, so she could help get William situated more easily. "Feiyan was wondering where you were." She said, wrapping her Spymaster into his seat with the factory installed restraints.

"Oh, you know me…" His eyes moved from mirror to mirror in case anyone tried to surprise them. "I had to find the right model then the right colour… it's a whole process."

"You make jokes at the oddest times." Zaliki observed as she sat on the other side of William, letting Feiyan ride up front with Damon.

"Humour - levity, if you will - helps me focus my mind when I'm in a group. It's a long story. Let's say my process is tried and true." Damon raised the hovercar above the ground. "Hold onto your hats folks, we're taking to the air."

"Good." Feiyan nodded her approval. "We will be much harder to track than we would be on any ground route."

"Gotta love getting the seal of approval from the most… um… seasoned agent in this vehicle." He suppressed a grunt when the woman beside him punched his upper arm. Not hard enough to bruise but he definitely felt the impact. Once airborne, Damon put the autopilot on after inputting the address. When that was complete, he turned in his seat in order to look at those in the back without making use of the rearview mirror. "How's he doing?"

"He's almost unconscious again." Scarlett answered in regards to William's condition.

"Alright. Just keep him steady back there. We won't be too long in the air if all goes according to plan."

"I can count on one hand how many things have gone to plan since all of this started." Scarlett observed. "We need him awake in order to get off the island."

"We should be safe for a few hours. I hope." Damon turned back to face out the windshield of the hovercar. "Hopefully that'll be enough time for whatever they dosed him with to get out of his system."

"Any chance you have some analysis equipment at this place of yours? Perhaps we could identify the substance." Feiyan inquired quietly.

Blowing out a breath, Damon shook his head. "You know if I did then it'd be black market. Not to mention illegal…"

"When has that ever stopped you?"

A soft chuckle left him as Damon nodded slowly. "A fair point. Especially since we're driving a stolen hovercar. Yeah. This place we're going to is, ugh I hate to admit this, fully equipped with everything we might need."

"Fully equipped?" Eyebrows raised in surprise, Feiyan turned her eyes to him once more.

"Don't get excited. What I have is nowhere near as good as what is available at the agency but should be enough for our current needs."

Feiyan shook her head upon hearing that. This man seemed almost as resourceful as a Spymaster. From the stories she'd heard about his alter ego of Tengu, she supposed she should have known better. And yet the news still managed to impress. In the back of her mind, Feiyan wondered if they would be able to get off the island even if William were able to lift the lockdown he himself imposed.

The remainder of the ride was conducted in silence. Something Damon wouldn't complain about as it reminded him of before Scarlett Wintyrs fell into his lap. He'd enjoyed his solitude during his time as Tengu yet... being back in the fold... he couldn't argue it felt good. Plus finding out the man who'd been his friend for years was actually the Spymaster for the Centurian Agency. Well, that made his answer to the question of 'will you come back' very easy. In a positive way.

When the small light blue cottage came into view, Damon disabled the autopilot and took the steering yoke in his hands. Lowering the hovercar into the parking space in front of the cottage, Damon turned off the ignition then jumped out and ran to the back to help get William inside.

"This is tiny compared to your beach house." Zaliki remarked.

"Yeah, yeah. Get the front door, will ya?" Damon retorted.

"Will it not be locked?"

"I got this place when you and I were, well, you and I. Press your right index finger where the key should go. I'd wanted to surprise you with this place then you broke up with me the same day I was going to bring you out here to see it." Dragging William out of the vehicle, Damon slung the man into a fireman's carry then started towards the cottage.

"You..." Zaliki stared at him, wide eyed. She'd never been shocked into silence before yet now here she stood with her mouth hanging open and unable to find suitable words for the situation.

"Yeah, yeah. I'm a sentimental kinda guy, what can I say. Could you get the door please? William's heavier than he looks. Guess he's been working out." Damon grunted out as he was only partially fibbing.

Quickly recovering, Zaliki set her right index finger against the sensor which appeared to be nothing more than a keyhole. A slightly warm, tingling sensation was the only indication she had that her fingerprint had been scanned. An audible click reached her ears and the white front door swung open on its own. She'd always known Raynott was security conscious just not to this extent.

"How many people can get this door open?" Scarlett asked as they each passed over the threshold.

"Myself and Zaliki." Going to the single three-person brown leather couch in the living room, Damon gently laid William down then carefully placed a beige throw pillow under his head and dropped a lightweight blanket over his body. "Don't try forcing the door to shut." He called over to Scarlett when he saw her doing just that. "It'll close on its own. Built-in timer of two minutes."

"Very interesting." Wintyrs stated while the door slowly closed, locking once the mechanism connected to the proper point. "But a whole two minutes?"

"Yeah, well, when I programmed it I never knew what I might be carrying. Of course I never for one second thought it'd be a body..." Shrugging, he shot the three women a smile. "And I have to apologize. This place is much smaller and only has rooms furnished for two people. I didn't think I'd be entertaining anyone here."

"We'll manage, Damon. I'm sure we've all had to deal with far worse conditions in the past." Feiyan patted his shoulder before pulling one of the kitchenette's chairs over to the window by the door in order to keep watch.

"She's got a point. Where's this equipment you mentioned?" Eager to try and identify the drug that was used, Scarlett's eyes roamed around but could see no overt signs of where the items might be.

"Let me get a sample of the drug then you and I will explore my little lab." Damon went to a small unit with doors then took out a slim silver, metal suitcase. He opened it on the floor next to the couch William was lying on to reveal the contents.

What she saw made Scarlett whistle in appreciation. "Damn, Damon. That's quite a collection kit."

"Yep." He took out what looked like a cotton swab and rubbed it along the collar of William's shirt and also put some on a piece of tape then covered it with clear plastic in order to ensure nothing contaminated it any further than it already had been. "But you ain't seen nothing yet. Ladies, I'm taking Scarlett to my lab - are you two okay to guard our dearly beloved Spymaster?"

"Something tells me we don't have much of a choice." Shaking her head, Zaliki's words sounded harsh however amusement could be seen in her eyes.

"Well you do but... yeah, no. Not this time." Giving the woman a wink, Damon packed what he collected up, placed them in the case then rose to his feet from the kneeling position he'd been in. "Come on, Scarlett. Let's see what we can find out."

Raising an eyebrow, Wintyrs shrugged before following him out to the small garage the cottage boasted. There was nothing special about the room where a car should be housed. As far as Scarlett could see at any rate. Knowing how Damon loved his hidden places, however, she suspected not all was as it seemed. She crossed her arms while watching him.

"Are you going to make me ask?" Scarlett eventually grew tired of the silence, knowing full-well he wanted to make this as much of a show as he could.

"Despite how tempting that is, no. I want to get William back on his feet as soon as possible." Damon placed the silver case on the single step leading into the house to ensure he wouldn't drop it. "This is something I only want you to know about in case we can't fully trust Zaliki or Feiyan."

"An odd statement considering we left them to watch over William." Pointing out the obvious was not a task she was fond of yet Scarlett knew the point was extremely valid.

"Okay, yes, fair point. But this is... well... different..."

"Why?"

"It's kind of my sanctuary." The admission wasn't one he made lightly. "And the only reason I'm telling you is because I know how much you care about William. I'm hoping that two of us doing the analysis will speed things up."

Surprised at his confession, Scarlett nodded once. As she watched, Damon moved over to the portion of the wall where the main garage door opener hung which was when she noticed a second item with it. One resembling an old-fashioned push button doorbell. While Scarlett wondered what the button could possibly do, Damon reached out and pressed it with his right index finger. When he did, a tired creaking sound reached her ears. A rectangular swath of floor in the centre of the garage lowered down into itself and transformed into a flight of stairs. Wintyrs took a step back in surprise then met Damon's gaze.

"Impressed yet?" Raynott's eyes glinted mischievously.

"Show me your layout first then I'll tell you."

Snorting softly at the noncommittal response, Damon grabbed the silver case. Before starting down the stairs, he motioned for Scarlett to take the lead. Scarlett raised her eyebrows at the gesture, shrugged and did as he bade. Arriving at the top of the stairs, she looked down only to see flickering lights at the bottom. Going underground was bad enough as it played right into her greatest fear of being buried alive. Not to mention her claustrophobia. Add a flickering light into the mixture and, for her at least, it became a recipe for disaster.

Seeing her hesitation, Raynott raised an eyebrow. "You alright? I swear it's safe otherwise I wouldn't keep my equipment down there." He placed his free hand on his companion's shoulder. "I'll be with you the whole time. It's basically one giant room. I didn't bother segregating anything. Besides it's faster to move from one machine to another without walls or doors between them."

"That makes a certain amount of sense." Scarlett acknowledged then started down the stairs, gripping the railings on either side tightly, aware her knuckles were turning white from the pressure being exerted on the railings. Staring straight ahead seemed to help a little as she continued the descent. Eventually arriving at the bottom, Scarlett took a deep breath to steady herself as Damon joined her.

"You doing okay?" Concern laced Damon's words. He'd never seen her like this. Not even when she found him in the underground tunnels. Of course, that being said, he'd kept her fairly well distracted then. Realization set in. "You're claustrophobic. I can do this on my own if you want to go back upstairs."

"As you pointed out, it'll go faster with both of us working on figuring out what the drug is." Scarlett answered softly then shot him a gentle smile. "But thank you for asking."

"Alright. If that changes, if you need to go back upstairs, let me know and go." Damon waited until she nodded before continuing. "Why don't you go to the microscope and have a look at the particles to see if you can figure anything out while I let the spectrometer have a look at part of the same sample. Just in case it's something unidentifiable by the machine or you, I want to run both. Better safe than sorry."

"Right." Taking the tape from him that he'd stuck some of the substance to, Scarlett headed over to the microscope. The setup here was more than any field agent had. At least as far as she was aware. That's why they had the lab at the agency. So places like this weren't necessary. Yet with the situation the agency now faced, having even a miniature lab in the field was welcome.

Heading over to the spectrometer which was across the small room from where Scarlett now worked, Damon prepared the sample and inserted it. Technology had come a long way but he always preferred the older models. Plus the newer ones were all linked together to share information which made tracking the user extremely easy. An event he, as Tengu, needed to avoid. And now, with a Spymaster in this cottage, the need for anonymity was even greater. He prided himself on this cottage. Not just for the lab but for the fact it was in no way connected to any network and remained completely untraceable.

Damon glanced over his shoulder to see how his partner fared. While they were far enough apart that he could detect no overt signs of how her claustrophobia might be affecting her, he instinctively knew the second she had nothing else to focus on she would again be in dire straits. Shifting his weight from foot to foot in order to prevent his soles from aching, he found the silence in the lab deafening. If he were on his own it wouldn't bother him however having another person there encouraged him to engage in conversation. If only to keep his mind off his feet. This was the first time he regretted having only a concrete floor in the lab, if this property remained in his possession after everything was said and done, that might change. He also began considering adding seating of some sort.

"Anything?" Jumping when Scarlett's voice came from right next to his elbow, he regretted allowing his attention to wander. He, in fact, had been staring blankly at the machine running the test. "Sorry. I didn't mean to startle you."

"We should have some results shortly. Did you recognize it?" He didn't turn to her as his eager eyes remained on the spectrometer.

"I've never seen anything like it to be honest."

Pursing his lips, Damon hoped the spectrometer might have better luck. Those hopes were dashed when the monitor connected to the device flickered to life to display the results. Which were no better than what Wintyrs determined.

"Damn it!" Damon slammed his hand down on the top of the metal table where the equipment rested.

"Let me guess. No results found."

Finally turning, keeping his frustration to himself as best he could, Damon locked gazes with her. "Whatever this drug is, it's brand new. What the hell kinda people are we dealing with here?"

"The worst kind. Ones who know us better than we know ourselves."

2

"Vargas is a Spymaster. We both know minds of those particular people work on a completely different level compared to yours or mine." Scarlett tried to reassure him. Unfortunately the result ended up being a rise in her own apprehension.

"Smart enough to concoct his own specialized drug, do you think?"

"Dream up the formula, maybe. Actually create? No. You know the old adage… if you have to ask…"

"I don't want to know, right. Of course, that being said, it's kind of odd. Okay, it's a new drug. The spectrometer should've been able to pick up on the elements involved in the creation."

Knowing he was right, Scarlett paused to look at the machine in question. "There's no chance someone could have found your little lab here and tampered with your equipment is there? It's the only explanation which makes any kind of sense."

Rubbing a hand over his face, Damon shook his head. "I designed this place so no one other than myself could enter."

"Buuuuuut?"

"This is Vargas we're dealing with. Given that… I guess anything's possible."

"Can you restore the spectrometer back to original factory specifications?"

"As long as the programming hasn't been drastically altered then yeah, I should be able to." Damon answered then moved closer to the machine in order to proceed with that course of action. Only a few seconds passed before a single loud beep indicated completion. "Alright you blasted thing. Let's try this again, shall we?" Ignoring the quiet chuckle from Scarlett, Damon inserted the sample for a second time then tapped his fingers impatiently while they waited.

"You do know what they say about a watched pot not boiling, right?" A touch of humour coloured her voice when Scarlett posed her question.

"Technically I'm not watching it, I'm watching the screen."

"Semantics."

"Yeah, yeah." Waving a hand at her, Damon stared at the screen when it came alive with what the analysis uncovered. "Oh, come on!"

"Still nothing?" Scarlett frowned.

"I don't get it. This bloody machine should recognize the smallest ingredient used as the base for whatever this drug is."

"Unless..."

"Don't stop there. I hate cliffhangers."

"Unless the entire drug was created from chemicals or other substances the spectrometer either doesn't or can't recognize. I hate to say this but maybe because this one is older than what's used now..."

"Right. The software may not be able to recognize newly discovered or created... elements for lack of better terminology." Feeling like he could have smacked himself, Damon shook his head. "You do realize the only way we'll get answers is from a more sophisticated lab."

With a sigh, Scarlett nodded. She'd already reached that exact conclusion. "There's just one option."

"I was afraid you were going to say that. Is there anyone at the Centurian Agency you think won't betray us to Vargas? Provided he's still alive and those grenades of ours haven't killed him."

"There's one person there I trust implicitly. And I can all but guarantee she'd shoot anyone on sight if they seemed to be working against not only the interests of the agency but those of the world." Scarlett stated solemnly.

Something in the tone of his companion's voice caused Damon to eye her closely. "Do I know this person?"

"Myrtle."

"Oh." Scratching his head, he pondered that for a moment. "So, yeah, I know of her. A hard-ass from the scuttlebutt that was going around. And definitely not the type who'd be lenient with traitors. If she suspects the agency is corrupted... what do you think our chances are of her helping us?"

"If I ask... probably pretty good."

"Because you're incorruptible?" Raising an eyebrow, Damon gave her a wry grin.

"Partly."

"Do I want to know the other part?"

"She knows she owes me one. Big time." When Scarlett saw him watching her, the question he wanted to ask was obvious. "I'll explain later. I don't suppose you have a means of communication that can't be traced?"

An involuntary chuckle left Damon's partially parted lips. "You, uh, do remember who you're talking to, right?"

"Depends. Are we talking about Damon Raynott or Tengu? I'm pretty sure they're both resourceful."

Damon shook his head. "You know which persona I'm talking about. Tengu, of course. Thanks to my time under that guise, I learned a few tricks that the Centurian Agency doesn't teach. Which, in my opinion, they should. Anyway - to answer your question - of course I have a way to communicate that can't be tracked. Are you worried about Vargas or the agency?"

"Both."

"Ah. Alright, follow me."

Cocking her head to one side, Scarlett shadowed him after grabbing the sample he'd left behind on the spectrometer. When he led her to a rather large screen hanging on the far wall, she wondered what he was up to. Damon moved right up to the wall and pressed a red button installed next to the monitor. A slot opened in the wall under the screen. On a mechanism which sounded like it needed either greasing or oiling, an older model keyboard slid out from the newly uncovered opening alongside a beige box-like contraption. Scarlett leaned down to the box in order to have a closer look.

"Figured it out yet?" Damon watched her. The entire setup was something most people would consider old-school. In fact, he felt certain very few would have the smallest inkling what the box was.

"I think I have a pretty good idea."

"Really?"

"Yep." Scarlett straightened up before turning to face him. "If I'm not mistaken, your little box here is a signal scrambler. Once you activate it, it should light up like the proverbial Christmas tree. How am I doing so far?"

A smile tugged at the corners of his lips while he raised an eyebrow at her. "Spot on. So far anyway. Look closer."

The way he spoke caused Wintyrs to take him seriously so she bent down in order to afford the device a closer examination as he suggested. Uncertain as to what she should be looking for, Scarlett shook her head a bit, returning her gaze to Damon. "Alright. I give up."

"You're sure?" He held his hands up in surrender when her eyes narrowed. Only then did he notice the tiredness in the woman's face. She seemed to be in desperate need of some rest and, if she were anything like him, never would she admit to such. "Okay, got it. You're sure. So, yes, it's a signal scrambler but it can also alter your voice and image should you wish. The agencies banned its use by agents because of misuse. I'm kinda hoping William might overturn that decision until, at the very least, Vargas is no longer a concern."

Scarlett traced the device with her index finger. "I've heard of these from Feiyan. This is my first time seeing one."

"I used to be in the same boat. At least until Jacques showcased this bad boy at the museum prior to putting it on the auction block. Funnily enough - I was the only bidder. It was all done on the forums in order to keep the purchaser anonymous. As far as anyone knows, Tengu is who managed to snag ownership of this lovely gadget."

"Can we get on with it, then?" Hearing how testy she sounded, Scarlett winced. "Sorry."

"Don't be." After giving her a reassuring smile, Damon activated the box in order to prevent their signal being traced then used the keyboard to connect to the Centurian Agency network. Once complete, he navigated to Myrtle's terminal where they stared at a blank screen as the system alerted the user to an incoming transmission. After a couple of minutes the screen flared to life with the image of the woman they sought.

"Hello?" Myrtle frowned at first then her eyebrows shot up when she saw first Scarlett then Damon. "Agent Wintyrs?? And..."

"Myrtle, this is Michael Malley." Scarlett quickly interrupted in case of eavesdroppers.

"He has a remarkable resemblance to..."

"We don't have time, Myrtle. I need you to analyze a substance for me. Our Spymaster has been exposed to it and I need to know if there's any reason for concern."

"Our Spymaster is there with you?? How is that possible?"

"A tale for another time, Myrtle. Can you help us? There are few people I trust right now and you're among them."

Myrtle's eyes widened and she blinked rapidly a few times, taking in what had been said. Struggling to find the right words to respond with proved impossible so instead she went with something unrelated. "How do you propose to send me a sample? I'm assuming you're not near the agency."

"Good guess." Scarlett said and looked at Damon, wondering the same thing. "And a good question. Michael? Please tell me you have an idea."

"Have I ever let you down?" Wincing after asking the question, Damon met Wintyrs' eyes. "Don't answer that. Myrtle, is it?" He pretended not to know the woman on the screen in order to help facilitate Scarlett's lie regarding his identity. Only when Myrtle nodded confirmation did he continue. "Do you have the ability there to receive a small sample via that new-fangled device called Scentsniff?" He hated the name of the thing but the capabilities it possessed.

"You mean that device able to detect a substance then transfer a breakdown to someone, shall we say, more knowledgeable than the sender? Along with a 3-D image?" Disdain coloured Myrtle's voice for machines such as the one described were close to being the bane of her existence.

Damon narrowly avoided rolling his eyes. "Yes. That."

Pursing her lips in thought, Myrtle remained silent for a few moments. "I'm pretty sure we can. It'd have to go through the main server."

"We're desperately trying to avoid that, Myrtle." There had to be some way for her to convey to the other woman - overtly and without outright saying it - that no one at the agency could fully be trusted. The question was how.

Myrtle's eyes narrowed further. Something Scarlett never suspected them capable of. "Hmm… I think I understand. Is there *anyone* else here you would trust with this?"

"None."

"Give me a few minutes. I'll see if there's a way we can do this and if anyone asks I'll tell them I need to run some tests without putting our entire network at risk. Everyone knows what it means when I say that." The screen went black before either of them could respond.

"Uh… what just happened? And what the hell did she mean by that?" Damon turned wide eyes to his companion.

Hiding a smirk behind her hand in case the other woman reappeared on the screen without warning, Scarlett carefully thought about her answer. "Myrtle's tests can be somewhat… explosive… at

16

times.   And if she doesn't do the proper tests then unwelcome consequences have been known to happen."

"Unwelcome consequences?   I gather you have experience with this?"

"One of her gadgets nearly decapitated me during a firefight."

"Okay - I really need to hear the story behind that!"

"I've opened a can of worms, haven't I?" Scarlett shook her head a couple of times.   "Let's save it for a rainy day when we're not on a commlink with the agency, okay?"

Pretending to pout, Damon shrugged.   "Fine but only if you promise."

"Are you serious?"

"Deadly." He gave her a toothy grin.

"I promise."

"There. Now was that really so hard?"

Scarlett opened her mouth to fire off a rebuke when the screen flared back to life.   "Myrtle, what's the verdict?" She ignored Damon's relieved look.

"What do you think? Would I be wasting my time here right now if I hadn't been successful?"

Scarlett bit back a sarcastic response to the clear disdain in Myrtle's voice. She needed to remember the position Myrtle worked could be taxing for someone who never went in the field. "I'm sorry. Do you think this will work?"

"Honestly? I have no friggin' clue. The tech said my terminal has its own number for the next few hours in order to facilitate my tests." Myrtle typed something on her keyboard just prior to a ten-digit number appearing at the bottom of their screen.   "Can you send your thing to that number please?"

"On it." Damon inserted the sample into the Scentsniff then punched in the number on the screen. "It's, uh, working on it."

"Working on it?   What kind of connection do you have there? Transfer should be instantaneous." Myrtle rubbed her forehead. "You do know how busy I am, don't you?"

"Oh, stop it, Myrtle." Having had enough, Scarlett snapped at the other woman.   "This is for the Spymaster and takes priority over anything and everything else. He was exposed to it. I need to know if there's a counter-agent we can use, if it's more dangerous than we thought, or if he just needs to ride it through until all the effects are over and done with."

Swallowing after the berating, Myrtle stared at them. No agent had ever taken that particular tone with her before and, for a few seconds, she was speechless. She gave herself a small shake. Their Spymaster needed her help. No way she could refuse the request. "Forgive me, Agent Wintyrs. What you've sent has arrived. Do you want to stay on the line or call back in a few minutes?"

"We'll wait." Scarlett crossed her arms to reiterate her point.

"Bear with me then." Myrtle switched the screen back to black as she couldn't work with people watching her.

"She's, uh, interesting." Remarked Damon when they were put on hold - again.

"You're the master of understatement." Scarlett paused, watching him thoughtfully. "Wasn't Myrtle there when you were at the agency originally?"

"If she was then she was just a tech. I tended to deal with someone else. Now I think on it though, I do recall hearing her name in passing. Patrick said she was the best he'd seen in years."

"Patrick?" Scarlett frowned, the name unfamiliar to her. "I've never heard of him."

"He left for another agency around the same time you started."

"Another agency? I thought that wasn't allowed except for extenuating circumstances or unless agreed upon by the Spymasters in charge of both agencies." Scarlett raised an eyebrow.

"Yep. And they did."

"Which one did he go to?" Even as she asked, Scarlett felt certain she knew the answer.

"The Orion Agency. And yeah, I'm pretty sure he's still there. Like Vargas, Patrick believes he's the best of the best. He does have a... oh, let's call it what it is... an evil streak. He's a right royal bastard. When he wants to be, that is. And he's damned smart when it comes to creating gadgets and stuff." Damon frowned. "Smart enough to make this drug actually."

"You think Vargas misled us when he mentioned getting his money's worth?"

"Wouldn't you? I doubt he'd want anyone to know or think his agency produced it." Shrugging, he glanced at the blank screen. "Knowing William as long as I have, I know how he thinks. I have no doubt Vargas plans things out in much the same way."

"An interesting point." Scarlett wanted to say more but was interrupted when Myrtle's image popped back up on the screen.

"Myrtle?"

"I have some answers for you. Do you want the good or bad news first?" Pushing her glasses back up her nose, she gazed at the two people on her monitor while waiting a reply.

"Just... either... I don't care."

"Alright, let's start with the bad news. I was able to identify the components used in the drug."

"How is that bad news?" Damon wondered how this woman defined bad news.

"Let me finish, please. There is no antidote that will work."

Scarlett groaned, rubbing her face with one hand. "And the good news?"

"Well to start - the drug isn't a poison so it won't kill him. Given enough time the effects will wear off. Finally, once it does, you need to make sure he doesn't become too active. If that happens the drug will reactivate if it hasn't completely left his system. What's more interesting is that it seems to have been biochemically engineered for a specific person's DNA. And I guess we already know for whom it was designed." Myrtle revealed then met Scarlett's eyes. "I don't suppose you have any idea who created it, do you?"

"Suspicions only... why do you ask?"

"I've seen something similar before. I'm trying to remember where." Taking her glasses off, Myrtle cleaned them absent-mindedly while wracking her brain. "So familiar..."

Pressing her lips together, Scarlett refrained from mentioning the name their suspect. She didn't want to lead Myrtle to an incorrect conclusion. "Take your time, Myrtle."

With a glance at the woman standing beside him, Damon wondered at her sudden shift from being hurried to what appeared to be complete patience. Then he hid a smile behind his hand. Of course. Now that she knew their Spymaster would be alright in the end, there was no reason to rush. Although Damon would argue the clock was still ticking. Even though the cottage he'd brought them to was technically off the grid and in his true name, concern lingered that Vargas would find them. And with the way their luck had been running, that would happen sooner rather than later.

"Patrick. I'll be damned. It has to be Patrick." Myrtle stopped herself before she broke her glasses in anger.

"Why would you say that?" Scarlett asked, eager to learn how the woman reached the same conclusion Damon had.

"Well, two things come to mind. One - he's the only one I know who might be remotely capable of crafting something like this. Two - I know the real reason he ended up at another agency."

"Are you going to share?"

"He's a sick bastard who wanted to start testing his creations on live humans."

3

Scarlett's eyebrows shot up. The practice Myrtle suggested her former supervisor wanted to implement had been outlawed a long time ago as being both cruel and inhumane. To hear someone - anyone - in their agency wanted to bring it back into play shocked her to her core. The silence from Damon let her know he felt the same way.

"Yeah. That's how I was when I first found out. We were ordered to keep it quiet." Myrtle revealed.

Blowing out a breath, Scarlett slowly nodded. "Thanks, Myrtle. For everything. Do me one more favour?"

"Of course."

"Pay close attention to the details."

The abrupt change in Myrtle's face told Scarlett she understood the message attempting to be conveyed to her. Passphrases weren't often used. This one was ancient. Even so, Wintyrs hoped the other woman would verbalize her thoughts.

"More than usual?" The question Myrtle posed in response indicated to those listening that she not only understood but sought to know how bad things were.

"Very much so."

"Consider it done. Is there a dedicated comms unit I can reach you on?"

"Michael will transmit some information to you. Do me a favour and don't reconnect to the agency network until after you receive, put somewhere safe, and then delete that from your system. Our Spymaster's life may hinge on your actions."

"Understood. If I come across anything I think might interest you, I'll be in touch." A beep from her monitor advised the trio the message

21

Damon sent had been received. "Oh, and Agent Wintyrs? Please be careful." Myrtle cut their communication before either of the other two could respond.

Damon shut everything down while thinking about his first real conversation with Myrtle. Even though he didn't really do much talking. After turning to the only other person in the room with him, he allowed his eyes to rest on her face. Some of the worry lines had vanished from around her eyes. The tiredness, however, clearly remained.

"Now that we have some answers, how about we head back upstairs? We should all avail ourselves of this window of peace and quiet to get some rest." He didn't think his suggestion would go over well despite how she obviously felt.

"You love jinxing us, don't you." Scarlett tilted her head from side to side, trying to stretch out the forming kinks.

"Maybe. Well? Shall we?"

"Yeah. Let's. Who knows how long we'll have."

Damon hid his surprise at the ease with which she agreed. Without another word, he led her back to the entrance and lowered the stairs once more in order for them to depart. He let her go first as he believed himself to be a true gentleman through and through. The second they reached the top he could see more of the stress leave her body. He needed to help her past whatever fear besides the claustrophobia surfaced when she entered enclosed spaces.

"You're unusually quiet." Scarlett observed while watching him close and secure the entrance to his lab.

"Am I? My apologies."

"Oh, not necessary. I was enjoying the silence." Teasing someone was not something she often did. So when it happened, she tended to wonder if she was doing it right.

Turning to his partner, Damon scarcely believed his ears. "Now I know you're tired. When we get back inside I think you should rest first. It's a double bed, we can move William in there and you can stay with him. One of us will take the couch and we'll switch off after a few hours."

"If Zaliki and Feiyan are amenable then yeah. I can live with that arrangement."

Damon nodded, leading her straight to the bedroom. "Before you say anything - don't bother. We both know the others will agree that you get to sleep here and now with William." He held up a finger when he saw her open her mouth to protest. "I said not to bother. It's an argument you're not gonna win. Get in that bed. I'll be right back with William."

Scarlett's mouth was still partially open when he vanished from the doorway. Rubbing her eyes tiredly, she quickly assessed her surroundings in order to take stock of entry/exit points or anything else which might prove to be or become a threat. One window and one door appeared to be the only access ports. The walls were painted a dark blue making the already small room feel even more so. If it weren't for the window, she'd find this bedroom a bit too much for her claustrophobia. In an effort to make the place a little more bearable, Scarlett moved to the window then cranked it open. The ocean air was as clean here as at Damon's beach house.

"We really need to talk to William about how much he's working out." Damon grunted, carrying their Spymaster in using a fireman's carry and gently placed him on the bed.

"Oh, stop. You're only complaining because you're not the one getting carried around." Scarlett gently covered William with a light blanket. "Thanks for bringing him."

"Get some rest." Raynott flashed her a smile then headed out, closing the door behind him.

Once he was gone, Scarlett climbed into the bed next to her Spymaster. She pulled the same light blanket over herself given it was large enough before carefully placing an arm across his chest, snuggling into his side. When she woke she needed to remember to thank Damon for placing William on his back.

Returning to the other two ladies of their little team, Damon released a deep breath. "Okay, I've got them both down for a nap."

"You sound as though they're children and you're a parent." Feiyan shook her head. "What were you two able to uncover about the drug?"

"Oh, you're gonna love this…"

Zaliki and Feiyan listened avidly as Damon recounted what they'd uncovered. When he finished, he was met with silence. Whether they were shocked or if they were processing what he'd revealed, he couldn't say.

"I keep a small supply of food here - of the frozen variety. You two want something?" Damon offered when his stomach grumbled loudly.

"That would be nice, thank you." Feiyan flashed him a smile. "I don't believe either of us is picky…"

"I'll heat up some personal sized pizzas. I have a few stockpiled." He left the room, needing a bit of time for himself.

Feiyan leaned back in the chair she'd been in since their arrival. With a soft sigh she steepled her fingers. Deep in thought, she didn't realize the only other occupant of the room was studying her.

"Do you believe what he told us?" Zaliki finally asked the biggest question on her mind.

Raising an eyebrow, Feiyan looked at her. "Are you saying you don't?"

"I'm having trouble swallowing it if I'm being completely honest."

"Why?" Curious as to the reasoning of how the other woman felt, Feiyan found herself compelled to make the inquiry.

"Not because the explanation comes from Damon... because of who, or what, they went to for the answers we needed." Zaliki pressed her lips together.

"You mean Myrtle?" A soft chuckle left Feiyan's barely parted lips. "She's a genius and can be trusted."

"Why do you say that?"

"I'm the one who vetted her for the agency before she joined. I carefully cultivated her way of thinking to coincide with both mine and Scarlett's. She. Can. Be. Trusted."

Blowing out a long breath, Zaliki nodded. Her muscles relaxed at the same time - a first since they'd made their escape from Dolus. "Then let's concern ourselves with the what. Myrtle was at the agency when they spoke with her. Even if her line had been separated and secured - that doesn't mean the conversation wasn't overheard."

"Unfortunately very true. If I understand Damon correctly - even if they listened in, they would be unable to trace the call back to this location. Plus Myrtle knows how to cover her tracks. Is there anyone within the Orion Agency you would lend the same amount of trust in that we do Myrtle?"

"There is one. For much the same reason as yours but Damon was correct about Patrick not being there. He'd be in charge of her section. I wouldn't be surprised if Vargas plans to do the same as William and purge his agency of those he considers bad seeds. Those who don't think like him. Though I doubt he'll merely fire them."

"You think he'll kill them."

"Yes, Feiyan, I do. I have a couple of others I trust there with my life as well."

"And you want to get a message to them." Twisting a loose strand of hair around her fingers, Feiyan contemplated Zaliki's dilemma.

"Preferably before Vargas resumes his throne, yeah."

"Then we ask Damon if he has a way to send one to those you believe will be in danger. What we should do is have everyone meet at a secure location. Like the Centurian Agency - after it's been purged of course." Feiyan said, thinking out loud. "And we should see what William's thoughts are as well."

"You know what I love most about this cottage?" Damon returned, deftly balancing three plates, each of which holding a small one-person pizza. "Sound carries depending on what room you're in." He handed each of the women a plate.

"So you..." Zaliki accepted the plate while mentally listing the implications of what he'd said.

"Heard every word, yep. On the plus side it means you don't have to repeat everything."

"It would also suggest we should have no expectation of privacy during our stay." Shaking her head slightly while at the same time taking the proffered plate, Feiyan believed this news should have been revealed to them upon their arrival.

"You shouldn't have that expectation anywhere. You, of all people, know that." Moving over to the only free seat in the room, Damon sat on the couch next to Zaliki. "So how many people are we talking about when you say you want to warn those you trust?"

"No more than five." Zaliki replied between bites. She hadn't realized how hungry she'd been until that first bite of the pizza hit her tastebuds.

Falling into thought, Damon gave her answer some consideration. One person proved no challenge to send something to but five? That was an entirely different story altogether. The more recipients, the higher the probability of the message being discovered and possibly traced. He chewed on his pizza while contemplating how he could go about accomplishing her request. For him, there was nothing more fun than doing what seemed impossible to others. Then it clicked. A randomizer. That's what he'd need to even consider making this not only possible but also successful.

"He's smiling." Zaliki had been watching Damon's face as his silence had been becoming a little unnerving.

"Not only smiling. He reminds me of the Cheshire Cat." An involuntary shudder ran through Feiyan. The character was one of the few things which haunted her nightmares whenever she thought of it.

"I need to go to the auction house." Damon said out of the blue.

"Are you kidding?? You'd be arrested as soon as any officer spotted you. Or worse."

"Feiyan, I need a randomizer and I don't have one. I've never had the use for it until now. If we want to get the word out to Zaliki's colleagues then I need to check out the black market merchandise. Jacques won't turn me in." At least Damon hoped he wouldn't. If he was still alive. Hopefully Vargas had been lying about not being able to get information from a corpse. The auction house owner was too much of a resource for Damon. He couldn't lose him.

"Perhaps not but what's to stop others from doing so?" The intensity with which Damon felt the need to do this radiated off him in waves and Feiyan knew she needed to break through in order to make him see reason. "Can you not access the auctions online? Like when you attempted to secure the painting from the fake Tengu - whom, I am guessing, was Amir?"

"Good guess." Finishing his pizza, Damon rubbed his chin, letting what she said roll around in his mind a for a little while. "I could try hacking into Amir's fake Tengu account..." following Feiyan's lead, he began thinking out loud, "there could be a chance Vargas has put an alert system on it though now Amir is dead..."

"Are we certain of that?" Zaliki asked out of the blue. "Yes, Vargas showed Scarlett and William a head in a box but can we be absolutely certain it was really Amir's? What if, like so many other things cropping up lately, it was an illusion." She was quite aware of them both now staring at her. "Don't tell me the thought hadn't crossed your minds."

"I'm not about to lie and say I had the same idea. That hadn't even occurred to me." Groaning, Damon rubbed his temples with both hands. "And now I won't be able to think about anything else."

"You're awfully quiet, Feiyan."

"Am I, Zaliki? Perhaps it is due to the suggestion you just planted in our heads."

"Well, we know how Damon feels about it... what do you think?"

"Yes, Feiyan." Supporting Zaliki, Damon looked at the other woman in the room. "Please share and let me not wallow alone in frustration."

No longer feeling relaxed, Feiyan rose to her feet in order to begin pacing. "What do I think? I think we have underestimated Vargas at every turn. I think we must agree that not only is he possibly more intelligent than our own Spymaster but that he is also resourceful beyond belief. And I think we need to consider the distinct possibility that he has anticipated every single move we have and will make. I cannot see how we will gain victory over him."

4

Scarlett stirred when she felt a finger lightly stroking her cheek. As wakefulness penetrated her dreams, she remembered where she was and kept her reflexes in check. Had she not then her companion more than likely would have found himself flying across the small room. Opening her eyes, she found William's face right in front of hers on the pillow, a tender smile on his lips.

"Hi." When the one word left his lips in the form of a whisper, much more than its true meaning managed to be conveyed. His warm brown eyes gazed into her blue ones the second her eyelids parted while he continued to stroke her cheek with his finger.

"You do know..." Scarlett kept her voice quiet for she had no desire for them to be disturbed just yet, "how lucky you are right now, don't you?"

"You mean because I'm not lying in a heap on the other side of the room?" The one corner of William's mouth twitched, fighting a smile.

"Yes." She confirmed, reaching up to cup his face tenderly with one hand. "How are you feeling?"

"Honestly? Still tired but my brain doesn't feel as muddled. Where are we anyway?" William managed to tear his eyes away from her face in order to cast a glance around at their surroundings.

"A cottage Damon had squirrelled away."

"Still on the island?"

"Yep."

"Huh. I only knew about his three large houses... interesting that he has a fourth, smaller one. It's not under Michael Malley's name is it."

"No, William, it's actually under his true name."

"Clever. Not even I would think to look for a property under your real identities. Especially not here. Were you able to get any answers while I was out?"

Sitting up and leaning her back against the headboard, Scarlett's brow creased into a small frown. It was becoming more and more apparent that this man's brain was always engaged. Almost as if, for him, the actual act of thinking was a drug. She doubted anything she said would be able to put a stop to it either.

"Yes. Thanks to Damon and Myrtle."

"Myrtle?? You risked contacting the agency??" His disbelief caused his eyebrows to shoot almost into his hairline as he sat up next to her. "We have no idea who we can trust there! Your call was probably traced and the location relayed to Vargas!"

"Hey. Relax. Contrary to popular belief, Damon and I do know what we're doing. I trust Myrtle implicitly. I know in my heart she'd never betray us. As for being traced, I wish them all the best of luck on that. Damon used a scrambler. I mean, come on, you know us better than that."

Taking a deep breath to calm himself, William nodded. "I'm sorry. You're absolutely right. Please continue." He knew this probably wasn't the right time for what must seem to her to be a debrief but he couldn't help himself. At least this round of sleeping together they'd kept their clothes on. A fact which helped ease his conscious. A bit.

"Anyway... what we found may surprise you." Scarlett hated talking shop in bed however obeying her Spymaster's wishes was deeply ingrained and she told him everything she, Damon and Myrtle uncovered. When she finished, the deep breath he released could not be missed.

"Wow." William fell silent, absorbing what she'd shared. "So Vargas really did have this drug engineered just for my DNA, huh? I wonder if he did the same for the other Spymasters." Shaking his head, he moved to get up only to find Scarlett's hand gently, but firmly, pressing against his chest to stop him.

"Didn't you hear what I said, William? You can't be very active until we're certain the drug has completely run its course and left your system."

"Believe me, I heard you..."

"But?"

"But I really need the men's room."

"Oh! I'm so sorry. It's in the hallway. From what I've seen this place only has one bedroom and one bathroom. Do you want, or need, some help?" Scarlett silently berated herself for attempting to guess his needs.

"I think I can manage." William covered the hand she kept on his chest with one of his own. "I give you my solemn word I'll come straight back here the second I'm finished, okay?"

With a nod, followed by a quick kiss, she watched him go then stood up from the bed and wandered back to the window. For the first time in awhile, she found her mind at peace. Knowing it wouldn't last only made her relish the feeling more. Scarlett stood there, staring out the window at the tranquil ocean water, losing herself in the scents as well as the sounds that came with the view. An arm wrapping around her waist from behind then pulling her back to lean against a solid chest made her sigh softly. Although she wondered yet again if the man holding her had a death wish.

"I really should stop doing that shouldn't I..." William remarked after feeling her muscles tense in preparation for defence.

A shiver ran through her body when his breath brushed against her neck. He made her feel weak in the legs, a feat no other man managed to accomplish. "I mean, if you want to see some of my moves, all you have to do is ask."

"Such a tease." Leaning his head down, he kissed her neck tenderly, pleased she'd decided to sleep with her hair tied back.

"William! You're supposed to be resting." Scarlett said, fighting back a groan of delight.

"You make it very difficult to follow those orders." He mumbled into her neck, grinning when he felt another shiver go through her.

"Okay, no." Turning in his arms in order to face him, Scarlett noted a mischievous gleam in his eyes. "Do you really want the drug you were given to reactivate and render you unconscious again? Helpless? At the mercy of whomever stumbles across you?"

That was akin to putting ice on a fire for William. He let his arms fall away from her waist with a sigh of longing. "No, of course not."

"Good." Wintyrs responded. Seeing his expression, she reached up and caressed his cheek. "We'll have time for us later. Right now we need to ensure you continue on the course you're on plus we need to get off this island. Which in turn means you're going to have to lift the travel restrictions."

"Mmh..." William moved back to the bed, sitting on the edge of the mattress. "I don't want Vargas being able to get off the same time we do..."

"Couldn't you just impose the restriction on him and his forces? Especially Mike?" Having a gut feeling it wouldn't be wise to sit next to him, Scarlett remained where she was with her back to the window, gaze lingering solely on him.

"It'd be next to impossible to restrict his forces. I don't know who they are. Even if I did, they could easily use fake identification. Travel doesn't require DNA identification or verification. Yet. Or they could use private travel arrangements like you and Damon did to get on the island." William shook his head. "I hate saying something's impossible but this one most definitely is. If we want off this island, I'll need to open travel up to anyone and everyone."

Scarlett crossed her arms. That hadn't been the answer she'd hoped for. She wanted to get a head start on Vargas. Those hopes were now dashed. Keeping her eyes on William, she could see the gears in his mind still turning. Finding a problem without a solution was annoying him. A fact he couldn't hide no matter how he tried. Not from her.

"Unless..." William perked up suddenly with a grin. "I think I've got it!"

"As long as it's not contagious..."

"Ha ha. Very droll." Rolling his eyes at her unexpected yet welcome teasing, he shook his head a bit before continuing his train of thought. "Theoretically I could lift the ban for the five of us only. Once we're far enough away, I can call back and lift it completely."

"How much suspicion would that raise? Will Vargas be able to figure out our mode of transportation and stop us before we have a chance?" A good agent knew that to get the best out of their Spymaster, they needed to pommel him or her with questions. Any holes in a complete plan needed to be weeded out prior to implementation. Which was precisely what Scarlett would do. Especially if it kept his mind busy so that his body could rest.

William blinked at the questions. As he hadn't been formally presenting an idea, expecting them wasn't part of what was going through his mind. Given with whom he spoke, however, he should've seen it coming. And he was impressed she'd found holes as quickly as she did. "Suspicion? Likely a lot. As for your other point... it really all depends on when I make the call. For example if I do it now then yes, he'll absolutely be able to have time to place men in strategic locations. That being said... if we wait until we're actually on board our chosen mode of transportation then the likelihood of him figuring out what we're doing drops - but doesn't vanish entirely."

Scarlett's attention shifted to the doorway when Damon appeared there without warning. "Damon, hey."

"I thought I heard voices." Raynott gave the duo a smile when William turned to face him. "Good to see you awake again, bud. An unconscious you is no fun at all."

"I'm not quite sure how I should take that..." Narrowing his eyes momentarily, William chuckled to let his friend know there were no hard feelings. "Scarlett's been catching me up on what you found out about the drug. Now I'm trying to figure out getting us off this blasted island."

"Good. The sooner the better. Especially with the crazy theory the three of us just came up with." Damon cryptically stated, leaning against the doorframe.

"Do I want to know?" William raised his eyebrows.

"Yes and no. the point has been made that Vargas is, well, diabolical to put it mildly." He looked at Scarlett then back to William. "We think Amir is still alive."

Scarlett had been about to sit next to William but froze where she was - only one stride from the window. "William and I saw his head. In a box."

"Are you sure? One hundred percent sure? Is there any way - any way at all - that what you were shown was fake. A hologram or even a fake head done up to look like Amir's with phony blood? How closely did you look?"

Trying to keep her breathing steady and even, Scarlett let herself look back into her memories. Once again, her photographic memory might come in handy for this mission. She knew both men watched her. They were well aware of her memory as well as her trick of replaying what she'd seen. After a few minutes, though, she blew out a frustrated breath.

"I can't tell. If it was a fake then it was a damned good one. What I can say is there was no pooled blood inside the box." Scarlett forced her feet back into motion, taking a few more strides to the bed then sat down beside William.

"Which could mean only one of two things. Vargas had Amir's head chopped off then waited for the blood to drain before putting it in the box..."

"Or?" Damon prompted William when the other man stopped speaking.

"Or you guys are right and what we were shown was fake. Which means Amir is alive."

5

Zaliki rose from the couch when she saw Damon returning with Scarlett and William. Motioning with her head, she indicated for the Spymaster to take her seat. No one needed to ask if Scarlett would join him there. Feiyan tapped her fingers on her knee while watching the others get settled.

"So now that we're all here..." Feiyan began, stopping when William raised a finger.

"I know Scarlett and I probably weren't in that bed long but please tell me you each managed to get some rest." William's eyes moved to the other three in turn.

"We rested enough." Feiyan answered for them. "Judging from your faces, I think I'm safe in assuming Damon shared with you what we have... reluctantly... theorized." When the pair nodded, the older woman took pity. Especially on William. The man looked as if his entire world was crumbling around him which, Feiyan guessed, in essence it was. "William, I do not think there would have been any way for you to have foreseen any of what has transpired."

"You can't be sure of that." The dejected tone in William's voice succeeded in drawing all attention to him.

"William..." Scarlett took one of his hands and squeezed gently, "don't beat yourself up over any of this. Please."

"Yeah, how about instead you fill us in on Patrick." Damon suggested, not enjoying seeing his friend the way he was. Although he couldn't deny feeling some of the same knowing they had undoubtedly lost Dolus.

"I don't know much about him except for the notes my predecessor left in his file."

"Which you've read, I'm sure."

"Of course."

"You never met him?" Scarlett frowned. "Even when you were..."

William gave her a warning look. "Can we not..."

"Don't you think they deserve to know? Haven't each of them proven themselves to you?" Shifting on the couch in order to look him in the eyes, Wintyrs refused to waver on her stance. "You've entrusted them with your true identity - you may as well share the rest."

"About him being the Shadow?" Feiyan asked innocently, looking non-plussed when William's head snapped around in shock. "Oh don't be so surprised. It didn't need a genius to figure it out. There's a way you hold yourself at times that screams you were once an agent. The fact the Shadow's antics both started and stopped the exact times you were an agent was way too coincidental. Remember - agents are trained observers."

William's mouth opened and closed a few times with no sound coming out. "Damon?" He finally recovered his senses, letting his gaze remain on Feiyan despite addressing the other man.

"Hmm?"

"Did you know?"

"I suspected. Although that didn't happen until I became Tengu. It made a certain amount of sense. New Spymaster, Shadow disappeared." He shrugged. "It's nice to know I was right though."

"And the Orion Agency... well we thought perhaps we'd been able to eliminate the Shadow once and for all. He was a menace to some of our agents." Zaliki winked at William as she'd been one of those agents.

"Wow... okay..." William's stunned silence broke once more. "Well... I can honestly say I thought I was far more discreet regarding my secret identity." Blowing out a breath, he wondered how many others held the same beliefs as the agents sitting with him here and now. "Alright, so now you know... yes... I ran into Patrick a few times when I was being equipped for missions however he wasn't my assigned tech. In passing he seemed nice enough, almost friendly even which is rare for someone in that department. They don't like creating attachments in case their assigned agent or agents are lost."

"Then can you share with us what your predecessor put in his file?" Damon pushed again.

Rubbing his eyes with his free hand, William gave the question some thought. Technically he shouldn't. However if Patrick was working for or with Vargas then, in the interest of cohesion, he needed to. "Genius level intellect, holier than thou, know-it-all attitude. Can say and make you feel as small as an ant with barely any effort... I could go on. Do you want more?"

"Ahh, no... I think we get the picture." The description William gave did absolutely nothing to assuage Damon's nerves. If anything, he felt more on edge. "Did the file say why he was sent to another agency?"

"I'm assuming Myrtle told you and Scarlett." Even if that hadn't been the case though, William knew by this point he'd have shared the information anyway. When Damon nodded to confirm his suspicions, however, it for some reason made him feel more at ease regarding divulging the sensitive information. "Well, as each of you know, changing allegiances to another agency is not only frowned upon but is also punishable - unless extenuating circumstances exist or the Spymaster of each agency agrees to the action. In Zaliki's case, we're using the extenuating circumstances condition. Which is what we'll also use for any of her compatriots that she trusts who wish to get away from Vargas. Patrick, from what I understand, was akin to a hot potato."

"So no agency wanted him?" Zaliki found that most interesting if that were indeed the case.

"Sadly, that's precisely what I mean. The methods he wanted to use were... barbaric to put it mildly. I saw some of his denied requests. The Orion Agency were the only ones to step forward. Their Spymaster promised to properly train and reform him. Obviously now we know the real reason - Vargas wanted him. Back then, my predecessor would've been relieved to have him taken off our hands. Otherwise..." Trailing off, William hated the thought of what the consequences were which the man faced.

"Patrick would've been executed, wouldn't he." Scarlett hazarded a guess. Judging from the look William gave her, she was right. One of the few times she wished not to be.

"Yeah. That's how dangerous he was deemed."

"So we just let the Orion Agency have him?? Shouldn't the fact they were the only agency to volunteer to take him have raised red flags somewhere??" Stunned over hearing this development, Damon couldn't wrap his mind around why it was allowed to happen.

"Damon... the order to execute an agency asset is one no Spymaster ever wants to make. The fact Patrick's case nearly arrived at that precise point tells me how desperate things must've been. So when the Orion Agency stepped forward offering what was tantamount to rehabilitation, of course it would have been accepted. Probably with no questions asked. As long as the life could be spared, then the promise they'd made would've been more than enough."

"Great. So add him to Vargas and we have a recipe for something beyond disaster." Bowing his head, Damon stared at the floor for a moment as he organized his thoughts. "If they've taken out every other Spymaster like what your computer programme told you, shouldn't you have received some kind of alert? You know, something along the lines of 'danger, danger'? There's no way Vargas could've programmed it to tell you what he wanted you to see?"

"You know... you questioning everything is making me doubt it all." Removing his hand from Scarlett's, William rubbed his face with both hands. Leave it to Damon to bring up what he did. "Feiyan? You designed it... could Vargas do what Damon suggests?"

Feiyan tapped her knee with her fingers again. "As we all know - anything is possible. But I would swear on the graves of my children that what's been suggested falls into the realm of impossibility."

William groaned. "He's not finishing with me..." he looked at Scarlett.

Shaking her head, Wintyrs met his gaze. "He's starting with you."

6

"Well, that changes the whole ballgame now, doesn't it." Remarked Damon, raising his face to peer around at the group again. "Diabolical doesn't begin to cover it if that's what Vargas has done." He started pacing the room. "If true, though, could you reach out to any of the other Spymasters to get help?"

"It's possible..."

"But?"

"There's only two places that can be done from."

Raynott stared at the other man, pausing his pacing. "Let me guess. Dolus or Centurian Agency headquarters."

"Yes..."

"Well we sure as hell aren't returning to Dolus..." Pausing at the expression on William's face Damon shook his head several times. "No. Absolutely bloody not! Do you have any inkling in that overly large brain of yours what a bad idea that is?? That's like pouring gasoline on a bloody inferno, mate! No way in hell should we be considering this course of action!"

"At this point, Vargas would never expect it."

Throwing his hands up in the air, Damon couldn't contain his exasperation. "And there he goes considering it. What happened to getting off this island, eh??"

"Damon..."

"No. Just... give me a bit." Raynott walked out the back door to stand on the deck. He didn't want to chance saying something he'd regret.

"How certain are you Vargas wouldn't expect us to go back to Dolus?" Scarlett's brain shifted into overdrive as she began planning ahead for the eventuality. "And do you need to be there or can you give one of us your credentials to log in plus what the message needs to say?"

The tapping of his toes was the only indication William gave of hearing her. "I suppose it's possible. The system is quite complex though. We'd need a way for me to be able to talk you through everything. Preferably without the signal being traced."

"We still have our ear buds. I'm sure Damon would have the microphone and receiver for a main hub somewhere around here."

"I can't ask this of any of you. We have no idea what could be waiting for us."

"William." Feiyan's calm voice penetrated the conversation with the force of a hammer breaking through rotting wood. "After all we have been through since this whole thing started - what makes you think you would have to ask any of us to do this? By now you should know we would willingly lay down our lives for our Spymaster. No assignment, or request, made by you would be refused by a single one of us."

"It could be a suicide mission if Vargas and his men are still there."

"Are you trying to talk us out of or into volunteering?" Damon asked, reentering the cottage as well as the conversation. He'd left the door partially open behind him when he'd left in order to hear what was being said.

"Honestly? Out of." Sighing softly, William graced each of his agents - he almost smiled when that term entered his mind - with an appraising look. What he saw made him realize he would be hard-pressed at this point to convince any of them not to accept the mission.

"Really?" Damon barked out with a laugh. "You mention the words suicide mission and you think we'd back down? You were an agent once - one of, if not the, best. So let me ask you this. If someone offered you an assignment and briefed you with the preface of 'it could be a suicide mission'... would you back down from the challenge or rise up, face and overcome if only to prove it could be done?"

About to refute the statement, William paused, locking eyes with the man who'd become the closest friend he'd ever had. In that moment, he knew Damon was right. A no-win scenario for any agent was like handing candy to a toddler. "You're right. I wouldn't have ever hesitated as an agent. But as your Spymaster..."

"Stop." Scarlett reached over and placed a finger on his lips to force him into silence. "I'll go. And don't try to talk me out of it. You know you'd never be able to."

"If it makes you feel better, I'll go with her." Damon volunteered before either of the others had a chance. "We've been working together since arriving on this island, we know how each other thinks. Which means the pair of us will have the best chance for success."

William wanted to scream no. To prohibit her from going. The look in her eyes, though, told him if he were to do that, she'd never forgive him. And that was something he knew he wouldn't be able to live with. What he needed to remember to do was separate his feelings for her from the mission. A feat proving more difficult with each passing second. There was only one choice available. At least one which wouldn't find him on the wrong side of her anger. "Alright."

Appearing satisfied with the answer, Scarlett looked at Damon. "When do you want to leave?"

"No time like the present but I don't want to risk using that hovercar we, uh, borrowed." Damon was pleased when he noticed she seemed as eager as himself to get things moving.

"We won't have to. You said my hovercar is at your place, right? The house we were at before this one?"

"Yeah... why..."

"In a garage?"

"Yes. With a closed door which I'd really rather not have to replace." Having a funny feeling he knew where this was headed, Damon gave her a bit of a glare. "So don't you even think about..."

"Already done. Sorry." Scarlett had been playing with her watch while he'd been speaking, sending instructions to her beloved vehicle. "Hey, at least when it gets here it'll park in the driveway." She added hastily when she saw his downtrodden expression.

"Yeah. Great. Do you have any idea how expensive that door was?"

"The agency will cover the replacement." William quickly intervened. "Speaking of the agency... Scarlett, won't they be able to track your hovercar? It's agency issue..."

"No it's not." Wintyrs grinned. "I use my personal one. Trust me - it can't be tracked by anyone except my Spymaster. You need your codes in order to enable tracking."

"She's got one of those super top of the line models." Damon seemed to accept William's offer then grew excited thinking about Scarlett's vehicle. "I've seen it. Coupled with some of Myrtle's tech, it's freaking amazing."

"I never knew you used your personal hovercar." Not knowing things of this nature irked William. He should be aware of everything like this in order to best lay plans and other thoughts out properly. "Is that something you've always done and plan on continuing to do?"

"Yes and yes." Frowning, she cast a worried glance at him. "I thought you knew."

"Did Amir?"

Pausing because she had to think about that, Scarlett eventually shook her head. "Not unless Myrtle told him."

"Then if he didn't know, neither do I." Not wanting to say more on the subject or risk sounding like he was disciplining her in front of the others, William let the matter drop. For the moment at least. "Do you have a plan for getting into Dolus and to my office undetected?"

"Undetected? Well, you just took all the fun out of it." Damon pretended to pout at the restriction.

"Yeah, yeah. I'm just one giant party-pooper."

"We'll figure one out on the way there." Scarlett broke in, rising to her feet. "Damon - do you have a microphone and speaker compatible with the communications units we're using?"

A sidelong glance from him should have been all the answer needed but Damon spoke anyway. "Seriously? Do I look like a parts warehouse??"

"I'm sorry I just thought…"

"Scarlett." He waited until she focused her attention on him. "I was kidding. But do you really think you have to ask?"

"I'd rather ask and get this type of response than find out you don't by accident." Scarlett smacked his upper arm gently. "Behave yourself."

"I don't know how." Damon laughed and jogged from the room before she could retaliate.

"Well he's in a good humour now." Zaliki stared after the man who had disappeared from the room.

"There's a mission to complete." Wintyrs answered. "He probably feels the same as I do. I'm sure you know the feeling. The euphoria. Your adrenaline pumping in anticipation, your heart beating faster to get you going, your reflexes coiling so tight they could spring at any moment and without warning…"

"Yes, yes, child." Feiyan waved a dismissive hand. "We all know the feeling however you seem to be… almost turned on by the thought of a mission."

Scarlett felt heat rise into her face as she blushed a bright red. "Feiyan!" The other two chuckling at her discomfiture caused her to follow in Damon's footsteps. She found him in a room next to the bedroom she and William had used. This particular space was small enough to be more of a closet than anything else.

"Having problems out there?" He didn't turn around to see who was there. Only a select few people could sneak up on him the way she had. And not one of the others could be counted among them.

"Right. Sound carries. No, I'm fine. I just..."

"Don't like being teased?" Damon glanced over his shoulder to see her nod then went back to searching through boxes he stored there. "I know how you feel, believe it or not."

"Have you found them yet?" Not wanting to discuss the matter, Scarlett quickly changed the topic.

"Not..." Damon stopped mid-sentence upon opening another box. "Never mind. Yes. Just dug up the right box." He handed her the small speaker while he scooped out the microphone and hub. "Alright... where do you think would be the best area to set these up for them?"

Given this was his cottage, Scarlett was taken aback to be asked her opinion. "Uh... well where they're sitting right now should be okay, shouldn't it? Depends what range those get as they look a little dated."

"Hmm... good point..." Turning back to the box after handing her the microphone, Raynott dug out one more thing. Swivelling around to face her, he watched as she stared at what he now held. "Range booster and signal scrambler so it can't be traced."

The explanation wasn't needed. Scarlett recognized the device as she had had to make use of one in the past. "Is there anything you don't have?"

Damon pursed his lips then laughed and shook his head. "Oh, probably. I wouldn't know until you asked though."

Together they walked back to the rest of the group in companionable silence. Damon dumped the range extender in William's lap without warning, chuckling when the seated man reacted on pure instinct to catch the device in order to keep it from falling. When he saved the extender from certain destruction on the hardwood floor, William released a relieved sigh.

"Nice catch." Damon remarked, carrying over a small table. "Good to see you still have agent reflexes."

"Yeah I... wait... why?" Narrowing his eyes, the hairs on the back of William's neck raised as suspicion permeated his words.

Ignoring the question, Damon took the items from Scarlett then set them up on the table which now sat directly in front of William. "You know how these work, right?"

"Yes of course. But why were you testing to see if I had agent..."

"Scarlett, can I borrow your earpiece?" Damon cut the Spymaster off again, trying not to show how much he was enjoying doing so.

"Sure." She handed the requested item to him after removing it from her pocket and cleaning it off with a nearby cloth napkin.

"Thank you, milady."

The room fell silent while Damon worked. Scarlett watched on in fascination while he adjusted the mic to match the frequency of the comm unit she'd handed him. When he was satisfied, he moved on to the speaker then connected the extender to both of them as well as the hub. Reaching over, Damon took the range extender/signal scrambler from William and set it on the table with the other devices. He stood up only when certain everything was ready to go and would work. With a wink to Scarlett, Damon handed back her device then looked at William who gave off the air of someone being extremely flustered and frustrated.

"Oh, I'm sorry William. You were saying?" Damon graciously asked, doing his best not to grin.

"The car's here, Damon." Scarlett announced. She leaned down and kissed William's cheek gently. "He asked because you may need those skills before this is all over." The words were whispered into his ear when she spoke so no one else would hear them. Backing away, she noted his posture had relaxed thanks to receiving an answer. "You three please stay safe. Stay hidden if you can and keep in constant contact. We'll be back as soon as possible."

7

When Scarlett walked out of the cottage to see her beloved hovercar waiting, her smile became one of almost childish delight. She hadn't seen the vehicle since before she'd been 'captured' by Zaliki and handed over to Feiyan whom, at the time, they thought was working for Amir. Ostensibly Vargas. Few things had gone right on this main mission of hers but the stuff that had was what brought this team of theirs together. A fact for which Scarlett was immensely grateful. After disabling the security system which automatically engaged when Scarlett used her watch to summon the hovercar, she gazed thoughtfully at Damon.

"You haven't told me yet how you managed to circumvent the security on this to get it to your place." She said while going to the driver's side and him to the passenger.

"Oh, I don't know. Don't you think it's nice to have some mystery in a relationship?" He shot her a grin right before entering the vehicle so he wouldn't hear her answer.

With a slight shake of her head, Scarlett climbed in behind the steering yoke and watched as he buckled himself in. "Are you really not going to tell me?"

"Mmm... nope." Damon thought of something else just then. "Do you have any weapons hidden in the trunk or somewhere for when we get to Dolus? I'm not sure your laser will be... quick enough if someone decides to take aim at us while also calling for help."

"The trunk is well-stocked. With more than weapons."

"Are you gonna share or keep me in suspense?" Damon rubbed his hands together in anticipation, unable to keep himself from asking the obvious.

"I think I'll opt for option number two." Starting the hovercar, Scarlett ignored the crestfallen look her companion now sported.

"You... are an evil woman." Damon crossed his arms while she engaged the vehicle, choosing to take to the airways instead of the ground routes. "We'd be better hidden on the ground, you know." He felt the need to point out even though he was sure she'd already taken that into consideration.

"While that may very well be true, our maneuverability up here is far better. If needed, we can drop down fast and change to the ground." Scarlett kept her eyes forward, paying close attention to any nearby traffic while taking them back towards Dolus. "Do you think our odds are high of Vargas still being there?"

"Nah. I'm sure his people got him free. He'll be off licking his wounds now and plotting his next steps. You know, if he really is going after William first, out of all the Spymasters I have to wonder why. Why choose him."

"A very good question." And one that'd been running around her head for awhile without an answer. "He didn't clue in that William was here, at least not at first, since he had Amir trying to ensare him so we can't blame it on convenience..."

"Maybe he somehow had a sample of... oh, of course. I bet Patrick grabbed samples of DNA for our previous Spymaster as well as for the most well-known agent at the time. Who else would fill a Spymaster's shoes. Somehow the little weasel must've realized William assumed the mantle and tailored the drug to him." Bouncing ideas off Scarlett was already almost second nature to Damon.

"If that's true then he could've also shared William's likeness before Vargas looked him up on the database."

"Unless..."

"Unless? Don't stop there." Scarlett prodded, wanting to know his complete thought.

"Perhaps Patrick didn't share an image. Maybe he wanted to see how resourceful his new employer was. Is. These are all answers we can only get from Vargas."

"Yeah." Her attention was divided though. Some of the things he'd said stirred something up in her thoughts. Speculation was all well and good but they really needed some cold, hard facts. The question was how to get them.

"We're almost there." Damon remarked, successfully pulling her from her reverie.

Not having realized how close they were to their destination, Scarlett swore under her breath. She didn't want to land right away so she circled the building a few times which would cause anyone looking up from below to think that either their car was malfunctioning or the driver had no idea where they were going. Likely the latter of the two would come up first given the area's touristy nature. Grateful for once to have daylight, Scarlett spared some glances out the window to the parking area below. Unlike their last visit, the area around Dolus seemed completely abandoned.

"We might be in luck." Scarlett said after activating her comms link so those at the cottage could hear what was being said.

"Can you describe what you're seeing for us?" William's voice filtered through the ear buds both Scarlett and Damon were sporting.

"Right now a completely empty parking lot. To the naked eye it'd seem like Mario and his minions have pulled out from Dolus." Damon answered, peering out his window.

"Then let's go beyond the naked eye." Scarlett said quietly. "Time to test out one of Myrtle's newer additions to my hovercar." She reached over to a blue button on the dashboard only to find Damon's hand covering hers to make her stop.

"Hang on. Whatever you're about to activate… you've never used before?" Wariness crept into his voice. Damon remembered their earlier conversation from the lab all too well.

"Nope. First time. Aren't you lucky to be here with me for it?"

"Depends on your definition of luck." He muttered, dropping his hand. "Just… try not to kill us, yeah?"

"Now would I do that to you?" Scarlett smiled slyly at the look he gave her then pressed the button.

"So… what's supposed to… whoa… okay this is awesome!" Damon grinned from ear to ear as the tinting on each window changed to a greenish substance, allowing them to identify all heat signatures around them. "Your car's windows literally just became radar and heat sensors. I'm going to have to talk to Myrtle about getting this feature on my lot."

"I forgot she was developing that." William's voice filtered through once more. "How's it working?"

"Nary a spark. So far." Wintyrs directed her gaze down to Dolus again. "I'm seeing a few heat sources inside the club but nowhere near the number that were here before."

"Manageable?"

"William... this is us you're talking to, mate."

"How could I forget." The rolling of his eyes could be heard in his voice. "Damon - don't get cocky."

"Me? Cocky? Never." Damon glowered at Scarlett when he heard what sounded like a snicker come from her side of the vehicle. "I heard that, Agent Wintyrs."

"You were meant to. You sure you want to do this?" She looked over the heat signatures once more.

"Hell yes."

Chuckling at his eagerness, Scarlett deactivated the sensors for the descent. Circling down slowly so as not to draw any unwanted attention, she maneuvered the hovercar into a spot in the main parking area for Dolus. Letting her eyes roam over the area, she ensured what her hovercar's infared sensors told them was accurate. As far as she could see there was no one waiting to ambush them. Outside the club's walls at any rate.

"Looks like we're clear." Turning to give Damon her attention, she kept her expression blank. "Shall we gear up?"

"Gear up? Just what do you have in this hovercar of yours anyway?"

"I think it's time you found out. Join me at the trunk?" Scarlett exited the vehicle without waiting for a response. Keeping her eyes peeled for anyone wishing them harm, she popped the trunk. When Damon appeared at her side a minute later, Wintyrs turned to him so he could peer inside.

"Uh, Scarlett, did you take a bump to the noggin' there, lass? That's completely empty. Hey, look, tumbleweeds are rolling around in there."

"You should take another peek." Wintyrs pressed her finger against the tail light closest to her. While they watched, the bottom of the trunk flipped over so the empty side faced down and what was once the underside now sat on top.

It wasn't often Damon was impressed let alone enough to make him speechless. This was one of those rare times. He stared at the inside of the trunk, blinking as he took in what he saw.

"Like what you see?" Scarlett tried to break the hypnotic spell seeming to weave over him.

Damon coughed at her phrasing but didn't validate the words. "This is... remarkable. I'm going to have to talk to Myrtle."

"Take whatever you want to use." Her offer was genuine since he'd given her the same choice when they were at his beach house.

"Are you sure?"

"Absolutely."

Grinning, he reached down to grab the holsters for two pistols. After strapping them on and holstering the weapons, he put his hands back in to take out a couple of knives as well. He wanted to be ready for close quarters combat just in case. Judging from what he witnessed out of the corner of his eye, his companion was preparing for exactly the same possibility.

"There's one thing I'm really looking forward to from this, you know." He finished prepping while making his comment.

"Oh yeah? And what's that?"

"Seeing you in action again, you've always had this... grace... about you. It's fascinating to watch."

"You find me fascinating?"

"Maybe that came out wrong..."

"You better hope that's what happened, Raynott." William's slightly annoyed voice filled their ears.

"Oops... I forgot you were listening, bud."

"Clearly."

"That's enough, boys." Scarlett broke into the conversation, gently closing the lid of the trunk. "We've got a mission to complete."

8

"Damon - main door or employee?" Scarlett wanted his input on entry method.

"Well, we've used the tunnel and employee. I say we go in the front door. Should scare the shit out of anyone in there." He grinned.

Wintyrs was about to voice her opinion when he started towards the suggested entrance without her. Sighing, she jogged after her partner, catching up quickly since he was just walking. Arriving at the doors at the exact same time, they parted with Damon going to the right side while Scarlett went left, both kept their backs against the building. Wintyrs blew out a breath and readied the pistol she'd chosen, preferring to go with a single ranged weapon coupled with a pair of deadly looking knives. She looked across the space between them to meet Damon's eyes. A slight nod was all the confirmation she needed. They were ready. At least, she hoped they were.

Taking another moment to centre herself, Scarlett felt everything in her body clicking into place. Her muscles tightened but not overly so. Just enough to be ready for anything. At the same time, her heart beat evened out at a steady rate. She reached out to the door with her right hand, thankful it was push to open, then moved swiftly to be in front of the doorway once the impediment was removed. A frown marred her face upon seeing no one waiting to give them a warm welcome. She sensed Damon join her side.

"Dare we hope our luck is changing?" He murmured softly.

"Mmh…" She didn't want to answer one way or another for fear of jinxing them.

"Are you two alright?" William asked, eager to stay informed of their progress.

"We're good." Scarlett whispered her answer. "No sign of a welcoming party. Not yet anyway."

The duo moved forward nearly in unison. When they reached the doorway to the first, and main, dining area, Damon signalled to stop. Peering around the corner of the doorframe, he narrowed his eyes. He could see two of Vargas' men inside with their backs to the entrance where he and Scarlett were. Pulling back without making a sound, he turned his head just enough to see his partner and held up two fingers. After she nodded acknowledgement, he motioned to let her know he would take the one on the left. Another nod. He was relieved to not have to explain any further as he might have had to do with an agent who didn't know him from a hole in the wall.

They moved without sound. As if one with the air itself. Vargas' guards remained completely unaware as the two agents swiftly came up behind them. So oblivious were the pair of men that Scarlett and Damon were able to use the butts of their respective pistols to knock them both out. They placed the blows strategically on the backs of the men's heads and caught them as they went down in order to minimize any noise.

"Well... that's two down..." Damon whispered, eyes darting around the room wondering if any of the others they knew were in the building had been alerted.

Scarlett didn't bother responding. Conversation, she found, during this part of a mission could be too distracting. And could potentially lead to deadly results. Checking over the guard she'd been responsible for taking down, she grew puzzled and glanced over at Damon. She wondered if he'd uncovered the same thing.

"Does yours have a communicator or radio of any sort?" Breaking the code of silence she so valued at this stage of the game did not come easily but the question needed airing.

Wondering at her sudden curiosity, Damon deftly searched the fallen man in front of him. Once complete, he shook his head slowly and wondered if he looked as perplexed as his partner. "No... nada, zip, zero, zilch. He's not even armed..."

What he said in response caused Scarlett's eyes to narrow. "William? Did you copy that?" She devoutly hoped he wouldn't be thinking along the same lines she was.

"I did. I don't like the sound of that." Their Spymaster answered quickly, not wanting to keep them waiting. "All I'm going to say is move as quickly as you can and get out of there."

"Roger that." Scarlett didn't say more as he'd confirmed her suspicions despite not giving voice to it. Vargas left these troops of his at Dolus to die. Which meant he either expected whatever infiltration team was coming to spare no one or he planned for something bigger - and much more final - to happen to Dolus. The latter meant he left the guards here either as a distraction or as a force to attempt to keep whatever infiltrators that came busy and without time to escape. Neither option was particularly appetizing.

"This way." Damon motioned for her to follow although by now she probably knew Dolus almost as well as he did. Almost.

"You get the feeling like we're rats in a maze?" Her remark made Damon stop in his tracks in order to turn and look at her.

"And you talk about me jinxing us." Of course the idea hadn't entered his mind until she mentioned it. Now he couldn't stop thinking about the possibility. "I really wish you hadn't said that."

"It's just a question." Scarlett continued to whisper, checking each room as they moved down the hall to William's office. She didn't spot another soul anywhere which only made sense to her if the hunters were funnelling their prey to a room with only one way in or out. "Where'd all those heat signatures we detected before entry disappear to?"

"Good question. Keep your eyes peeled."

"Nah, thought I'd have a nap while we walked." The snarky response passed her lips without any thought.

"Sarcasm, huh. You lot have definitely been hanging around me too long."

Scarlett rolled her eyes. Letting the retort die on her lips, she peered into the last remaining room between them and their objective. Still no one to be seen. Nothing she thought of could be used to create artificial heat signatures like what they saw - if she dared believe they were fake. Which, until they were on their way back to the cottage, she wouldn't. When the pair reached the closed door to the office, they bracketed it the same way as they'd done the front door. Without needing to confer with her partner, Scarlett reached out and slowly turned the doorknob.

"Ready." Damon whispered, giving her a nod to go ahead.

Nodding, Wintyrs pushed the door open, letting her partner enter first to check for resistance. Yet again none was encountered. Casting a glance behind them to make certain no one tried to sneak up to surprise them, Scarlett relaxed seeing no other souls in the hallway.

She entered the room after Damon, closing the door as she did.

"Well… the weapons and what few explosives we left behind are gone. Looks like Vargas or his men did a pretty extensive sweep." Damon shook his head. "I wonder how thorough they were."

Scarlett knew he referred to the arsenal they kept in a room within their emergency tunnel system. There was no doubt in her mind anything it used to house would be gone. Part of her wondered if more traps might have been left behind but given the lacklustre reception they'd received on their return, she quickly quashed those thoughts.

"Are you two still there?" William's voice in her ear made her pause her cursory examination of the office.

"Yeah, we're here." Responding to him almost automatically, Scarlett went to his desk and sat down. "I'm at your computer, William. Are you sure I'll be able to access what we need without alerting anyone to our presence?"

"I'm going to talk you through the back door system I installed in case of a situation like this. In theory, it should be untraceable."

Pausing with her finger hovering over the power button of the unit, Scarlett raised an eyebrow. "In theory??"

"I've never used it. I haven't needed to until now."

Closing her eyes for a brief moment, Scarlett wondered why it was that she always seemed to come across untested inventions. Perhaps this luck of hers was more bad than good. "Damon?"

"Don't worry. I've got you covered. Do what you need to do."

Giving him a nod, Scarlett resumed speaking with William. "Okay. Turning the unit on now."

"Booting up shouldn't take long. Once complete, you'll be in a normal, or guest, user mode. I'll guide you into where you need to be when you tell me it's done loading. You'll know when - there should be a chime to advise you." William stated, visualizing the screen in his mind in order to talk her through what needed to be done.

The chime sounded so quietly that Scarlett strained her ears to hear it. He'd been right on the money though. His system booted up in under a minute. "Out of curiosity… if we were to take the unit with us, can it be utilized wherever there's a network connection?" She swore she could hear the gears in her Spymaster's mind turning the second she made the inquiry.

"I suppose something like that could be possible. We can make the attempt after we've done this portion if you'd like and only if you don't think you've been discovered."

"If we did then we wouldn't need to worry about infiltrating Dolus again. So let's speed this up, shall we?"

"Yeah, the faster you two get through this, the happier I'll be." Damon chimed in.

"And here I thought you liked watching my back."

"I like it better when I'm behind you."

Scarlett shot him a dirty look while William choked on whatever he'd been swallowing at that moment. "Damon, please behave. I'm sorry, William. I'm ready when you are."

With a shrug, Damon moved back to the closed door of the office. He didn't pay any attention as the instructions were provided over their comms. His entire focus rested on determining if their enemy had located them. Thinking he might have heard a noise, Damon opened the door a crack to peer into the hallway. Nothing. Of course that wasn't to say someone couldn't be hiding in one of the doorways. He decided to remain where he was until his partner finished her assignment.

After a few tries, Scarlett was able to claim success as she gained entry into the database used by the Spymasters. "I'm in, William. Third time's the charm. What next?"

"Look for a file called SOS. Go ahead and click to open when you find it."

"Gotcha. Standby." Deciding to take the easy route, she brought up a search bar then typed in the file name. "Found it. Opening now and... I'm in." Quickly realizing this was a messaging system, she smiled to herself.

"Are there any new messages posted there?"

"None that I can see. If that good or bad?"

"Actually very good. We may have been on the right track with our one theory at least. Go to post new message - it's an older model programme based on 20th century technology." William explained without giving her a chance to ask about the interface.

"That explains a few things. Won't Vargas see this though?"

"No. Once we type up the message, we'll reset the privacy so it can't be read by the Orion Agency. Doing so will indicate to the others that that agency has been compromised and they shouldn't trust anyone from there until further notice."

Pausing again, Scarlett frowned at the screen. "And what if Vargas has already posted his own message to that effect about the Centurian

Agency and you? Altering the privacy so we can't see it?" Silence greeted her. "Maybe we should just bring the unit to you so you can do your thing."

"I'm starting to think that may be a good idea." He answered quietly. "I have a couple of ways to check to see if what you suggested has happened. Although if it has then I won't be able to read the content of the message. No one from our agency would."

"Then it's a good thing we have someone from the Orion Agency on our team. Can a normal agent access this SOS board?" Scarlett hoped it was possible.

"Not easily but... connected to a different comms hub... and knowing how to do it... yeah. Only one agent per agency is able to read those messages aside of the Spymaster. We should be able to fool the system long enough to read the message if it's there."

"Fool it long enough?" The phrasing bothered Scarlett when she heard it.

"We can discuss that when you're back here as we get ready to do what we talked about. For now let's get the unit prepped for mobile use."

Pursing her lips at the lack of response from William, she filed it away to ensure they would re-visit the subject as he promised. "Damon? Are we still clear?"

"Yeah, you're good. But I'd suggest speeding this up if we can. I wouldn't put it past Vargas to magically appear out of thin air." He replied without compromising his position.

"Okay, William. Talk me through what needs to be done."

Damon tuned the duo out again. What they were discussing he filed under need to know. And he didn't. The same sound as before reached his ears, seeming closer than the last time. His eyes never left the vantage point of the hallway so he knew whatever the noise was emanated from one of the rooms. Curiosity began to get the better of him. He glanced back at Scarlett to see how she fared. Eyesight alone, however, wasn't enough to determine if she was nearly done or not.

"Going to interrupt here." Damon finally said. "How much more time do you think you're going to need?"

William was the one to answer over the comms. "Maybe another five to ten minutes." He paused, analyzing the tone of his friend's voice. "What's got your hackles up?"

"I'm not sure. I've heard something - the same sound - a couple of times now. The last occurrence seemed closer." Wondering if he sounded crazy, Damon returned his gaze to the corridor. "I dunno. Maybe I'm hearing things. Wouldn't be the first time."

"What's your gut telling you?" Scarlett asked while her fingers worked on the step William had just given her instructions for.

"That there's something amiss."

"Then you need to check it out. I'll be fine here." She nodded confirmation of her assurance to him. "Go. Check it out."

"If you're sure..." The thought of leaving her alone didn't sit well given everything that'd happened. Not to mention the fact Vargas was dead set on getting William - and her.

"I'm sure. There's only one entry point for this room and if I have to, I can easily hide under William's desk."

"You? Hide?" Damon scoffed at the thought.

"As in - use for cover. Do I have to spell everything out for you?"

With a sly grin, Damon exited the office. Working with a partner wasn't new to him but it had been awhile. Since before he'd been forced to fake his death in order to stay alive. It was a nice change from the solitude he'd experienced since becoming Tengu.

Moving down the corridor in complete silence, Damon went to the first door. Peering through the circular window with caution, he could see nothing out of the ordinary. Knowing that meant very little, Damon continued watching. Still nothing moved. About to open the door, he stopped when he heard the noise yet again. This time, though, it sounded further away.

"Oh now I know someone's messing with me." Damon muttered under his breath. "And I'm not finding it at all amusing."

Standing still where he was, he waited to see if it repeated. This time, however, he was looking at his watch. Something he should've done the second he'd first heard... whatever the hell it was. If a pattern existed then the implications of what the source could be would become significantly lower. There. He tapped his watch when the sound occurred yet again. It was hard to describe. Somewhere between a chirp and a chime yet with the aspects of both. He could safely say he'd never heard anything quite like it before. When a gentle hand touched his arm from behind, Damon nearly jumped out of his skin in surprise.

"Bloody hell, Scarlett." He breathed out once he realized who stood behind him. "I never heard you coming."

Wintyrs raised an eyebrow at him. "You weren't supposed to. What were you timing?" Having caught him staring at his timepiece, she knew right away something was amiss. He wasn't the kind of man to watch a clock so closely.

"A sound. It's… I dunno, weird. Almost like a bird chirping but also like a wind chime."

"Can one of you remove your earbud to let me hear?" William asked.

"Yeah, hang on a sec, mate." Damon removed his earpiece, holding it up just as the unknown note occurred again. Placing his comm unit back in his ear, he frowned at the silence on the other end.

At the cottage, William rose to his feet when the sound carried to his ears. All colour drained from his face. It was a noise he'd hoped never to hear. There was only one thing he could do. One warning he could issue. He shouted into the mic hoping to convey his sense of dread and urgency.

"SCARLETT! DAMON! GET OUT OF DOLUS! *NOW!!*"

9

When William's words came through the comms, Scarlett and Damon met each other's eyes then took off running to the nearest exit.

Meanwhile at the cottage, William paced back and forth, his agitation obvious to the two women with him. That sound. He knew of yet not heard it. Now that he had, he would likely never be able to forget. His breathing came out raggedly while continuing to pace. The only hope he clung to now was that his warning reached his agents in time.

Damon grabbed Scarlett's hand the second he thought she might be slowing down and pulled her along behind him. He couldn't recall ever hearing what sounded like near-panic in William's voice. A fact which spurred him on. Whatever noise they made now mattered not. If they ended up with an army chasing them then they'd deal with it as soon as they left the building.

Scarlett kept pace with her partner as best she could, not complaining when he took her hand to help her even though she didn't need it. When a Spymaster gave an order, an agent was expected to obey without question. And when an order such as the one William issued came forth - no agent would pause to consider why. The second they got outside, the duo continued straight to her hovercar and climbed in, locking themselves inside. They both turned their attention to Dolus as what seemed like a wave of energy rushed through the building from top to bottom and back. The air around the club was displaced slightly which was the only reason they could see the wave. Otherwise it would have been invisible to the naked eye.

"What the bloody hell was that??" Damon couldn't believe his eyes.

"Are you both there? You're both okay??" Anxiety flickered through William's words. He'd remained silent as he'd not wanted to be a distraction.

"We're here." Scarlett answered, only a little out of breath. "We're in my hovercar and just saw... I don't even know how to describe that to you..."

"Let me guess. A wave of what would've been invisible energy save for the displaced air around it?"

"Yeah... that. William? Do you know what the hell that was??"

"Sadly, Scarlett, I think I might. Get your asses back here - preferably in one piece. I'll brief you all at the same time."

Locking eyes with Damon again, Scarlett started up the hovercar. "We're on our way."

Damon scratched his chin while she maneuvered them into the airways. Belatedly, he noted a system in the vehicle's dash he'd not seen equipped on a hovercar prior to this moment. The fact he hadn't made note of it during his previous rides in this vehicle surprised him enough that he nearly forgot to put his safety restraint into place.

"This may be an odd question - what's that thing in the dash?" Damon needed to satisfy his curiousity.

"It's kind of like a radar. I can see what's around us without having to look plus it alerts me when another vehicle gets a little too close for comfort. Also if there's any projectiles heading our way."

"Yeah I really gotta get Myrtle to outfit one of my rides." Even so, Damon kept glancing at the mirror on his door to see if they were being followed. When they arrived back at the cottage he quickly climbed out in order to scan the skies. No other vehicles were around but that didn't ease his nerves as he ushered his partner into the domicile.

"You're back." William had been pacing the entire time and stopped only when he saw them come through the front door.

Scarlett tossed a small device to him which he easily caught. "Your computer stuff as requested and instructed." She waited until Damon stood next to her before continuing. "Now... do you have *any* idea what that thing was and why hearing it made you yell for us to get out of Dolus?"

William licked his lips. This was something he'd hoped never to have to confront. "I have a theory which I'm pretty sure can say has been proven." Sitting back down on the couch, he rubbed his face with both hands while being aware of all eyes resting solely on him. "I remember when I was going over Patrick's file, he'd listed designs for a device... a weapon of sorts."

"What kind of weapon...?" Scarlett asked although she wasn't entirely sure she wanted to know.

"One able to deconstruct anything organic, breaking it down right at the molecular level. He called it the Eliminator."

"And you think that's what we encountered at Dolus?"

"I'm afraid so."

Damon blew out a breath. "Vargas."

"But of course. If he green lit that project then he has the potential to eradicate everyone on this island just to get to us."

"Do you really believe him capable of mass murder??" Feiyan spoke up finally. She'd heard rumours of someone designing a weapon of this nature but never believed anyone would be brazen enough to risk its construction.

"When it comes to Vargas... I wouldn't put anything past him. This goes beyond even that." William sighed softly. "Alright... there's something else I may as well share with you guys about this weapon."

"Well, that sounds rather foreboding..." Crossing her legs, still sitting in the same chair she'd been in since arriving at the cottage, Feiyan continued her line of questioning "Do we want to know?"

"Honestly? Probably not. That being said, if we're facing this weapon then you should know everything."

"Full disclosure?" Amazement entered Feiyan's voice. A tone none of them had heard on any previous occasion.

"Full disclosure." He watched as they each gave him their unwavering attention. "Well, at least what I can remember from the file."

"Let's hear it then." Damon leaned back against the nearest wall, crossing his arms.

Leaning forward and placing his elbows on his knees, William looked down at the floor for a long moment. "Okay... in for a penny, in for a pound. I remember seeing potential specifications, what it could be capable of but - and most importantly - my predecessor initialed it for further review."

"He... what? What on earth could have been his reasoning behind that??" Nearly choking on his own spit while swallowing, Damon tried to come to terms with what he was hearing.

William spread his hands apart in a gesture indicating he had no idea. "I wish I could give you an answer. The truth is - I haven't the foggiest notion. As a whole, Spymasters from all the agencies banned weapons like this years ago. Even investigating the potential of one, the schematics, anything really is breaking the ban. Not bending - breaking. Seeing my predecessor initial his interest in exploring Patrick's research on this 'Eliminator' makes me wonder about his intentions. Did he want to see if it could be created and work or did he plan on turning Patrick in to the authorities under a trumped-up charge like we do with anyone we need punished by the law."

"Wait... I never knew the agencies did that..." Damon stared at William in shock.

"Spymasters do. When and if the need arises." Shrugging a bit, William sent his friend a silent apology. "Eliminating assets only happens if no other recourse is available. For example if we couldn't trap or catch up to the targeted asset to implement the arrest option... then the kill order is given."

"Is that why your predecessor sent agents after me? Originally to arrest me?"

"Damon, I honestly have no clue. All I can tell you is - be glad it was me he sent."

Falling silent, Damon continued staring at the other man. He'd had no idea what agent had been sent for him and to learn it was the man he'd cultivated a close friendship with baffled him. Opening and closing his mouth a few times, he couldn't figure out what to say.

"Can we backtrack to this Eliminator weapon?" Zaliki broke the silence.

"I don't have much else to tell you. In fact, as of this moment, you know what I do." William responded softly.

"I have another question." Scarlett finally spoke up then waited until their Spymaster met her eyes. "Could the Orion Agency have made their offer regarding Patrick because of this invention? Did we ever have a data breach between the time of its inception and when the offer came through?"

Steepling his fingers together was the only indication the small group had that William needed a few moments to think about his reply. "Not that I was made aware of."

"So it's possible and they never advised you when you took over as Spymaster."

"The chance exists that what you described may have come to pass. Why they wouldn't have briefed me on it, I have no idea."

"Plausible deniability." Damon interjected. "I mean think about it. We had the schematics and everything related to this device on our servers. First mistake. Second was not deleting them. But if other agencies know it's being used and that you had prior knowledge of both it plus a data breach then they would probably issue a kill order on you. Am I right?"

"Well... you're not wrong."

"Is there any way we can track it?" Brainstorming wasn't one of Scarlett's favourite pastimes but she sensed they were in sore need of that precise activity.

"Maybe. First thing's first though. The messages. Damon, I need a computer with network access please."

"Drawer in the end table next to you. Itlooks like a tablet. Before you ask, yes it'll be able to read your storage thing or whatever it is we brought you." Raynott answered swiftly.

"Thanks." Turning slightly, William retrieved the tablet, powered it up and attached the drive unit from Scarlett. "Now to make them think we're from another agency." He cast a glance at Zaliki. "Can you get us onto your main network?"

"As long as Vargas hasn't blocked my credentials then it shouldn't be a problem" She replied, getting up from the floor to take the tablet from him. Once in her hands, Zaliki attempted to log in with her information, taken slightly aback when it actually worked.

"I'm not sure if it's good or bad that you were able to get in." Scarlett stated softly upon witnessing the other woman's success.

"Neither am I." The admission came not from Zaliki but rather William. "This shouldn't take long though since I know what I'm doing."

The group fell silent to allow the Spymaster to focus on his task. Damon disappeared for a few minutes without a word. Wondering where he'd gotten to, Scarlett rose to her feet from the couch just as he returned carrying a tray filled with cool drinks. Gratefully taking one, Wintyrs shot him a smile and returned her eyes to what William was doing. To her, it appeared the process neared completion. He wasn't typing as fast as when he'd started out. While she watched, the screen changed to what an older model message board might look like.

"Alright. I'm in." William announced into the round. When his face fell, he didn't need to tell them what he'd found.

"Let me guess." Placing a gentle hand over the one of his closest to her, Scarlett kept her eyes on his face. "I was right, wasn't I? Vargas already told them he's the one in trouble, we're the ones after him, and for the cherry on top - he's said we have the weapon and are using it. How'd I do?" Him turning his head to face her with his eyebrows raised was all the answer she needed. "Yeah... that's what I was afraid of."

Logging out as quickly as he'd gotten in, William placed the tablet on the nearby end table with a frustrated sigh. "This gives us both bad and good news. Which do you want to hear first?"

"Let's go with good." The suggestion came from Damon.

"Another theory proven - the other Spymasters are alive and well after all. Vargas must've hacked the system to feed me false data to make me feel isolated."

"And the bad?" She really didn't want to ask however Scarlett knew they needed to know.

"I've been blacklisted." The words were said so quietly that even Scarlett, who sat right beside him, strained to hear what he'd said.

"Blacklisted?" Scarlett repeated for the others. "Please tell me that's not as bad as it sounds."

"Probably worse." William pinched the bridge of his nose and closed his eyes for a moment. "A capture or kill agent will be sent after me now. From every agency save for ours. That's around fourteen different agents. And the emphasis was on kill."

"Because they believe you had the Eliminator built and tested." Scratching his chin, Damon started to wonder what else could go wrong.

"So we have to clear your name." Scarlett shrugged. "I don't think that'll be too hard to do."

"I'm not quite sure how you propose we do that. Our agency and all associated agents have also been blacklisted. They'll come for me first though as they are of the opinion if you cut off the head of the snake then the rest will die."

"We go to the source."

"Scarlett..." William stared at her.

"He's the only one who can get you off that list. As much as I hate to say this..." Wintyrs released a deep breath. "We need Vargas."

10

"You can't be serious." Zaliki's heart skipped a beat when she heard Scarlett's suggestion. "After everything we have done to escape his grasp, now you say we need him?!"

"If he recants what he said or told to the other Spymasters then we should be able to clear William's name."

Scoffing, Zaliki looked up at the ceiling to organize her thoughts. "What makes you think Vargas would consider doing what you suggest. He'd have to admit to being involved. Never in a million years would my former Spymaster do anything of the sort."

Scarlett was about to protest, to defend her plan, when William put his free hand lightly over the one she had holding his. "Zaliki's right. As much as I want to agree with you... I need to side with her this time. Vargas would never allow himself to be implicated in this mess."

"Then what do we do?" Wintyrs met his brown eyes. "Please tell me you have an idea. Any idea."

William wanted to lose himself in her eyes and touch. Moreso when she used her other hand to caress his face. "I... I need a bit of time... because right now - no. No, I have no ideas or plans of any kind. I just... excuse me for a few minutes." He rose from the sofa, leaving the room in the direction of the bedroom.

"You all do realize what we now must protect him from, yes?" Feiyan asked the team. She knew the answer, however maintained a slim hope that perhaps she'd misheard some of the conversation.

"I'm not sure I want to say it out loud. If we do then it'll be real." Damon responded sullenly.

With a shake of her head, Scarlett looked at her hands then at each of them. "Every agency will send their best agent to attempt to apprehend him. Their *best*. Numbering fourteen. Vargas wanted William to see that thread of conversation. That's why he left Zaliki's credentials alone. And not just William, either. Mario Vargas wants all of us off our game. Doubting ourselves. We can't let him see that's precisely the effect it's having." Standing up, she crossed her arms, wearing a set expression. "If any of you want out before this starts going down then this may be your only chance. I'm not going anywhere. I am a sworn agent of the Centurian Agency and it's my duty to protect my Spymaster from *any* threat. That's precisely what I'm going to do. Even if that means making the ultimate sacrifice."

Raynott eyed her for a moment. Her words resonated and stirred something within him. Instinct screamed to run while he still could. His heart and head, on the other hand, said otherwise. William was his friend. Eyebrows rose as he realized the other man was actually more than that. He was his best friend. Someone he would, without hesitation, lay his life down for. "I'm staying with you."

"Child, you know I never back down from a fight. William's chances of not only evasion but also survival rise exponentially because of those of us in this room right now. I, too, shall remain." Feiyan smiled. "After all… I'm not getting any younger."

All eyes in the room moved to Zaliki who released a long sigh. "Vargas probably already has plans for my head to be delivered to him on a silver platter. I don't intend on making that easy for him. I, too, shall stay by William's side."

"And here I thought you'd stay for me." A wolfish grin appeared on Damon's face.

"Please do not make me regret this decision."

"Who, me? Never."

"Uh-huh." Zaliki shook her head at his response.

"For the record, though," Damon suddenly grew serious, returning his attention to Scarlett, "sure they'll be sending their best agents but I think we have the Centurian Agency's best in our presence. I'm staring right at her."

"Given that I trained her - I am in complete agreement with Damon." Feiyan held up a hand to stave off the protest she knew Wintyrs was about to make. "You may disagree because I am still an agent as well however you must remember you bested me in hand to hand combat."

"Wait… I thought you planned that…" Scarlett cocked her head at her former mentor.

"Only partially. Most definitely not to the extent which you managed." Smiling, Feiyan gave her a satisfied nod. "You've earned the title of best agent at our agency."

Scarlett felt heat rising in her cheeks. The mantle they'd gifted was not one she desired. Then there was the way they now looked at her. Not really reverence although fairly close. Never since the beginning of her career had she wished for this to happen. And now that it had, she desired nothing more than a way to reverse it.

"Feiyan, Zaliki - what say we do a quick perimeter patrol?" Damon suggested, noting the uncomfortable look on Wintyrs' face. After a nod from each of the two women he'd addressed, he led them outside.

Scarlett sighed when they left her alone in the room. Rubbing her face with both hands, she moved to the single window and looked out. While not right next to the ocean, they were still close enough to the water to see it from this vantage point. She took solace in the waves which were as turbulent as her thoughts at the moment.

"They're right, you know." William's quiet voice came from just a few feet behind her.

"About what" Scarlett's words were hushed, her eyes lingering on the waves beyond the window.

"You being the best agent of the Centurian Agency. Why else would I want you to be my right hand?"

Eyebrows knitting together in a frown, Scarlett turned to face him. "So that wasn't because of our newfound relationship?"

"What? No, of course not." Although he understood why she might think that. "Just because we're... together... now doesn't mean you'll curry any special favour with me. If you weren't the best of the best, I guarantee I'd not have asked you to assume the role."

"Well... that's a relief." She smiled then closed the distance between them in order to give him a gentle kiss. "How are you feeling?"

"I assume you mean in regards to the drug?" William enjoyed the kiss, brief though it was. When she nodded her response, he shrugged. "I feel good. I think maybe it's finally run its course. At least I hope so. I have way too much to think about now to let a drug induced sleep interfere."

Wintyrs caressed his face gently with both hands while staring into his eyes. She could see fear in their depths. "Hey, we've been in tougher scrapes than this."

"Have we?" William raised an eyebrow. "Why can't I think of any?"

"Okay, maybe not tougher scrapes but you know we're up for the challenge."

"You do understand the danger we're in, right?"

"More than you probably realize. We're sitting ducks on this island. We need to get out of here."

"You're right, Scarlett. Absolutely right. Which means we need to get to the airfield as soon as possible." William knew the sooner they were in the air, the better. There was no telling when the first agent might strike or if Vargas would finish them first.

"First, we need a plane. I'm hoping Damon's friend will let us use hers again." When Scarlett noticed the bewildered look on his face, she quickly explained. "It's our best option. She has the underside coated to reflect the surrounding sky but the rest of the plane is quite... colourful."

"Only one profession would be bold enough to do that kind of scheme on a plane."

"I didn't ask, William. He was helping me and at that point we were still earning each other's trust."

"Fair enough. Let's call the others in. I want to get on the road to the airfield."

"Well, I like hearing that as a greeting for our return." Damon said, startling the duo. "Sorry, there's only so many times we can walk such a small perimeter without looking conspicuous." He chuckled. "So it sounded to me like you've come up with a plan?"

William moved to stand next to Scarlett, taking her hand in his once more as he looked upon the rest of the team. "More like revisiting our original one. Scarlett mentioned you two arrived on a... special... plane? Any chance it would still be available for us to use?"

A sly smile spread across Damon's face. "You bet it is. When are we leaving?"

"Right now."

11

The group elected to utilize both hovercars - the one they'd 'borrowed' as well as Scarlett's. When William suggested splitting up, he'd been met with heavy resistance. Yet Scarlett agreed one of them needed to fly or drive hers - and she was the only option for that given she knew of what it was capable. After some persuading, the others eventually agreed as that solution still left William with three protectors in the same vehicle as he.

Once that was settled, Scarlett suggested they take the ground route allowing her to shadow from above. When the point of her being able to see any approaching threats and intercept them was made, the group readily accepted her proposal. True to his word, when that was sorted, William had them get on the way. Scarlett managed to get airborne while the others squared themselves away in the second vehicle.

Scarlett kept her hovercar above and slightly behind theirs with her 'radar' activated. She had the unit's comm system linked to the one in the other vehicle for quick and easy communication. Finally alone again, she found the silence comforting. Realization set in that she'd missed being on her own. Rather, working solo. Most of her career, even her life, had been spent this way. Not having to worry about other people or a partner made her job all the more simple. Now she found herself as the first, and most important, line of defence for their Spymaster.

A beep from her radar interrupted her thoughts. Glancing at the screen, Scarlett noted a blip trailing the hovercar below - rapidly closing the distance between them. Two more dots appeared on the radar on either side of the first, making her swear under her breath.

One, even two, she could handle albeit with some difficulty. Anything upwards of that number would be a challenge. All she really needed to do was keep them busy. Long enough for the rest of the team to board the plane.

"Damon," Scarlett spoke out to the open comms, knowing the man would've refused to give up the yoke to anyone else, "you need to put the pedal to the metal."

"I gather we have company incoming?" His voice came back at the same time she noted their vehicle pulling away as he increased their speed.

"Affirmative. Three bogeys on your six."

"Grrreat... how the hell did they find us..." Damon trailed off and she could hear someone in the background talking quietly to him. "Seriously? I thought we were waiting until we were on the plane for that! And why didn't I hear the call??"

"What's going on?" Wintyrs maneuvered her hovercar into position between her team and whomever was incoming.

"Apparently William lifted the travel ban just before we left and didn't tell us. I'm willing to bet those are Vargas' men coming in hot. Do you have a visual?"

Inwardly groaning at the news about William's call, Scarlett glanced around. "Negative. I see them on my radar but they're not close enough to see with the naked eye yet. I've placed myself between them and you. No matter what happens, keep going and get on that plane. Don't stop for anything. Understood?"

There was a moment's silence before Damon responded. "Understood."

"We'll maintain the open comms - I don't want to have to shift my focus to activate it."

"Don't worry about us. I remember my evasion techniques. The longer you can keep them off our tail, though, the happier I'll be."

"Copy that."

Scarlett backed off her speed a bit, wanting to get more distance between the two vehicles. With luck, those approaching would have no idea about her hovercar nor who was inside. She wanted the element of surprise on her side. Glancing in her rearview mirror, Wintyrs finally noticed the outlines of the three vehicles in pursuit.

Setting her hovercar on auto-pilot for a minute, she prepared what she hoped would be a warm welcome for their uninvited guests and when she looked in the mirror again Scarlett couldn't decide if she was relieved or not. The approaching hovercars were indeed employed by the Orion Agency's Spymaster. Luckily they were police vehicles and likely not equipped with any spy toys - hopefully - however they wouldn't hesitate to use brutal and deadly force.

"Okay, guys. I can confirm it's Vargas' men."

"We hear you, Scarlett. Be careful but, uh, give 'em hell for us."

A small smile played over Scarlett's lips. "With pleasure."

With some measure of amusement, Wintyrs noted the police cruisers maintained a 'V' formation. Even when coming up alongside her. There ended up being one unit on either side of her hovercar while the third remained at the rear. Without hesitation she activated the window tinting, making it impossible for them to peer inside and see her. She rubbed her hands together in anticipation. This was going to be fun.

"You there in the red hovercar." One of the units broke into her comms. "You are impeding a lawful pursuit. Please pull over and remain in your vehicle."

Scarlett stifled a guffaw. Like that was going to happen. She gave them kudos, however, on the fact they successfully broke into her comms unit to give a warning. Of course if they had any inkling of who was behind the yoke, they'd never have wasted their breath. Pressing her lips together, she contemplated giving them a verbal response when her hovercar jolted a bit from being hit from behind.

"I guess I took too long to answer." Scarlett muttered while being aware the others would hear. "No one has any patience anymore."

Wintyrs reached out to her dash and pressed a grey button. After a quiet chirp of acknowledgement, a billowing dark grey cloud exuded from her exhaust pipe, completely enveloping the cruiser on her bumper. Even with the soundproofing installed inside her vehicle, she could clearly hear theirs bang into something - likely a tree - before crashing down on the road below. Both occupants climbed out and when Scarlett risked looking at them she could tell they were not harmed from the impact. Their vehicle, on the other hand, had not been ready to land. The hovercar blew apart at the seams on landing. One down. The problem which now lay ahead was the other two units knowing whomever drove her hovercar wasn't about to cooperate. And had some tricks up their sleeve.

"Red hovercar, you are now ordered to pull over. Driver, you will be arrested by any force deemed necessary."

She gave them credit. They were still trying to take her out of the equation peacefully. This time she felt they deserved a response. Even if it wasn't going to be what they wanted to hear. She activated the comms channel to them.

"Attention, police units. This is the driver of the red hovercar. I graciously decline your invitation to pull over for a party at your place. Catch me if you can."

Scarlett laughed into the channel then shut it down as the hovercar jolted from side to side when each to the remaining two units took turns hitting her. She wanted to wish them luck with that endeavour for they wouldn't even be able to scratch the paint. All they'd succeed in doing is causing damage to their own vehicles. And when she looked over each one, Scarlett noted dents already forming.

Deciding to focus on the one on the left, Scarlett pushed back before pulling to one side and hitting them a little harder. The patrol unit veered slightly off course. She was about to follow when she realized the second one wasn't taking advantage of the opening. A knot formed in the pit of her stomach as she moved her attention forward only to see it in pursuit of the rest of her team. And William.

"Damon, one slipped past me."

"No shit!" Raynott yelled through the comm. "They're shooting at us!"

"Hang on! I'm coming!"

"I can evade. I think. If only this tub of lard was more maneuverable!"

"Just… sit tight. Continue on course, I'll get him off you."

Damon glanced at the comms speaker when a burst of static came through. He didn't want to look in the rearview mirror but felt compelled to. What he saw made his stomach turn. A fireball falling with a small mushroom cloud when what was left of the vehicle smacked into the ground at high speed. Slamming his fist on the dash told the others something was wrong. Very wrong.

"Damon…" William met the other man's eyes in the rearview mirror. "Do I want to ask?"

"One of the hovercars behind us just went down in a literal ball of fire." He answered in a tightly controlled voice.

"Damn it!" The Spymaster closed his eyes, automatically thinking worst case scenario.

"Now hang on, William. We don't know it was Scarlett. There's no way to tell from this distance. We'd have to circle back to verify and no - before you even think about asking - we're not doing that. We still have one of Vargas' units after us so what we're going to do is exactly what Scarlett told us to. Get to the airfield and board that plane." Damon returned his attention to what he was doing.

"How much further?" Feiyan inquired, lowering the window she was seated next to.

"We're almost there. Why?"

"They are firing upon us once more. I don't take kindly to that." Taking the pistol Damon handed her while being glad she chose to sit up front next to him, Feiyan leaned out the window and returned fire.

"Damn it. We're so close. I'm going to pull right up to the plane and we hop on board. I'll cover us until the hatch closes. No arguments." Damon yanked the yoke suddenly, causing the hovercar to jerk left, nearly knocking Feiyan out her open window. Only Damon's hand quickly grabbing the waistband of her pants kept her in the vehicle.

For the umpteenth time Damon wished he'd borrowed a more maneuverable hovercar as he attempted to evade the weaponsfire directed at them. The airfield quickly approached. Damon pushed the vehicle to the highest speed it could muster while carrying four people. Frowning at the closed gate, Damon tightened his grip on the yoke.

"Hang on, folks!"

"You're not seriously about to do what I think you're..." William jerked in his seat restraint when the hovercar smashed through the gate, nearly causing their driver to lose control, "never mind..."

"They are nearly on top of us!" Zaliki called out, looking out the back window. "We will not be able to board the plane!"

Damon was about to answer when a voice came from the comm speaker.

"Yes you will!"

"Scarlett??" William's eyes widened when he heard her voice. "But... how??"

"Later. Time for these guys to finally get it through their thick skulls that we're not to be trifled with."

Having hidden herself slightly behind and to one side of the patrol unit, Scarlett knew the sun blocked the corrupted officers view of her. They had no idea she was there. And she would use that to her complete advantage. The timing needed to be perfect to get the unit off the bumper of her team in order for them to get on the plane. A small smile played once more over her lips. The fun wasn't over yet.

"We're pulling up to the stairs to board, where are you?" Damon's palms were damp with sweat, his hands continuing to grip the yoke tightly.

"Do what you need to do. Relax. I've got this."

Damon's question died on his lips when he glanced in the rearview mirror briefly to see Scarlett's hovercar streak between theirs and the patrol car, making the officers veer off to avoid a collision. "She's got their attention!" He pulled up beside the stairs leading to the plane then parked, turning the engine off. "Everyone out and get boarded. Tell the flight attendant you're with Michael Malley and he'll let you on. I'll lay down cover fire then join you once you're all through the hatch. Go!"

When Damon hopped out, his pistol already sat comfortably in his hand. He kept next to the hovercar, using it for cover. His eyes were glued to the sky, watching as Scarlett led the patrol unit on a merry little chase. Some of the aerobatics she was pulling off would've made him sick to his stomach. Yet, even so, her pursuers remained focused on her instead of them. If they survived, he'd have to remember to ask her how she managed it. When he heard someone shout his name, Damon looked over his shoulder to see Zaliki beckoning. Knowing she'd only do so if they were all safely aboard, he rose from his position of cover and ran for the stairs just as bullets peppered the pavement from behind as a fourth patrol hovercar entered the fray. Damon ran fast enough that each one missed but had to duck on the stairs themselves as the newcomers flew close enough to have cut off his head had he remained standing.

"Run, Damon!" Zaliki shouted, giving him what cover fire she could with the rifle she carried. She grinned when one of her shots hit the mark - the hovercar's hood. Smoke rose from the engine and the driver obviously struggled to maintain control, landing the unit on the other side of the airfield's fencing. "Gotcha."

"Nice shooting, Zaliki!" Damon jogged up the remaining stairs to enter the plane. Pressing the comm unit which still sat in his ear, he opened a channel to their absent team member. "Scarlett, we're aboard! Get your pretty ass down here so we can take off!"

Scarlett swerved, the latest weapons fire from behind barely missing her hovercar. She smiled when she heard Damon's news. But there was no way she'd be able to board that plane. At least... not in the traditional fashion. The thoughtful expression turned to one of unbridled excitement as she realized what she'd need to do.

"I won't shake them. Begin takeoff." Scarlett responded.

"We're not leaving without you!"

"I never said you would be. Lower the cargo door then start taxiing. If you reach takeoff speed, get airborne. Just don't close that hatch. Trust me."

Eyes widening when it dawned on him what Wintyrs wanted to attempt, Damon shook his head while eyeing her car a moment longer. "And I thought *I* was crazy." He muttered, kicking the stairs away before locking the main hatch. Once complete, Damon jogged up to the cockpit where he informed the female Captain of his colleague's plan. He sympathized with her the second he witnessed her reaction. A rather large gulp followed by a visible shudder.

"Is your friend insane?" The pilot asked, lowering the cargo hold ramp and starting the plane's engines.

"No more than I am." Damon didn't wait for her response, leaving the cockpit and going down the aisle. "You lot should buckle up. This is going to get bumpy."

Already someone who, at this stage in his life hated flying, William's whiter than normal face turned to follow Damon when the other man continued down the aisle towards the rear of the plane. "What about you?"

"I'll be fine." Damon called over his shoulder. He went into the cargo section of the plane and stared out the open ramp, almost hoping he could will Scarlett's hovercar into existence. Under his feet, he felt the plane picking up speed. It wouldn't be long before they were airborne and he knew the pilot wouldn't be able to keep the ramp open for long after the wheels left the tarmac. "Come on, Wintyrs, pull that rabbit out of your hat already. You know I hate being kept waiting." Although he believed he spoke only to himself, Damon forgot he still had an open comms with the woman in question.

"Well when you ask so nicely, how can I say refuse?" Scarlett replied, her hovercar suddenly wheeling into view behind the plane and giving chase. "Please tell me you're not in the cargo hold."

"I'm not in the cargo hold."

"Liar."

Scarlett set her sights on the ramp the plane was literally dragging behind it. She wasn't quite at her vehicle's top speed and she was gaining - one patrol unit still valiantly giving chase. When she noted the wheels of the plane starting to leave the ground, Wintyrs switched to air mode and took the hovercar up, matching the angle of ascent the winged beast took. She was losing ground. Her heart hammered in her chest while her finger hovered over the one button Myrtle told her to use only in emergencies. As far as she was concerned - this definitely qualified. She pressed the red button. Almost immediately the hovercar gained a burst of speed powerful enough to push her back in her seat and keep her there. The cargo bay of the plane approached at an alarming speed. Scarlett removed her finger from the button and hit the brakes the second she was on the ramp, managing to get the hovercar stopped just before Damon became a fly on her windshield.

Damon cringed when the vehicle came flying - literally - into the plane. When it continued sliding towards him, he brought a leg up to his chest, trying to make himself as small as possible. As the hovercar finally came to a rest, Damon glanced down at the one leg on which he balanced to see that the front bumper of the vehicle gently rested against the side of his knee. Releasing the breath he'd inadvertently held, Damon rested the foot he'd raised on the hood of the car as the female driver finally emerged.

"If you were aiming to pancake me - you missed." Damon remarked, throwing her a smile.

"I said not to be in the cargo hold." Scarlett closed up her hovercar while she spoke.

"Nooo... you said 'please tell me you're not in the cargo hold' not to get the hell out of the cargo hold."

"Oh..." She paused then shrugged with a grin. "My mistake."

"Your..." shaking his head, Damon climbed over the hood of the car to regain his freedom. Once accomplished, he walked over and gave her a gentle hug.

"Uh... what'cha doing there, quick draw?" Scarlett teased, laughing when he pulled away quickly. "I'm kidding. I didn't hurt you with that landing, did I?"

"Nah, I'm made of pretty resilient stuff. In all seriousness, though, that was some pretty amazing driving. Flying?" His voice held a note of admiration when he spoke.

"Thanks. A lot of that was Myrtle's doing, to be honest. She put an emergency speed boost on the hovercar."

"And that fireball we saw during your little dance with Vargas' men?"

"Oh... that... I didn't know Myrtle added a rocket launcher to my car's arsenal. Heat-seeking to boot. While it didn't destroy that patrol car, the resulting small explosion was more impressive than I thought it would be. So I used that to my advantage and bided my time for the perfect opening to take on the third." Wintyrs explained.

Damon held up a finger. "Hang on... did you use us as bait?"

"Um..."

"You used us as bait."

"Maybe..."

"You. Used us. As bait."

"Yeah, I kinda did." Making the admission with a wince, Scarlett tried to ignore the disbelief written across his face.

"Unbelievable." He shook his head then grinned. "I'd probably have done the same thing."

"I know you would have." She chuckled quietly. "Does our pilot have our heading?"

"I was about to head up to the cockpit to provide her with that when a certain someone tried to pin me against the wall with a hovercar." He teased gently.

Scarlett was about to retort then realized he'd been precisely where he'd not only needed but also wanted to be the entire time. "Why don't we both head that way? I'm sure the others are wondering what's going on."

With a silent nod, Damon led her through a hatch to the main area of the plane where the rest of their team sat, anxiously awaiting news. "Hey guys - look who I found." He stepped to one side to reveal who followed in his wake then strode to the cockpit to fill their Captain in.

"Scarlett." William breathed out her name when he saw her standing there. Before anyone could stop him he was out of his seat and taking her in his arms.

Wincing, Wintyrs very gently pushed him away. "I'm still known as Katriona Malley on this plane." She said, ensuring her voice was loud enough for only the three of them to hear. "Michael's wife. We need to keep those covers active if we want the crew's to cooperation."

Dropping his arms from her as if he'd been burned, William backed off. He kept his face carefully schooled in case anyone had eyes on them. A fact he should have thought of sooner. "Forgive me, Katriona, if I overstepped any boundaries."

"You are forgiven." Scarlett replied in German, noting the slight surprise of each of her companions when she changed languages. "The crew of this vessel as well as the owner believe me only able to speak German but capable of understanding English." She quickly explained while Damon rejoined them.

"We're on our way back to merry old London. I'm assuming that's where we wanted to head." He stated, appearing non-plussed at hearing Scarlett's change of languages.

"We can go to Raven's Way once we land." Feiyan said. "I can easily provide a safe place to rest at my home there for all of you... if you and your lovely wife would care to join us of course, Mr. Malley."

"We'd be delighted, madame. Thank you." If he were startled at her referring to him as his cover identity, Damon did a remarkable job of hiding it. "You're certain we wouldn't be a burden?"

"I wouldn't have offered if I thought you would be."

"Fair enough."

Scarlett shook her head silently, moving to one of the windows to peer outside. No matter how she tried, worry lingered in the back of her mind like a constant companion. That last patrol unit of Vargas' witnessed her maneuver. Of that she had no doubt. Which meant they'd be able to identify the plane she boarded. If what she did could be called boarding, of course. Depending on Vargas' reach as Spymaster, he could alert all airports to be on the lookout for them. Even label them fugitives to ensure local authorities would make an honest attempt to apprehend them if a local agency couldn't send one of their assets.

The only thing currently working in their favour was the destination Damon chose. London, at least, was their own agency's territory. That gave them some ground to stand on. Even if it was shaky. If indeed Amir still lived and made it back to the Centurian Agency... then that changed everything. Leaning her forehead against the fabric lining the inside of the plane's hull, Scarlett sighed quietly. Weariness penetrated every pore of her body, including her bones, but she dare not rest. Not yet.

"Are you alright?" Zaliki's voice coming from right beside her caused Wintyrs to jump in surprise.

"I'm fine, thanks." Scarlett replied in German. She instinctively knew the other woman understood her. "Why do you ask?"

"Dam... Michael..." Zaliki flinched at the slip of her tongue, "told us what you had to do to get on the plane. I have to say - I don't think any of the rest of us could pull off a stunt like that."

"I think you could. You just need the right incentive. And the right tech outfitted on your vehicle."

"Plus skill."

"True."

Zaliki studied the face of the woman next to her. "Do you wish to speak about whatever it is that's on your mind?" She lowered her voice so only Wintyrs could hear her.

"I wouldn't know where to begin." She sombrely admitted.

"Even if it's jumbled, I would be honoured to assist if I can."

Taking a moment to let that sink in, Scarlett wasn't sure what to say. A virtual stranger was offering to hear thoughts she wasn't able to follow herself. It was an offer the likes of which she'd never received on any previous occasion.

"Thank you, Zaliki." She felt like once the words started they wouldn't stop. "I'm worried about what could come next."

"Tell me. And be glad I speak German fluently. Do you wish for me to do so or to continue as we are?"

"Continuing as we are is absolutely fine." Scarlett let her gaze to linger on the clouds floating below them. "By any chance... do you know how long your former Spymaster's reach is?"

"Mmh... a question I have often pondered. In truth you know as much as I do. Having met and seen of what he is capable, I would say his reach is possibly longer than any of us - save for perhaps William - can imagine. Why do you ask?"

"Because I don't believe anywhere we think might be safe will be."

"Keep going." Eager to hear what was going through the woman's head, Zaliki gave her her undivided attention.

"We're heading to London. Our home turf, if you will. Who's to say our landing area will be safe? If we're right and Amir is alive, odds are he'll have run right back to the agency as soon as he could. I'm willing to bet he's mobilized everyone there whose loyalty can be guaranteed."

"You think he'll have agents on the ground waiting for us."

"Vargas' men can identify what plane we're on." Scarlett gave voice to the biggest concern on her mind.

Zaliki fell silent then nodded slowly. "Something we should have anticipated." Her voice didn't waver despite the news causing adrenaline to surge. "We should bring this to William."

"Because he's a Spymaster? We could. Or we do our jobs and figure it out ourselves as if he's just another asset to protect." Feeling like she'd already been relying on her Spymaster too much already - like he were a crutch - Scarlett decided to solve this one without his assistance. Like she should have been doing from the get-go. "Our job is to think on our feet. To adapt to any situation. And that's exactly what we're going to do." Wintyrs turned around, catching a glimpse of Zaliki's stunned expression as she did, to see if the other three were all seated in the cabin. Which they were.

"Scarlett?" Willam spoke first, seeing her watching them unnerved him. "Is everything alright?" He realized too late he'd called her by the wrong name and winced, knowing it was too late to take it back.

Damon sighed, covering his face with one hand. Of all the people he thought might slip up - William had not even made the list. "Good job there, mate."

"Sorry Michael."

"Forget about it. I forgot you knew my nickname for my darling wife. She does love that colour. Especially when it's draining from someone's body."

Relief passed through William's face, lasting only an instant, when Damon managed to cover up his error. "It completely slipped my mind you hate anyone else called her that. Can you forgive me?"

"This transgression only. Do it again and there'll be hell to pay. Even if you're my best friend. Got it?"

"Got it." His voice grew soft, pretending to reel from the reprimand. Anyone who might be listening in would think his feelings of regret were genuine.

"Back to why my wife's staring at us though. Darling? Care to share?" Damon returned her look.

"We need to change our landing plans." Scarlett stated matter-of-factly.

Having taken a sip of water, Damon spat it out in surprise and coughed, trying not to choke on the few drops that managed to escape the mass exodus. "I'm sorry. I thought you said we have to change our landing location."

"I did."

"Why??"

"How about you trust me on this. We can't risk landing at the same airfield we left from. There's a strong chance doing so could be hazardous to our health."

"Do what she says, Michael." The support came from William. The tone of her voice told him that she believed this to be of the utmost importance. He couldn't deny her instincts.

Blowing out a breath, Damon scratched his head. "I'm not sure if there's an airfield we could class as 'under the radar' near London - or

Raven's Way for that matter."

"Really, Michael? Are you forgetting you told me who owns this plane? I'm sure an arms dealer has at least one location to put this bird down undetected." Now was no time for the other man to bluff his way out of a solution. William studied his face. If Raynott lied to him, he'd know.

"Do you have any idea what I'll owe her to get the information never mind making use of it?"

"We can deal with that later." Pausing for a moment, William tilted his head as part of what Damon said sunk in. "Her?"

"Yeah. Her." Slouching in his seat, Damon procrastinated going to the cockpit in order to answer his friend's questions better. "She's the one arms dealer who always manages to elude any agent that any agency sends after her."

"You don't mean…"

"Yep. Nightingale is what she goes by. And she can be just as ruthless as Vargas if she chooses."

12

"So after you left the… organization you were working for legitimately you, what? Got in bed with her?" William stiffened in disbelief.

"Are you talking literally or figuratively?" Damon shot back. He thought there was no need to defend anything he might have had to do to survive after cutting ties with the agency.

"Either. Both." William noted out of the corner of his eyes that all three women paid keen interest in the conversation. A discussion teetering dangerously on the edge of interrogation.

"I don't have to explain myself."

"On the contrary. You agreed to come back to the organization. That means you have to explain yourself if I ask. And I'm asking. Nightingale is another enigma. One a lot of people have been trying to put a stop to for years. So yes or no - were you or are you intimate with her?"

Bowing his head, Damon chewed the inside of his cheek while carefully considering his answer. He wanted to point out he hadn't signed the papers swearing him back to being loyal to William yet. At the same time he didn't want to jeopardize his chance to return to the fold. That last thought cinched his answer. "Both. How else do you think I had access to this plane? She doesn't lend it out to just anyone who asks."

Wishing for a different response, William nodded. "Would you be willing to sketch her face for us later so we know who we have to thank?"

"No." Damon didn't need any time at all for that inquiry. "Once I'm officially back, I'm going to get her to… help… us. She'd be an amazing asset to have." Hopefully William would understand. Even if they weren't being eavesdropped on, turning people into informants was challenging enough.

Scratching his chin, William mulled over Damon's words. When they rebuilt their agency he knew they'd also need to connect to some new contacts. Nightingale, though... he couldn't decide if she was worth the risk. "What makes you think you can trust her, Michael?"

"Not a damned thing."

The answer startled William and he made eye contact with the other man. "Go make the call. We'll deal with the consequences later. What I know right now is that this bird can't stay airborne indefinitely."

"Alright, William, I'm going. But be warned, I may end up offering her a, uh, date... with you."

William would've choked had he been eating or drinking. "Michael, you know full well I have a girlfriend. I doubt she'd take kindly to me going on a date with another woman."

"Beg to differ." Damon interrupted his friend's train of thought. "If it helps save your life, I'm sure she won't mind a bit."

A feeling of helplessness rushed over William as he turned his eyes to her and noted a smirk on her face. "Katriona, help a guy out here, would ya?"

"At some point we must all pay a price." Scarlett answered, trying not to laugh. Not an easy feat given the nearly comedic expression of shock on the face of the man she loved. "I'm sure if she loves you she'll understand."

"I hope you're right." William's eyes softened then he nodded to Damon. "Promise her what you feel you need to, Michael."

"Understood. I'll be back in a few minutes." Rising from his seat, Damon jogged off to make the call.

Scarlett shook her head, watching William run his hands through his incredibly short hair. If push came to shove, she knew he'd do whatever he had to. Even if he didn't want to. Just like so many things hidden in each of their pasts. The fact something he hadn't done yet bothered him so greatly increased the admiration she felt for the man.

"If Vargas can identify this plane and pass its description on to others," Zaliki needed to air her concern, hoping - in a convoluted way - that she wasn't the only one amongst them who felt troubled, "would it not stand to reason that anyone who knows of this Nightingale might put two and two together? If the agencies have attempted to take her down or disrupt her operation in the past, they'd be able to link this plane to her."

Wintyrs frowned but agreed with what the other woman said. The concern was valid. Also one she hadn't wished to burden the team with. "The thought crossed my mind, yes. And I'm sure we're not the only ones. I think the risk is worth it. So what if they connect the plane to her? I'm certain she has many places we could land and even the best agents can't cover them all."

"Agreed." Damon said upon his return, his call not having taken as long as anticipated. "And that's exactly why, when I made our request, I asked for one which wasn't completely isolated but also not the busiest. The pilot's being informed as we speak and also being advised to not relay our course change and to turn off our transponder in order to avoid any attempts at tracking us. Now... because I had to ask for so many things..." he held a hand up, "I know, I know. It doesn't seem like a lot however I was assured all of what I requested would take some doing. Anyway - William, old buddy, you've got yourself a blind date when we land."

"Great."

"I do mean that literally, by the way."

"Meaning?"

"You have to be blindfolded. The entire time."

"I'm sorry... I think I misheard you..."

"You didn't."

"And what of his bodyguard?" Feiyan spoke up. "Surely this Nightingale understands that someone of William's influence must be protected - at all times."

Pressing his lips together, Damon shook his head. "Not gonna happen, I'm afraid. The date will take place in the hanger of the airfield we'll be landing at. We can stand outside but are not permitted to cross the threshold. If we do so at any time during the date then we're signing our own death warrants, as well as William's."

"A blindfolded date in an airplane hanger. Gives new meaning to the phrase 'blind date', doesn't it?" William hid his nervousness by cracking, what he hoped, was a funny joke. Not one of his companions smiled. "Look, I'll be fine. Nightingale obviously wants to keep her identity a closely guarded secret. Something each of us can appreciate."

"How long until we land?" Scarlett changed the topic of conversation, much to everyone's relief.

"Even on this jet of hers - a few hours." Raynott immediately responded. "We won't be anywhere close to Raven's Way though."

"Where will we be close to then?"

"Near to what used to be called Chester. In the middle of Devil's Run."

"Lovely. You sure know how to show a girl a good time, husband of mine." Scarlett slipped into character when the co-pilot joined them from the cockpit.

"Oh, everyone, this is our co-pilot." Damon snapped his fingers a couple of times as if trying to recall her name. "Shyleen... right?"

"Yes, Mr. Malley. I was asked to let you know we've altered course as requested. Our transponder has been deactivated and no one knows we've entered a new heading." The young brunette said, her clipped words revealing a subtle French accent.

"I appreciate the update, thank you." Damon gave the young woman a smile. Unfortunately for her it happened to be the one which tended to cause women to swoon. Her facial expression softened considerably while her cheeks reddened with a blush borne not of embarrassment but of arousal. The poor girl cleared her throat then vanished back to the cockpit as quickly as she'd appeared.

"You're cruel, Michael." Scarlett said, shaking her head in amusement. "That poor girl."

"I can't help being irresistible, darling."

"Oh, I'm sure you could. If you wanted to."

"Maybe. If, as you say, I wanted to. Which I don't."

"I take it back. You're not cruel. You just hate being tied down. Begging the question - why did you marry me?" If he wanted to act the way he was, then Scarlett had no qualms over exhibiting similar behaviour.

"I, uh..." Caught off-guard, Damon stared at her, looking like a deer caught in the headlights.

"Well? I'm waiting." Scarlett crossed her arms, tapping the toes of her right foot impatiently.

"Cause I love you, of course." Maintaining the character of Michael Malley was becoming exhausting.

"I think we should discuss a divorce." With a fling of her hair, Scarlett looked up at the ceiling of the airplane which was when her eyes caught a glimpse of a fairly well-hidden camera. Seeing it made her glad she, Damon and William continued to play out their cover identities to the best of their abilities.

Feiyan silently chuckled at the display. Especially when the man in question appeared speechless. "I believe you have made your point, Katriona."

Deigning to grace Damon with a smugly superior look, Scarlett scoffed. "We shall see. I could always re-introduce him to my knives..." she trailed off, letting him fill in the blanks with his imagination.

"Katriona, darling, forgive my wandering eye." He didn't need to see the camera to know necessity dictated to act like the married couple they claimed to be.

Narrowing her eyes, Scarlett pretended to scrutinize him for a few moments before relaxing her stance. "Oh, very well. You're forgiven. This time. Should I bear witness to such an... indignity... again then rest assured I will be terminating this marriage. Permanently."

It was all Damon could do to keep himself from laughing. Michael Malley would never laugh at such a comment. He'd be genuinely terrified of his so-called wife following through on her threat. "Yes, dear."

"Good. Now that that's sorted out..." Moving across the cabin, Wintyrs sat herself on Damon's lap, wrapping her arms around his neck then leaned in so she could whisper in his ear in English. To anyone watching it would look as though she were kissing his neck. "Will William be in danger?"

Damon turned his head towards her, to appear as if he were trying to capture her lips with his own. "I honestly don't know." He whispered back. "Speaking of William... he looks ready to beat me to a pulp. Maybe we should stop what we're doing for his sake?"

"Is that what Michael Malley would do?"

A soft groan escaped Damon's lips. "Woman, do you have any idea what you're doing to me?"

"What makes you think I don't? But in all seriousness, would Michael Malley be able to stop cold if a woman he was with was doing this to him?"

"Hell no." His voice cracked slightly then he finally captured her lips with his own, holding her tightly against his body to prevent her escape.

William stared at them. He couldn't help himself. When his fingers began to cramp, he looked down to see he was clutching the arms of his seat so tightly his knuckles were turning white. In fact, he gripped them so hard his nails left indentations in the fabric. With great effort, he relaxed his fingers though he thought his nails might be permanently stuck, such was the effort needed to pull them free. Giving himself a moment to calm down, William peered at the areas on the arms where his nails had been and thanked whatever powers that be they hadn't broken through the fabric itself. Although he did worry that the indents might now be a permanent feature.

"You may not wish to stare at them so intently lest your jealousy be observed." Zaliki mumbled under her breath from her seat next to William.

Using everything in his training, William quashed the feelings the green monster within brought forth. "Thank you, Zaliki." He replied softly once he had himself back under control.

Nodding once, Zaliki then swallowed when the plane hit some turbulence. "Oh joy…"

William glanced over at her, noting her sudden sickly pallor as well as the same tight grip on her arm rests she had talked him out of. "Zaliki? Are you alright?"

"It has been some time since I last flew on a plane. I'd nearly forgotten how much I despise the activity." She was ashamed to note her voice quivered when she spoke. "And I am also not a fan of heights."

William raised his eyebrows. Reaching over, he covered her hand with his. "There's no shame in admitting you have a weakness."

Snorting softly, she shook her head and lowered her voice to a whisper only he could hear. "You're very different from my previous Spymaster. From Vargas." She amended. "Weakness is not tolerated in the Orion Agency."

"You'll find a lot of differences between two agencies, never mind two Spymasters." William gave her an encouraging smile while keeping his words the same volume as hers. "Everything you feel, every fear, every strength and - yes - every weakness, comes together to make you who you are. I want my agents to embrace that. To embrace all the broken bits inside them and acknowledge you wouldn't be where you are today without them. I know it's a big ask of someone who's been trained to believe the complete opposite but I think you'll find once you try, you'll wonder why you never did before."

Having closed her eyes at a particularly strong jolt from the turbulence, Zaliki reopened them, wanting to see his face. The kindness she saw there nearly caused tears to well in her eyes. Nearly. "Thank you, William… you do realize…"

"That if there're listening devices on this plane I just revealed my true identity as well as your own? Yeah. I'm fully cognizant of that and should something come of it, I'll deal with it then. I think... I think I'm done living in the shadows. Hiding behind a mouthpiece and my agents."

"What exactly are you proposing?"

"I'm not sure. But when I figure it out, you lot will be the first to know."

13

The remainder of the flight transpired without incident. That one bout of turbulence had been the only literal bump in their journey. Upon landing, their co-pilot rejoined them in the cabin, only this time with a little surprise.

"William? Will you join me, please?" Shyleen politely made the order sound like a question. A loaded one given the handgun she now sported in her right hand. "The rest of you are to remain on board until my employer completes her... business... with your friend."

"Now just one moment, dear." Feiyan rose to her feet, eyes on the weapon when it trained on her the second she moved. "We were advised we could wait outside the hanger while this event took place."

"Plans change."

"Then you have a problem, dear girl. I am his personal bodyguard. If I am not nearby then he will not be attending this so-called date."

Shyleen stared at her, obviously not having expected to encounter resistance. She chewed the inside of her lip while thinking about the older woman's provision. "I'm not sure I can..."

"You know what the original arrangement was, Shyleen." Damon added his two cents. "We lot wait outside the hanger while William dines with your employer. Please don't tell me she's reneging on our agreement."

The young woman stared at him. She'd been assured having a weapon in hand would cause the passengers to comply. Swallowing, she glanced over her shoulder when the pilot joined them. "Ma'am... they won't cooperate... Mr. Malley raises a good point..."

"I heard." The pilot cast her gaze over her passengers. "I can guarantee she won't like it but I say stick to your original arrangement.

Just get off my bird before bullets start flying. I don't need to waste time patching holes."

"Thank you, Eliza." Damon bowed his head to her respectfully.

"Just… go… before I change my mind or my employer changes it for me." Eliza waved a hand at them, wanting them to disembark with all haste.

Scarlett wasn't about to question their good fortune. With a nod to the others, she led the way to the hatch and was pleasantly surprised to find it open with the stairs already hooked up for them to descend. Her eyes scanned the tarmac, what was visible to her at any rate. Despite the cloud cover eliminating natural sunlight - which would have been of immense help - she saw nothing amiss. She even let her eyes roam over the tops of the nearby buildings. If there was a sniper anywhere then they were extremely well hidden.

"What's the verdict, Katriona?" Damon came up to stand behind her, doing the very same sweep.

"No threats visible to the naked eye. I think we're good - for now at least." She answered while descending the steps. "I am, however, slightly surprised at the lack of welcoming committee from Nightingale. Not even an airport crew. Thoughts?"

"She owns the entire airfield. Any crew that were here to place the stairs are already off to the next project until Eliza recalls them to refuel the plane. I'm sure once we're all on the tarmac her bodyguards will appear out of thin air. Actually, they'll probably come right out of that hanger straight ahead. Otherwise, based on past experience, Eliza would've pulled us right inside. The fact she didn't tells me whatever Nightingale has cooked up for her 'date' with William, we can confirm it's happening in there."

A tall pale man wearing a dark suit, complete with a black dress shirt, exited the hanger and met the group at the bottom of the stairs. "Only William was to disembark."

Scarlett noted the man appeared to avoid sunlight at any cost such was the paleness of his skin. The short platinum blonde hair he had only added to, what she considered to be, the unhealthy pallor he sported. "Our original arrangement is the one we are standing by. And the one your employer should honour." Since she detected his voice held a distinctly German accent, she felt no qualms in speaking her cover identity's native language.

"I prefer to speak in English. If you are unable to converse in that tongue then you may remain silent. I also prefer to deal with men.

There is only one woman who has earned my respect."

Even Damon's eyebrows rose at not only what the man had said but also the tone with which he spoke to Scarlett. "I'd be careful if I were you, mate."

The pale man turned his attention to the man who spoke. "And you are? After you tell me your name, you will explain your comment."

"Michael Malley. And that's my wife you disrespected. You're going to apologize right now or I won't be responsible for what happens next."

"I have no reason to apologize. You may call me Leopold."

"Like I said Leo..."

"Leopold."

Damon smiled maliciously. "Leo. I can't be responsible for what happens next."

Leopold was going to answer when, seemingly from out of nowhere, the sharp edge of a blade found itself against his throat. Scarlett stared into his light blue eyes, keeping the knife in place and allowing outrage at being treated the way he had done to reflect in her face. Hearing of such things occurring always angered her but having it directed at her? Well, that was something else entirely.

"Issue your apology. Unless you *want* me to slit your throat. I'm given to understand it can be a very painful way to die - if done correctly." She could see Leopold grinding his teeth, his adam's apple bobbing up and down while he processed the position in which he now found himself was by no means ideal. There was something else in the man's eyes. Knowledge he knew and none of their group were privy to. She slowly lowered the blade. "You wanted to see how I'd react to how you spoke to me. Why?"

Spreading his hands apart in front of him as a way of attempting to placate their guests, Leopold smiled. "One has to know where one stands when coming face to face with Scarlett Wintyrs."

Shocked silence descended over the entire group, Wintyrs being the first to recover spoke up in English. "How..."

"With your renowned memory, you don't recall our last meeting?" Leopold grew smug. "Well, now I feel somewhat vindicated at least. Oh... and I won a bet. Thank you for that."

"I don't understand. Katriona? You lied to me?" Damon turned to her in his guise of Michael. "To both William and I? Is that what this man is saying??"

Pursing her lips while attempting to appear annoyed her cover had been blown, Scarlett avoided eye contact with either of the men on her team. "I'm sorry, Michael."

"Was everything a lie? Was nothing real? Not even your love for me?" Anger coloured Damon's voice to maintain his cover. An action which caused Leopold to shake his head slightly.

"You are, of course, joking. Are you not - Damon Raynott?"

Nearly choking, Damon glared at the newcomer. "I don't know who that is. I am..."

"Damon Raynott." Leopold finished for him. "The only one of you whose identity we believe is William. Speaking of which..." He held up a wide, thick black cloth, "it's time for your meeting."

Moving past the others, William could almost hear Scarlett's silent plea for him not to go. "Is the blindfold really necessary?"

"Non-negotiable." Replied Leopold. "Turn around."

William did as he was bade, closing his eyes as the cloth wrapped around his head. He hissed quietly when it was tied nearly too tight. Unable to open his eyes under the cloth, William realized it had been secured that way to render him completely blind. What didn't help matters was the cloth was so wide it ranged from the top of his forehead right to nearly the tip of his nose. A rough hand grabbed his right arm in a vice-like grip, turned him around and forced him to begin walking.

Scarlett watched Leopold escort their Spymaster into the hanger, anger suffusing her face. An emotion she barely managed to keep in check as two men - who were so burly they were obviously bodyguards - closed the door behind Leopold and William then took up positions in front of it. "Damn it!"

"How the hell did he know who we are?" Damon growled, sounding ready to murder someone.

"A good question." Zaliki said softly. Feeling like a change of topic was necessary, she did just that in order to try and distract both Wintyrs and Raynott. "Were you blindfolded whenever you met her, Damon?"

"Each and every time."

"Really? Even when you and she... you know..."

"Like I said - each and *every* time. I have no idea what she looks like so please don't ask." Damon wondered if he sounded as distracted as he felt.

"Ah... sorry. I've been wondering that since the plane..."

"No need to apologize. But who told her about us..."

"Leopold inferred he'd encountered Scarlett before." Feiyan's calm voice penetrated the conversation. "Perhaps Nightingale has as well."

"What's frustrating is that I don't remember him. At all." Scarlett's frown deepened, creating deep wrinkles in her forehead. "I don't think the encounter - whenever or wherever it happened - was face to face. But if I was on assignment, I would've been using a cover identity."

"Which circles us right back around to how the hell does he know both our true identities." Shaking his head, Damon thought of something else. "And is he the only one who knows? He referred to 'we', inferring at least one other person shares the knowledge. But is it Nightingale? Or someone else entirely?"

The point he made was good, Scarlett realized. She looked at the hanger. What had their Spymaster just walked in to?

14

William flinched when the door to the hanger closed behind them. He cocked his head when he heard a lock slip into place. The urge to pull away from the hand guiding him was strong but he quelled it as best he could. If something went awry during this meeting - or whatever was about to happen - then backup would be slowed by not only that lock he'd heard but also undoubtedly by the guards Nightingale was certain to have.

"Ahh… there's our guest of honour." A woman's voice echoed through the hanger to his ears. The words held an accent he couldn't quite identify.

"Nightingale, I presume?" William asked while Leopold sat him down in what felt like a wooden chair.

"Very good guess. Leopold, please ensure he is… comfortable."

Eyebrows drawing together at the odd turn of phrase, William moved to stand again only to find a second set of hands on his shoulders pushing him down and holding him in place. "Now wait just a damned minute here…" he said as someone grabbed his left arm then the other person his right. Before he knew what was happening, his wrists were put in leather cuffs and tightly secured to the arms of the chair.

"Relax, William. This is as much for my protection as yours." Nightingale smiled as the process that had been completed on his wrists was repeated for his ankles. One ankle tightly restrained to each of the chair's front legs. "Thank you, gentlemen. Leopold, please bring the food. The rest of you are dismissed. Take up your positions outside and ensure we are not disturbed." Gazing upon her guest, her smile remained, watching while he struggled with the restraints.

"Comfortable?"

No matter how he twisted, William felt no give in the leather cuffs. He couldn't move. His body stiffened nearly of its own accord when arms went around his waist and another leather strap wound around him in that same area, effectively completing his captivity. It was official. Unable to see or move, with backup unable to reach him with any sort of ease, William knew he was in dire straits if this went sideways.

"Can you explain to me, please, how this is for my protectiommmmph!" William's question was cut off when food was placed in his mouth.

"Eat first. We can talk later. I'm sure you must be famished after your flight." Nightingale spoke softly. "Please don't think you're getting some kind of special treatment by being bound and blindfolded in that chair. All first meetings begin the same. The dinner part, however, that's just for you." She helped him drink some of the red wine she'd chosen to go with the roast chicken.

William pulled his head back after swallowing some of the wine. "I'm sorry. I'm not really a fan of wine in general to be honest." Although felt some relief about the restraint system not being unique for him. He'd been worried that perhaps they'd figured out who he really was.

"And here I thought as part owner of Dolus you'd like all sorts of alcoholic beverages."

"That's Michael's purview. Mine's the decor, the food and the ambiance."

"Do you mind if I ask why you and Micheal both needed to get off the island?" Nightingale opened a beer for him then gently held the bottle to his lips for him to take a sip. "Better?"

"Much. Thank you." William replied after swallowing some of the familiar liquid. "As for why we had to leave... the local authorities decided I wasn't paying them enough so they targeted both us and Dolus." Knowing the lie would be believable for her made it easier for him to say.

"Vargas still the Chief of Police there?"

"Yeah. As corrupt as they come."

Nightingale chuckled softly. "Don't I know it." A soft sigh could be heard. "Tell me why you're travelling with Scarlett Wintyrs and Damon Raynott." Annoyance flickered through her voice upon saying Damon's name.

"Hey, I had no idea that's who they are. As far as I knew he was Michael Malley and she was his new wife. When your man out there said those other names I nearly shit my pants. Especially when Wintyrs' name came into play." William easily maintained his character - mainly because his answer did bear some semblance of truth. He really did nearly shit his pants.

"I see…"

"You don't believe me?" The answering silence spoke volumes. "I ran Dolus. You, of all people, know the kind of clientele I catered to. Do you really think I'd relish a visit from, let alone board a plane with, the world's self-proclaimed best agent??"

"Interesting." Her voice held a chill to it causing a shiver to run down William's spine.

"What is?"

"That you would risk such a bold-faced lie when being as helpless as you are."

"I'm not lying." William was pleased to note his voice remained steady despite the heavy pounding of his heart.

"Remember to whom you speak." Reaching over to him, Nightingale gently ran a hand through his hair. "I'm certain Michael - sorry, I of course mean Damon - told you everything he could about me. Including the transactions I facilitate. I have to wonder why he'd share that with you. A mere business partner." Taking a handful of his hair, she yanked his head back hard and smiled when he groaned at the unexpected strain on his neck.

"I needed a new weapons broker." William grunted out, finding it somewhat difficult to speak. "He told me about you. It was just a fluke he'd been using your plane. I wanted him to arrange a meeting - I just wasn't anticipating one so soon."

Nightingale grew silent, staring down into the portions of his face which weren't obstructed by the blindfold. After weighing his words, she eventually released her grip on his head. What he said made a modicum of sense yet, at the same time, believing him didn't feel right. Trusting her instincts always proved the safest option. And they told her there was a lot more to this man than what her eyes saw. Which also suggested he could potentially be extremely valuable.

"Tell me, William, why is the Centurian Agency so very interested in you? Not to mention heavily vested in your safety given your travelling companions."

"I already told you…" Alarm bells rang in his head. William felt certain this mysterious woman was adding all the clues together despite his best efforts to achieve the contrary.

"You told me exactly what you thought I wanted, or needed, to hear. But the way you all acted on the plane... well... a picture says a thousand words. And what I witnessed spoke absolute volumes."

"What about what you heard?"

"Please. I don't have mics on my plane. I don't want to hear if anyone becomes... intimate. If you get my meaning."

"Only too well." William winced when he felt a pinprick in the back of his neck. "What was that??"

"A new, and very powerful, way to get the truth out of you." Nightingale gently dragged her fingertips along his neck, moving to sit in front of him again. "No more games."

William shook his head, mind growing hazy. "What... exactly... did you just dose me with?"

"A new concoction my boys wanted me to test out. I'm told it's a unique blend of ethanol, scopolamine and amobarbital."

Hearing her list managed to elicit another groan. Any of those on their own he could battle - and potentially win. All three mixed together? That was another story entirely. Sweat beaded on his forehead as he knew whatever she asked of him next, he would be compelled to speak only the truth.

"Tell me your true first name." Nightingale knew as soon as she saw the top of his forehead glistening in the light that the drug concoction was already at work.

"William." He answered, twisting his wrists desperately in the leather cuffs.

"Are you part owners of the Dolus club?"

"Yes." No matter how he tried to stop them, the answers passed through his lips of their own accord.

"What else do you do?"

He groaned and pulled harder on the restraints when she asked the one question he hoped to avoid. Trying valiantly not to answer, he pressed his lips together as hard as he could and winced when it felt like someone took a match to his brain.

"The more you fight it, the more painful it will become. Answer the question. What else do you do?" Seeing him struggling against the drug told Nightingale she was on the right track. He'd been lying to her.

A cry of pain left him at the same time as his reply. "I'm the

Spymaster for the Centurian Agency!"

15

A feral grin spread across Nightingale's face when it sunk in what prize she'd managed to rope in. She watched when he bowed his head after revealing his identity and knew some measure of shame must be coursing through his veins. A priceless treasure. That's what the man bound to the chair across from her just admitted he was. Absolutely priceless. Oh the secrets she could get from him. The things she could force him to help her plan. Then there were the capers he'd be able to help her get away with.

"Why did you seek me out?" Now she knew his true self, she needed to understand the intent he held towards her.

"To establish a connection between you and the Centurian Agency. We may need someone like you soon." No matter how he tried, William couldn't stop what, for all intents and purposes, was a bad case of verbal diarrhea.

"Interesting. We'll have to discuss what you had in mind. For now, though, we're going to load you up in our truck and head out." She paused thoughtfully. "Can you see any problems that course of action might bring about?" Given who he was, Nightingale figured she shouldn't let his talents go to waste.

"Several. One of them worse than any other."

"Tell me."

"Agent Wintyrs. She'll stop at nothing to get me back."

"Won't the others as well?" Doubt entered Nightingale's mind, knowing he couldn't lie to her with what coursed through his veins.

"Yes. But not with as much tenaciousness as Agent Wintyrs." Breathing hard, William told himself to shut up. To no avail.

"Now why is that?"

"She and I are... together..."

Nightingale fell silent again. Anything other than that. If only he had said anything other than that. Despite being a woman herself, the desire to draw the wrath of another female by taking her man from her was quite low on her list of things she wanted. Add to that Wintyrs being his best agent and the recipe for danger was pretty much all-encompassing. Rubbing her forehead, Nightingale began reconsidering the plan she'd formed. Although admittedly, it was still quite tempting - despite the risk.

"Were you in my shoes, William, and you had a Spymaster fall into your lap - would you take him with you and use him to your own advantage?"

'No!' William begged his mind to say. That's not what came out. "Yes."

"Why?"

"The advantage outweighs the risk."

"How long, do you think, before Agent Wintyrs catches up to us? And what will she do when she does?"

"Depends on the variables. As for what she'd do - she despises killing however I think she'd make an exception in this case."

"Thank you for being so transparent, William. Now, unfortunately, you did manage to convince me to have you join us on our journey, for you were definitely right about one thing. The advantage outweighs the risk." Nightingale very gently inserted another needle, the contents of which would counteract the serum already going through him.

William grunted upon feeling the sting of the needle in his neck. Very soon afterwards, his mind cleared as quickly as it had fogged over. "I'd urge you to reconsider."

"No reason I should."

"Except for the communicator Agent Wintyrs slipped into my pocket before I came in here. She's heard everything."

"What?! Why didn't you tell me that?!"

"You didn't ask. So, even under your drug's influence, I had no compulsion to inform you." The hanger door slamming open couldn't have been more perfectly timed.

"Nightingale!" Scarlett's voice rang clearly across the breadth of the hanger. "Leave now and I won't give chase - providing William there does not go with you. Lay one more hand on him, however, and all bets are off." She didn't move any closer than just over the threshold of the door for two reasons. One - if the woman decided to harm or kill

William then she was too far away to prevent it. Two - Scarlett knew Nightingale placed high value on her anonymity and Wintyrs wanted her to see she respected that. If only because she was fully aware of William wanting to cultivate her as an informant.

"How did you get past my guards...??"

"With skill. And a bit of guile. Oh, don't worry, they're just a bit tied up right now. Not a single one was harmed beyond what first aid could treat nor are any of them dead. In fact I would've been in here much sooner but I must give you credit. Your men are remarkably well-trained. I'm a bit disappointed none of them were female. I thought you believed in equal rights."

"I do. Just as I believe in being prepared." Nightingale smiled. "After all, I wanted to see what you were capable of before I unleashed my more skilled - and deadly - guards." With a snap of her fingers, Nightingale called forth her most elite. Dressed head to toe in black, each of the ten to fifteen distinctly feminine figures stepped out from the shadows where they'd been perfectly camouflaged. "Now, to revisit what you previously said, if you come any closer - I'll kill your Spymaster. Right here, right now. Stay put and he comes with me without being harmed. My guards - and I mean these lovely ladies here - will ensure our safe departure. They will only attack to defend themselves or me. Any questions?"

"Do you have any clue what will happen if you go down this path? The lengths myself, and others, will go to in order to retrieve him? You'll be signing your death warrant." Scarlett crossed her arms, taking another step inside the hanger. She felt more than heard the other three members of the team follow her inside and array themselves next to her on both sides.

"What she said." Damon stated, his eyes quickly taking in the situation. "Hello, Nightingale. Nice to see you again."

"Michael. Oh, I'm sorry. I suppose I should be calling you Agent Raynott. Who're your other friends?" Moving behind William, she gently placed the muzzle of her pistol against the helpless man's temple. "While introductions are made, I'd suggest you all remain right where you are."

The feel of cold metal against his temple made William flinch. Again he tried to no avail to free his wrists. Whatever grade of leather the restraints were made from, he couldn't get them to stretch in even the slightest.

"Zaliki." The woman standing to the left of Damon stated.

"And I am Feiyan." Came the response from Scarlett's right.

That final name drew Nightingale's attention to the older, Asian woman. Hearing what she had was as unexpected as anything could get. And as dreaded. Moreso than hearing Wintyrs' name. Her hand shaking with this new information, Nightingale slowly lowered the weapon from William's temple. Even her guards were looking back and forth between themselves, a cloud of uncertainty drifting through their ranks. After a few tense moments, each and every one of the black-clad women bowed deeply to Feiyan with a respect no other in the hanger could have imagined.

A low whistle echoed through the large space. "I think they know you, Feiyan. Or know of you." Remarked Damon, somewhat awestruck.

The older woman remained silent, the display having stunned her as well. Seconds turned to minutes before she regained enough composure to speak. "I thank you for the honour you show me. Something which must not have been easy for a group such as yours as I would imagine you honour each other above all else." Feiyan bowed gracefully in return. "That being said - if William is not returned to us then you will all see - first hand - of what I am truly capable."

One of the masked women stepped forward. "If we are asked to fight, to defend, then that is what we must do. That is what we have been hired for. What we have trained for. We would prefer not to fight you if it can be avoided."

"Believe me, the feeling is mutual." Feiyan took one step forward.

"Then please allow our employer to depart. With the male in contention."

"An event we cannot allow to come to pass." Reasoning with this group of masked women seemed to be the best solution Feiyan could see. If such a thing were possible. "Can you not see you are on the wrong side? You seem an honourable bunch of women. There is no honour to be had in defending one who brings harm down upon others."

The one who'd taken responsibility to speak for the group came forward, raking Feiyan with her gaze. "What would you know of her?"

Blinking rapidly, for the response had not been anticipated, Feiyan risked a quick glance at Scarlett who nodded once, almost imperceptibly, for her to continue. "The woman you've pledged yourselves to is known to us as an arms dealer. She goes by the name Nightingale. While I cannot say with any certainty who she has sold weapons to, I feel safe in assuming many deaths that have happened should not have." Feiyan hesitated briefly before finishing her thought. "Including those of children."

Those final words had an effect. Not the one Feiyan expected but she wouldn't look a gift-horse in the mouth. Half of the group of masked women turned to face Nightingale while the remainder maintained their focus on Scarlett's team. Wintyrs watched, being cautiously optimistic that perhaps the tide once again turned in their favour.

"Feiyan is not known to be deceitful in situations such as this. Speak true to us. Has she lied regarding you and what you do?" The woman who had been speaking with Feiyan continued in her role when she faced Nightingale. "Your answer will dictate the direction in which those events that are to follow take shape."

"So if I say the wrong thing, you'll turn on me? I've paid your group good money to ensure our safety." Nightingale growled out.

"Answer incorrectly or choose a path which proves unwise then your funds will be returned to you."

"Before or after you kill me."

"Answer my question and we will go from there."

After swallowing a lump of bile lodged in her throat, Nightingale gave in. "Fine. Yes. I'm an arms dealer. I sell weapons. Once in my buyers' hands, though, I wash my hands of any responsibility over what they're used for. Or how they're used. That... Feiyan... spoke the truth." She shrugged. "Everyone has something they excel at. It just so happens selling and brokering in the weapons trade is my greatest strength. I won't apologize for that."

"Before all hell breaks loose, can I say something?" William startled everyone when he spoke.

"Speak." The masked woman responded. "You have that right given you are the cause of this dispute."

"Uh... thanks. I think." Still vainly pulling on his restraints, he wasn't quite sure how to take the answer he'd been given. "Look, I can't see a damned thing but I've been listening. None of you want this situation to escalate to bloodshed no matter the bravado you might be trying to put off. Scarlett - tell the newcomers who we are. Let them see us as we truly are." William believed he knew who the group was and, if he was correct, then Feiyan had been absolutely right in bringing up the subject of honour.

Scarlett sighed heavily. Revealing the information William asked wasn't a plan she would normally back. "Just how many people are we sharing that information with, William?"

Licking his lips, William wondered why she seemed so hesitant to follow his orders. "Uh… well Nightingale already knows so I'd say the leader of these lovely ladies. Perhaps she'll be kind enough to allow you to whisper it in her ear?"

Wintyrs' attention shifted to the spokeswoman of the masked group. After what felt like an eternity, the woman nodded and came to stand in front of her. Taking a deep breath, Scarlett leaned in and uttered three words.

"The Centurian Agency."

The woman pulled away from Scarlett as if she's been burned. After moving backwards a few steps, she looked into Wintyrs' eyes, wondering if she were being lied to. Nothing in their depths indicated deceit. With a small wave of her hand, the rest of her troupe stood down - much to everyone's relief save for one person.

"What are you doing??" Nightingale couldn't believe what she was seeing.

"Recognizing an old ally." The woman responded, turning back to the one who had employed their services. Then she redirected her attention to the man bound in the chair. "An ally who was once there for us when we needed one most yet failed us at a most inopportune time."

"If we did then you have my most sincere apologies." William had forgotten about that event. "We, at the time, were trying to diffuse a situation that threatened to destroy every living being on the planet. We had to make a hard choice that day. One with dire repercussions."

"Our sisterhood was put to the brink of extinction."

"I… didn't know it had been that bad…" How could he tell her it was before his time without revealing who he was. The short answer was - he couldn't.

"Now you know. After such an occurrence, though, why would you think for one second we would take you back as an ally?"

"Because of your honour. Plus… we're trying to save the world. Again." Not wanting to go into any further detail, William hoped they had heard enough. He opened his mouth to say something else only to find a sticky substance pressed over his lips to prevent him from speaking. He shook his head but couldn't dislodge the obstruction.

"I think that's quite enough of that." Nightingale rubbed her thumb over the gel-type item she'd affixed to the bound man's mouth, ensuring it maintained a properly strong grip. "Only I know how to remove that, by the way." She ensured her face remained in the shadows so none of the others in the hanger could identify her. "If anyone else tries, it will expand over his nose, suffocating him."

"Damn it, Nightingale, we're trying to give you a chance here! Can't you see that?" Damon responded, unable to comprehend why the arms dealer continued on her original course. "If you take him then any offer we have for you is off the table. All we wanted was someone who could help us obtain information. In exchange, you'd get to keep doing what you're doing."

Nightingale frowned upon hearing his words. "How can I be certain that's not a ruse to get your boy here back?"

With a sigh, Damon shook his head. "You can't be. But I can tell you if it was then Ms. Wintyrs wouldn't still be standing beside me doing nothing. She'd be taking action. Yet here she is. Right next to me, letting me be all diplomatic-like. Which, if I might be so bold, I'm damned good at."

Biting her lower lip, Nightingale realized he was right about one thing at least. Wintyrs hadn't made a move. A fact which suggested he might be telling the truth. "Alright. Keep talking, I'm listening."

Damon breathed out in relief. Her answer could have easily gone the other way. "I'm not sure what else I can tell you. The deal's not mine to make. It's Williams. And you've ensured he can't say a damned thing."

"So make the deal yours. I'm sure William will honour anything you promise." Nightingale tapped the weapon's barrel against her captive's cheek. "Won't you, William."

William grunted quietly into the stuff on his mouth. His biggest concern was Damon writing a cheque they couldn't cash - so to speak. He supposed it was a chance they needed to take. When the barrel of the gun tapped his cheek to indicate she wanted his answer, William nodded.

"There you have it, Damon. He agrees. So make me an offer I simply can't refuse."

Giving Scarlett a sideways glance, Damon saw her nod concordance. He rubbed his brow, wondering what all he could put on the table. Then a thought struck him. "What would you like to see in the deal?"

"Two things. Access to all the weapons you use - past, present and future. I want full immunity from prosecution and assassination with all agencies and police forces."

A soft groan left Damon's lips. He knew not even William could promise or guarantee the second one. Then there was the first request. Agency weapons in the hands of an arms dealer was a disaster waiting to happen. There was no doubt in his mind that he needed to negotiate those two demands. But what could he propose instead? From his vantage point, Damon witnessed William shake his head slightly, confirming what he already knew.

"Right. I think you know full well not a single one of us can say yes to those demands." Damon stated softly. "Perhaps we could negotiate something similar."

"I'm listening."

"Of course you are..." Raynott wished he could consult with William about what she wanted. He sure as hell didn't want to over-promise on anything. "Full immunity with our agency is the best I can offer. The weapons are off-limits but I'm sure we could share some of the other tech we've created or have in our possession." There was a soft, affirmative utterance from Scarlett which confirmed his counteroffer was doable. Knowing she approved eased his conscience somewhat. Plus, Damon knew if she did then William was likely to as well. All he needed now was for Nightingale to accept.

The arms dealer allowed the silence to drag out. While not what she'd asked for, Damon Raynott offered precisely what she wanted. However she had no desire to make life easy for him. Not after he'd lied to her for so many years and led her on. So she allowed the tense quietness to continue, noting with a small smile that the longer it dragged on, the more uncomfortable the man who made the offer appeared. Finally feeling the urge to put Damon out of his misery, Nightingale sighed loudly, making them think she was giving in.

"You're certain you can guarantee what you've offered?" Breaking the silence, she asked the only real question still on her mind.

"You can be assured of it." Scarlett answered when she noticed Damon hesitate with uncertainty.

"Mmmh... a promise made by Scarlett Wintyrs is normally a sure thing..." Nightingale reflected upon all she'd been told. "Very well. You have yourselves a deal."

"You'll release William?"

"As I have your word, you now have mine. I will remove the restriction over his mouth but leave the other restraints for you. I want to ensure I have time to leave this place without any of you trying to follow me. The sisters here," she used her hand to indicate the black clad females, "I'm certain will have no issue blocking the door for me for at least ten minutes. Raynott knows how to reach me - I expect to receive your offer in writing within twenty-four hours or all bets are off. I will consider you all my enemies and take any measure I deem necessary to remove everyone involved with your agency from the face of the earth."

"That... sounds fair." Scarlett knew the threat was genuine while also believing the woman had every right to give them the ultimatum she did.

Nightingale smiled, knowing they couldn't see her face - nor how victorious she felt. With her left index finger she caressed the top edge of the thing over William's mouth and watched in drop into his lap. Smirking, Nightingale reached down, picking it up while letting her fingers brush gently between his slightly parted legs. She had the extreme satisfaction of seeing him stiffen in the chair before blending completely into the shadows and slipping out the back door.

William heard the door behind him click shut followed closely by the distinct sound of a lock sliding into place. "She's gone." He called out to those in the hanger with him. An unfamiliar touch made him flinch and the restraints fell away. Once his right hand regained freedom, William reached up, ripping the blindfold off to find two of the black clad women finishing untying him. "Thank you."

"You are, of course, most welcome." The spokeswoman of the group moved forward to stand directly in front of him. "Do you then know who we are? Given what has been said, I am assuming you do."

"The Sisterhood of the Jaguar." William answered. There was no doubt in his mind about their identity. Especially once he saw what they wore. "Still hiring yourselves out to the highest bidder?"

"We do what we must to survive. As do all who live in this world. Including yourself." She gave him a brief bow. "Although her time is not yet up, we now depart. Should you ever have need of our sisterhood, our alliance remains despite what transpired in the past. We will know should a need of us arises however we have also transmitted how to contact us to Feiyan." She said, backing into the shadows.

William opened his mouth, wanting to thank them again, but the group of women were gone. Almost as if by magic. "Okay, that was a humbling encounter."

Scarlett rushed over to their Spymaster, the other three members of the team hot on her tail. Placing one hand very gently on his arm, Wintyrs raked her gaze over him to reassure herself he'd come to no harm. "Are you alright??"

"A bit dizzy from those drugs she gave me but I'll be fine. We have to find somewhere we can lay low while we figure out our next steps."

"My offer remains." Feiyan stated. "However it would take us awhile to get there from here and the only mode of transport we have at the moment is Scarlett's hovercar."

"Damn. I forgot about that." Willam muttered. "Damon?"

"I'll see what I can find."

"Just... hold that thought." Spoken so softly the others at first had no idea it was her, Scarlett rubbed her face with one hand.

"Scarlett?" When she paused his actions, Damon's curiosity was sparked.

"There's a closer place we can use." She replied softly.

Feiyan moved to her former pupil's side, her face a mask of concern. "Are you sure of this, child?" Knowing what the younger woman was about to propose caused Feiyan no small amount of worry. Solely because she knew what was coming and that she'd been the only one at the agency Scarlett entrusted with this information.

Wintyrs closed her eyes for a moment then nodded slowly. "The option is our best one, Feiyan." Meeting her mentor's eyes, she noted the pain in their depths. Not the woman's own but instead a reflection of her old pupil's. "It's for the mission."

"Please don't tell me we'll need to break another of your cover identities..." William didn't want to do that to any of his agents.

"No... nothing like that." Scarlett's voice grew soft once more. What she was about to say to them needed all the courage she could possibly muster. Moreso than ever before. "I have a place nearby. It's where I grew up. And the last place I saw my parents alive."

16

Devil's Run, as the area was now known, was almost as bad as Raven's Way. Although not as dark, it still drew the unsavoury and those wishing to stay under the radar. That type of place, albeit dangerous, could also be a treasure trove - depending on what one was looking for. In this case, another hovercar. Damon left the others in the hanger, wanting to be as inconspicuous as possible. He only needed to find one which wouldn't stand out. They needed to blend in. And he didn't want another encumbrance like they'd had on the island. His eyes roamed the street yet again.

"Wonder why there's not many here... usually this street is positively brimming with parked cars." Damon softly said to himself.

"Wrong time of day." Scarlett's voice answered in his ear.

Damon winced. He'd forgotten he still had the comms unit. And that it was activated. "I only have vague knowledge of this area." Loathe to admit the weakness, he did so anyway.

"Given your alter-ego of Tengu, I thought you'd know Devil's Run like the back of your hand."

"Remind me to tell you more of what I did under that guise later." Flinching at his wording, Damon quickly corrected himself. "In terms of travel. I'm still not saying a damned thing about my exploits."

"Understood."

When she didn't give him a hard time about that last part, Damon knew Wintyrs was having a rough go of it. He couldn't blame her. In fact, he was certain he'd be in the same boat if their positions were reversed.

"So if now's not a good time to find one, why didn't you stop me?" He wasn't upset, only worried about wasting precious time.

"Even though it's not the busiest hour, there'll still be a good selection. You may need to traverse a few streets to find them though."

"This'd go a hell of a lot faster if we went 'shopping' for one using yours instead of me using my..." His words were cut off by two short beeps of a hovercar horn behind him. When Damon turned he found Scarlett's vehicle right there with its owner behind the yoke giving him a small grin. He ended up standing there and blinking for a few seconds in surprise.

"Are you going to get in or not?" Scarlett raised an eyebrow at him while at the same time pressing the button to open the passenger door.

Not wanting to miss the chance at saving his feet, Damon quickly walked to the door she'd opened and peered inside. "You sure you want to be involved with grand theft?"

"You're not going to steal one."

"Look, lovey, we need a ride big enough for the rest of us. We've already been over this."

"Which is why we'll find a suitable one and purchase it from the current owner for a reasonable price."

Damon climbed in and closed the vehicle's door, looking at her as if she'd grown a second head. "With what money? We can't use agency funds, we'll be tracked down in a heartbeat."

"Open the glovebox."

Raising an eyebrow, he did as she requested. "I see your handgun and some spare ammo..."

"See the gold button?" Scarlett kept the hovercar in park while giving him instructions.

"Gold button... gold button... maybe I'm blind but there ain't no gold button in here, love."

"Stop calling me that." She gave him a dirty look at the new pet name he seemed to have adopted for her. "Inside the cover, there's a gold button. If it were any closer to your face it'd bite you on the nose."

Damon kept the smile from his lips. He'd accomplished what he'd set out to do. Sure, she was annoyed, but that was far better a place for her to be than the edge of depression he'd been sensing her teetering on. As soon as the cover for the glovebox swung all the way down on its hinges, the button in question was quite plain as day. So he took the opportunity to get her out of the hole threatening to consume her.

"Oh! That button." Damon pressed the round, shiny control.

As soon as it was pushed all the way down, Damon could hear -

barely - a whirr then a click. He watched as the platform holding the weapon slid down as if on an elevator to be replaced by another 'level' holding a clear case. Swallowing involuntarily, he used both hands to carefully extract the plastic box while staring at the contents inside.

"There has to be fifty thousand pounds..." His voice sounded weak even to his own ears.

"Actually there's fifty thousand in every world currency in there. I believe in being prepared so I always have cash on hand in case of emergencies. And, no, not cash from the agency. Those bills are clean and completely untraceable from my personal bank. Yes..." Scarlett held up a finger, watching his wide eyes threaten to bulge out of his head, "it's all mine. You know the hovercar is mine so you should be well-aware that I'm not exactly on the poor list."

Recovering as quickly as he could, Damon nodded. "Yeah. This money, though... all I can say is wow... but yes, someone in Devil's Run could absolutely use this cash."

"I'm glad we're in agreement. Let's find that person, shall we?"

Waiting until she saw him nod, Scarlett reached over and pressed the button again to bring her weapon back into sight. There was no going back on this path she'd set them on. Which meant very soon they would all - save for Feiyan as she already knew - see her in a completely new light. She only hoped they wouldn't treat her differently. The decision to keep what they were about to discover away from agency eyes had been made with ease. After all, Scarlett wanted her reputation built on her merits, not seeming like she purchased it.

"Hang tight a second." Damon gently took her hand in his when he noticed her about to start the hovercar back up. "I think our ride just pulled up. And I even like the colour."

Wintyrs opened her mouth but before she could say anything he was already back out of the vehicle. A quick glance at the passenger seat he'd vacated made her smile. He'd left the box behind and took only the stack of bills in the currency of the region. Fifty thousand pounds. Watching him, she saw his path led him to a light turquoise hovervan. A vehicle similar in looks to an old-fashioned minivan. Definitely not new given the many dents she could discern from her vantage point. It was covered in a layer of dust though so she couldn't see what other flaws it undoubtedly sported.

Maintaining a her gaze on the unfolding scene, she watched the driver exit their hovervan then stop stock-still when Damon approached. After a moment, Scarlett could tell the driver was another male. Judging from a cursory glance, he appeared to be about the same height and build as Damon. Much to her surprise, the driver took the cash Damon offered and handed him the keys. After watching the other man walk around the corner, Raynott jogged back to her, indicating with one hand that he wanted her to roll down her window. When she did, it was with raised eyebrows.

"That looked... easy..." Scarlett remarked quietly.

"Yes. And it only took ten thou."

"Why didn't you give it all to him? I'm sure he could've used it."

"No point in bleeding you dry." Damon shrugged. "I gave him far more than what that piece of junk is worth."

"Trust me, you don't need to worry about 'bleeding me dry'."

Damon frowned at the less than cryptic remark. "I'm going to grab our new ride. I'll meet you back at the hanger then later you can explain to me what you meant by that." Turning on his heel, he quickly walked back to the hovervan without giving her a chance to respond. She could, of course, say something to him over the comms but he suspected she wouldn't.

Scarlett shook her head, watching him go to the 'new to them' vehicle. Without a word into the comms, she started up the hovercar. When it purred to life, she smiled. Damon should have known better without her needing to point it out. After all, he knew full well this vehicle was her own. That fact, even when not having any other insight, should have been enough for him to see she wouldn't easily be devoid of money.

Keeping the wheels of her hovercar on the ground instead of taking to the air, Scarlett pulled a u-turn and drove back the way she had come. Given their location she knew using the ground route would be much safer and far less conspicuous. A fact she'd relay to the rest of the team when they were ready to begin the last leg of the journey - for this day at least. Just as when she'd come out to locate Damon, the return trip to the hanger took only a few minutes. The nearly deserted streets contributed nicely to that timing as did getting what few traffic control lights there were on green. When the airfield drew close, she altered her heading slightly in order to go straight to the hanger. Once there, she parked alongside the longer edge of the building, turning off her vehicle then got out. She decided not to re-enter the hanger just yet. Part of her knew the others had been dreaming up questions for her. Some of which, hopefully, Feiyan fielded in her stead.

A rumbling reached Scarlett's ears, causing her to raise her eyes to the sky. Not a cloud as far as the eye could see so the sound wasn't thunder. Groaning quietly, she turned her attention to the road. The hovervan Damon took possession of wheeled into sight. And the closer it came, the louder the noise grew until it parked next to her. Right before smoke billowed from under the hood. Damon turned off the ignition, jumped out and ran to the hood, throwing it open in an attempt to cool the engine. His eyes met Scarlett's who was doing everything she could to contain her mirth. This tickled her funny bone for some reason.

"I think your 'deal' may have been overpriced." Scarlett finally said, eyes dancing with the strain of keeping her laughter behind closed lips.

Slowly, and quite deliberately, Damon turned his head to look at her. When he saw her face, he couldn't help the ironic chuckle followed by the shake of his head. "Do not, I beg of you, say the word karma."

"How about…"

"No. Nope." He laughed in earnest now. "How much you wanna bet that if I'd offered him the entire fifty grand, he'd have at least warned me about… well… this…" Gesturing at the slowly dissipating smoke, Damon leaned back against the hovervan, watching her.

Scarlett wiped the tears from her eyes, her shoulders shaking with silent laughter. "Honestly? I doubt it." She swallowed, trying to choke back what felt like an endless supply of giggles. "It's Devil's Run, Damon. Folks here need whatever money they can get their hands on. And they'll do or say whatever they have to to get it."

Rubbing his forehead, Damon nodded. "This is where people come when they can't afford Raven's Way is what you're saying."

"Precisely."

"Alright… well, I'm not exactly what one might call a master mechanic but I might be able to get this baby running enough to get us where we want to go."

"Or…"

"There's an or?"

"Absolutely. I say we bet on the sure thing instead of just a possibility." Taking a hair elastic out of a back pocket, Scarlett quickly pulled her hair back into a ponytail. "Find me a hovercar toolkit."

Damon stared at her as if seeing her for the first time. "Are you telling me that you…"

"I prefer to rely on myself whenever and wherever possible so yes, that's precisely what I'm telling you." Being able to surprise any of their group with her range of skills continued to delight her.

"Of course you are…" The statement was followed by another shake of his head, this time in amazement. "Out of curiousity - and just between us - is there anything you *can't* do?"

"Never ask me to cook." Wintyrs caught the odd look he shot her and smiled. "Not only do I hate cooking, I'm also terrible at it."

"I doubt that very much."

"I can burn water."

"Never mind, I stand corrected." He gave her a nod. "Let me check out what the previous owner left in the back of this hovervan. I don't think the hanger will have anything we could use."

"I can make things work if push comes to shove. Although I really would prefer proper tools for the job."

"Let me have a quick look then."

Wintyrs placed her hands on her hips as he disappeared from view around the back of the hovervan. She decided not to wait to find out if he discovered anything useful. The second he vanished from sight, she bent over the engine in order to begin a visual inspection. It didn't take long before she spotted the problem. Thankfully, the issue was one with a relatively easy fix - provided she could get her hands on the stuff. Approaching footsteps caused her to pull her head out from under the hood to find Damon had returned, carrying a rather large toolkit.

"You want another laugh?" His voice was completely devoid of any humour.

"Uh… sure?"

"I'm going to guess the guy I paid off wasn't the actual owner of this hovervan."

Blinking a few times, Scarlett recovered from the surprising revelation before daring to speak. "What makes you think that?"

"A hunch. This is a proper mechanic's kit. No one who owns one of these would let this to happen to their vehicle. I think the guy I paid was taking it for a test run to see what was wrong so he could fix it."

Scarlett groaned. That wasn't news she wanted to hear. Even if it were only conjecture. "Ten to one odds the real owner will call the authorities and register it as stolen if that's the case. I don't suppose you happened to turn off the transponder before driving here?"

"What do you think I am? A complete rookie? Of course I did." Damon placed the large, grey metal toolkit on the ground next to her.

"Did you already figure out what's wrong with the engine?"

"Yeah. Something a proper mechanic should've been able to spot without needing a test ride." Flattening her lips together, Scarlett crouched down to the toolkit and threw open the lid in order to start her search.

"Are you going to tell me or do I have to guess?"

"I honestly wasn't sure you'd be interested. This lovely..." she did her best not to cringe at the description, "hovervan has a cracked gasket."

"Oh... and how bad is that?"

Squinting when she looked up at him, the sun currently at its worst for dusk and glaring right into her face, Scarlett couldn't tell if he was having fun at her expense or not. "You're pulling my leg, right?"

Eyes widening at her question, Damon shook his head once. "Just because I'm a guy doesn't mean I know mechanical or engine stuff. I haven't the foggiest notion what any of those parts are or what they do."

"Then why'd you offer to try and fix it??"

"To be a gentleman. My plan was if you'd said yes to wait until you were off doing something then run and grab William."

Scarlett continued squinting up at him until the sun became too much. Averting her gaze, she looked back into the toolkit then began digging around. "Well, I can honestly say you managed to fool me. Well done."

"It's a talent." Damon noticed her hands pause then pick up a spray can of some sort. From his vantage point the canister looked to be red with a black label and white lettering. Unable to stifle his curiousity, he had to ask. "What is that?"

"Consider it a glue of sorts." Scarlett answered, giving the can a few good shakes in order to ensure the contents were well-mixed. "This is going to seal the crack for us and the best part is it'll keep its hold for a very long time."

"So are we talking hours? Days?"

"Better. Years."

"Yeah... that should do us."

Scarlett let him have the last word on the subject, finishing up her repair job. To be on the safe side, given who would be being transported by this vehicle, she gave the crack a few extra squirts in order to make the repair that much thicker. The stuff smelled absolutely terrible so she left the hood open for a few minutes to give the odour time to dissipate prior to the engine starting to prevent the stench from circulating in the cabin.

"You want to grab the others?" Scarlett inquired of him. "I'll clean up here then we can hit the road."

"Sounds good. Back in a few."

She started her cleanup after hearing his steps fade in the direction of the hanger door. Putting the can back where she found it, she closed the lid and secured the latch. The toolkit was quite impressive. Obviously its owner had put a lot of effort, not to mention money, into ensuring the kit was well-stocked. Taking care to run her fingers over the metal lightly, Scarlett wondered why the man Damon purchased the hovervan from hadn't requested the toolkit back. Unless he'd, perhaps, felt bad about not mentioning the full story of the vehicle. Maybe he'd wanted to leave them a way to repair the problem when it cropped up. And, just maybe, the amount Damon paid him would more than cover the cost of replacing everything. She placed the weighty kit back in the trunk, closing the hatch just as the others exited the hanger.

"Damon tells us he accidentally got us a vehicle in need of repair?" William got to her first, needing to know if they had to go in search of another.

"Repairs are done. At least as far as this poor thing's current problem is concerned. There's likely other issues lurking but without having time to give it a proper inspection I have no clue what else could be going on. If something pops up, we'll have to deal with it."

Reaching up to her face, William used the thumb and forefinger of this right hand to gently wipe away some dirt on her cheek. "I had no idea you were a grease monkey."

"There's a lot you don't know about me." She replied, her voice hushed.

"Clearly." He gave her a tender smile before clearing his throat. "We should get going. Scarlett, is it safe to assume you'll be leading our little caravan?"

"Unless Feiyan wants to drive…"

"Absolutely not." Came the older woman's resounding 'no'.

"Then I guess I'm leading. Mount up everyone. Let's get this show on the road."

114

17

Sticking to the speed limit, only because drawing any undue attention wouldn't be wise, Scarlett kept them on the ground, leading the others to the one place she never wanted anyone to know about. Having told Feiyan, plus physically showing her, still weighed heavily on Scarlett. In an odd way, sharing this secret felt as though she were betraying her parents. Anyone who ever understood how she felt tended to be those with the same emotional scars.

Going by ground roads, as well as keeping the speed down, meant the journey took a little longer than usual. It didn't help that Wintyrs needed to keep a map up on her display to see where they were. She'd never gone this way to their destination. In fact, she preferred the airways - if only for the fact there was more room to maneuver. Rounding one last bend in the road they were currently on brought them before a large set of intricately designed old-fashioned wrought iron gates with flowers etched into the metal. Not to mention tall. And they were held up on either side by rock walls which were the same height and looked as though they would be able to withstand the strongest battering ram. Or even a collision with a truck at high speeds.

Glancing in the rearview mirror, Scarlett could see the awestruck faces of Damon and Zaliki who were sitting in the driver and front passenger seats, respectively, of the hovervan. Her lips twitched while Scarlett fought a smile, even though she knew they wouldn't see if it won out. If they were already in awe... well... they hadn't seen anything yet.

Scarlett placed her car in front of the gate next to the small panel located on a stone pillar at the side of the driveway. After rolling down the driver's side window, she held her wrist against a glowing green panel in order to be identified by the small chip implanted there. Simultaneously another scanner looked into her eyes. A beep reached her ears and she hit the number '2' on the keypad to indicate how many vehicles the sensors should expect to pass through.

Although the security system was fairly new - and state of the art at the time of installation - the gates themselves were quite the opposite. No signs of rust could be discerned anywhere on the wrought-iron. Even the stonework seemed immaculate. Only Scarlett knew their true age, and it was something she'd only reveal if asked.

The second the gates swung open to their natural stopping point, she took her hovercar through while keeping one eye on her rearview mirror to ensure the van behind kept pace. Large trees lined both sides of the 'S' shaped driveway, successfully keeping the house hidden from view as the vehicles approached. Scarlett's stomach twisted and turned as she rounded the final bend. The house - if the structure could be called that - filled her vision.

A year had passed since her last visit. Everything looked exactly the same which made her glad to have maintained her family's staff of four to look after the place. Large enough to rival a small castle, the house was constructed of red brick with a darkly shingled roof. A couple of the second floor rooms boasted double doors leading out to a balcony that wrapped around the entire building and also had a staircase leading to the ground level. Scarlett sighed, parking her hovercar near the front door. A lump formed in her throat, only vanishing when she forcibly swallowed it down. With a deep breath, she exited the vehicle at the same time the hovervan parked on the right side of her car.

Damon gave a low whistle of appreciation when he climbed out from behind the steering yoke. "I never knew this place existed... it's not on any maps that I can remember. It's yours?" He looked over the roof of her hovercar to see her looking a tad more pale than usual. When she didn't answer right away, he frowned. "Scarlett?"

"Hmm?" Meeting his gaze, Scarlett realized she'd heard the question but neglected to answer. "Sorry. Yes. It belonged to my parents and their parents before them." Her eyes moved back to the house. "I always have trouble believing it's mine now."

"It appears well constructed." Zaliki murmured, moving closer in order to admire the flower gardens bordering the entire ground level. The only time there was a break in their continuity was wherever a door or pathway was found. "These blossoms are quite lovely as well. An impressive array of species."

"I'll have to take your word on that." Wintyrs said, walking up the main path to the set of double-doors which served as the main entrance. "The only thing about plant life I know is identifying poisonous ones. I can't grow a thing. In fact, where others have a green thumb, mine is most assuredly black."

Scarlett pressed her index finger onto the keyhole in the brass handle of the left-hand door. A beautifully dark brown oak door with a stained glass window depicting a winter's night which continued on the glass on the other door. She heard the quiet beep of recognition before the lock clicked off and the door opened. Given the slowly setting sun, the inside of the house already grew dark. To save anyone from potentially breaking any bones, Scarlett reached over to a row of switches along the nearby wall. Finding the one for the entryway, she pressed down until it clicked on. A crystal chandelier dangling from the ceiling brightly came to life, nearly blinding any who were unfortunate enough to be looking up at the time. In the centre of the main landing sat a wide spiral staircase leading to both the upper floor and the basement.

"Jeez..." Damon recovered first. "William, can we make this place the agency's new headquarters??" He marvelled at the white marble floor of the entry, veins of gold and grey creating the marbled pattern. The grey stood out a bit more due to the light grey paint on the walls.

"I'd be open to the concept if Scarlett is." William replied diplomatically. The golden bannister on the spiral staircase had successfully enamoured him. A railing complimented by the beige carpeting on the stairs themselves.

Glancing over her shoulder at her companions, Scarlett raised an eyebrow. Uncertain she'd be able to emotionally handle the idea, Wintyrs' didn't mention the thought also crossed her mind. "We can talk about it after. Do you want to explore on your own or have a tour?"

"I think I can safely speak for all of us." Feiyan spoke up. "Please allow us to explore on our own - we, each of us, enjoy learning our way around new and strange places. Perhaps you could give us a general overview of each floor?"

"Sure." Scarlett turned to face them. "We're on the main floor. Here you'll find the kitchen, dining room, main office including library, indoor pool with whirlpool and sauna, as well as the main living room used for entertaining company. Downstairs - which only runs about half of the house because of the pool - you'll see the games room and a sitting area with entertainment centre. Oh, and the gym as well as a smaller office setup. Upstairs are all the bedrooms - each with their own ensuite washroom. You'll each have your own room by the way. We do have a cook on premises as well as a groundskeeper, housekeeper and a valet."

"You have a butler?" The astonishment in Damon's voice couldn't be disguised.

"Valet." Wintyrs quickly corrected him.

"But you have one…"

Rolling her eyes, she nodded. "Yes, Damon. Along with everything else I mentioned. Anyone have any questions?"

"Are there any security measures in place we should know about?" William inquired. Given to whom the house now belonged, he thought the question reasonable.

Despite how she felt, the inquiry managed to draw out a small smile. "There are. Once the gate and door both recognized me though, everything deactivated. If we come under assault, the measures are easily reactivated including some additional features designed to protect anyone inside. I'll have to add all of you to the system so you have access to it."

Gently grasping her hands, William searched her face while wishing yet again the woman in front of him weren't so good at concealing her emotions. "If you want to talk…"

Scarlett forced a smile back to her face, squeezing his hands. "I'll let you know. Just… not right now. I'd suggest going upstairs first and choosing your rooms. The one with the dark red walls is mine."

Waiting until the other three vanished up the stairs, Feiyan turned to find Scarlett watching her with an unspoken question in her eyes. "I'll go in a minute. Are you alright, child? The others may not be able to see it but I know you far better than they. Being here again - even with all the upgrades you have done - is hurting you. I'd go so far as to say tearing you up on the inside."

Chewing the inside of her lower lip, Scarlett contemplated how much she wanted, or needed, to share with the older woman. "It's nothing I can't deal with."

"Scarlett…" Feiyan could see she wouldn't get anything more from her. "Have you come back often?"

"I try to visit once a year." Scarlett relented. "I was planning on returning more. That's why I sent some plans to Jerome a few months ago for a specialized workspace to be housed in a separate building on the property."

"And how do you feel about the proposal made by our two male companions?"

Casting her eyes around the entryway, Scarlett let the question stew for a moment. "An interesting concept. And something I'm open to discussing…"

"You have reservations."

"Wouldn't you?"

Unable to argue the point, Feiyan smirked. "I believe you know my answer."

"Indeed." Scarlett released a sigh, forcing tense muscles to relax as she did. "You should go and see what room they left for you. I'm going to check in with Cheyanna so she can let the others know we're here. I don't want to startle any of them."

Feiyan watched the younger woman disappear through one of the three ornate doorways leading from the entryway. Somehow she would get Scarlett to open up about her emotions. Another thought struck her as she climbed the stairs. If she couldn't crack Scarlett's shell then perhaps the person who managed to capture her heart would have better luck. William. Reaching the top of the stairs, Feiyan noted three of the five doors were closed which indicated what rooms were spoken for. One, however, remained open a crack and upon peering inside, she found whom she sought. Gently pushing the door open, Feiyan stared at William's back. The Spymaster's attention was focused on looking out the window and not the pale grey walls of the room he'd selected.

"William?" Feiyan called to him quietly so as not to startle him. A slight turn of his head towards the sound of her voice intimated he'd heard her. "May I have a moment of your time?"

"Have you ever wondered how it is that things always seem to come full circle?" He replied, not turning to face her. There was a deep pain etched in his words.

Hearing that, Feiyan moved into the room, closing the door behind her. "I believe fate always has a plan. Beyond that… no… I haven't really given it much thought." She joined him at the large picture window which took up the better part of one wall of the room. The four-poster king-sized bed whose light brown frame blended nicely with the room's colour scheme detracted nothing from the size of the bedroom. "What is troubling you, William?"

"Fate's twisted sense of humour." His voice was hoarse with emotion. "I've been here before. I didn't recognize the place at first... she's had some redecorating done."

"Why..." Feiyan stopped when she witnessed a single tear make its way, unbidden, down the cheek closest to her. "William? What is it?"

"Has she told you how her parents were killed?" He inquired of her, his eyes never leaving the view of the grounds.

"Only that it was an accident. She's never gone into detail." Feiyan paused, an unexpected feeling of dread washing over her. "Why?"

"It was no accident." William hoarsely responded, finally turning his head to look at her. "I killed them."

18

Shocked silence greeted his admission. Feiyan knew they each had skeletons in their closets but this... she, for the first time in her life, had no idea what to say. Blowing out a long breath to centre herself, Feiyan took a moment to gather her thoughts. This news shook her to her very core.

"William... what do you mean you killed them?" Trying to fathom how this could be possible, Feiyan laid a gentle hand on the man's arm.

"Exactly what I said." Voice cracking with emotion, he gave her the only answer he had. "It was my first solo assignment as an agent. I can't tell you everything but what I can say is that at the time I was given the mission, they had betrayed our agency and were being actively recruited by one of our rivals. And they'd stolen some of our agency's tech to take with them." Closing his eyes, William leaned his forehead against the cool glass of the window, the soul-crushing pain of the admission obvious to anyone observing them.

"You're telling me that you, as a brand new agent, were able to take out two seasoned agents without getting yourself killed." Scorn was dominant in her tone, causing the man to finally look at her. "I would guess your mission was, in fact, to retrieve the stolen technology at any cost, correct?" Feiyan waited until he silently nodded. "They found you and threatened to kill you, didn't they." Another nod. "You reacted and allowed your training to guide you in order to survive?" She inhaled deeply when he repeated the head motion. "Then do you not believe you acted in self-defence? That you had no other choice?"

"There's a bit more to it than that, however does it even matter? They're dead because of me." William looked out the window again.

"She tells anyone who asks that they died in a fire or a car accident."

"William... why has it taken you so long to make this admission? How could you be her Spymaster - now her lover - without revealing this?"

"I only knew them by their codenames and first names at the time as well as by the address I'd been given." He closed his eyes, trying to relax tense muscles to no avail. "I didn't know they were her parents. Not until we arrived at that front gate and entered this house. That's when I realized..." Sighing softly, William found he couldn't finish the sentence.

"That you were the one responsible for her parents' demise. Did she see the bodies, do you know?"

William shook his head slightly. "No. I knew they had a child. When I came here, the child was at a friend's for a sleepover. So after I... you know... I placed them in their car and affixed an incendiary device on the engine. As far as anyone could tell, they died in a freak accident when their car caught fire."

"You ensured no one could tell any differently? That all they would be able to attribute the deaths to was an accident?"

"Yeah."

"Which is why she says either car accident or fire." Feiyan rubbed her eyes. "You know you have to tell her."

"How can I?" His eyes began watering with how great the despair within him was. "How could I do that to her? She'll hate me."

"At first, yes. I will be at your side when you decide the time is right - if you wish me to be. Keeping this from her would be far worse. Especially if she somehow ends up figuring it out on her own."

That remark caused his eyes to fly open. He turned to face her, a note of alarm in his face. "You sound like you know something I don't..."

Feiyan met his gaze. "I know she never believed their deaths to be accidental. Just as I know she looks at everything dealing with their case whenever she has a spare moment. Interestingly, I don't think she's ever discovered they were in the same line of work that she's now doing."

"Wait. You're saying she has absolutely no clue that her parents were agents as well?"

"If she did then I have no doubt the information would have been confided to me. Now, the hired help she mentioned... could they be the same as what her parents employed? Did anyone see you that night?"

William groaned, moving to the chair sitting in the corner and sank onto its soft cushion. "The groundskeeper would have seen me exit my vehicle as I arrived here under the pretence of a business meeting. The valet let me inside but after that I made myself scarce. I don't know if they're the same people as now. I won't know until I see their faces."

Feiyan stared at him. "How did you leave?"

"The same way I arrived. My car had remote operation as well as a holographic double of me. I faked getting into the car after a reasonable 'meeting' time elapsed and had it drive off. I caught up to it down the road a bit. Don't ask me how I managed to get past the gate or fencing."

"You know I must."

Blowing out a breath, William relented. He was surprised to note telling her all of this made him feel as though a giant weight had been lifted from his shoulders. "I had their car explode right next to the gate which caused enough damage that it swung right open."

"An interesting, albeit messy, tactic." Feiyan muttered softly. "Now for my next question - why are you telling me all of this?"

Narrowing his eyes, William shook his head. "I have no idea. I... felt compelled to..." A coldness settled over him, enough to send a shiver through his body. "Nightingale said that last injection was the counteragent..."

"Perhaps it was. I don't think she administered enough."

William covered his face with both hands. "Damn it."

"We're going to either have to wait it out or see if Scarlett might have something here we could use to neutralize the remnants of the drug cocktail in your system."

"I... I can't be near anyone until it's been rendered inert."

"Except for me. At least that would be my assumption."

Slowly returning his hands to his lap, William mulled her statement over. "If we stay on a certain topic then that'll work."

Knowing he couldn't lie to her, Feiyan went to him and gently covered his hands with her own. "I'll make sure no one else enters this room until we solve this. And we will get through this. The last person you should be near is Scarlett so do us all a favour? Stay. Put."

Looking into Feiyan's eyes helped anchor him and he nodded to her. "I'll be right here waiting for you to return. Well... in this room at any rate."

Scarlett wandered the main floor after speaking with her valet, Jerome, who welcomed her back warmly and assured her he would pass along the news of her arrival and that of her friends to his colleagues. Without thinking about where she was going, Wintyrs found herself in the main office. Once over the threshold, the large portrait of her parents with herself as a child captured her attention and held her frozen in place. The painting had been commissioned the year before the accident then brought to her in its completion as a token of remembrance at the memorial service. It always managed to elicit a mixed emotional response from her. No matter how she felt, Scarlett could never take it off the wall even if she wanted to. For reasons only one other person knew - Jerome.

The painting ended up so large that instead of hanging it for admiring visitors, her family made it into a special door. After the death of her parents, Scarlett had taken to wandering the house. She'd wanted to discover everything, most especially the areas her parents had forbade her to peer into. What she'd uncovered shocked her. Inadvertently discovering the portrait could move, she'd opened it to discover that hidden behind sat a small wing of four interconnected rooms. Every one of which contained equipment she hadn't bothered to look at too closely at the time, or since. Those hidden rooms, though, and what appeared to be specialized gear, told her exactly what her parents had done. It was what inspired her to become who she was now. And the only person who knew any of this - including what she did - was Jerome.

Wintyrs freed herself from the frozen state she'd entered, moving to stand directly in front of the portrait and staring into the eyes of first her father then her mother. "I miss you both so much." She whispered hoarsely.

"They loved you more than you could ever dream." Jerome's lightly accented Scottish voice came from the doorway behind her. "They'd be so proud of you, you know. Of who you've become and of the lovely young woman you've grown into."

"You tell me that every time I come back." Scarlett responded softly, turning to face him.

Jerome had been with her family for as long as she could remember. His short, black hair was now mostly grey and wrinkles pitted the pale face. The black suit he preferred to wear did absolutely nothing to help with that. After doing some quick mental calculations, Scarlett figured the valet had to be in his late seventies now. Yet he showed no signs of slowing down.

"Maybe it's my way of trying to get you to come home more often."
He smiled, the dwindling sunlight causing his dark blue eyes to
twinkle.

Scarlett shot him a sly grin. "Now, how did I know you were going
to say that."

"Years of repetition?" He entered the office, setting down the silver
tray he'd been carrying. "I brought you your favourite."

"Earl grey?"

"But of course. Do you still take it with milk and sugar?"

"I do. Thank you, dear friend."

Jerome doctored her tea in silence. "The people I saw you arrive
with on the cameras - are they part of the agency?"

Her response came as a slow nod. Scarlett had always been glad
that Jerome knew everything - including what agency she worked with
- it gave her someone to talk to when needed. "For the most part."
When a shadow passed over his face, she moved the conversation
along. "That bothers you. What's wrong?"

"It's not my place to say, dear Scarlett." Jerome handed her the cup
of tea he'd prepared.

"Thank you." Scarlett gratefully accepted the drink, taking a careful
sip for she knew the liquid was scalding hot. "Now... please tell me
what's on your mind. You know you can tell me anything."

Hesitating a moment, Jerome wondered how much to share. He
believed it was not his place to reveal all of what he knew. "Very well.
The one male you're travelling with - by any chance is he from Texas?"

Having been about to ask which male he was inquiring about,
Scarlett quickly pivoted into a different question. As well as answering
his. "He is, yes. How'd you know without talking to him?"

"I've spoken to him before."

"What? When? About what?"

"On the visit prior to this one. The day your parents died."

19

Rapidly blinking, Scarlett absorbed Jerome's revelation. "That was twenty years ago, Jerome..."

"And a day I'll never forget." He rearranged the tray to ensure even distribution of weight for when he was ready to pick it up again. "Miss Scarlett... you and I have never discussed that day. I'm thinking we should."

Scarlett watched him for a moment, taking in his body language as well as the undertones of his speech pattern. The conversation he proposed wasn't one she wanted to have at the moment. Or ever. "Jerome..."

"Madame, I do beg your forgiveness, however I don't think waiting is an option."

After taking a very deep breath, Wintyrs nodded. "Let's keep it general if we can, without too many details, alright?"

"If that's your wish, of course, madame." He bowed his head to her. When he hesitated it quickly became obvious he wasn't sure where to start. "Miss Scarlett..."

"Would you feel better if we proceeded in a manner where I ask questions and you answer?" Scarlett inquired, sitting down behind the desk while motioning for him to take one of the chairs across from her.

Jerome shook his head but accepted the invitation to sit and did so. "That's alright, Miss Scarlett." Breathing deeply a couple of times to steady his nerves, he continued - determined to share what he deemed important for her to know. "That man arrived saying he was here for a business meeting. Given I knew the nature of your parents' 'business', I didn't question him. As far as I knew he could've been part of a case they were working or from the agency itself. Either way, I knew better than to indulge my curiousity. His arrival wasn't strange but I can't recall seeing him leave. Just as I don't remember your parents getting into their vehicle to go somewhere. They always told me if they were going out - especially if you weren't home. Which, on that night as I know you recall despite trying not to, you were not. Everything about that event, that entire day, was odd."

Scarlett grew quiet while he spoke, sipping her tea every so often. When he paused, she looked over the rim of the teacup at him. Her assumption could only be that he couldn't be certain what else he should reveal or what she'd want to know. "When you say you don't remember... do you think it's a gap in your memory or..."

"Absolutely not, madame!" Jerome frowned deeply. "I know I'm getting older but rest assured, my age isn't interfering with my memory. Not yet anyway."

Scarlett placed her tea cup, along with the matching saucer, onto the desk with great care. Her mind raced with what he'd told her. What could William have been doing here? Why had he never made mention of knowing her parents? "Thank you for sharing all of that with me, Jerome. You've given me a great deal to consider."

"Perhaps, madame, instead of attempting to determine the answers yourself, you might take the matter directly to the source given he is once again in attendance."

She graced him with a gentle smile. "It's nice that you and I still think along the same lines."

Jerome rose to his feet, eyes lingering on the young woman he'd watched over and witnessed grow into adulthood. "When you do - I'd urge caution. When I last encountered that man, he struck me as being capable of great violence if he desired."

"Thank you for your words of wisdom, as always, old friend." Scarlett trailed off at the nearly timid knock on the closed office door. "Yes?" Wintyrs called out only to find Jerome already at the door, opening it to allow admittance to whomever stood on the other side.

"I'm hoping you might spare me a few minutes to talk." Feiyan stated, looking into the room after giving Jerome a nod of acknowledgement.

Part of her wondered how Feiyan managed to locate her but Scarlett had a feeling the older woman, whom appeared to be in her sixties in Scarlett's estimation, must have planned to go through the entire house until she located her target. Her former mentor was nothing if not tenacious when on a hunt. "We just finished, come on in and have a seat."

Feiyan entered the office, doing as requested, but waited until Jerome left with the tray before speaking. "I think you and I should talk."

"I have a lot on my mind right now, Feiyan." Rubbing her forehead, Scarlett wondered how much more she could handle. She was already on the verge of teetering over the edge.

"I can tell." Watching the other woman, Feiyan questioned her motives for wanting this conversation. After weighing all the options, though, she still believed this to be the right course of action. "Scarlett... dear girl... I'm not sure I should even be the one telling you this. Perhaps it would be better coming from the original source..."

"Oh for the love..." Scarlett shook her head, left foot beginning to tap impatiently under the desk. "Just spit it out, Feiyan. I'm in no mood for riddles."

"It has to do with William." Relenting upon observing the young woman's behaviour, Feiyan reached the conclusion that keeping her in the dark would do far more harm than good.

Scarlett's gaze started to wander the room but at her guest's words, her eyes - and attention - snapped right back to the woman across from her. "What about him?"

"It would appear Nightingale didn't administer the proper amount of the counteragent to the truth serum cocktail she gave him."

"I see." Scarlett's voice grew quiet.

"I think we should all give him space until we're certain the drug has run its course." The silence which greeted her suggestion caused Feiyan some measure of worry. "Scarlett?"

Wintyrs tapped her fingers on the desk's surface. True, her mentor raised a good point. Due to his position they should indeed leave him alone. However, that being said and now armed with the information provided by Jerome, Scarlett couldn't deny the timing was perfect for her to find out more about that fateful night from her Spymaster. "I concur, Feiyan. And leave him alone we shall. After I speak with him."

"Scarlett, I can't allow that. He has asked me to keep everyone from his room save for me since I won't ask him anything which might compromise past, present or future missions."

Rising from her chair, Wintyrs shook her head. "No. I need to speak with him. Now. While I know he can't lie to my face."

Feiyan jumped up. "Don't make me fight you on this! I'm sworn to follow his orders! As, I might point out, are you!"

"I'm not going to fight you, Feiyan. You also won't stop me. I need some answers. Ones I'm sure he'd lie about under other circumstances. I'll beg on my hands and knees if you make me, Feiyan, but I'll not fight you over this."

Having never heard such conviction mixed with genuine resignation from her former pupil, Feiyan felt thrown for a loop. "Does it have anything to do with what you and that man - whom I assume is the valet you spoke of - were talking about prior to my untimely arrival?"

"It does, yes. And I swear it's only that which I wish to speak to William of. Please."

"Tell me first."

Scarlett sighed with frustration. "Fine. Jerome remembers William being here the night my parents died. If he was... well I'm hoping he might be able to give me some closure. There's always been so many questions surrounding what happened. I need answers. Truthful answers."

"I understand why..." Feeling torn between duty and friendship, Feiyan closed her eyes. "Go. If he asks, don't tell him you saw me. I will forget this conversation took place."

Scarlett stared at her former mentor for a moment. Not for a second had she expected to hear anything of the sort from the other woman. The fact she was willing to disobey orders from their Spymaster for her spoke volumes. "I... thank you... Feiyan." Racing from the room, Wintyrs ran upstairs and paused. She stared at the three doors which were closed. Each one led to a guest suite. Belatedly, she realized she should have consulted Feiyan about which room William elected to claim as his own for the duration of his stay. Given how he felt towards her, one door made more sense than the others. Only one of the suites bracketing her own had the door closed. Feeling confident about her decision, Scarlett strode over and rapped her knuckles on the surface a few times.

"Feiyan...?" William opened the door a crack then swore under his breath when he saw who stood without. "Scarlett. Now really isn't the best time."

One of her perfectly sculpted eyebrows rose upon hearing his whispered curse. "Make it a good time, William. We need to talk. Right now."

"Scarlett..." The weak protest died on his lips when he saw the determination in her eyes. And it was mixed with something he couldn't quite identify. Doubtless he would regret this decision. Not saying another word, he opened the door to allow her admittance. "Come on in."

With a small nod of thanks, Scarlett moved into the room. She remained silent until he closed the door. In a way, she wanted him to start the conversation. If only to give her an opening as she wasn't quite sure how to broach the subject.

"So, uh, something tells me this isn't a social call." William observed after the door clicked shut. He returned to the chair he'd occupied during Feiyan's visit and sat back down.

"Good guess. First... how're you feeling? Any aftereffects from the truth concoction or the antidote Nightingale gave you?" Scarlett perched on the edge of the bed nearest to him to look into his eyes in order to determine if anything he told her was a lie. If anyone had a chance of fooling her, it was him.

William shook his head. "Whatever was in the counteragent either wasn't quite strong enough or the dosage wasn't right."

"So you're still feeling the effects of the serum?"

Stomach twisting for he had a feeling he knew exactly where this line of questioning was heading, William wished he could just not answer at all. "It comes in spurts but yeah."

"Then I have some questions. Ones I need truthful answers for." When she saw his expression, a cold feeling of guilt ran through her. "I'm sorry. If I thought you wouldn't hide the truth from me about this then I'd leave you be. I have to know though. Were you here twenty years ago? On the day my parents died?"

All blood drained from his face giving the appearance of him being as white as a ghost. Yet even if the serum wasn't still affecting him, he felt fairly confident he'd tell her what she wanted to know. That's how much he loved her. He had no desire to base their relationship on a lie. "Yes. I was here. And I'll tell you anything you want to know about that day - with or without the serum's effects."

Momentarily studying him, Scarlett sensed what he said had nothing to do with the drug. "You really mean that, don't you?"

"I do."

"Thank you... in that case - what were you doing here? Jerome said you told him you were here for a business meeting. What can you tell me? Is your meeting why they died? Do you know?" The questions spilled out without a filter. She couldn't help herself.

William leaned forward, resting his elbows on his knees, looking into her eyes. "I can answer all of those questions - and I will - first, though, I need to know how much you know of what your parents did and of that day itself. No games. Let's put all our cards on the table. We need to remember who we are and what we do for a living, alright?"

That hadn't been the response she'd been expecting. Yet she supposed she should have. Especially given to whom she spoke. "I know they both worked for the Centurian Agency. Jerome knows too and he knows I do." Why was she telling him that? Maybe some part of her realized lying to him, even a lie of omission, wouldn't help her case. "As for that day... I was at a friend's all day so I only know what I was told. A story I'm sure you're already familiar with given it's in my dossier."

"Indeed. For the record, I know all about Jerome and what he knows. He's, and I'm surprised he hasn't told you this, an agency asset. Former field agent. I familiarized myself with his dossier - as you so eloquently termed it - in preparation for my meeting that day. Jerome joined your household staff after he'd been severely wounded in the line of duty. Badly enough he could no longer work in the field but he still wanted to be useful and remain with the agency." William explained softly.

"Hang on... Jerome... why didn't he tell me..."

"He was sworn not to. His sole responsibility was your protection while you were in the confines of this property."

"My protection?? Why?"

"There's not many agents who marry and have a child or children. When they do, the child gets protection, S.O.P. - something we've done since the agency's inception."

"What about when I wasn't here? Like, for instance, when I was at my friend's that day?"

"You were always watched over. Guarded, if you will. When you were out and about, other agents took over the responsibility in order to keep you or anyone else watching from growing suspicious." With a wince, he realized part of what he'd just revealed was thanks to the serum. "Damn it. Okay, you weren't supposed to know that."

"Tell me about your meeting with my parents. Why did you come here, of all the places you could've met?" Taking pity on him, Scarlett moved the conversation along.

William rubbed his face, feeling the serum taking effect which he hoped wouldn't happen for this particular inquiry. "The meeting was my cover story" The words left his lips of their own accord. "My mission was to retrieve a project stolen from the Centurian Agency…" taking a deep breath, he risked looking at her again, "and to *talk* to Troy and Kristi who sought to defect to another agency with said technology."

Scarlett sat still as a statue. Nothing wanted to work, even breathing normally proved challenging. Speechless, the only thing she could do was stare at him. Two things wandered through her mind. One - she wanted to scream. Loudly. The second… she felt as though time had taken her back twenty years to that fateful day. How could she respond? If her understanding of what he'd said was accurate then the man she loved just confessed to his involvement with the death of her parents.

"I know this'll be hard to hear." William continued despite being concerned about her silence. "At the time I didn't know who they were. I honestly didn't know until you had me set foot in this house today."

"Then how did you know about my being watched over?" Scarlett recovered from her initial shock to find her voice. Nothing made any sense.

"I researched when time permitted but their surname had been completely wiped from our records. Jerome I was able to find from facial recognition when I first arrived here all those years ago. My favourite gadget at the time was a pair of glasses which would scan the face of whomever you looked at then provide you with any and all information the agency had. When I tried to use them with your parents, the sole result I received was one-worded. Blacklisted. So of course I knew when that popped up my mission parameters had changed. Drastically." Growing more concerned, as her normally pale face grew even moreso, William reached a hand out to her. Dismay filled him when she pulled away from his touch as if the contact had somehow burned her. A reaction he'd kind of expected but knowing it could happen didn't make it hurt any less.

Rising from her perch on the bed, Scarlett went to the window. She hated herself for how she'd reacted to his touch yet the memory of his skin making contact with hers made her nauseous. At the same time, however, she realized he'd only been following orders. As any of them would have done. How could she fault him for that? There was also the awareness that most of what he'd shared had been done thanks to

Nightingale's serum. Something in his eyes told her he hadn't wanted her to know every single detail he'd walked her through.

"Blacklisted, huh?" Wintyrs' winced when her voice cracked on the word.

Remaining where he sat, William nodded even though her attention seemed focused on whatever was outside at the moment. "Yes." He verbalized his head motion. "And I know you know what that means."

"You had no choice." Scarlett responded in a whisper. "Had you disobeyed then you, too, would have been placed in that category." She turned back to him. "Just tell me this... did you make it painless for them?"

"That was my top priority, yes. I can't stand seeing anyone suffer."

Being honest with herself, Scarlett hadn't imagined how painful for her this discourse would, or could, be. What she'd felt before disappeared, replaced by an overwhelming desire to cry unstoppably. An urge she shoved down as far as possible. Payback entered her mind and left just as quickly. Guilt over what he'd done was obvious even to an outsider. As was the fact that it was tearing him up on the inside. To which Scarlett longed to say *good - I hope you choke on that feeling* - another thing she managed to quash. Dare she utter the words she knew she'd want to hear if their positions were reversed? If she did... could she follow through with the sentiment? And, most importantly, could their love survive this? Possibly the ultimate test of anyone's love.

"Scarlett? Please say something..." The longer any of her silences stretched on, the more worried he grew. "I know you're probably seeing me in a totally new light right now but I really need you to talk to me."

"Begging doesn't become you." Her steely gaze found his, ensuring he dare not look anywhere else. "Do you have any idea how much pain you've caused me? Both then and now?"

"I don't." William meant the admission to show her he wanted to understand although doubted those two words alone would do the trick. "Help me to."

"It's like having someone rip your still beating heart from your chest and crush it with their fist before they put it back in." Describing emotions, merely talking about them, was never something she enjoyed. Emotions were a weakness. At least most of them were. In her mind, anyway. "I'm no good at trying to talk about that stuff."

Releasing a heavy breath whilst allowing her shoulders to slump, Scarlett knew she couldn't hold him accountable for an event he had no choice over. "Thank you for making it painless for them. I... I think, given what you've told me, I can forgive you. It may take some time though."

"I get that." His words were solemn. "Is there anything I can do..."

A slight shake of her head was the only response he received. William expected something along those lines. What had been the surprise was her revealing she could forgive him. In time. That went far beyond his wildest imaginings. For her to say it must have taken a remarkable amount of courage. Which made him respect her even more, despite thinking that wasn't possible.

"I'll let you get some rest. Oh, did you recover the tech the agency said they took?"

Pausing for the briefest moments, William realized this was yet another question he'd hoped she wouldn't ask. Rubbing his hair, while carefully avoiding his faux-hawk, he tried desperately to keep the answer to himself. And failed. Miserably. "No."

"Then where is it? What was it they took? Do you believe the tech taken is now outdated or will it still work?"

"Troy discovered my true intent before I was able to recover what they'd stolen. I don't believe the tech will be outdated to be honest. In fact it may even work better now than it did back then."

"What was it?" Scarlett narrowed her eyes when he managed to avoid the singular most important question.

"A targeted EMP pulse rifle."

20

Well, this day was proving to be one of the most eventful - not to mention newsworthy - of Scarlett's life. She stared at William until he began shifting uncomfortably on the chair, her intense scrutiny making him nervous.

"You're telling me that my parents stole a pulse rifle capable of emitting a targeted electromagnetic pulse from the Centurian Agency?" Scarlett waited until he nodded confirmation. "And you were unable to recover said weapon during your mission even though it clearly should have been your main priority?"

"Scarlett, I told you..."

"Yes, yes. Your priorities changed when your glasses advised you that my parents had been blacklisted." Chewing the inside of her cheek, Scarlett replayed their conversation in her mind. Nothing stood out to her as being a lie. As near as she could tell, he'd been truthful about everything. The only reason she was certain of this was because her Spymaster had a tell when he lied. His left eye twitched. Albeit very subtly. One had to watch closely for it. Like she had been doing from the second she walked into this room. "I'm going to assume it's probably still hidden here somewhere."

"Here or one of their warehouses or stashes. Teams and agents have been trying to locate it for twenty years. There hasn't been any sign or mention of it anywhere. We've taken that to mean they didn't get a chance to sell or pass it off to the rival agency they intended to defect to." William's taut muscles started to relax as he came to the conclusion the woman in the room with him wasn't about to yell or scream at him. Sitting back in the chair, William steepled his fingers wondering where her interrogation would lead them next.

"I don't suppose you have a diagram or picture, do you?" Perhaps what she asked was too optimistic. Nonetheless, Scarlett held out hope for a positive answer.

Raising his eyebrows in surprise, William silently applauded her thoroughness. "No... but I might be able to draw a reasonable facsimile if you'd like me to try."

"Don't trouble yourself. I have a feeling I'll know when or if I see it." A thought struck her out of the blue. "William... an electromagnetic pulse would disrupt any electronics in its path. Could we not use this rifle to eliminate the Eliminator, for lack of better terminology?"

Given his mind had recently been preoccupied with a great deal of other things, William was utterly astonished he hadn't considered what she suggested. "That... might actually work."

"I'll begin searching with Jerome's help. Between us we know every inch of this mansion including all of the secret areas my folks thought they'd keep hidden."

"I'd like you to pair with Damon and Jerome with Feiyan then please." William winced at her expression. "Look, I'm sorry but right now if there's talk of splitting up, I don't want anyone going off on their own."

"Worried Jerome or I will keep it for ourselves?" Scarlett's words came out with a sharpness she didn't intend however also couldn't control given the circumstances of the conversation.

"What? No! I just don't think anyone should be 'exploring' on their own."

"Yet you allowed Feiyan to do so, didn't you?"

"Hang on, how'd you know about that?"

"I have cameras in some areas of this house and she went past several." Scarlett expertly covered up the slip of her tongue. "Not to mention - this is my home."

"Scarlett, please, I'm asking for safety's sake. I swear there's no other reason." William tried again. The last thing he wanted was to experience her wrath.

"Very well." Turning her back to him, Scarlett headed for the door. Before exiting the room, she glanced back over her shoulder. "I'll want more details about the rest of our conversation at a later time."

"Of course." William promised. Even if all of the serum had worn off by then, he'd tell her anything she wanted to know. For the most part. The deciding factor would be what questions she might pose.

Satisfied, Wintyrs left his room to find Damon leaning against the wall in the hallway. "Were you eavesdropping?"

"A good spy always does." Damon replied, rapidly continuing when he noted anger rising in her eyes. "Except in this instance. No, I heard your raised voice. Not what was being said. Given how upset you sounded, I wanted to be here when you were finished in case you needed an ear to bend or a shoulder to cry on. Also, since it was William you were speaking with, I made every conscious effort to afford you both the privacy any Spymaster expects to have when engaging with one of their assets."

"Mmh."

"So are you?"

"Am I what?"

"Alright?"

Forcing her mind to stop making her feel so guarded was exhausting. For some reason, she couldn't unwind from the talk she'd had with William. Scarlett made herself remember that this man wasn't the one who deserved whatever happened to him. This was Damon talking to her now. Not William. "I will be. I'm sorry for snapping at you."

Damon shrugged. "I'd say I'm used to it but honestly I've never been on the receiving end of a woman snapping at someone. Either way, though, no apologies needed. What's going on?"

"We have to go on a search. Let's find Feiyan and Jerome first. I don't want to have to explain twice."

"Who's Jerome?"

"That'd be my valet."

"Ahhh... gotcha. When do we get dinner? I'm starving." Giving her a wry grin, Damon did nothing to hide the rumble from his stomach the second food was mentioned.

"An announcement or chime will sound through the intercom when dinner is ready. Give Andrea some time. Our visit was totally unexpected after all." The noise did manage to elicit a smile from her despite everything.

Scarlett led Damon back down to the entryway. She was glad when he didn't try to hold a conversation. Which actually gave her pause. He loved to hear himself talk - that much she had gleaned from the time they'd spent together. So for him to be this silent meant, to her at least, that he must have picked up whatever signals her body was sending regarding her current state of mind.

When they arrived at the bottom of the stairs, they found Jerome and Feiyan already there waiting for them. A sight Scarlett doubted to be merely coincidental. Stepping from the carpeted stairs to the marble floor, she eyed first her former mentor then her valet. Something wasn't sitting right until she noticed Feiyan's communicator in her hand.

"You've already spoken with William." Scarlett stated, crossing her arms over her chest.

"Only long enough for him to ask me to grab Jerome and meet you two here. Would one of you care to tell us what's going on?" Feiyan replied casually. Feeling as though her friend, and pupil, was trying to lead her into a trap that would result in an argument, she refused to rise to the bait. Arguments were the last thing any of them needed. Except for maybe Scarlett who, to Feiyan's eyes, looked ready to rip someone's head off.

Emotions were getting the better of her. Wintyrs knew that. She was doing everything she could, using every technique she knew, to keep them in check. Especially her anger. Only one person deserved that and he wasn't among this small group.

"Miss Scarlett? Are you in the know about this?" Jerome watched the young woman with eyes like a hawk. He knew her well enough to pick up on when she was hiding things.

"I am." Scarlett answered, all eyes now on her. "I'll fill Zaliki in later. For right now - Damon and Feiyan there's two very important things you need to know before I tell you why we four are meeting here. One, my parents also worked for our agency. Two - Jerome still does, if I understand William properly, operating as my guardian or protector since I was a child."

"You know??" Jerome gaped at her.

"I do."

"How did you figure it out? I've been so very careful. Even your parents didn't know. The only person aware of my assignment was the Spymaster at the time. After his death the files would have then passed on to... the... new..." His face blanched when realization struck. "The man you're calling William. You said he told you of me?"

"Indeed I did." Scarlett kept a straight face when her valet concluded what that could only mean.

"He's the Spymaster?" Bug-eyed, Jerome could only whisper the question. "You're saying we have our Spymaster in this house at this very moment?"

"That's exactly what I'm saying. Are you alright?" When the older man she'd been addressing put a hand out to brace himself against the wall, Scarlett wondered if perhaps she'd taken the conversation too far. Reaching out to the man who'd basically raised her, she gripped his shoulder, watching him closely. When he just stared at her, she gently squeezed the shoulder she held. "Jerome?"

"We've... we've never had a Spymaster grace these hallowed halls, Miss Scarlett." Jerome lifted a hand and gave the one she was using to hold him a light pat. "Don't you worry about me, dear girl. I'll be right as rain in no time. Given his presence, though, do you not think it wise to activate the external gate security system?"

"What will that do?" Damon inquired. If there were additional measures they could take to ensure William's safety then he was all for it.

"An alarm will sound in the house if anyone tries to open the gate or climb over the fence. The gate will be electrified. On top of the fence are pressure plates which will also be electrified." The valet quickly explained.

Impressed, Damon risked glancing at Wintyrs to see her thoughts but her blank expression gave no indication one way or the other about her opinion. "I'd love to see that system on... what do you say, Scarlett?"

"Very well." Scarlett nodded to give Jerome the go-ahead then watched as he pressed a button on the timepiece he wore on his right wrist given he was left-handed.

When the system was armed, an announcement sounded throughout the house given by an obviously mechanical female voice. "External gate security system activated. If leaving the premises, system must be disengaged to prevent injury or death."

"It's nice you give your guests that warning." Feiyan remarked when the announcement ended. "Now - why are we four here?"

Looking around the entryway saddened Scarlett. There used to be pictures of her family everywhere she looked. Now, though, not a single frame adorned the walls. She couldn't even tell where the holes were that used to hold the nails for the hooks to hang the frames. Seeing the moments gone had her wondering why they had been removed without anyone consulting her. A subject she'd have to take up with Jerome. Giving herself a small shake, Wintyrs looked at the other three. "We're going to search this house from to bottom and everything in between. We're looking for an EMP pulse rifle stolen by my parents when they planned to defect from our agency to another. The main reason we're conducting this search now is because William believes the rifle may actually be able to stop the Eliminator."

"Hold up a second. Your parents were agents with the Centurian Agency too?" Damon flinched at her glare. "Alright, alright. I'll shut up." He held his hands up towards her, pretending to fend her off.

"Jerome, please take Feiyan and search the east wing including the basement. Damon and I will go west. And we need to include the secret rooms my parents added to the house." Scarlett finished her instructions for the team then waited to see if there were any questions. When none arose, she gave them a bleak smile. "Alright then, let's do this."

Wintyrs turned to the wing she and Damon were to search and led him through the doorway. Once again the silence from her companion struck her as odd yet, as before, she felt in no mood to question his choice to not speak. Knowing where she wanted to check first, Scarlett took him to the office Feiyan found her in earlier. She ignored his low whistle of appreciation, turning to find him right behind her - staring at the portrait on the wall.

"Those your folks?"

"Yeah."

"Troy and Kristi were your parents." Taking hold of her shoulders, Damon made her look into his eyes. "How long have you known about what they did for a living."

"For awhile." Scarlett tried to shake off the tight grip he had on her but his hands refused to release her. "Damon, you'd be wise to let go of me before you get hurt." The dangerous undertone in her words caused his hands to fall from her faster than she'd ever seen him move. "What's your problem, Damon??"

"Troy and Kristi." Damon shook his head at her. "You never heard the rumours then?"

"That they were going to defect? I found out about that today. From William."

"Did he tell you..."

"That he's responsible for their deaths? Yes."

Blinking back his surprise, Damon stared at her. "And he's still alive?"

Frowning at his behaviour, Scarlett moved behind her desk in order to press a small red button. Once she did, the portrait swung open to allow them access to the hidden rooms beyond. "Of course he's still alive. Why? Did you think I'd seek revenge? Against not only our Spymaster but also the man I love?"

"Yes. Hell hath no fury like a woman scorned, remember? I've experienced my fair share of that to say the phrase holds true." When the portrait opened, he fell silent, bewildered. "I've only seen that trick twice now. Here and back at the auction house on the island. Wonder if the same person did both... so what's back there?"

In a way Scarlett wished he'd fall back into the silence he'd maintained until they entered the office. "Why don't we just wander go in and you can see for yourself?"

With a shrug, Damon jogged around the desk to join her. "After you, milady."

Once over the threshold of the previously hidden doorway, darkness enveloped them penetrated only by some glowing blue light - the source of which Damon could not see. Only when the portrait closed again did the area become awash in white light. Normally he found this hue hard on the eyes due to its harsh brightness. This seemed different though. Softer yet just as strong. It certainly didn't bother his vision. A fact he was immensely grateful for. Especially when what greeted him in the area beyond that portrait gave his own little lab setup a serious run for its money.

"Did you set all of this up?" Damon's tongue thawed enough for him to ask.

Scarlett silently shook her head. "No. My parents must have. Probably with Jerome's help." She paused, running her fingers along the edge of a keyboard. "I've never been so far into this area. I think part of me was afraid of what I might find if I came too far." Voice growing soft, Wintyrs' eyes roamed the once-hidden room. "All of this equipment looks like it's from our agency, not scrounged like yours. You know... I don't understand how they could have a setup like this. They had everything they needed here to not only run their own missions but have a fully functional base of operations."

"You sound like you're leading up to something there."

"Maybe I am." She said softly. "I'm not sure I entirely believed William when he told me my parents were defecting to another agency. Let alone that they stole tech from the Centurian Agency..."

Moving around the small rooms comprising the hidden lab setup, Damon stopped next to a cupboard which - to him at any rate - seemed out of place. When he realized she was waiting for him to say something, he responded with the only thing that came to mind. "And now?"

"Now… I'm not sure what to think."

Damon winced. He'd probably feel the same way if he were in her position. Testing the door to the cabinet, he found it locked. A locked cabinet in a hidden lab which had been owned by spies. What were the chances what they sought lay beyond that metal door. Thinking the odds might be in their favour, he searched the immediate area for a key as the lock on the door was surprisingly old-fashioned and simplistic in nature.

Cold, white walls did nothing to detract from the lab feeling as Scarlett continued looking around. When she heard drawers opening then closing paired with her companion muttering under his breath, Scarlett raised an eyebrow. "You okay over there?"

"No. Blast it. I have a cabinet here needing a key which I have yet to find. And I don't have my lock picking gear with me." Damon answered, slamming his fifth drawer shut. "I bloody well hate searching a spy's lair. People in our line of work are too damned good at hiding things."

"Very true." Wintyrs' eyes landed on the only picture hanging on the walls of this place. The image was of her as a child, sitting on a swing and waving to the camera. It was an odd feeling. Seeing a likeness of her younger self. In fact, she'd always hated her picture being taken - a fact making her look at this one closer. She couldn't remember it being taken. An oddity in and of itself. Combine that with her aversion to being immortalized in such a manner could only lead her to one conclusion. The image had been fabricated. But why? And to what end? Reaching out, Scarlett plucked the thin silver frame from the wall in order to take a closer look. Many of the pixels were different sizes as well as densities. It was a Frankenstein image. Pursing her lips, she flipped it over to look at the back only to find a key taped to the reverse side.

"Damon? I think I may have found what you're looking for." She called out to her partner, carefully removing the tape holding the item in place then letting it fall into her open palm.

Peering around some of the larger equipment to locate where her voice came from, Damon saw his companion standing next to a wall not far away but her positioning raised something interesting in his thoughts. That wall might indicate the edge of this secret lair, or whatever it was called, but she was smack-dab in the exact centre of it. Raynott walked over to her, noting how tense she was.

"You found the key?"

"Well… I found *a* key. Only one way to find out if it's the one you're in need of." Handing it to him, Scarlett flipped the frame over again to look at the picture.

"Cute kid. That you?" Damon asked after glimpsing the image.

"It is and it isn't."

"How very Freudian of you." When he noted the tease seemed to miss its mark, Damon shrugged and took the key over to the cabinet which had been frustrating him. A victorious whoop left his lips after he successfully fit the key into the keyhole and a slight turn released the lock.

"We're in!" A metallic clink echoed through the lab to Scarlett's ears. "So, uh, you know how you said you weren't sure what to think about what William told you about your parents?"

"Yeah?"

Damon moved back into her line of sight, holding up the sought after rifle. "How about now?"

21

When the weapon entered her sight, Scarlett's heart dropped into her stomach. Every instinct told her what met her eyes was undeniable. Then there was her heart. These were her parents they were talking about. Her family. How could she not defend them?

"Are you sure that's the EMP rifle?" Scarlett knew what his answer would be. She still had to ask.

"Oh, I'm pretty sure. I mean, short of testing what it does I guess we can't be one hundred percent but I'd stake my reputation on it." Damon eyed her. "You're really hoping it's not, huh?"

"They're my parents. I... need... to give them the benefit of the doubt. Wouldn't you?"

"Yeah... I guess I would." A pang of guilt shot through him for what she must be feeling. "Look, we can't go back in time to right the wrongs our loved ones did. All we can do is move forward. Keep those good memories at the forefront of your mind. The theft, the defection - those weren't the parents you knew and loved."

His words threw Scarlett off-balance. "Uh... thanks?"

A wry grin adorned his face. "What can I say? I'm hungry. That makes me kind of philosophical." Moving over to where she still stood, Damon let her take the rifle to examine. "Scarlett, we're kinda going out on a ledge here. We can't fire that thing without knowing for sure that's the right rifle and we can't be sure it's the right rifle without testing it."

"No... William indicated we should be able to tell by looking at it. Which tells me there must be something that sets it apart from any other weapon despite its age." Scarlett's eyes narrowed. The rifle, now that she held it, seemed cumbersome. Probably why she favoured pistols or knives. Bulkiness aside, the weapon appeared unusually large for the class in which it had been placed. There were also what looked to be lights near the trigger mechanism - not currently lit up but definitely out of place for a normal rifle.

"You find something?" Having been watching her examine the item in her hands, Damon noted when her gaze lingered on one particular area.

"Possibly. I'm certain this is what William hoped we'd find."

"Awesome." Raynott picked up the framed picture she'd placed facedown on the nearest desk surface when he'd handed over the rifle. "Ah, now I see what you meant. This picture is yet isn't you."

"Hmm? Oh, yeah, that. Honestly just thinking about that image gives me the creeps."

Damon sure as hell couldn't blame her. Even to his trained eye the piece of art - if it could be called that - was like something out of a horror film. Everything about the picture was off. The pixels as she'd mentioned however there was more to it than that. Much more.

"In your search of this lab... I don't suppose you came across a magnifying glass of some sort?"

"No... why?"

"I think there's more to this picture than just you being the subject. If I can get my hands on a magnifying glass, I can look deeper." Sounding distracted, Damon rummaged through the nearby desks and drawers. "Eureka! Found one." He held up a lovely magnifying glass with a brass frame and an ivory handle. "Were your folks fans of old time mysteries? I haven't seen such a beauty of one of these in anything except auctions or places with antiques."

"Possibly. I'm kinda questioning everything I thought I knew about them though. Right now I feel like I never knew them at all."

Damon nodded once, not pushing the issue. Holding the glass up to the picture, he peered closer at the image then pulled back abruptly. "Whoa..."

"What is it? What did you see?"

Taking another look, Raynott pressed his lips together, wondering how much he should tell her. "Let me put it this way... between that rifle and this picture... there's no doubt what William told you was true."

Scarlett put the rifle down on the nearest surface then took both the picture and the magnifying glass from the man she found herself calling partner now. Not saying anything, she looked through the glass at the picture. Pulling back after seeing what he'd seen, she swallowed hard.

"Scarlett. We have to take this to William." Damon's gentle voice penetrated her thoughts like a knife cutting through softened butter. I know you're not talking to him or you're mad at him or whatever but this *has* to take precedence."

Hearing him be the voice of reason was enough to shock her into responding. "You're right. Can you find Feiyan and Jerome to let them know we located the weapon please? I'm going straight to William."

"If you'd rather I go..."

"They were my parents. That makes this my responsibility."

Wintyrs noted the conflict in his eyes. He wanted to stay by her side. To support her however he could. Yet at the same time he saw the value in her words. Eventually he bowed his head in acquiescence then jogged from the secret lab. She followed in his wake shortly after, locking the door back up while carrying the rifle, picture and magnifying glass. Once everything was secure, Scarlett headed back upstairs and knocked on the door to William's room.

The sound didn't startle him for William expected it. Albeit not quite this soon. Moving to the door from his position at the window, he opened it and raised his eyebrows at who stood there waiting. "Scarlett." A blush crept into his cheeks at the way her name came out. He'd made it sound like he was ready for more than just a kiss. Which, as that thought crossed his mind, William uncomfortably realized was closer to the truth than he'd like.

"Can I come in?" How he'd said her name hadn't registered with her, only that he'd said it. "And you may wish to stick with Agent Wintyrs for this one."

William's brow furrowed but he stepped aside in order for her to go past him. The fact she didn't seem mad with him hadn't gone unnoticed. Nor did what she carried with her. "You found the rifle! Excellent work, as always."

Scarlett moved further into the room, not turning to face him until she heard the click of the door being secured shut. Only then did she finally dare look in his direction. "I never should have doubted you." The words came out as a whisper. "I may not have said I did but I did." She let him take the rifle in order to place it down.

"As far as I'm concerned you had every reason to." William walked back to her after placing the weapon on the desk in the room. "What's made you change your mind? And so quickly?"

"You were right. My parents were defecting to another agency. Worse... they never really worked for the Centurian Agency. I think they were always part of another agency. At the top of my list is Orion. And they stole a lot more than just that rifle." Scarlett let the words come out in a rush, worried if she didn't then fear would stop her later.

"Okay so they were infiltrators not defectors." William went back to the chair in the corner and sat down heavily.

"That's... that's what it looks like from everything we've found so far." Scarlett handed him the portrait as well as the magnifying glass.

"What's this?" A smile crossed his face. "Is this you as a child?"

"In a way..."

"What do you mean?"

"Use the magnifying glass. Take a closer look."

Narrowing his eyes, William concluded she wasn't going to say anything else until he did as asked. He held up the picture and the magnifying glass, taking the requested closer look. What he saw, he couldn't quite believe. The image he thought was a picture of Scarlett was comprised of hundreds of smaller images. Putting his eye even closer, William blew out a breath.

"I'm guessing you and Damon didn't spot what I'm seeing now. You saw the smaller images, yes?"

"Yeah."

"Did you see each one has a microchip embedded in it?"

"What?! No!" Scarlett's eyes widened. "There has to be at least a hundred of those smaller images!"

"And each one appears to have a microchip." William repeated and saw how faint she looked. With a speed he'd forgotten he could move with, William jumped from the chair. He grabbed her in his arms to keep her on her feet. "Hey, stay with me here."

Gripping his arms to keep herself steady, Scarlett swallowed the lump forming in her throat. "I can't believe this is happening."

"I know." His brown eyes searched her blue ones. "Scarlett, one of the images had a phrase on it. I need you to tell me if it means anything to you, can you do that for me?"

Squeezing her eyes closed for a moment, Scarlett slowed her breathing. She kept her grip on his arms, not wanting him to let her go. "Yeah. Yeah I can do that."

"Good. 'Wintyrs' Caress'. Any idea what that might mean?" He kept his gaze locked with hers.

"No." Scarlett answered truthfully. "I mean it must be something personal though if Wintyrs is spelled the same as my surname."

"Which it is." With the knowledge that for some reason she needed to feel his touch right now, William kept his hands where they were. "If all the images have a microchip then it's plausible to assume it could be the name of a specific file. Perhaps one of great importance."

"That makes sense... if there's encryption though... maybe it's a cypher." If it was a file, she couldn't fathom what it might relate to given the name. "We should find some way to read those chips."

"We'll add that to our list but you and I both know that's not our top priority." William watched her nod then straighten her shoulders. Taking the motion as a sign, he released his hold on her. "First though..." He looked around in alarm when a loud chime interrupted what he'd been saying.

With a smile, Scarlett touched his arm gently to reassure him. "It's alright. That's the meal chime. Dinner's been served. Shall we head down?"

William blinked. An actual dinner bell? He'd never experienced anything like it. "Uh, yeah, sure. No, wait." Tentatively taking her hand in his, he needed to finish his question. "Are you and I going to be alright?"

Scarlett had been half-expecting the inquiry which meant when he finally got around to posing it, she wasn't taken off-guard. She did, however, blow out a long breath. "I know what you did and why you did it. With the why becoming more clear with every discovery we make." Noting the sadness in his eyes, Scarlett squeezed his hand. "They say love conquers all. There's no denying what I feel for you is love. Whenever you touch me - even if by accident - I feel like an electrical current runs right through me. When you have your arms around me, I feel safer than I ever have in my entire life. And when you look at me, when our eyes meet, nothing else exists. You complete me."

"Then..."

"Yeah. I think we're going to be alright. Despite what you did." Scarlett moved in close, gently placing her lips on his. "Has the truth stuff worn off yet?"

William longed to tell her how happy what she said made him. Looking at her face, though, told him she already knew. He wrinkled his nose at the last question. "Ask me something that I wouldn't normally lie about."

"Okay…" Wintyrs thought about what to ask then nodded once to herself. "Are you the Spymaster for the Orion Agency?"

Trying not to smirk at the inquiry, he shook his head. "I absolutely am." He grinned broadly. "I'd say it's worn off."

"Good. That means you can join the rest of us for dinner without worrying about spilling your guts about anything classified."

"Uh yeah, we should be good. Plus I'm starving."

Scarlett kept hold of his hand, dragging him from the room. She stayed close to him while they went down the stairs to the main level and even as they made their entrance into the dining room where the rest of their team were already seated. Surprisingly, they'd left the head and foot of the solid walnut table for her and William, ranging themselves along the sides. The high-backed chairs made anyone who sat in them feel small and insignificant. They were the same wood as the table with thick cushions on the back and seat covered with a dark burgundy fabric. A stark contrast to the classic beige walls. Noting Zaliki also sat at the table suggested to Scarlett that either one of their team retrieved her or one of the staff had. Either way, Wintyrs was happy to them all there. Obviously she and William took too long to arrive as the table held plates at each sitting location which remained covered with silver lids in order to keep the contents warm.

William pulled Scarlett's chair out for her, gently pushing it back in once she was sitting down. He smiled at her quiet thank-you. "You're welcome." He gently caressed the back of her neck before going to the other end of the table to take his place there. "Something smells really good."

"We know, mate. We've been waiting on you two. I'm pretty sure there's a puddle of drool under my chair." Damon stated disdainfully. "What took so long anyway? I even had time to run upstairs, grab Zaliki and bring her back down for pete's sake."

"Well, we apologize for keeping your stomachs waiting but you never have to stand on ceremony for me like that." William said in response. "Please - eat."

"We weren't standing on ceremony for you, William. No matter how important you think you are just because you were so powerful on the islands." Feiyan interrupted, shifting her eyes to a younger woman none of them had yet spoken to, cocking her head slightly to acknowledge the nod of confirmation from the Spymaster. "Are you feeling more like yourself now, William?"

"I am, yes. Thanks for asking." William could have smacked

himself for not noticing the woman in the room with them.

"Good. Anyway, further to your earlier comment - we were waiting for Scarlett since this is her house."

Falling back into the persona he'd created for life on the islands, William snorted in response. "Come now. She may own this place... and may be the most gorgeous woman in this hemisphere, but I'm the one everyone looks to and you damned well know that."

Damon chuckled, almost feeling like they were back in Dolus with William assuming his disguise once more. "I'm going to interrupt now. Can we please eat? I'm starving."

"You're always starving. Every time I see you, you're eating." Glancing at his Dolus business partner, William smiled.

Scarlett clapped her hands together lightly to gain the attention of those sitting around the table. "Let's put the conversation on hold for a bit. Dig in, folks. Cheyanna..." she shifted her gaze to the woman they'd each donned covers for, "could you please get us a nice Reisling to accompany this dinner?"

"Right away, Miss Wintyrs." The diminutive brunette left the room swiftly, her white sweater making her sun-tanned face seem more bronze than any other colour would.

"Cheyanna?" William repeated the name. "I don't recall her presence here on my last visit."

"She joined our staff last year. After our previous housekeeper, Sylvie, passed away. Sylvie would've been the one you likely saw." Scarlett explained.

"Strawberry blonde, right?"

"That was her."

"I managed to avoid being seen but I definitely saw her. I'm sorry to hear she passed. Can I ask how?"

Feiyan, Damon and Zaliki were pretending to be engrossed with the delicious food they'd been served. A meal consisting of chicken cordon bleu and scalloped potatoes. It was one of Scarlett's favourite dishes. Doubtless why Andrea had whipped it up upon hearing of her arrival. Despite the rest of the team seemingly focused solely on their food, both Scarlett and William were well-aware they were far more interested in the conversation.

"The coroner ruled it natural causes." Scarlett answered quietly, seeing the housekeeper returning with the requested wine.

Cheyanna opened the bottle at the buffet, the pop of the cork echoing in the silence of the dining room. Each glass was then filled with the Reisling, starting with Scarlett's and finishing with Feiyan's. When she completed her task, Cheyanna left the dining room again but Scarlett knew she wouldn't be far in case she was needed.

"How soon after you lost Sylvie did you find Cheyanna?" William returned to the subject as if they hadn't been interrupted.

"The turnaround was fairly quick. I managed to hire her before I had to return to the agency after Sylvie's funeral." Scarlett frowned at him. "Why?"

"So she's been fully vetted?"

"Jerome looked after that for me. Since she's still here I have to assume everything came back clean." Pausing, she noted the closed expression he now wore. "What's wrong?"

"We can discuss it later."

Digging in to her own meal upon realizing the conversation was over for now, Scarlett ended up deep in thought. Her Spymaster's mind worked differently than her own and she knew he could, at times, see things his field agents missed. Be they subtle or not. What had he seen about Cheyanna? Why had he questioned Sylvie's death in the manner he did? When her fork clattered to her plate without warning, Wintyrs found everyone's eyes on her. She gave them what she hoped was a reassuring smile. If her parents managed to not only infiltrate but also fool the Spymaster who hired them, who was to say others weren't as talented. Especially if they were affiliated with the Orion Agency. After all, they'd seen first hand how good that agency's Spymaster was. And if Cheyanna worked for him...

Scarlett jumped out of her chair, racing over to the buffet. She placed her right hand against what looked like a normal section of the wall. The part under her palm glowed orange and a small panel emerged from the wall right beside her hand after a slot slid back out of the way. Her fingers flew across the panel quickly enough they were nearly a blur.

When Wintyrs left her place at the table with such alacrity, the other three agents nearly followed suite. In their minds such haste indicated a threat. However when she merely went to the wall, they relaxed again. The only one who hadn't been spurred to action was William. Instead he watched Scarlett, knowing if she needed any assistance she would let them know. One of his eyebrows raised when the wall revealed the panel but he kept his mouth shut. He didn't want to distract her from what he surmised was an important task.

"What're you doing, Scarlett?" Damon inquired, watching the

woman's back.

"Disabling all outbound comms traffic as well as activating a damper I had Jerome install last year to make this place safer if needed. And right now I'm really glad I had that foresight." Scarlett replied, finishing up. Once completed her self-appointed task, she touched the wall again and the panel slid back into its hiding place.

"Okay… why?" Zaliki finally spoke up, her curiosity winning out.

"If what William thinks is true then Cheyanna is in fact part of the Orion Agency just as I suspect my parents were." Rejoining them at the table, Scarlett noted the only one who seemed shocked was Zaliki.

"Wait… what??" Food all but forgotten, Zaliki stared at Scarlett.

"Yeah that about surmises all of our reactions when we found out." Damon drawled out. "Sorry, I thought she might've put two and two together when I briefed her on the way here - OW!" Rubbing his upper right arm, Raynott turned to Zaliki. "How is it you can punch so damned hard?"

"How is it you are weak enough that such a light touch hurt?" She countered.

Damon paused, still rubbing the spot. "Fair point." He answered then turned back to the table nursing what was sure to be a bruise forming on his arm not to mention his damaged ego.

Scarlett merely shook her head at the pair's interaction. William attempting to keep his amusement under control didn't escape her notice. Nor did Feiyan's smug smile - whether over Zaliki's reaction or Damon's supposed injury, she couldn't tell. "Maybe we should consider dividing and conquering?"

"We need to get Myrtle here." William stated. "And for that we need to be able to send out a comms. Which we can't do until Scarlet lets us."

"You know there's only one way that'll happen." Wintyrs said, finishing up her meal.

"I do." His gaze moved around those seated at the table. "We have to expose Cheyanna."

"How the bloody hell do you want us to do that??" Damon looked back and forth between the Spymaster and Scarlett, feeling as though he were at a tennis match. "Short of us catching her in the act…" He trailed off when his words resulted in William giving him a large grin. "Why are you looking at me like that? You look like you won the lottery or something."

"Maybe because you just hit the proverbial nail on the head. We have to catch her in the act, like you said. Incontrovertible proof she's with another agency and knowingly infiltrated the staff of this household in order to obtain Centurian Agency secrets." William elaborated in a soft voice.

"Great. But again we're left with one very important question. How?" Damon wanted answers which meant he ensured he was the first to speak, not allowing the women a chance.

"With bait." Scarlett spoke up. "We allow her to see that we found the EMP rifle. Let slip within her hearing what my parents planned to do. Leave it unguarded. She won't be able to refuse the temptation, she's young enough she's probably still trying to find a way to prove herself. What better way than by completing a mission started twenty years ago. She'd probably think they'd give her a hero's welcome upon her return."

Not having expected an answer from that quarter, Raynott glanced over at her. "Why do I get the feeling you've done this before?"

"Yeah. Not my first rodeo. William?"

"Do it." Knowing Wintyrs was more than capable of the task, William wondered if she shouldn't have backup anyway. "Maybe have one of the others with you in case she's more than you can handle?" He flinched at the look she shot him in response. "She's younger than any of us here in this room, which means her reflexes will be better not to mention other things, I'm sure."

"I can handle it." Annoyed at the suggestion, Scarlett downed the rest of her wine in one large gulp before leaving the room in order to begin preparations.

William puckered his lips, feeling as though he'd bitten into something extremely sour. "Zaliki... you know Orion Agency training and protocols..."

"I can help sell this if you want me to." Already thinking ahead, Zaliki rose from the table. "Cheyanna won't know about Scarlett's parents' mission without being able to communicate to the agency herself. An older agent, though, would possess such knowledge. As the Wintyrs' infiltrated your agency, I shall do the same with the Orion Agency - at least for this purpose."

While not what William had in mind, the idea was a good one. "I like it. Damon, Feiyan - remain at my side please, just in case."

"Awww how come those two get to have all the fun?" Damon crossed his arms, pretending to pout.

"If the shit hits the fan the way I think it will, there'll be enough fun for all." William replied wryly. "Actually you two can start helping me figure out getting Myrtle here and away from Amir. I'm worried about what could happen to her if she starts questioning or resisting orders."

"I could see her doing that." Feiyan said while Zaliki left the room. "I will begin crafting an extraction plan."

"Work with Damon please. I know you both prefer working alone but this time I want both of your input for the best way to do this."

"As you command." She bowed her head to him, indicating her respect for his request.

"Happy now, Damon?" Smirking, William glanced at him.

"Yeah, yeah. Where do you plan on riding out this so-called storm you're expecting to blow in?" Getting up from the table in tandem with the other two, Damon walked alongside his friend as they left the room.

Cheyanna stood in the hall outside the dining room, shooting the trio a smile when they exited and arrived where she waited. Although she hadn't been able to hear absolutely everything the group discussed, she'd heard enough. Only when they had passed her did Cheyanna school her expression once more. Coming into this house she'd known the Centurian Agency would have people here. Especially given Scarlett Wintyrs' reputation. What she hadn't counted on was how many had arrived. It would certainly make what she had to do far more difficult. If she could only get Wintyrs alone, away from anyone else in the house, then perhaps she might stand a chance. And maybe she'd finally be allowed to go home. All she had to do was complete her mission objective. Kill Scarlett Wintyrs.

After all, how hard could it be?

22

Scarlett jogged up to William's room to retrieve the EMP rifle. When she arrived, the hairs on the back of her neck stood up for reasons unknown. Pausing in the doorway, her eyes roamed the room, searching for the source of her uneasiness. Given there were no overt signs of anyone else nearby, she was forced to conclude something else was the driving factor. Perhaps something her peripheral vision captured but her mind had not yet registered. So intent was she on the room that Scarlett didn't hear someone come up behind her.

"Stay like this any longer and people will think you're a statue." Zaliki said in her ear.

"You do like sneaking up on people, don't you." Scarlett responded, pleased she'd been able to hide her surprise at the other woman's presence.

"It's a talent. What're you looking for?"

Wintyrs shook her head in response, the uneasiness slowly evaporating. "I don't know. Just a feeling. It didn't last long. Like someone unseen was here."

"If your instincts are telling you that then we should heed what they say." Stepping next to Scarlett, Zaliki narrowed her eyes and let her gaze roam the room as the other woman had done upon her arrival. "Given who is staying in this room, perhaps we should examine things more closely?"

"Agreed."

Moving inside further, the feeling returned. Scarlett couldn't shake it no matter how she tried. Keeping her pace slow, she peered everywhere she knew she'd hide a listening device. Nothing stood out. She slid her glance over to Zaliki who busied herself with searching the other side of the room. When their eyes met, Zaliki shook her head, indicating she had found nothing as well.

"I'll check the ensuite." Zaliki offered, moving into the smaller room without giving Wintyrs time to protest.

Instead of following the other woman, Scarlett gathered the EMP rifle as well as the picture. When she picked up the frame, the phrase William asked her about again rolled through her mind. Wintyrs' Caress. Not knowing to what the phrase referenced gnawed at her. Could it really be a file name as William suspected? Or something else entirely. Bringing Myrtle here could take ages and she sure as hell didn't want to wait that long.

Drawing herself back to the task at hand, Scarlett's eyes moved up to the ceiling. The one place no one ever really thought to look was up. Frowning, she examined its length, eyes trailing back and forth until she spotted the anomaly. Carefully placing the rifle and picture on top of William's bed, Scarlett resumed giving the hole in the ceiling her scrutiny. Not a gaping hole by any means, the size seemed to fall in line more with the circumference of a pencil-thin surveillance camera. Likely with audio.

"Nothing noteworthy in the ensuite." Zaliki commented, exiting said room. Taking in Scarlett's position, she raised an eyebrow. "Are we praying for help now? You didn't strike me as the religious sort."

"Huh? Oh, no, nothing like that." Scarlett replied, her eyes locked on the hole still. "However I think I just found what we were looking for."

"Really?" Intrigued, Zaliki meandered over to peer at what the other woman now pointed to. "Interesting… you know if there's one in here then chances are pretty good there'll be one in every room of the house."

"On this floor yes, definitely, because of the attic… the other two floors would be far more difficult to do something like this."

"Then the question arises - did who we suspect do it or could it be older?"

A chill settled in her stomach as Scarlett considered that. The point was well-made considering the Centurian Agency knew her parents were stealing technology from them. Could the devices be from their own employer? There wasn't even a guarantee that the Orion Agency was behind them. Any agency could have planted the devices if they were aware of the Wintyrs family's association.

"Anything's possible. After things are put into motion and our suspicions about our suspect are either confirmed or not, we can verify with them if the devices are theirs or not." Scarlett didn't want to reveal what gender or even the name of their suspect in case Cheyanna was listening at this very moment.

"Agreed." Immediately picking up on Wintyrs' turn of phrase, Zaliki kept her answer short and sweet. She needn't be told that the device they uncovered could be in use. Which also suggested she put her part of William's plan into motion. "Is that the EMP rifle your parents stole from the Centurian Agency? The one they planned on turning over to their true employer?"

Sensing a ploy she hadn't been made aware of was afoot, Scarlett cocked her head to one side, deciding to play along in order to see where this was heading. "Yes. Apparently they were killed before they had the chance to complete their mission." When Zaliki took the weapon into her hands, Wintyrs clamped down on the protest she wanted to make.

"Are you planning on locking it up someplace safe to make sure it doesn't fall into the wrong hands - again?" Running an admiring hand across the barrel of the rifle, Zaliki sighed quietly. "I must admit this is an absolute thing of beauty."

"I have a weapons safe in the office. I'll lock it up in there until we're ready." Thankfully Scarlett already considered that part of the plan which made answering the question easy.

"Combination lock?"

"Keypad lock. Why do you ask?"

"No reason."

Wintyrs shot the other woman a wink then led the way down to the office to ensure Zaliki knew where it was. "Have you done any exploring of the house?"

"Not really. I took the opportunity before dinner to have a quick rest. My thoughts were to wander around and burn off some of those calories we were fed. How safe are we here, anyway?"

Revealing the weapons safe in the large armoire which was the same wood and colouring as the desk, Scarlett scratched an eyebrow with her thumb. Buying herself some time, she keyed in the access code then pulled the heavy metal door open which resulted in showcasing the incredible array of weapons inside. They didn't want Cheyanna to have an easy time locating the EMP rifle so Scarlett tactfully placed it amongst some of her other rifles which were visually similar. Before closing the locker back up, Scarlett gave the weapon another once over to assure herself of its positioning. The green indicator light next to the keypad lit up as the lock activated. Only when she saw that did she close the doors of the armoire.

"Are you going to answer my question?" Zaliki prodded, sounding somewhat impatient. And given how long she'd taken so far to provide a response, Wintyrs couldn't fault her.

"Next to our own agency, this is quite likely the most secure building on this continent." Scarlett turned to meet the other woman's stunned eyes. "And I don't say that lightly." Keeping things brief, she filled Zaliki in about her parents in case Damon missed anything.

"I suppose, if they were part of Orion and managed to infiltrate Centurian, it would stand to reason they would make this place as secure as any agency building." Zaliki paused, pursing her lips before continuing. "What were their names again?"

"Troy and Kristi."

Recognition flashed through Zaliki's face. "I wondered. I'd heard tales of them when I was training and can confirm they were Orion assets. They were two of the agency's best. There've been no infiltrators like them since. Their skill was so great they were likened to chameleons. At least, that's what new recruits are told. I'm curious about one thing though."

"What's that?" Scarlett picked the picture back up from the small table she'd set it on while dealing with the rifle.

"How did you end up with the Centurian Agency and not Orion when both your parents worked for the latter? Our Spymaster at the time of your recruitment age should've been all over you. Even begging you to join us."

Scarlett smiled reminiscently, leading Zaliki from the office. "I received invitations, when I turned eighteen, from four different agencies to test for potential recruitment. The only agency to make me an offer was Centurian."

"Four agencies vied for you? That's unheard of from what I understand." Zaliki followed Wintyrs closely. "I've always been told only one agency at a time is permitted to send those invitations."

"Be that as it may, that wasn't the case for me. Anyway, the entrance exam for each is the same but the answers may vary between the agencies as you know. My answers only impressed Centurian."

"Why is that do you think?"

"Probably because my answers tended towards solutions intended to keep targets alive whenever possible. I said I'd only kill as an absolute last resort."

"Yeah. Orion Agency wouldn't have liked responses like that. In fact that's where I've always admired Centurian - they let live whenever they can." Shrugging, Zaliki grinned. "Makes me even more glad over what's transpired between all of us."

Cheyanna bided her time. Waiting patiently until the two women left the office. Having had a thorough tour of the house when she was hired, she was fully cognizant of where everything was. Including the weapons safe. Even though that hadn't been part of the 'official' tour. Once the hallway emptied, Cheyanna inched along the wall until she reached the doorway. After ensuring the room was devoid of life, she slipped inside and moved right over to the armoire. The combination for the safe had been fairly easy for her to guess. Agent Wintyrs' 'parents' date of marriage - two digit year, month and day in that order. If she hadn't studied up on Wintyrs and her family history then things would have been a lot harder.

Curiousity as to what her target put in here drove Cheyanna to checking out the safe. When the door clicked open, the light on the keypad turning red to let the user know the lock was disengaged, she pulled on the handle and watched the door swing open. Cheyanna ran her fingers lightly over all the weapons, finding herself jealous of the selection sitting right in front of her. Sadly, there was only one she wanted. All thanks to the eavesdropping she'd done.

So the famous Agent Wintyrs' parents hadn't worked for the Centurian Agency but for the Orion Agency. Her agency. And they failed to complete their final mission. To bring this weapon to their home agency. Cheyanna's fingers stopped on one rifle which stood out to her over all others. Dragging the weapon from where it had been stored, a smile tugged at the corner of her lips. If she could bring this back to the agency in addition to completing her own mission to eliminate Wintyrs then she would rocket to the top. A favoured agent. One whom could pick and choose which missions to take.

"Hello, Cheyanna."

The voice from behind made Cheyanna whirl around with wide eyes to see from whence it came. "Miss Wintyrs!" Feigning innocence, she stared at her 'employer' who stood just inside the office doorway. Odd she hadn't heard her enter considering she'd locked the door after entering the office.

Scarlett's gaze took in the open weapons safe as well as the rifle in her housekeeper's hands. "What are you doing, Cheyanna?" Reaching behind her, she pushed the door closed once more.

"Cleaning, Miss Scarlett."

"Mmh." Scarlett crossed her arms. "In here? At this time of day? I gave you set hours when you started here. Technically you're off the clock. Try again."

Blinking rapidly, Cheyanna's mind worked quickly in an attempt to find a plausible explanation. "I apologize, Miss Scarlett. I shouldn't have lied." Pushing her glasses back up her nose to their proper position, the blonde and mahogany-streaked brunette tied her long hair back out of her face. "In my spare time, I familiarize myself with areas of the house I'm not in every day."

"Mmh." Repeating her earlier noise, Scarlett leaned back against the closed door and clapped her hands a couple of times. "Oh...you're good. I'll give you that."

"Ma'am?"

"If what you say were even the slightest bit true, you wouldn't know the code to that safe. Nor would you be holding what is arguably the single most dangerous weapon that was in there." Clucking her tongue in disappointment, Scarlett wondered at the woman's resolve. "I'm going to go out on a limb and say you're a newer recruit to the Orion Agency. Probably training as an infiltrator. I'd hazard a guess you showed so much promise, your superiors devised the hardest test - mission - they could come up with for you. Infiltrate my staff, learn what secrets you could and then... what? What would be your crowning achievement." Wintyrs tapped her right index finger against her lower lip, pretending to consider all options while in fact waiting to see if this infiltrator would break her cover or not.

Cheyanna sighed, placing the weapon on the desk. "They said you were good. Maybe even the best - which I highly doubt. You hit every single point right on target." A malignant smile appeared on her face. "You want to know what the final part of my mission is? What did you call it... my crowning achievement? Well, that's quite simple really. Your death."

"Somehow I knew you were going to say that." Her muscles were already anticipating what would soon be coming. "They didn't warn you that by attempting to complete your entire mission you'd be the one dying, not me?"

"Please. I'm good. So good I've been equated to following the footsteps of our greatest. Kristi. Oh, wait, wasn't that your mother?"

Cheyanna laughed lightly.

"Don't you dare bring her into this." Uncontrollable anger rose in Scarlett's throat.

"I just did." Cheyanna's smile turned cruel. From her research prior to infiltrating the household staff, she knew the more emotional Scarlett grew, the easier literally everything would become. "I have to wonder though. If she was so great, same with her husband - Troy, wasn't it? - then how could they have been killed by a measly accident?" Seeing Wintyrs' face growing red with her suppressed rage let Cheyanna know she had found the woman's weakness. "I mean, seriously. A car accident took out two of our so-called best..." Forced to trail off when Scarlett lunged at her, she side-stepped easily, letting her assailant crash into the desk with her waist.

Scarlett winced when she landed against the edge of her desk. The air knocked out of her from the sharp impact, she wasn't fast enough to avoid the hand grabbing her hair and yanking her back into a chokehold. Reaching up with both hands to the arm tight around her neck, her back pressed firmly against Cheyanna's chest, Scarlett managed to gasp in a couple of short breaths before her airway was closed entirely. She clawed at the arm but it wouldn't budge. Eyes landing on her desk, she grunted and lifted her feet, planting them firmly against the solid piece of furniture. Then she pushed with all her might, throwing Cheyanna off-balance and knocking them both to the floor.

The second they landed, the pressure around her throat vanished, allowing Scarlett to drag in air while coughing and rolling away from her opponent. Wintyrs swiftly jumped back to her feet. When she turned to face Cheyanna again, she saw the housekeeper grinning like a madman.

"What're you so happy about?" Scarlett rubbed her neck with one hand, gaze taking in how the infiltrator stood in order to be prepared for the next onslaught.

"You." Cheyanna sneered. "I know your weakness now. You were sloppy just then. I could've snapped your neck."

"Why didn't you?"

"I figure you deserve a fighting chance. But what would your parents have thought if they had seen that? I mean, come on. I'm sure you were trained better than that."

Clenching her teeth, Scarlett fought the urge to rise to the bait. Instead she expertly blocked the swing heading for her face, grabbing the woman's arm and using her own momentum against her to throw her across the room. "You got under my skin once. Trust me when I say it won't happen again."

Cheyanna groaned when she slammed into the armoire. A sickening crack told her at least one rib broke upon impact. Facing the open safe, she grabbed the edge and used it to fake needing help to stand. Knowing Wintyrs' view of the weapons was blocked, she picked up a smaller pistol. "And you underestimate me." She whirled, firing the pistol in several bursts, smiling when she realized it was a fully automatic model. Newer. And much deadlier.

Cursing, Scarlett ran for her desk - the only source of reasonable cover in the room. She felt a burning sensation in her abdomen as she dove behind the piece of cumbersome furniture. "You need to work on improving your aim!" She called out over the desk. When she heard a click followed by a snap, Scarlett realized Cheyanna had unloaded an entire clip trying to get her.

"You think so? You might want to check yourself over - I see some lovely red stuff out here on this white carpet." Cheyanna replied with some amusement. "Maybe you're getting too old for this game, Wintyrs. You're slowing down."

Looking down, Scarlett was shocked to discover her attacker was right. With one hand, she pressed down on the wound in her abdomen, trying to slow the bleeding. Unfortunately, the bullet was still in there which meant she would have to be incredibly careful with her movements or risk the projectile moving and causing more damage. With a wince, she reached over to the lower drawer on the right where she kept a first aid kit. With the injury more on the left-hand side, the stretch she had to do made the wound pull causing her to groan quietly. Wintyrs pulled out the first aid kit with one of her bloody hands then removed a couple of gauze pads, tucking them into the waistband of her pants as a temporary fix.

"I'd be careful who you're calling slow." Scarlett called back, focusing on the task at hand in order to keep the pain at bay as best she could. Footsteps told her Cheyanna moved around the room but it seemed as though she planned to remain as close to the weapon safe as possible. A tactic which effectively blocked Scarlett's own path to get a weapon for herself. After muttering a curse, Scarlett fumbled around in the same drawer she'd already been in. Her hand found what she sought and, gripping it tightly, she pulled out the silver letter-opener gifted to her parents when they married. Pressing her lips together, she leaned down to peer under the desk in order to gain some sort of idea where her opponent was.

"I hope you're still alive back there." Cheyanna called out. "I've been looking forward to killing you and I don't want only one bullet to do the job."

"A mistake on your part." Getting to her knees while keeping herself in cover, Scarlett could still feel blood trickling from her wound like a faucet that hadn't been shut off properly.

"Judging from your voice, I'd tend to disagree." Arming the pistol once more, Cheyanna took aim at the desk. "Come on out, Wintyrs. Time for you to face the music."

"You're going to wish you hadn't said that." Pushing the pain away, Scarlett fell to her left side so her head and shoulders cleared the side of the desk then threw the letter-opener like one of her knives. A yell of pain told her she'd hit her mark so she rolled to her feet, launching herself across the desk's surface and ramming her shoulder into the middle of Cheyanna's back. Never had she been thankful of someone turning around to double over in pain before. After they both fell to the floor, Scarlett could see why. The handle of the letter opener protruded from the other woman's stomach.

Cheyanna bit back a loud curse as she fell to the floor. Instinct told her to remove the foreign object from her stomach but she overrode that knowing if she did then she would bleed far more. And she had nothing with which to staunch the flow. Instead, she crawled away from Wintyrs then turned back to her, pistol armed, and fired again.

Seeing the business end of the barrel coming around to bear once more, Scarlett managed to get to her feet then rushed to grab the weapon. She heard it go off as another burning sensation reached her brain. This time from her left thigh. Blocking out the pain as Feiyan taught her wasn't as successful with two rounds now inside her. Yet it did help - somewhat. A small cry left her lips as a third bullet entered her - this time in her lower back. Her breathing grew harsh as she refused to give in. If Cheyanna found out about William... no. Even with what he'd done, she would protect him until her dying breath.

Rising to her feet, Cheyanna strode over to where Scarlett lay on her stomach, a blood pool slowly forming around her. She kicked the woman in her side, smiling in delight at the resulting moan. Lashing out with her foot once again, she succeeded in rolling the wounded woman onto her back.

"You're going to die alone, Wintyrs." Cheyanna sneered, putting a round into Scarlett's other thigh, relishing in the cry of pain. "We're up to four bullets now. How many do you think you can handle, hmm?" She fired one into her target's left shoulder next.

The pain grew blinding as a fifth went into her right shoulder. With each successful shot, Cheyanna drew closer to her prey. Wintyrs' vision swam as her attacker knelt down next to her, placing the barrel of the gun against her forehead.

"Any last words, Agent Wintyrs?"

"Yes." Scarlett gasped out. "You shouldn't... play with... your assignments... especially not... dangerous ones..."

With that, Scarlett used all of her strength to yank the letter-opener from Cheyanna's stomach and plunged the blade into the side of her neck. A startled look flashed through her rival's eyes as she realized what happened. Parting her lips, blood dripped freely from the corners of her mouth before Cheyanna fell on top of Scarlett. Dead.

The fight now over, pain overwhelmed Scarlett's senses and the last thing she heard before blackness claimed her was William shouting her name.

23

William chuckled, listening to Feiyan and Damon bicker over the smallest details while trying to come up with a plan to rescue Myrtle and any other agents who may still be loyal to their agency and himself. They sat in the living room that Scarlett told them was on the main floor. He'd elected to sit in a recliner so he could put his feet up for a little while. Feiyan and Damon were on the eight-person L-shaped sectional. Both pieces a beige leather which complimented the lavender walls.

"William - back me up here, would you?" Damon looked over to his friend then shook his head. "Were you even listening?"

"Hmm?" Rousing himself from the brink of sleep, William gave the pair his attention. "Sorry, I think I was daydreaming. What was the question?"

Leaning back into his seat, Damon crossed his arms with another shake of his head. "You *think* you were daydreaming. Either you were or you weren't, pal. Which is it?"

"I was… kind of… listening. I just wasn't paying attention and for that you have my deepest apologies."

"Mmh." Crinkling his nose, Damon let the gesture tell the other man how he felt about that. "I was asking you to back up what I suggested however if you weren't listening then there's no point."

"Sure there is. Does what you said contradict anything that Feiyan mentioned?"

"Kind of."

"Then it's easy."

"I don't follow…"

"Simple. She's right, you're wrong." William laughed when Damon sputtered in anger. "Relax, Damon! I'm teasing. Sort of."

Damon tossed a throw pillow at the Spymaster, snorting when it was caught with ease. "Shouldn't you be doing this? Come up with the main plan and let us poke holes in it?"

"As much as I hate to agree with anything Raynott says…" Feiyan spoke up, "I'm afraid on this point I must. The base of the plan should be given by you."

Blowing out a breath, William closed his eyes for a moment. When he reopened them, he noticed Scarlett going past the doorway carrying the rifle and picture with Zaliki in tow. To see they were already implementing the trap for Cheyanna pleased him greatly. Now he only hoped the young woman would fall for it.

Returning his attention to the pair sharing the room with him, he found his mind completely devoid of any ideas for what was needed. "Let me be honest. I am utterly exhausted thanks to everything that's happened. I've been wracking my brain since our original discussion at dinner, and this is a first for me, I can't devise a single thing."

Feiyan eyed him in sympathy. "That is understandable. You have been through much recently. Far more than any Spymaster is expected to endure. Perhaps you would be better served if you went to bed and came at this fresh in the morning?"

Rubbing his face with both hands then slapping his cheeks lightly, William gave Feiyan a charming smile. "I appreciate the sentiment, Feiyan, but it's too early for me to hit the hay. If I did then I'd be awake at the crack of dawn. No, I'll push through." He glanced at the doorway when Jerome entered with a serving tray carrying a carafe and three mugs. "Jerome?"

"I thought you might all enjoy a spot of tea." Jerome answered, pouring out three mugs worth. "If you need milk or cream, there are some located in the mini-fridge in the end table next to you, sir." He motioned to the table beside William. "Also on the shelf of that same unit you'll find a small variety of sugars and sweeteners."

"That's very kind of you, Jerome. Thank you." William took one of the steaming mugs and gently had a sip. Over the valet's shoulder he saw Zaliki going back the way she'd come with Wintyrs but no sign of Scarlett. He figured she was probably going to wait around the baited trap for awhile to see if they had any nibbles.

Jerome finished handing out the mugs then locked eyes with William. "I'm always happy to serve my agency. And my Spymaster."

William swallowed his mouthful of tea the wrong way and began coughing. With watering eyes, he saw Jerome had already departed. "How did he...?" The question left his lips when the choking subsided somewhat.

"Don't ask." Damon answered. "He kind of figured it out on his own."

"Kind of?"

"Hey, he may be older but he's still sharp as a tack."

"And you blabbed."

"Not me. Your girlfriend did."

"Just because Scarlett's not here to defend herself doesn't mean you can..." William trailed off when a loud bang reached his ears. "Was that...?" Several more followed.

"Gunfire!" Feiyan exclaimed, rising to her feet, prepared to shield William with her body to protect him if necessary.

Jumping up, William put a hand on Feiyan's shoulder before he stepped around her and ran towards the sound. Despite his position at the agency, he refused to turn away from a fight. He would always run towards the danger. Especially if his agents might be in trouble. Stopping in the hall, William strained his ears, listening for a sound of any kind to lead them in the right direction. There was no need for him to look to know both Damon and Feiyan stood slightly behind him, bracketing his body with theirs.

The sound came again. Closing his eyes, William focused on it then turned to the hallway he'd seen Scarlett vanish through a little while ago. His heart dropped into his stomach. "Scarlett..." Her name left his mouth as a harsh whisper and he took off down that hall like a shot.

Feiyan moved swiftly after the Spymaster, Damon at her side. "The office is down this way." She called up to William.

"So's the place we found the rifle." Damon added as another series of shots reached their ears followed by complete silence.

Deafening. That was the only way William could describe how quiet it was now. Finding the door to the office locked, he rammed his shoulder into it but it didn't give. Glancing at Damon and receiving a nod in response, he timed his next hit to coincide with the other man's. After a couple more hits, the door finally gave in, creaking open. The scene that met their eyes made all three stop and stare.

"SCARLETT!!" William shouted then saw her head loll to one side as unconsciousness claimed her.

24

Damon pushed past William, running to their fallen comrade. Once there, he dragged Cheyanna off Scarlett, not even bothering to check the Orion agent for a pulse. As far as he was concerned she could die a slow and painful death. If she wasn't dead already. Both women were coated in blood. He couldn't tell whose it was though.

While Damon pulled Cheyanna to a spot across the room where she would be out of reach, William knelt next to Scarlett and felt for a pulse. Relief flooded him when he felt a gentle flutter under his fingers. But the feeling didn't last long. He raked his eyes over her body and grew pale.

"We need medical supplies. NOW! She's bleeding out! I count at least five bullet wounds in her front. I'm afraid to roll her to check her back." William tried to keep his voice calm however knew there was a quiver in his words he could not keep in check no matter how he tried.

Feiyan rushed from the room only to discover Jerome searching for them. "Jerome! Scarlett's been badly hurt. Where do you keep your medical supplies??"

For a brief moment, Jerome stared at her then snapped into action and pressed a button on his watch. An alarm sounded throughout the residence with a sound resembling that of an ambulance siren at a volume which easily alerted those in the building yet remained at a level which was not deafening. A woman Feiyan had not yet met came running around the corner, her long red hair plaited into a thick braid that went down to between her shoulder blades. The paleness of her skin was unmatched, adding a porcelain-like quality to her appearance.

"Jerome? Who's hurt?" The newcomer inquired, out of breath.

"Miss Scarlett! Where's your kit?"

"Here." She brought the hand that had been behind her back forward to reveal a large black bag resembling a doctor's kit.

Turning back to Feiyan, Jerome motioned for her to lead the way. "Andrea is not only our chef, she was a doctor for our agency years ago."

Feiyan nodded, instinct telling her to trust his word. Not wishing to delay longer for fear of losing Scarlett, she led them to the office at a run - pleased when they both kept pace with her. Proving both their training and professionalism, neither the valet nor the chef emitted so much as a gasp upon seeing the scene. Andrea immediately moved to Scarlett while Jerome headed for Cheyanna only to be stopped by Damon's bloody hand on his arm.

"Don't bother, mate. First off, she's already gone. Second, she's the one who did this to Scarlett." Damon growled out softly.

Jerome met the other man's eyes in utter shock, nodding in understanding. "How is Miss Scarlett, Andrea?"

Working feverishly, Andrea shook her head. "She's lost a lot of blood. I need to get her to the medical bay with all possible haste or we may lose her."

"Do you have a stretcher or anything?" William managed to keep his voice steady despite the heavy pounding of his heart. Dread filled his soul upon seeing not only his best agent but the woman he professed to love lying in an ever-growing pool of her own blood.

"Not close enough. Someone will have to carry her." Andrea replied, her voice even as she worked to staunch the flow of blood from the wounds she could see. "I need to roll her on her side to see if there's any injuries to her back. Can one of you prop her there for me?"

"I've got you covered." Answered William. He helped her roll Scarlett onto her left side and winced when he heard the newcomer swear under her breath. "How bad?"

"One in her back. Thankfully nowhere near her spine. Let me see how deep it is." Taking out a medical laser measuring device, for she believed in having all the latest medical gear even though she was a chef now, Andrea held it to the hole then nodded to herself when she saw the result. "It's shallower than the others. I want to get this one out and bandaged before we try to move her. I've managed to slow the bleeding of the other wounds."

"Do what you have to do, doc." William stated, noting the hint of surprise from the woman when he said that. "I know who you are. And I trust you. Implicitly."

Fighting back the cold shock that settled over her, Andrea spared one second to give him a nod. While new tech was wonderful, and in most cases a time saver, for a shallow bullet extraction Andrea much preferred using a set of old-fashioned forceps. Completely focused on her patient, Andrea made short work of the bullet retrieval, throwing the offending piece of lead to the side after working it free. In an unexpected turn, she found one of the Texan's hands covering the wound to stem the flow of blood in order to give her time to pull out another piece of tech from her bag. At that moment she couldn't recall the name of it but its purpose was far more important. It sealed wounds that were ready. Giving the man another nod, Andrea activated the device the second he moved his hand away, closing that particular wound in about a minute. One less for her to be concerned with at least.

"Now that we don't need to worry about that one shifting closer to her spine, I feel safe saying we can carry her to the medical bay." Andrea threw the bloodied items in a bag while the other instruments found their way back into the main satchel.

"Alright. I'll bring her." William rose to his feet, suppressing a wince as the nearly forgotten knife wound and his injured ribs protested the movement.

"Let me do it, mate. You're obviously still in pain from... earlier events." Damon noticed his friend's discomfort despite him trying to hide it.

The protest died on Wiliam's lips. He knew Raynott was right and they'd probably move faster if they followed the other man's suggestion. Stepping aside to give him room, William nodded to Damon then watched him pick Scarlett up gingerly and cradle her limp form in his arms as close to his own body as possible.

"Lead the way." Damon said, surprised at how easy it had been to lift Wintyrs. The injured woman seemed lighter than he would have guessed. He doubted she would've lost so much blood that her weight would be so drastically altered. Though he'd been wrong before.

Damon ran right behind Andrea. This woman who seemed capable of so much felt familiar to him though he couldn't quite place her. His eyebrows nearly rose into his hairline when she activated a hidden door beneath the spiral staircase which led into what he could only describe as a hospital - built for just one person. Questions could wait, he knew, and he lay his burden gently on the single occupant bed the room boasted. Once done, he backed out of the area, rejoining the rest of the group just outside the hidden door.

"This feels so... surreal." Damon eventually stated, shattering the silence which had befallen the team.

"I agree." Feiyan said. "I must say - our dear Scarlett must have an incredible will to live. I don't think anyone else would have lasted this long."

"We all know she's special." William spoke up, clearing his throat before continuing. "We need to deal with Cheyanna's remains then shift our focus to Vargas and his Eliminator as well as getting anyone who's still loyal to the true Spymaster of the Centurian Agency out of headquarters and brought here. Scarlett wouldn't want us to stop our duties just because she's injured."

Feiyan nodded. "William's right. Which begs the question - out of those, what is our top priority?"

"We need not worry about those you mentioned at the agency's headquarters." Zaliki startled everyone when she spoke. "Covert communications are my speciality. Even when there's a dampener on. I have already sent a message to Myrtle with instructions on implementation." Seeing they were staring at her as if she'd grown a second head, she continued. "When I'm bored I tend to tackle a known problem." She shrugged. "It's also how Orion trains their assets. No one is ever to have idle hands. Either way, that particular problem has been dealt with. Myrtle will reach out to me with any questions or problems."

William couldn't believe his ears. Knowing one of the matters he'd been worried about had skillfully been taken off his hands - and without his prior knowledge - was something new for him. It was quickly becoming clear that if he were rebuilding their agency from the ground up with this team, he'd have to alter not only how he did things but also his way of thinking. "Zaliki... I don't know how to thank you."

"No need. Unless you wish to tell me how you know this Andrea? You said you trust her implicitly."

Looking down at himself, William winced as another priority sunk in. "Ah. Yeah. That." He sighed softly. "Let me go get cleaned up first. I don't want to be covered in blood when Scarlett wakes."

"Yeah, I'm with William on that score." Damon chimed in, longing to rid himself of the slowly drying fluid of life.

The two women watched the pair rush upstairs. Feiyan glanced at Zaliki after the men departed. A question burned in her mind.

"Zaliki, how were you able to send a message to Myrtle if Scarlett locked down all communication?"

Smiling, Zaliki wondered who would be the one to ask. "Simple. I did it prior to the lockdown." She chuckled when Feiyan's surprise was clear. "Before dinner when I was supposedly 'resting' in my room. That is when I did it."

"But from what you said…"

"Feiyan, did I say *when* I conveyed the message?"

The older woman thought about that for a moment then chuckled. "No. No, you didn't. We assumed and you didn't correct us."

"You lot believed I could do the impossible. Why on earth would I want you to think otherwise?"

Smiling wryly, Feiyan shook her head. "A very good answer, Zaliki. I must applaud you for how you handled that." Looking around them, Feiyan realized something. "Odd. Where did Jerome disappear to I wonder."

"I suspect he might be taking care of the mess in the office. I caught a glimpse of him and another man heading in that general direction. Do you not find it interesting that Scarlett's valet and now her cook were both part of the Centurian Agency?"

"Not in the slightest." Feiyan remarked. "Jerome doubtless was assigned. After all, our agency believed Scarlett to be the product of two of our agents. Those special children receive certain protections." Her eyes wandered back to the door of the medical bay. "I wonder how it's going in there."

"Andrea will tell us as soon as she can." William answered while coming down the stairs, Damon at his side.

"You two were quick considering how much blood you were covered in." Eying them up and down, Zaliki could not spot any overt sign of the dreaded red stuff.

"William and I are pretty good at cleaning up… messes… such as the one we were both in."

"Good to hear." Zaliki locked William in place with a cold stare. "Now, please tell me how you know Andrea."

Deciding he couldn't avoid answering forever, despite every instinct in him saying he should, William launched into his explanation. "Andrea left our agency, oh, I guess about ten years ago. She was likely our best medical tech. Even came to us with an actual doctorate.

She was given the position of head of medical. Within her first month she saved more lives than our entire medical team had in a single year. Which, honestly, wouldn't have taken much but it's still an amazing feat."

"I'm gathering it's safe to assume your life was among those she saved?"

"Yes, Zaliki. It was. And that's a tale for another time."

"Spymasters love that turn of phrase." Zaliki ruefully chuckled. "Very well, I shall hold you to that. How about, instead, you tell us how at least two of Centurian's assets came to be working here. Or do you not know?" She wondered if he would answer the question. Somehow she felt like she was inquiring about a trade secret.

"I honestly only know about Jerome. I suppose it's possible that after Andrea left the agency, Scarlett may have sought her out and made an offer she couldn't refuse. It could be entirely coincidental as well." A small shrug lent strength to his claim of ignorance. "Truthfully - I don't much care why she's here. I'm just glad she is."

The group fell silent when the door to the medical bay opened. Andrea slipped through then paused, watching them. "Miss Wintyrs is going to be fine. Thanks to modern technology." When a collective sigh of relief rose from the group, she allowed herself a small smile. "It was very close. Due to the amount of blood loss... well... we almost lost her. We always keep some of her blood type on hand in case something happens. Be grateful she insisted on that. She was shot a total of six times. Amazingly not a single shot hit anything major. In that regard, she's a very lucky woman."

William took a single step forward, causing Andrea to focus on him. "How long until she's up and about?"

"You don't understand what I'm saying about her injuries..." Andrea sighed when she saw the look in his eyes. "I don't know. With the bullet wounds she sustained, even with me being able to mend the holes they made - and I mean right down to the most minuscule of damage - recovery is patient-dependent. The more incentive she has, the faster things are likely to go."

"I need her back on her feet as soon as possible." William said. "We have an agency situation and we need all hands on deck."

Andrea paused, looking the man who spoke in a new light. "So you're the Spymaster, huh?"

"How..."

"Relax. Only Spymasters say things like what you just did. Look, your agent needs time to recover both mentally and physically. Pestering me won't change a thing."

"I understand but…"

"No buts. You know how I work. I remember you. I remember saving you from the very brink of death itself, much like I've done for Agent Wintyrs. And you damned well know that my patients come first and foremost to me. Not their duty. I'm sure the four of you can handle things without her for awhile." Crossing her arms, Andrea made sure they could see she wouldn't back down.

Licking his lips to hide his surprise at the way she spoke to him, William nodded once. "We'll heed your advice, *Doctor* - as long as you accept reinstatement."

Taken aback by his tactic, Andrea stared at him. "Things are that bad?"

"Worse."

"The agency?"

"Headquarters will be moving here. We have to rebuild, Andrea… when you were with us did you by chance have dealings with Patrick?" William mentally crossed his fingers.

"Frequently… why? I was under the impression he'd been terminated. In every literal sense of the word." Cocking her head to one side, Andrea continued to study him. She'd known the previous Spymaster quite well and was not yet impressed with his replacement.

"We believe he's alive and well. And working for the Orion Agency who've been dogging our every move. They're also the ones who've infiltrated our agency at nearly the highest level. There are very few souls there now I can trust. The people in this house are among the ones I know would die for me if the situation called for it though not exactly something I'd ever want to see come to pass." William stopped to take a breath only to be interrupted.

"So why ask me about Patrick?" Andrea took the opportunity to inquire, surprised he'd shared so much with her given how Spymasters liked their secrets.

"Because it seems you're one of the very few who had, as you called it, frequent interactions with him. But… perhaps we can talk about him after. Could I see Scarlett, please?"

"No."

"No??"

"Not until you let me examine you. You've been wincing nearly every time you move. I have the tech here, you may as well take advantage of it. Sit in that chair please - after you remove that lovely loose button-up shirt you have on. A shirt that leads me to suspect you're unable to lift your arms above your head. Am I correct?" Andrea turned to the medical bay, reached in to her desk and pulled out her satchel.

William raised his eyebrows, too stunned by how accurate her guess was, to give any type of response. Spurred on by Damon lightly punching his arm, William quickly undid the buttons of the shirt but didn't remove it completely. He blushed at Zaliki's whistle of appreciation.

"It's so comforting to know our Spymaster keeps himself in shape." Zaliki said, eying his chiselled chest. "Impressive. You should strive for that, Damon."

"What? Hey! I look just as good - no, scratch that. I look better than that!" Damon sputtered out the protest.

Covering her mouth, Zaliki managed to muffle her giggle. "Sure you do. You just keep telling yourself that and perhaps one day you can will it into existence."

"Zaliki. Damon." William quickly put an end to their banter. "Can you please see how the mess in the office has been handled. We don't want any fallout traced back here."

"Aye, aye skipper." Damon gave him a mock salute and followed Zaliki towards the office.

"Is your team always so... cavalier...?" Andrea inquired while placing gentle hands on his chest and abdomen in order to conduct her examination.

"Yes and no. I don't mind to be honest. It functions as a coping mechanism during times like... well, like this one." William answered with a small shrug. He tried not to flinch when she moved her hands over his skin - a feat hard to accomplish given how cold they were. When her hands reached his injured ribs, William hissed quietly and goosebumps popped up on his arms.

"Ticklish or painful?" Andrea asked, aware of the older Asian woman scrutinizing her every move.

Grunting quietly before answering, William swallowed. "Painful."

Nodding silently, her skillful hands continued to probe then paused when she found the knife wound. "Now *this* you should have mentioned right off the bat." Investigating the area gently, she took mental note each time his muscles jumped, indicating discomfort. "You know, I don't expect my patients to keep their pain to themselves."

"I, uh, don't like doing otherwise if I can help it."

Shaking her head, Andrea muttered one word under her breath. "Men."

The utterance caused Feiyan to chuckle softly while watching the proceedings. When Andrea glanced at her again, she relented, knowing the red-haired woman undoubtedly wondered who she was to be here and monitor what was happening. "Forgive me, doctor. I am Feiyan. His safety is my priority."

Andrea's hands froze when she heard the name. Overcoming her shock, she continued examining the stab wound. "This was well looked after. No infection. I'll help it along like I did for Miss Wintyrs. Your ribs as well given you appear to have three that are broken."

"Thank you. Then can I see Scarlett?" William asked in a soft voice, the woman's reaction to Feiyan's name not being missed. It was something he'd ask her about at another time. Unless someone beat him to it, of course.

"You know my name." Feiyan observed, watching Andrea treat the Spymaster's injuries. "You seem frightened. Why is that? Unless you bring harm to the man you are helping then you have nothing to fear from me."

"Let's say I've heard tales of your exploits and leave it at that. It should be enough for you to know I have a healthy respect for you."

Feiyan kept her surprise to herself. "Did you leave the agency before or after we lost our previous Spymaster?"

"After. Immediately after."

"Ah." A nod of understanding, even though the woman's back remained towards her, was Feiyan's answer. Doubtless she, as all who were there and not privy to that Spymaster's plan, believed the story of Feiyan beheading him.

"Are we almost done? I really want to see Scarlett." William spoke up. Although glad to be rid of the pain at least, he wanted to check on Wintyrs. To see with his own eyes that she would be okay.

"Just finishing with your knife wound here. A couple more seconds and...... done!" Andrea stepped back, admiring her handiwork for a moment then gave him an approving nod. "Alright. You can go see her. If she's sleeping, please don't wake her."

William bowed his head in acceptance of her request. "You have my word. Thank you, again, for all you've done." He paused before entering the medical bay, glancing at her over his shoulder. "You never gave me an answer."

"Didn't I?" Looking innocent, Andrea met his eyes then sighed. "I suspect very few are able to say no to you. Very well, Spymaster. I'll accept reinstatement as your head of medical. At least until you have the agency back to full strength."

He didn't bother fighting back the smile her words elicited. "I'll take it. Thank you, Andrea."

"Mmh... save your thanks. I already have a feeling I'm going to regret this."

25

William moved as quietly as possible upon entering the medical bay. His eyes rested on Scarlett's face the second he saw her in that bed. She lay on her back, eyes closed and breathing deep yet even. He couldn't remember ever seeing her face so pale as it was now. Spotting a slender wing-backed armchair next to the bed, he moved to it and sat down.

"This wasn't supposed to happen." William whispered, placing his right hand on the bed near hers while bowing his head. "None of this was supposed to happen." He put his left hand over his eyes, finally feeling the burden of everything that had thus far transpired settling over him like a weight. And it threatened to bury him under its enormity. A light touch on the back of his right hand made him first raise his eyes then his face when he saw the distinctly feminine hand covering his own. His gaze moved up the bed to see the woman lying there watching him. "Scarlett."

Scarlett squeezed his hand with what strength she could muster, concern flickering through her face. "Are you alright?" She winced at how hoarse her voice sounded.

Raising an eyebrow, William leaned forward, taking her errant hand in both of his. "You're the one who nearly died and you're asking *me* if I'm alright?" He chuckled softly as he made the inquiry, not quite sure he believed his ears.

She smiled. "Yeah. I guess I am."

Shaking his head, William gently squeezed her hand. "I'm more concerned about you. And don't you dare tell me you've had worse because, as your Spymaster, I damned well know that's not true." He kept the volume of his voice low so no one outside the room could hear them. Or at least, that was his hope. "How are you feeling?"

Scarlett deliberated over his question, evaluating what her body was telling her. "Tired. A bit achy where the bullets were. Maybe a bit weak."

"Then get some rest. Recover. Andrea got you all fixed up. Somehow I don't think she'll want you undoing all her hard work, do you?" He gave her a tender smile then reached out and gently pushed a locket of hair out of her face before cupping her cheek with the same hand. When she leaned into his touch, warmth spread throughout his body.

"Can you stay?" She asked plaintively.

William bit his lower lip. There was still much for him to do but nearly all of it only required him to think. Something he recently discovered he did much easier whenever she remained near. After careful consideration of his duties as well as his feelings, William finally nodded. "I'll stay as long as you want me to." He caressed her cheek with his thumb, a smile on his lips. "Go to sleep, sweetheart. I promise I'll be here when you wake up."

"You called me sweetheart..." Scarlett murmured as her eyes closed and sleep claimed her with a small, happy smile on her lips.

He returned his hand back to hers, holding it gently while stroking the back with his thumb, a soft sigh escaped him just as he heard someone slowly enter the room. Glancing over his shoulder, William saw Feiyan standing there and acknowledged her presence with a nod.

"How is she?" Feiyan spoke quietly, seeing the injured woman asleep.

"She'll be okay." William answered, keeping the volume of his words on par with hers so as not to disturb Scarlett. "What's up?"

Feiyan moved further into the room in order to crouch down next to the chair the Spymaster occupied. Her eyes took in his posture and noted he appeared much more relaxed now he knew Wintyrs would survive her ordeal. "Damon has advised me the... scene... has been cleaned and the body disposed of."

"Already?" He snapped his mouth shut after realizing it had fallen open. "What did they do with Cheyanna's remains?"

"Took them outside and Scarlett's gardener - I think his name is Daniel - had some lye. They put the remains in a tub and poured on the lye. There will be nothing left by the time the chemical has done its job."

"Thorough. Excellent." He watched her for a moment before his brows knitted together. "You have something else?"

"I do. Zaliki did her thing again and checked in on Myrtle."

"And?" Prompting her the way she was making him do annoyed him. It was the same with any agent - regardless of who they were. In his opinion, he shouldn't have to feel like he was pulling teeth to get the information they had for him.

"Myrtle managed to escape headquarters undetected along with one other tech and two agents."

Pulling his head back slightly, William tried to hide his shock. And dismay. "Those are the only ones still loyal to me?"

"It's possible there are many more however you must consider they could be in the field."

William used his free hand to pinch the bridge of his nose, sighing as he did. "Maybe. I did hire some agents personally - no, they never saw my face - it depends who's with Myrtle."

"We'll find out soon. According to Zaliki they should be here in about an hour."

"Thank you for the update, Feiyan. Please make sure you all get some sleep as well."

"You need to do the same." She responded kindly.

"I'm not leaving her side. I made a promise and I plan to keep it." William gave her a small smile to lessen the harshness he knew his words held. "I can sleep sitting up."

Feiyan rose from her crouch and gave his shoulder a gentle pat. "We'll set up a rotating guard outside this room to ensure the safety of you both." Holding up her hand to stop the protest she saw he was about to make, she continued. "This is not up for debate - no matter how powerful you believe you are. Let us do this, if only to ease our own minds."

William felt his chest loosen, accepting her words. "Alright. Thank you. Again."

Smiling, Feiyan nodded then departed the medical bay to brief the others. The three of them easily worked out the needed schedule. Damon would take the first watch so he could also greet the newcomers when they arrived. Due to his time as Tengu, he'd become excellent at reading people and if, for some reason, any of those who were on their way gave him a bad feeling, he'd take care of it. By whatever means necessary.

Grateful Jerome had brought a semi-comfortable chair for them to man their guard post, Damon leaned back and sighed. He knew

William wouldn't be thinking great until Wintyrs was back on her feet. Which meant his agents needed to pick up the slack. Damon leaned his elbows on the arms of the chair then steepled his fingers just in front of this face. They needed to find the Eliminator in order to disable it with the EMP rifle. That meant drawing out Vargas. A thought struck him out of the blue. One which made him smile broadly.

Leaning forward, Damon nodded to himself, staring at the marbled floor. The plan forming itself in his mind was almost like a high from a drug. It was no wonder William and other Spymasters loved their job. He understood now. Having your brain work things out was a rush. When a pair of white high heels entered his line of vision, Damon raised his head so fast he was surprised he didn't hurt his neck.

"Uhh… hi Myrtle."

"Michael Malley, huh?" Myrtle pushed her dark, horn-rimmed glasses back up her nose, shaking her head. "I can't believe I fell for that. Aren't you supposed to be dead, Agent Raynott?"

Damon rose to his feet, his eyes widening when the newcomer wrapped her arms around him and gave him a tight hug. "Uh, yeah. I got better. I'm afraid tales of my demise are greatly exaggerated." He smiled. When he returned the hug only to find her shaking like a leaf, his eyebrows knit together in a frown. "Hey, hey. You're alright. You're safe here." Rubbing her back gently, Damon felt the tremors calm somewhat the more he spoke. "There you go. You're safe."

"I, uh, I'm sorry." Myrtle pulled away, seemingly embarrassed by her show of affection towards him. "I never expected anything like this to happen. And how did you lot manage to recruit an Orion agent to our agency? That's expressly prohibited."

"Well, when we met her I wasn't with Centurian anymore. I was dead, remember?" Damon grinned. "Anyway that's something you'll have to take up with the Spymaster."

"He's back at HQ and is the one you told us to run from if we were truly loyal. I'm confused."

"Yeah, I'll let him explain to you and… who else did you bring with you?"

"One of my assistants and two agents."

"Which agents?" Damon was curious to know.

"Alec Storme and Karishma Bakshi."

"Nice. They're two of the top tier. Which of your assistants? I'm kind of already assuming Karishma's husband."

"Good guess. Yes, Jayesh is here as well. The man who answered the door made them wait outside until I talked to someone in here." She quickly attempted to explain.

"Alec, Karishma and Jayesh. That's a damned fine start." With a nod to himself, Damon paced absentmindedly. "Oh, right, sorry. Yo, Jerome!"

Jerome entered the area and gave Damon a look suggesting he'd be better off never calling for him like that again. "You bellowed, Agent Raynott?"

"I did. Please allow Myrtle's travelling companions entrance. They're with us."

"You're certain? I don't relish the thought of the earlier incident repeating itself."

"I am. And it won't. Now, if you please...?"

"Ugh. Very well." With a rolling of his eyes, Jerome departed and, after hearing the front door open and close, Myrtle's companions wandered in.

"Nice digs." The younger male with blonde hair stated as he came in. When he saw who was waiting to greet them he stopped in his tracks causing both of those behind him to accidentally bump into him. "No. Way. Damon Raynott?? You're supposed to be dead! Well... I have to say... death suits you."

"Alec Storme!" Damon went to the other man and clasped his arm in brotherly camaraderie. He'd always liked this American. Not as much as William but they got along almost as well. "I can't believe you're still alive and kicking."

"What can I say? I'm just that good."

"Did you say Damon Raynott?" An exotic female with long, flowing dark hair entered behind Alec, her flawless caramel complexion glistening with a light sheen of perspiration, despite the temperature of the building being quite comfortable.

"Karishma." Damon's voice softened considerably. "You look radiant as always. Beautiful sari... I particularly love the gold embroidery and the green cloth compliments your skin tone wonderfully."

Karishma's smile was so bright it reached her brown eyes. "You're always so sweet."

"Stop flirting with my wife." A surly male whose looks were similar to Karishma's said, standing next to her.

"Jayesh. Always a delight." Damon struggled to not roll his eyes.

The man was undeniably brilliant and, next to his tall wife who wore stiletto heels, seemed shorter than his 5'7" height. Unfortunately his brilliance also made him look down on everyone he deemed not as smart as he.

"We just returned from vacationing back home in India when Myrtle asked us some strange questions then demanded we escort her here." Karishma tucked a stray lock of hair back behind her ear. "Can you please tell us what's going on."

"Not my place. Enough for you to know our Spymaster is on premises and, as always, his protection is top priority."

"Damon. You're supposed to be dead. That means you're no longer part of the agency which also means you can't give us orders. Nor have you given us any reason to believe you." Alec crossed his arms over his chest, staring at the man he once considered to be one of his closest friends.

"Alec's right, Damon." Karishma was quick to agree with her fellow agent.

"Who would you believe then?" Keeping his voice calm, Damon tried to keep himself the voice of reason.

"Off the top of my head? Oh, I don't know... maybe our Spymaster?" Jayesh stated with a shake of his head.

"He is otherwise occupied. Perhaps I might suffice?" Feiyan inquired as she descended the stairs with a gracefulness belying her age

Karishma turned in shock. "Feiyan!"

"Oh, great." Jayesh rolled his eyes. "A dead man and a murderer."

The door to the medical bay opened, William came out looking annoyed. "What the hell is going on out here? She can't sleep." He looked at the assembled faces. "Ah, I see. It's good to see you all." Seeing the confusion on the faces of the new arrivals made him smile. "Allow me to explain. My name is William. And I'm your Spymaster."

26

"Yeah. Right." Jayesh laughed. "The Spymaster would never reveal himself to us unless he's on the run from assassins or the agency has... been... compromised...." Trailing off, he stared at the Texan. "Oh shit..."

William nodded. "That's right, Jayesh. And unfortunately both of those things are true."

"Can you prove you're... you? Cause you're not who gave us our missions." Alec spoke up again.

"Amir was my mouthpiece. Alec - you were interviewed by the Spymaster due to your talents. That also means you'll only accept what I'm saying from another agent. One whom you all know and trust." Moving to one side, William reached into the medical bay and helped Scarlett walk out, letting her lean on his arm.

"Wintyrs!" Disbelief coloured Alec's voice when he saw her.

"Convenient you have the one agent on hand all of us would believe." Jayesh snorted quietly.

"Shut up, Jay." Scarlett glared at the tech until he raised his hands in surrender. "Everything *anyone* in this house tells you is true. Especially William. He *is* our Spymaster whom we are sworn to protect - with our lives if necessary. Our agency has been infiltrated to nearly the absolute highest level. Amir - the man we were led to believe was our Spymaster in order to protect William's identity - actually works for the Orion Agency. And he's carefully been inserting their agents and assets into our ranks. The questions Myrtle gave you were to ensure your loyalty - to William. That's why you're all here. Only people we know we can trust absolutely are on this property." She finished speaking, leaning so heavily on William's arm that he was

184

struggling to remain standing straight.

"Hey, easy there." William wrapped his arm around her waist and led her to the chair previously occupied by Damon. He nodded to Raynott who leapt to their assistance, helping get Wintyrs seated.

"So... you're really..." Nearly speechless, Karishma stared at him with wide eyes and watched the man in question nod. "Holy shit. Okay so things are worse than we thought. So... what do you want us to do?"

William stood up straight and rubbed his head thoughtfully. "We have several fronts we need to chisel away at but there's one I'm placing a higher priority on. Mario Vargas, Spymaster for the Orion Agency, has built a weapon we need to disable as soon as possible."

His words drew Myrtle's unwavering attention. "What weapon? Do we have any schematics?"

"Myrtle - it's the Eliminator." Scarlett answered softly.

Blinking rapidly, the tech shook her head in denial. "No... Patrick would never have gone so far. Not even he is that... that... insane! I need somewhere to work."

Clearing her throat, Scarlett nodded. "You'll have it. This place was my parents' - which is another long story that we really don't have time to get into. But, Myrtle, we have a solution for the Eliminator. We just need to ensure it's in working order as it's fairly old."

"The missing prototype EMP rifle??" Myrtle hazarded a guess while trying to hide her excitement. "I mean, other stuff went missing around the same time but that'd be the only one that makes any kind of sense when used in conjunction with the Eliminator. So? Am I right?"

"Take a breath, Myrtle." William gave her a kind smile. "Yes, it's the EMP rifle we need you to check. We don't have access to the schematics for the Eliminator nor anything else on our databases at the agency..." When he felt a gentle hand gripping his wrist, he looked down to see Scarlett looking very thoughtful. "Agent Wintyrs?"

"Don't count our databases out just yet." She said softly.

Raising an eyebrow at her, William chewed over the implications of what she'd told them. "Ahhh... okay."

"What would you have us do, boss?" Alec still couldn't quite believe he was actually talking to the Spymaster. Face to face. In person. It was mind-boggling for him.

"Damon and Feiyan will brief you and Karishma. Jayesh, please work with Myrtle as you're used to. Scarlett and I will show you where you can do that."

"We'll use the dining room. It's a good size for a briefing room." Feiyan stated. Motioning for the agents mentioned to follow her, she led them away.

"What about Zaliki?" Scarlett glanced at William again. Feeling safe in expressing her thoughts given Myrtle and Jayesh were talking amongst themselves, Scarlett decided to be frank with him. "When they find out who she is… it may not go over very well."

"Yeah, that crossed my mind too. Which is why I hope Damon and Feiyan will touch base on what's happening regarding the agency with Alec and Karishma." Giving himself a small shake, he crouched down next to her. "Are you up for showing these two that lab setup you found the EMP rifle in?"

Taking a moment to give her body a self-evaluation, Scarlett honestly couldn't tell. Just sitting here made her feel like she probably could. Doubtless that would change the moment she started walking. Not because of the now healed wounds though. Rather, it was the blood loss and subsequent transfusion. On the other hand, the only way she'd regain her strength would be to actually move around and do things. Not just sit or lie around doing nothing. Which would end up driving her crazy.

"Yeah. Let's go."

Scarlett rose to her feet, noting the two techs ceased their conversation the second she did. Instinctively knowing they would follow without being asked, she led them away from the medical bay towards the office. Once they stepped foot inside, Wintyrs stopped in her tracks. Whomever had looked after the cleanup after her fight with Cheyanna needed either a profuse thank you or a raise. Her eyes scanned the room again. Save for some bullet holes in the walls and her desk, there wasn't a single sign of a fight having occurred here. Not even her keen eyesight could find a drop of blood anywhere.

"Who…" She began only to find herself unable to finish the sentence.

"Damon and Jerome with someone named Daniel." William answered softly. "Along with Zaliki, of course. I have to say… they did an amazing job."

"Yes. Yes, they did." Giving herself a mental shake, she moved to the portrait and opened it. This time, though, she propped it open so they'd have time to go in and out as needed. After doing that she then went to the weapons locker in order to retrieve the rifle in question.

Hearing a low whistle, Scarlett turned to find Jayesh staring at the array of weapons.

"Don't let Karishma see that. She'll be jealous and then want me to make her something similar." Giving Wintyrs a playful wink, Jayesh headed for the portrait to see what lay beyond since Myrtle had already vanished inside.

"I think he likes you." William teased, helping her close up the locker again. He took the rifle from her willing hands so she wouldn't be burdened. "Allow me." After flashing her a smile, he held his arm for her to link hers through. Which she did almost right away much to his delight.

"Afraid of a little competition?" If he was going to tease, Scarlett would give as good as she got.

"From Jayesh??" A light-hearted chuckle left his lips. "Nope. Especially since he's married."

"You don't know?"

"Know what?"

"They have a completely open marriage because of her agent status." Scarlett shook her head at his look of confusion. "Meaning they can sleep with whomever they wish as long as they renew their vows at the end of the day or mission."

William fell into a stunned silence. "Oh... so then..."

"He can flirt and go further without repercussions - yes." Knowing he must be feeling a tad out of his element, Scarlett took pity on him. "Relax. Believe me, even with what you did, you'd always win the battle for my heart." Pausing to let that sink in, she grinned when his face lit up like a Christmas tree. "Although I do admit I'm surprised you didn't know that about them."

"Just because I'm a Spymaster doesn't mean I know everything. Though there are times I wish I did." He replied, walking into the lab setup with her, an awed expression on his face. "Like now. Now is definitely one of those times."

"Scarlett! This setup is... amazing for a home installation. Even if some of the equipment is out of date." Myrtle wandered back after having a cursory look around. "You said your parents owned this place? So that means they built this?" When the other woman nodded, she raised her eyebrows. "Well, it's impressive. Although I never knew your parents were agents." Being as easily distracted as she was, the second her eyes caught sight of the weapon held by William, she lost all interest in the inquiries she made. "That's the EMP rifle? Let me see." Without waiting for permission, Myrtle took the rifle from him then went to a nearby table with Jayesh joining her right away.

"She never changes." Scarlett mumbled, leading William to an adjacent room which was smaller. Inside was a desk with a computer. "This is our back door to the agency."

"Hold that thought." William didn't relish the idea of her standing for long given her recent ordeal. With that in mind, he left the room and returned a couple of minutes later carrying two stools he'd located in the lab. "Here..." he placed one in front of the desk for her and the other one beside it, "I thought this might be better than being on your feet."

"Always thinking." Scarlett waited until he sat down next to her then planted a gentle kiss on his cheek. "Alright... so," she activated the computer, "while this wasn't designed specifically for this task - we can make it work."

Frowning at what he saw on the screen, realization struck like a bolt of lightning. "This computer has the framework to start an agency. Your parents were looking at forming their own. That explains the size of this place and this lab setup..."

"I have no idea. I just know about this computer because it shows up on our network - our house network - as 'downfall'. I may have accidentally hacked it once and obtained its location but I was never able to come see it in person. After I found what our family portrait concealed... I was never able to come any further than the threshold. Perhaps because of my emotions or maybe I was afraid of what I'd find."

"Then how'd you know about the 'back door' part of this system?"

"My parents weren't *that* great with technology. When I found out about this unit during my hack, I may have.." Scarlett cleared her throat then continued, "done some exploring of its databanks while I had access."

At those words, William turned his face from the screen to look at her. "You know what? Maybe it's better if I don't know."

"I won't tell if you won't." Scarlett stated distractedly, typing away on an older model keyboard. "This mainframe is far more advanced and detailed than I anticipated." Her words were muttered as she toiled away. "That should theoretically work in our favour, making it easier to create and use the back door."

"I thought your parents had one."

"That's what I thought but I couldn't find it. It'll be faster to make a new one." She explained, her fingers flying across the keys.

"I'd almost forgotten how talented you are."

"What can I say. I'm well-rounded." Wintyrs felt, not for the first time, extremely grateful to be so good at multi-tasking. "Plus, if they did it would have been created with Orion Agency techniques and I'm sure if Amir didn't spot it then Vargas would. Or maybe one of the other infiltrators who snuck past our screening processes."

"And you don't think anyone would be suspicious if they spotted unauthorized access using Centurian coding?"

One corner of her mouth twitched as she fought a smile. "I'm not using coding that any agency has in place."

That stopped William cold. "Wait… what?"

"Myrtle designed a special coding system with my help. Only the two of us know how to use it."

"Do I want to know the reason behind the creation of this code??"

"Isn't it enough to know that right here, right now this code is what's going to get us some answers?"

Sighing softly, William gave her a nod. "Go ahead."

Scarlett flashed him a smile then finished her coding. "Done. We're in." The screen changed to reflect the main hub of their agency. It's what every agent, tech and anyone who worked there saw after logging in. Only she'd gone one step further. They were seeing the information as if the Spymaster signed in.

"Incredible. You didn't need my credentials."

"Nope."

"I'm not sure how I feel about that."

"Don't think of it as our agency, think of it as part of Orion."

Appearing a little less stressed, William steadied himself. "Alright. I can do that."

"You're sure?" She quirked an eyebrow at him. To her ears, he still sounded somewhat uncertain.

"No but let's do this before I change my mind."

Wintyrs started looking at the listed files. "There's one about Patrick."

"There'll be one on everyone working at the agency but…" he narrowed his eyes, "I didn't make that particular one."

"Interesting…" Without him asking, for she had a strong feeling they were on the same page, Scarlett opened the file in question. As her eyes skimmed the details, concern gnawed at the edge of her mind. "This is… extremely… detailed. And you're saying you didn't make it?"

William mutely shook his head then realized with her eyes glued to the screen she wouldn't see he'd answered her. "No. Look at the file creation date. Whoever made this did so *after* I assumed the mantle of Spymaster. Without my permission or knowledge. Which is extremely difficult to do."

"So now we have even more questions." Backing out of Patrick's file, Scarlett moved on to another. The title of which had some disturbing implications.

Project Scarlett Sunset.

27

"What the hell...?" William stared at the name for the longest time.

"I gather you have no idea what's in this folder?" Although suspecting she already knew the answer, the need to hear him say it out loud drove Scarlett to ask.

With a shake of his head, he motioned with his hand for her to open it. In truth, he wasn't entirely certain he wanted to know. Mainly because of her name being part of it. At the same time, though, William grew hopeful. If luck happened to be on their side, this would tell them what Vargas planned.

Knowing his silences always meant something, Scarlett opened the file only to gasp. She felt William stiffen as he, too, read what she did. The file was more than just one item. From what she could tell, the directory held files - and more - about everyone in their agency, every piece of tech their team had created, and more. Scarlett felt safe in saying the directory, for calling it a file was no longer accurate, held literally everything about their agency.

"My god." William overcame his initial shock. "All our assets... all our plans, our tech... can you tell who made this?"

"I already checked the metadata. Amir's behind it but there's a second associated set of credentials. Judging from the username, I think it's Vargas."

"What's the username?"

"Blood_runs_red. I can't really see anyone else coming up with one quite like that, can you?"

"Uh... no... no definitely not. Scarlett, can you open the one for the Eliminator?"

"Of course."

After she did as requested, William gave a low whistle. "I don't know how smart Vargas is to have put the actual schematics on here… literally everything about the weapon for that matter." Pausing when the woman next to him gently placed her hand on his, he looked at her. "What is it?"

"Vargas isn't the one who put those documents on here."

"Amir?"

"Nope."

"Then who?"

"From the looks of it… Patrick."

"Why on earth would Patrick put every single piece of information about the Eliminator on the agency's server…"

Scarlett shrugged. "All I can tell you is he added all of this yesterday. The same day it was used on Dolus."

"I wonder if his conscience got the better of him. Still… he couldn't have known we'd be the ones to find this information."

"I can't believe you just used Patrick and conscience in the same sentence. And with a straight face."

William snorted softly. Although she did raise a very good point. Even though he was only a tech, Patrick had never - to his knowledge anyway - shown any kind of remorse over his inventions and the harm some of them were capable of causing. "Yeah… anyway… I have to wonder who he might have left it for…"

"Well he thinks Amir is the Spymaster thanks to Vargas but… I don't know… maybe he suspects you exist. He does have a genius level IQ after all."

"He left it for me." Karishma poked her head into the small room they occupied. "Sorry, you left your secret entrance open. My curiousity got the better of me."

"Why would he have left it for you, Karishma. And on a level only a Spymaster can access." William turned on his stool to face her wearing a deep frown.

"He contacted me yesterday. Lord knows how he got my information. Told me he'd created something he deeply regretted and he'd uploaded all the information to, well, there." She pointed to the screen. "He gave me his login info so I could access it."

"Why you…" Scarlett wondered out loud.

"And not you? He thought - thinks - you're dead. Killed by his creation. Your supposed death is what made him grow a conscience." Karishma explained.

"Why would my death..."

"I think he may have a crush on you. Just a guess though."

William covered his mouth to hide his grin then coughed, pounding his chest with his fist, hoping Wintyrs wouldn't suspect how humourous he found the thought. The glare he received, however, advised him that he failed. Miserably. Giving her an innocent smile, he quickly moved the conversation along. "What all did Patrick say when he made contact with you, Karishma?"

"Not a whole heck of a lot. In fact, at the time, I thought he was a raving lunatic. Something about not all is as it seems, his login stuff... I still have his written communication if you'd like to see for yourself."

"Please."

Karishma nodded and handed him her personal comms unit after bringing the written correspondence from Patrick up on the screen. "There it is in black and white. He's pretty straight to the point about things as well. No small talk and, this surprised me the most, he didn't try to conceal what he was talking about."

Reading the message, William felt the same way. He read the words three times before handing the unit back to his agent. "He's definitely blunt about things, just as you said."

"What do you make of what he wrote?" Karishma dared to ask. This was her first in-person conference with the true Spymaster and she wasn't about to let Wintyrs hog the discussion. At least not yet.

William rubbed his chin, silently going over what had been sent. "Sounds to me like he hadn't realized until recently how bloodthirsty the Spymaster for the Orion Agency is. Nor to what lengths he's willing to stoop. And now that he has..."

"Don't tell me he wants back with Centurian." Scarlett turned to stare at him.

"No. This almost reads like we'll never hear from him again. The end sounded very... final."

"I thought the same thing." Karishma added.

"So... what... he's going to take his own life?" Wintyrs looked back to the screen. "If you two believe that then I can tell you you're sorely mistaken. That man loves himself too much to consider going that route. I could see him trying to hide though. From the world. Or, at least, the people he believes would exploit his intellect."

"He may think he's a dead man if Vargas uncovers what we did. Which would depend on how much attention he's paying his computer when he's on there." Following Scarlett's lead, William moved his gaze to the screen. "Any chance anywhere in there he gave thoughts on how to disable or destroy the Eliminator?"

"No. Unless it was already found and deleted by Vargas." Backing out of the file for the Eliminator, Scarlett looked to see what else might be in the directory which could be of some assistance to them. "If only we knew where he was keeping it or where he plans to strike next."

"Well, we know who at the agency - our agency - might be under his thumb..." Karishma sounded thoughtful, "there is a club not far from here that some of them frequent. Perhaps Scarlett and I can go and try to... pry... some information from a couple of them."

"You're assuming Vargas might have shared his plans with one of them." William said. "Although it's not the worst suggestion."

Hating missions like the one proposed, Scarlett knew she was actually pretty good at them. A fact which annoyed her. "We should take Damon or Alec as well. It won't just be men there and no guarantee if there are women present that they'll be interested in what Karishma and I have to offer."

Doing a double-take at Scarlett, William remained silent while he processed what had been said. "If nothing else, having them there would give you both some backup." The startled looks he received from them caused him to swiftly amend his statement. "And of course they'd also have the best backup available."

Scarlett grinned. "Smooth, William. Very smooth."

"I'm glad you think so." Rubbing his hands together, William nodded to himself. "Do you think you'd be up to proceeding with the plan tonight, Scarlett?"

"I think so." Wintyrs responded after contemplating how she felt at that precise moment.

"But, sir, I haven't a thing to wear." Karishma complained, folding her arms over her chest.

"That's not a problem." Scarlett decided to address the concern before their Spymaster spoke up. Considering she already had the answer, she didn't think he'd mind. "We're the same size I believe. Alec and Damon are similar in size as well which means I've got them covered too."

"Question." William raised his hand, wanting to ensure he had the attention of both ladies. "How exactly do you have it covered?"

"If my parents were prepared enough to have this place set up as a base of operations then don't you think they built a wardrobe section as well? Up in the master bedroom, there's another... hidden... room.

One I've made use of because of what's in there. And one I've added to as well. It's well stocked. Trust me when I say everything we need is literally in this house."

28

A silver Aston Martin hovercar pulled up in front of the Dark Lotus nightclub. A place where both the wealthy and the corrupt rubbed elbows, partying until they could party no more. The dark purple bricks of the exterior gave credence to its name. And the line up of people to get in stretched around the building.

"Welcome to the Dark Lotus." Alec Storme said, putting his hovercar in park. His medium length blonde hair had been slicked back and his blue eyes danced mischievously. The black tux he wore accentuated those features. Just as Damon's succeeded in making him look debonair. "Wait here, ladies. Allow Damon and I to show you what true gentlemen we are." Both men hopped out of the vehicle, going to the doors the two ladies sat next to.

Scarlett winced slightly as Damon helped her out of the vehicle. The action wasn't due to any pains she may have been in, however. It was because of what she heard upon exiting the hovercar. Even though they were still outside, her ears already picked up the thumping of the bass from whatever music was playing. At times Wintyrs hated having sensitive hearing - this was one of those moments. Then there was the din of those lined up to gain admittance. They already spoke louder than necessary. She waved her hand in front of her nose in a vain attempt to make the cloud of cigarette smoke dissipate but nothing happened.

"You look stunning tonight." Damon whispered in her ear, his hot breath caressing the nape of her neck. "That blue sequinned gown you have on... did you know it matches your eyes perfectly? Although I'd love to know how you managed convincing William to let you come out in that. You look like you had to paint it on."

Scarlett smiled. He wasn't wrong. The floor length gown was indeed skin tight in order to accentuate her figure. Add the plunging neckline and the fact only a thin strap winding around her neck held the outfit up and she knew anyone she approached would be putty in her hands. Karishma wore a black version of the same type of dress only with actual shoulders, not just a strap or two. The other woman had pinned her hair back to keep it out of her face and off her neck whereas Wintyrs left hers down but held back on one side with a clip matching her dress.

"You didn't answer." Damon entwined his arm with hers. "Plus how can you even move in that outfit?"

"Easy. There's a slit in the skirt which goes up to my thigh on each side. Believe it or not, moving isn't the problem." Scarlett replied.

"That what is?" Not commenting on the fact she continued avoiding his inquiry about William, Raynott was curious about what she'd said.

"Keeping unwanted attention at bay."

Damon glanced at Alec to see him nod confirmation he'd heard her last remark. Both men were quite willing and able to run interference for their 'dates' if necessary. Just taking her past the line and up to the door, Raynott could tell the challenge had already begun. Every male eye was on Scarlett and Karishma save for the odd one or two who openly gawked at himself and Storme. Whether for their looks or because their group were bypassing the line, Damon couldn't say. He was just following his partner's instructions from the ride in. She'd said to go straight to the door and she'd handle things from there so that was precisely what he was doing. When his eyes landed on the overly-muscled male bouncers on either side of the entrance, though, he nearly froze in his steps. He thought the bouncers hired for Dolus were large. These guys were even bigger.

"I'd really like to avoid tangling with those guys if we can." Alec said just loud enough for Damon, who was in front of him with Wintyrs, to hear.

Damon nodded once in agreement then moved his eyes back to the woman on his arm. "Whatever you're going to do, do it now please." He muttered to her.

Scarlett was smiling broadly as they made their approach. "Antony, Mikhail - so good to see you again!"

Both bouncers returned her greeting then the one whose name badge identified him as Antony kissed each of her cheeks once, very gently. "It's very good to see you again, Miss Wintyrs. You always make the club more elegant with your presence. These fine folks are with you, I presume?"

"Indeed they are, Antony. Can we go in?"

"Absolutely. Remind Ramone your drinks are on the house. For all four of you. The place has been really jumping as of late so he may not remember you or who you are. Although how anyone could forget a beauty such as yours is something I can't fathom."

"Flatterer." Leaning in, Scarlett gave Antony a light kiss on his cheek. "Say hi to your parents for me." With that, she led her team into the club all while being aware of the looks they were shooting her which ranged from awe to outright astonishment. Therefore it came as no surprise to her when Damon moved his lips close to her ear again, obviously dying of curiosity.

"Alright, spill Wintyrs. How in the bloody hell do you know the employees here?"

"You and William aren't the only ones who needed to subsidize their income." She answered, leading the group past the dance floor and the sweaty, gyrating bodies moving to the beat of the music. "Follow me."

Damon's jaw dropped upon hearing the insinuation that she was behind Dark Lotus. "Uh... sure..." He motioned with his head for Alec and Karishma to follow.

Scarlett made her way to a staircase in the back then up those stairs to a large room at the top. After Alec crossed the threshold with Karishma, Wintyrs closed the door. The sound of the music died away to the same dull thumping they'd heard upon their arrival outside despite the fact one of the room's walls was made entirely of glass. This had been done in order for the occupants to be able to look out over the club and guests. "It's one way glass and bulletproof." She answered the unasked question.

"So, uh, you own this place?" Damon found his voice working again. He moved to the glass, looking out over those on the floor below. The walls of the first floor appeared colourless at first. At least until the lights flared up briefly before dimming again. When that happened he could see they were the same colour as the exterior of the building.

"Not precisely. I financed the construction and concept in return for rent and a small share of the profits. I guess you could say I'm a silent partner." Wintyrs responded, moving along the back wall of the room which was another dark colour whereas the two end walls contrasted by being pure white. She sat at a large black desk the room housed.

"Impressive." Alec stared out at the club-goers as well. "Can anyone down there see us if the lights in here are on?"

"No. I ensured that this room would be private if the lights came up." Scarlett depressed a button on the desk. When she did, the ambient light in the room grew in intensity which resulted in the glass altering from clear to tinted on their side to the point where they couldn't see out.

"Uhhh... what if you both want to have the lovely brightness in here and see out there at the same time?" Karishma, though clearly impressed, decided to ask.

"Damon - on the wall beside you is a green button. Could you push that for me, please?" Sometimes Scarlett believed showing was better than telling. Such as now.

The other agents watched in awe as the glass on the inside hummed to life and the club-goers downstairs became visible. Only now they appeared more like green entities than anything else. Clothing was indistinguishable from skin although men could definitively be told apart from women. Alec cocked his head while watching the new way to observe the crowd. He wondered how, if one were to be up here when or if something happened, an individual could be set apart from the rest. Absolutely nothing he witnessed answered his question which meant he'd have to ask. He just hoped he wouldn't become an annoyance to Wintyrs. She was the one agent he'd always looked up to and admired.

"Cool. So how do you tell the blobs apart?" Alec resigned himself to asking.

"Look at their hands." Scarlett said absentmindedly, busy rummaging through the drawers of the desk.

Doing as his fellow agent suggested, Alec smirked after spotting what she'd hinted at. "The stamp everyone receives on the back of their hand when they arrive. Invisible to the naked eye but with the filter activated on this glass... I'm guessing an ultraviolet filter?" He turned his head to see her nod. "That makes them visible to whomever is in this room. And each stamp has a number. But how do you equate the number from here to the bouncers?"

"Simpler than you might think. Did you notice the glasses Antony and Mikhail were wearing?"

"Yeah..."

"The inside of the lenses have the same filter as this glass. Only the glasses are permanently that way. You can't turn them on or off."

Alec stared at her for a moment. "Damn. Okay. I'm officially impressed."

"How is it they know your true name?" Karishma moved over to also peer out the glass but that wasn't where her focus was.

"Because that's the name I used. And that was before I joined, well, you know what. I had an inheritance from my parents. I invested a portion in the club. After I found our employer - or they found me I should say - I had some security upgrades installed. Like that glass."

"What is it you're looking for?" Damon wanted to start circulating with the crowd as soon as possible to see if they could uncover anything.

"Relax, Damon." Scarlett stood up, a wooden case in her hands. "I know how badly you want to find a different date." She teased, placing the box on top of the desk and opening it. "New comm pieces. Never before used so they haven't been tampered with or tapped in to. One for each of us so we can keep in contact. They are always on so we can monitor each other continuously."

"Where did you acquire these?" Karishma walked to the desk and caressed the box with light fingers then selected one and put it in her ear.

"I'd rather not say just yet." Nodding to Alec and Damon, Scarlett watched as they each selected one then hooked themselves up. "Alright. We're transmitting. Let's go see what we can find. I'll come out last. If you need help… well, what SOS word do we want to use?"

"Is there a drink that's not served here?" Asked Damon.

Pursing her lips, Scarlett had to think about that for a moment. "Mimosas. It's the only one I thought made no sense to have given the club's hours of operation."

"Makes sense. Alright - if anyone gets in trouble or needs rescuing from whomever they're with, say mimosa however it makes sense too. Now, let's do this." Damon flashed them a grin then left the room with Alec and Karishma right behind him.

When she was alone, Wintyrs took a deep breath to centre herself. Normally a mission like this didn't bother her - even though she didn't like them. This time felt different. Finally she realized why. For the first time in her life her heart belonged to someone. The thought of wooing another person for information made her feel as though she were cheating. Even though she knew he knew what she was doing. Not to mention what she might have to do. Steeling herself, Scarlett left the room. As she descended the stairs, she became aware of the many eyes on her. Squaring her shoulders, she took each step as sensuously as possible. More flies could be caught with honey than nothing at all.

When her foot came off the final step, Scarlett discovered a young man bowing with an open hand held out towards her. Recovering from the surprise of such a gentlemanly act, Wintyrs gave the man a kind smile which hid her further astonishment that it was, in fact, Alec who offered the gesture.

"Thank you, kind sir." Scarlett leaned in, pretending to kiss him while actually whispering in his ear. "What are you doing?"

Alec appeared non-plussed by the attention, holding her vibrant body close so he could respond in kind. "With all the admirers you have, some might be too shy to make an approach. Jealousy can be a powerful tool. One I love to use in situations like this. Trust me - you'll have someone proposing marriage in no time."

Scarlett inclined her head to him, hearing Damon mutter something through the comms about wishing he'd thought of that. A song with a slower beat began playing. Without asking permission, Alec took her hand and led her onto the dance floor. He was smooth, she gave him that much. Plus he'd been right about one thing - there were a lot of eyes on them as he led her through a slow, intimate dance which kept their bodies close. When the music ended, Alec backed away a few steps, giving her a respectful bow.

"Thank you for the dance." Alec stated. "To say it was a privilege to be with a creature as lovely as you for the duration would be an insult to you. A thing I could never do. So instead, please allow me to say I hope you'll save time for another dance with me later this fine night." He gave her a slow wink before retreating into the crowd.

Keeping her head held high, Scarlett hid how much his compliment flattered her. There was no doubt in her mind the rumours swirling around the name Alec Storme were well-founded. Even though he was the youngest of their four-person team, Scarlett could see not only how much experience he'd already had but also the potential he hadn't yet tapped into.

Scarlett headed for the oblong-shaped, crystal-like bar in the middle of the club. Once there, she took a seat on one of the bar stools which were white in order to stand out against the dark colours surrounding them. Lights had been placed inside the clear structures which constituted the bar, giving it a dark purple glow. She nodded to the bartender, Ramone, who flashed a brilliant smile in her direction. Apparently Antony had been in error when he suggested the man tending bar might not remember her for before she could place an order, her drink of choice appeared in front of her as if by magic.

"Cranberry juice and vodka, ma'am." Ramone slid a coaster under the glass, giving her a wink when he did. He moved on to the next customer before she could thank him.

In her ear, Scarlett could hear conversations being held by the other members of the team and she smiled. Which she quickly hid behind her glass, taking a sip of her drink. It sounded like Damon might be having some luck. Same with Alec. Karishma, on the other hand, had a lilt in her words suggesting whomever she was speaking to was boring her. No one said the safe word though.

"What is such an attractive woman doing sitting all by herself at the bar?" A male voice said.

Pretending to have been engrossed in her beverage, Scarlett didn't look at him. The mirror in the centre of the bar was all she needed. For the moment. "I'd think it obvious. I'm enjoying my drink."

"Hmmm, indeed. I imagine after that dance you must be extremely thirsty."

Scarlett kept a flinch in check when she felt a light touch gently moving from the right side of her neck to her shoulder then down her arm. The mirror let her see a streak of grey in his otherwise black hair. A feature which gave the slender man the air of a distinguished gentleman. As he sat turned in her direction, though, his facial features remained somewhat of a mystery. "You saw that, huh?"

"My dear, everyone in the club saw. I believe we all stopped what we were doing in order to watch. You're a very… sensual… creature, aren't you." He traced her arm back up to her neck, amazed at the softness of her skin and greatly encouraged when she didn't pull away from his touch. "Do you have a name? Or shall I endeavour to give you one myself?"

"Katriona." Using the name she'd adopted for when she'd been partnered with Damon felt right to Scarlett in this instance. Over the comms, she heard Damon pause his own conversation when the name was used. Wintyrs could only imagine how it must have made him feel. It was a good identity, in her opinion, and one well-suited to the current environment.

"A beautiful name for a beautiful lady." He ran his fingers down her arm again. "Come now, won't you let me gaze into those eyes of yours?"

Putting on her most charming smile, Scarlett swivelled her stool in order to fulfill his request. His piercing green eyes met hers and she noted his nose seemed nearly too large for his triangular face. "You know my name - what's yours?"

"You, my dear, may call me Henri." A sheen was visible on his slightly sun-kissed skin which was obviously perspiration. Likely from nerves. Or at least that's what she hoped.

"Henri. A strong yet old-fashioned name."

"Well, Katriona, I'm a strong yet old-fashioned kind of guy." His smile revealed rows of perfect teeth so white they nearly sparkled even in the darker lighting of the club.

Scarlett cocked her head at his obvious attempt at flirting. "You're not very good at this are you..." she remarked with a raised eyebrow.

Flustered at being called out, Henri felt his cheeks grow warm. "Am I truly that obvious?"

"I'm afraid so. Your voice is shaking."

"Perhaps because I am completely besotted by the amazing beauty next to me."

"Henri. Please. All you're succeeding in doing is embarrassing yourself. If you'd like to skip the awkwardness and ask me to dance then, by all means, please do so."

"You aren't a fan of small talk?"

"Not in a club where you can barely hear yourself think. At least on the dance floor we would be closer. Easier to talk that way." Scarlett gave him a kind smile, holding her hand out to him to see if he would accept or not.

Seemingly startled at her boldness, Henri took her hand and led her out onto the dance floor. The DJ had elected for another slow song so Scarlett moved her body closer to Henri's. Heat radiated from his body telling her this was something he wasn't used to. Whether that related to the way they were dancing or her take-charge attitude, Wintyrs couldn't say. And though the effort had not been great on her part, the man was already putty in her hands. The way he looked at her was a dead giveaway. All she needed to do now was see if he had the knowledge they sought.

Doubt coloured Scarlett's mind. Mostly because she'd never been that lucky. After all, he was only her first 'approach'. Though admittedly it'd be nice if, for once, something like that would happen for her. When the hand around her waist slipped down to cup her buttocks, she reached behind and forced the errant appendage back up. This man wasn't as debonaire as he believed himself to be. With looks that he'd obviously worked on cultivating, she also didn't find him attractive. Beauty was in the eye of the beholder though. She always tried to look past a person's appearance to what they had on the inside. Something about Henri made her shudder internally. Not because of how he'd been acting but an underlying intent.

"Tell me about yourself, Katriona." Henri leaned in, speaking into her ear - thankfully the one without the comms.

"Not much to tell. Just a girl looking for a good time."

"I see…"

"What about you?"

"Just a guy looking for a good time."

Glad her dance partner couldn't see her face, Scarlett narrowed her eyes. That was the second time he'd rephrased her response and parroted it back to her in the apparent hope she'd not catch it. In the span of her career she'd only come across an individual doing the same thing in very specific occasions. The only thing any of them had in common was what they did. Fellow spies or the bad guy she'd been sent to find. Mentally crossing her fingers, Scarlett tried again to open a dialogue.

"What kind of good time?" Scarlett asked as they continued their dance.

"A little bit of this and a little bit of that. I guess you could say I'm kind of a jack of all trades. How do I know I can trust you?"

"You don't. But I'm still here, aren't I?"

"Which makes me wonder what's wrong with you. Usually by now, in my experience anyway, a woman runs. Nearly screaming. Yet here you stay."

"I have the same problem. Men or women. They find out I have a thing for knives and the pain they're able to inflict and my dates tend to vanish with some lame excuse."

Henri raised his eyebrows even though she couldn't see his reaction. "Really? Most women abhor violence such as that. You enjoy it??"

"Blood and death turn me on." Her whisper grew softer, more amorous - to the point of teetering on pornographic.

Swallowing down the sudden desire rising in his throat, Henri took a second to process her words. "You should join me tomorrow night. There's going to be a very special weapons test. If all goes to plan, there will be a lot of casualties. But no bodies left over. I've been told we get to watch their panic as they realize what's happening."

It wasn't lost on Scarlett that Henri was telling her literally everything she wanted to hear. Whether to make himself appear more desirable or for reasons more nefarious was the question she couldn't answer. Hopefully she'd be able to get him to slip up and reveal his true intent before it was too late. "You're telling a complete stranger all of this? I have to wonder why." She grunted softly when he pulled her closer so there wasn't even a gap of air between their bodies.

"Perhaps I'm hoping you'll spend the rest of the night with me then join me at the demonstration after which we will go for dinner then have another round of sweet love together." Henri replied in her ear, letting his lips nibble her earlobe when he finished speaking.

Scarlett closed her eyes. If there was one thing she had trouble with, it was someone touching her ears. Much to her surprise another slow song began and Henri did not release her. Wondering if she'd need to extract herself, her eyes roamed the crowd as he continued their dance. She saw Alec standing at the edge of the dance floor, ready to spring into action if she needed him. Another whirl around and her eyes landed on Damon who stood with Karishma - both tensed up just as Alec was.

"I believe the dance I agreed to is over." Scarlett said, trying to pull away without offending him.

"As long as my arms are around you then it has not finished." A tone entered his voice which made Scarlett grow wary. Not so much dangerous as it was possessive.

"Henri…"

"Give me an answer and we can cease this dance. Until you do…" he pulled her back in tight against him, "you remain in my arms."

Wintyrs shook her head at Damon when she noted he'd taken a step towards them, anger gleaming in his eyes. "How about this, Henri. I'll give you your answer when you let go of me. I assume you'd like to be both conscious and breathing when I say it. I'm dangerous. Very dangerous. And I don't like anyone trying to manipulate me. Especially into sex. So if you want to remain alive, you'll take your hands off me this very instant." She kept her voice soft, whispering in his ear while ensuring her words were filled with ill-intent. Her team obviously heard her for when her eyes next landed on Damon, his expression had changed spectrums and he was fighting back a grin.

Henri jerked away, his eyes wide with shock that she'd spoken to him thusly. Never had he encountered anyone like this woman. "You have my apologies, Katriona. Here I thought you were like other women here - speaking your mind with no gumption to follow through. Evidently I was wrong. I've met your demands, now honour your word."

Placing her hands on her hips and putting a sensual curve in her body as if to show him what he was missing, Scarlett eyed him closely. "We part ways tonight. You tell me where this demonstration is taking place and I'll meet you there. When it's finished, you may then escort me back to my place where we will fulfill the rest of your request. If you behave yourself during the test. This is the only offer I'll make and it's non-negotiable."

Shivering with anticipation, Henri nodded. His desire to have her now so strong, he could barely speak past the lump in his throat. "Deal."

"Give me the address of the demonstration and where to meet you tomorrow." Scarlett allowed him to lean in in order to whisper the information in her ear. After thanking him, she parted ways then headed outside the club, knowing the others wouldn't be far behind. Damon went to retrieve the car and brought it around to where the others waited. No one said anything until the doors were closed, sealing them inside.

"So??" Karishma spoke first. "Where's it going down?"

"And why are you paler than normal?" Damon frowned at his partner.

"Because I recognize the address he gave me." Wintyrs replied in a hushed voice.

"Well don't keep us in suspense..." Alec chimed in.

Scarlett turned slightly in her seat, given she was now up front with Damon, in order to look at each of them in turn. "The Centurian Agency."

29

The silence following her statement was unlike anything she'd encountered. Scarlett couldn't even hear the others breathing. It was nearly like they were frozen in time. Damon moved first, taking the hovercar to the air and heading for the mansion.

"We need to brief William and Zaliki. If they're targeting HQ they'll undoubtedly get anyone who might be loyal to them out first and kill everyone else." His hands clenched the steering yoke so tight his knuckles turned white. "I don't suppose he gave you the time this demonstration is scheduled to start?"

"Noon exactly." Scarlett answer. "Which only leaves us a safe window of... it's 10pm now... let's say twelve hours to give ourselves a cushion. In the grand scheme of things - not a whole hell of a lot of time."

"How the hell are we going to get our people out of there?" Alec asked, not able to see a solution that didn't get at least one of them killed.

"That's what we need William for." Wintyrs stated. "And maybe Zaliki can use the way she contacted Myrtle to somehow send a message... I don't know." Exasperation started to set in. "I don't do plans very well. Like you guys, I'm better thinking on my feet. Improvising as I go. Especially if the Spymaster's plan fails."

"Just be glad the airways will get us there faster." Damon told them as he pushed the accelerator to its max. "Let's hope there's no law enforcement around looking to make their quota!"

Scarlett glanced over to see their speed and winced. He wasn't kidding. She'd gone fast before but he was quite literally pushing this hovercar to its limit. The gauges hovered near the red zone for both speed and engine temperature. If they were to have any sort of collision right now... there'd be nothing left. Of either vehicle.

"Drop me at the door. I'll fill William in while you guys get changed. Feel free to utilize any of the clothes in that wardrobe we got these outfits from." Scarlett said out of the blue. Since she was the one who experienced the conversation first-hand, she figured it best that he received the information directly from her.

"You sure you don't want one of us there to corroborate your story?" Karishma cocked her head to one side, glad she was sitting behind Damon. In this position she was better able to study the other woman.

"William will believe me."

"Why would you think that with something of this magnitude?"

"Trust her." Damon quickly lent his support to his partner. "He'll believe her."

"Seriously - why would he unless... oh!" Feeling a sense of superiority, Karishma smiled smugly. "And how long did you think you could hide *that* from us?"

"Okay... what'd I miss?" Eyes moving between the two women, Alec sat forward as far as his safety restraint would allow.

"Our dear Agent Wintyrs is involved with our Spymaster." Not waiting for confirmation, Karishma continued. "Things make a lot more sense now. Why, though, didn't you tell us?"

Scarlett released a deep breath. She'd been apprehensive about how the two newcomers would react if they found out about her and William. But besides Karishma's superiority complex, she could hear genuine curiosity in the words. "I guess I was worried about how you might take the news. And honestly, the whole thing between us is still relatively new. I'm not sure either of us is really ready for too many people to know."

Karishma waved a dismissive hand. "Please. If anything, I'm happy for you both. Love is a genuinely wonderful thing. If you've found it... then you need to fight to the death to hang onto it."

Biting her lip at the strange metaphor, Scarlett nodded slowly. "Thank you, Karishma." The silence from the other half of the backseat grew concerning. "Alec?"

"Huh? Oh, yeah - of course I'm cool with it. It's just..." He trailed off, embarrassed to admit what he'd only just started to say. "Never mind."

Studying the man sitting beside her now instead of Wintyrs,

Karishma laughed lightly when she realized what he wasn't saying. "Alec Storme - you like her, don't you."

Growing red in the face, Alec turned his head and looked out the window next to him. "No. Yes. Maybe." He stumbled over each word. "I mean, how could anyone *not*?"

Allowing himself a small chuckle at Alec's discomfiture, Damon directed the hovercar down to the mansion. He pulled them up to the main door, giving Scarlett time to get out before heading to the parking area.

Wintyrs quickly walked into the house, bumping into Jerome the second she stepped over the threshold. "Jerome, where's William?"

"I believe he's still in your hidden lab or whatever it is." Jerome's eyes were wide at the haste with which she both spoke and moved.

"Thank you!" Scarlett called over her shoulder, wishing she could run in the dress she wore but even with the leg slits, she couldn't move as quickly as she'd like. Much to her surprise, she found the Spymaster back in front of the computer and making use of the back door into their agency. "William!"

William turned when he heard her call his name. There was a hint of what he could only describe as panic in her voice. "Scarlett? What's wrong?"

Scarlett took a few deep, controlled inhalations to help even out her breathing. "We have the target and when it's going to happen!"

"Okay." He patted the stool next to his to get her to sit down. "Come on. Sit and catch your breath. Tell me what's going on."

Obeying his request, Scarlett took the seat beside him and met his eyes. "We have very little time. The Eliminator will be used tomorrow around noon."

Swearing under his breath, William nodded. "Where? What's the target?"

"Centurian Agency headquarters."

William was speechless. A cold feeling of dread settled over him and a heaviness formed in his stomach. He shook his head slowly in denial. "We have to get anyone else loyal to me out of there. Safe to assume Vargas will get any Orion Agency sympathizers and assets out - or even tell them not to show up tomorrow altogether. Which means we'd be safe putting a building broadcast out."

"Why do I sense a 'but' coming?"

"Because you do. A big one."

Taking a deep breath, she gave him a nod. "Spill."

"Such a broadcast can only be done from the office of the Spymaster. In HQ."

Scarlett stared at him, absent-mindedly rubbing her forehead. "You're not setting foot near that building. I can guarantee not one of us here will let that happen. However," she put a finger up to stall his rebuttal, "I've got an invite to be there. I have reason to be in the vicinity. I'll get there super-early and go straight inside to initiate the broadcast." She grew thoughtful. "Can it be pre-programmed?"

William shook his head slowly. "No. Not unless Amir upgraded it without my knowledge. Although, given everything else he's done, I suppose anything's possible."

"Alright. We operate on the premise that he hasn't touched it. I'll go first thing in the morning when the most staff will be there."

"I don't like it but I can't think of anything better. Once you're in the building, you'll need to initiate a one-way lockdown. That'll let people out but no one else will be able to enter."

"You'll have to show... wait... can't we do that from the backdoor I created here?" Scarlett watched him shake his head again. "Okay, why not?"

"Security initiatives like the announcements as well as the lockdowns are housed on a separate data network. Only my codes can enable full access - well, Amir can use the announcements but not the lockdown - and they have to be input using an older model interface. I kept the setup like that in order to dissuade anyone outside of the agency from gaining access."

Raising an eyebrow, Scarlett pointedly looked at the monitor. "Don't you think maybe that should've been done with everything?"

"Not possible. You know agents need access when they're in the field. There's no way I could've kept everything on a closed network or database. Too many lives would be put in jeopardy."

"Unlike now when there's lives in jeopardy."

William groaned, putting a hand over his eyes. "Yeah, I see your point. Once we're out of this mess, I'll work with Myrtle to see if we can't figure something out for the new HQ. In the meantime..."

"In the meantime, I'm going to change into something more comfortable and then you're going to show me how to do what we discussed." Scarlett stood, placing her hands on her hips until he finally looked at her and gave her yet another nod. "Alright. I'll be back in ten minutes. Don't go anywhere."

Only after he gave her a mock salute did Scarlett head upstairs to the wardrobe room hidden in the master bedroom at the back of the large walk-in closet. The thought of sleep crossed her mind the second she laid eyes on the bed but sadly, with so many things going through her head, she'd never see the inside of her eyelids. Just the idea of potentially losing people she knew and worked with managed to tie her stomach up in knots.

Hitting the button under the closet's light switch, Scarlett watched as the tall, wide, shoe rack slid aside to reveal the wardrobe room. The one thing Wintyrs felt grateful for was that she could wear many of the clothes her mother added to the collection. Although, every so often, Scarlett did purchase a few items and sent them to the house for Jerome to add to what already existed. Finding a pair of dark denim jeans without the fashion which seemed to be trending - holes everywhere - Scarlett took them from the rack. No one could ever convince her to wear pants with holes in them. Especially if they were designed that way. They might be all the rage and, yes, she did have a few different pairs and sizes on hand in case push truly did come to shove but she'd only use them as the ultimate last resort. Given how dark the jeans she chose were, her fingers went through some of the hangers and found a sequinned red tank top which would pair nicely with the white leather jacket she'd bought.

Glancing in the full length mirror on the nearby wall, what she saw made her smile. People - like Vargas - might recognize her if they looked at her face. But in this outfit... no one would be directing their gaze above her neck. She grabbed an elastic and tied her hair back in a braid. The style was one of the few that suited her face while keeping errant strands out of her eyes. Since she didn't plan on sleeping, she wasn't worried about it getting messed up. Once satisfied she'd look good for a 'date' while also wearing something she could easily move in, she headed back down to William.

"Sorry, couldn't find my white heels." Scarlett stated by way of apology, her shoes clicking loudly on the tiles as she entered the room. "I couldn't show off this outfit without them."

William looked over his shoulder at her then swivelled his stool around, afraid he'd hurt his neck. "Is there anything you *don't* look stunning in??"

Scarlett flashed him a smile. "You're always complimenting me, haven't you noticed?"

"I can't help it. Are you saying you want me to stop?"

"Hell no. You're giving my confidence a much needed boost. Not to mention my ego." Moving closer, Scarlett leaned down and gave him a passionate kiss. When she pulled away, she grinned at his closed eyes and slack jaw. If only she had that effect on all the men. "You okay there, boss?"

Opening his eyes while flicking his tongue over his lips, William stared at her. "That's not playing fair." He whispered with a voice filled with passion. Shifting uncomfortably on the stool, William swallowed the lump which had formed in his throat and glowered at her when she chuckled at his predicament.

"I never said I play fair." She commented, one eyebrow raised.

Clearing his throat, William shook his head. "We should get started before…"

"Before everyone we know at the agency vanishes without a trace." Scarlett finished for him. "Let's do this."

30

Dawn arrived all too quickly in Scarlett's mind. She'd had William run through the steps she needed to take for the lockdown and announcement several times despite her photographic memory. They couldn't afford any mistakes. After giving him a tender kiss, Scarlett went to Myrtle. The two techs had been working on the EMP rifle all night, neither of them even stopping for food. Which had been why Scarlett asked Jerome to bring in plates for all four of them just before dawn.

"Myrtle?" Scarlett tentatively said the lead tech's name, not wanting to startle the other woman as she snapped a latch closed on the rifle before turning to gaze upon Wintyrs with a satisfied look.

"Agent Wintyrs." Myrtle smiled. Even though she had that air of satisfaction, Scarlett could see how tired both techs were. "You're just in time."

"Good because I'm about to head out. How's the rifle look?"

"Given the age, it's in surprisingly excellent condition. I've already shown Agent Raynott how to use it."

That caused Scarlett's jaw to drop. "What? But..."

"No buts." Damon rounded the corner into the lab. You're not doing this alone. More to the point - you *can't* do this alone. So while you're working in the building, I'll hunt down the Eliminator and use the EMP. Or, at least, that's my plan. We just have to hope I find the bloody thing before it's activated."

"If you don't, by the time of the test I should be the only one left in HQ anyway."

"Oh no. Don't you even think like that. Neither of us is dying today."

"Let's hope not." Scarlett planned on going alone but he'd raised an excellent point. She couldn't be in two places at once. Plus, judging from his expression, there was no way he was staying behind - no matter what she said.

"Which hovercar should we take?" Damon was already dressed - black jeans, black t-shirt and matching shoes. A black leather jacket completed the ensemble. It was quite apparent he planned on sticking to the shadows.

"The Aston Martin. Doubtless Alec has had it completely decked out. Especially since I know he's fan of a certain fictitious spy."

"Gotcha. Well then, let's go save some lives."

"You going to let me drive this time?" Scarlett raised an eyebrow at him.

"Uhhh... I *really* want to say no. That car handles like a dream. Nothing I've driven before can come close to comparing..."

"And yet, technically, it does belong to Alec..."

"Correction - it's an agency asset given the agency was the entity who made the purchase for Agent Storme's use." William said from the doorway to the computer room they'd been in. "Which means it's fair game for any agent to use."

Scarlett shot him a glare at those words. "Seriously? Are you planning on saying the same thing about my hovercar?"

"Nope. You bought that one with your own money. Although it's tricked out with agency tech, I'm not going to force the issue. I can't play favourites." He said as an apology. "Flip a coin but do so quickly because all your arguing is doing is making us lose time."

"Debating. Not arguing. Given they expect to see me in the neighbourhood..."

Damon shook his head. "We can switch spots after you drop me off. Come on - William's right. Every second is precious." Grabbing the rifle before she could argue against him driving any more than she already had, he ran to the garage with Scarlett. He'd seen Jerome park the sought after vehicle in there after taking the keys from his hands. Once inside the garage, Raynott led the way to the hovercar and held the door for her as she climbed inside. The second she was settled he closed the door, ran to the other side of the car and got in, reaching behind to gently place the rifle on the backseat. All while avoiding her eyes for he had a pretty strong inkling all he'd see in their depths right now would be anger.

"Well if you want to drive then drive. Don't spare the horses,

Damon. Get us there as fast as you can."

Words he'd been hoping his partner would say. Also ones Damon knew she'd probably come to regret. This brand, not to mention model, of hovercar was the fastest on the market. Add the Centurian Agency upgrades and it couldn't be caught by anything less than the exact same model. He didn't give her any warning. After all, where would the fun be in that? As soon as the large garage door was up, secure and out of the way, Raynott started the engine. Gunning it, he took them into the air with all possible speed.

Scarlett grunted as the sudden, albeit expected, burst of acceleration pressed her back into her seat. Part of her wondered how many G's they were pulling because it was apparent they were. "You do know I know what this vehicle is capable of, right?" Feeling she had to raise her voice, she hoped it didn't sound like she was mad.

Damon laughed. "Does that matter? You know. I know. A machine like this though..." he released a low whistle, "she's a racehorse. Meant to be free. You can't keep her caged up or on a leash. She has to be free. Be fast."

Wintyrs turned her head to stare at him. "You just inferred that this hovercar is a wild animal."

"Really? After what I said, *that's* what you focus on?" Amusement coloured his tone. "I'm not sure I want to know where your head's at."

"Very funny." Scarlett smirked then, finding the perfect opportunity to say something she'd always wanted to, the smirk turned into a mischievous grin. "Are we there yet?"

Glaring at her, Damon raised an eyebrow. "How much sleep did you get last night?"

"None. I had to have William train me on a couple of things." When the car swerved slightly, she knew precisely where his train of thought went. "Work related, Damon."

"Well... technically that could be..."

"And you were complaining about *my* mind." Scarlett snorted quietly. "Computer work-related. Not sexually related."

"Sure, kick my imagination where it hurts." He had the pleasure of hearing her chuckle which made the entire conversation worthwhile. "Back to your earlier question - we should be there in about ten minutes if I continue at this speed."

"Good. Then keep it up. The speed I mean." Scarlett quickly clarified upon hearing his chortle.

"Yes, ma'am. When we get there, I'll pull into an alley a couple of blocks down and get out. We don't want them seeing me until it's too late. Vargas should be in for one hell of a surprise though." Damon caught her giving him a puzzled look so he kept going. "He thinks we're dead."

"Does he? If he's worth his salt as a Spymaster then he'll suspect we escaped that death trap of his. In fact, that's probably why he chose HQ. He knows I wouldn't be able to sit idly by and watch our friends and colleagues be murdered."

Damon groaned softly. "Is there a reason you didn't think to mention that before now?"

Scarlett chewed her lower lip, knowing William was also part of the conversation via the communicators they each wore in their ear. "Yeah. I didn't want it to influence who would be sent on this mission."

"William knows the risks involved in every assignment. I know your relationship is new to you both but he doesn't play favourites. He'd assign whomever is best suited for what has to be done."

"Damon's right." William said softly in their ears. "Emotions aside, you two are the ones we need for this."

"Then you already knew…"

"What you suspected? Not for certain. Unfortunately the theory does have merit. No matter how I try to twist it to make the facts seem otherwise. I'm pretty sure you're walking into a trap. And I had a feeling you already knew which is why I didn't bother bringing it up before you left."

"I'm guessing it's also why Damon got the notion in his head to come with me." Scarlett responded to William however when the man next to her winced, she knew she hit the nail on the head. "You two really are tight, aren't you."

"When you've been best mates for as long as we have… you'd do almost anything for each other." Damon answered in a soft voice. There was something in his tone which only served to reinforce his words.

Raising her eyebrows, Scarlett paused in order to reflect on what he'd said. For the first time, she realized what she'd been missing by never letting anyone get close to her. Friendship like what the two men implied they had had always been just out of reach for her. Wintyrs wished she'd been able to cultivate a relationship like theirs. Which led to another emotion she'd never confronted. Jealousy.

"We're closing in on my drop-off coordinates." Damon's voice drew her from her thoughts. "You ready for this, Agent Wintyrs?"

"I'm always ready. What about you, Agent Raynott?"

Giving her a toothy grin, Damon set the car down in the semi-dark alley he'd mentioned earlier. "This is me you're talking to. What do you think?" He gave her a sly wink, grabbing the rifle and jumping out of the hovercar. Then he waited while she slid over to the driver's seat and gave her a mock salute after which he jogged off.

Scarlett watched him go via the rearview mirror. They both had tough assignments but somehow she felt he would have the worst. Then, as she started to pull away, another thought struck her. One, she wondered, if their Spymaster had considered.

"William?"

"I'm here. Is everything okay?" William's voice volume remained quiet in her ear which told her he was also monitoring them on the computer.

"I had a thought about the Eliminator."

"I'm all ears."

"Will it be emitting some sort of electronic signature even if it's not currently in use?" Scarlett asked. Hearing some clicking in the background, she knew he was quickly re-opening the file on the weapon. That fact alone made her glad she'd downloaded what they'd uncovered. She worried if the backdoor was used again someone might notice and put a trace on it. One of the reasons she hadn't minded leaving Alec and Karishma behind in addition to Feiyan and Zaliki. Their presence ensured William had protection just in case.

"Yes. Yes it will be…"

"Can we not track that signature to within some kind of search radius to help Damon?"

The silence greeting her follow-up question told her he hadn't thought of that. Although, he deserved the benefit of the doubt given how much he undoubtedly had on his mind. Someone stood in the background on his end - Wintyrs could hear them speaking in hushed voices then realized he must be talking to Myrtle to see what they could do.

"Okay, Scarlett, I'll admit - I should've been the one to think of this but thank you so much. Myrtle is installing a tracking program on the computer you have here. I think we can do this. If nothing else, as you said, we should be able to narrow the search radius."

"Good. I'm approaching the lower parking garage now. I'll let you know once I get to the Spymaster's office."

"I've added your prints to the allowed agents database for the lock on that particular door."

"When did you do that?"

"When you and Damon were on your way there. I quickly hopped on through the backdoor. Don't worry - I was only online maybe two minutes."

"You do realize…"

"I might've triggered some kind of alarm? It was a risk but had to be done. And I'm pretty sure I got out of there scot-free."

"Alright." Scarlett climbed out of the hovercar after putting it in park and turning off the engine. "I'm heading inside."

"I'm here if you need me."

Those words brought a smile to her face. Heading for the elevator, she was glad knowing taking this route meant she could avoid going through the Diamond Exchange which acted as a front for the building's main entrance. A nasty surprise waited for her, though, when she arrived at the double doors. After pressing the button to call the lift - nothing happened. Scarlett frowned then pressed the round protrusion again, this time harder, with the same result.

"Well. That puts a wrinkle in things."

"Scarlett?" William's voice remained calm yet the concern he held for her started to seep through. "Report."

"The damned elevator's not working. Moving to the stairs, standby." Wintyrs paused when she reached the door for the stairwell. A tug at the back of her mind screamed to not open that door. Her hand stopped halfway to the handle. "This isn't right."

"Something wrong with the stairs?" Wishing, yet again, that he was still an agent, William longed to be next to her. "Can you put your glasses on so I can see what you see?"

"Sure, hold on." Scarlett put her hand into the zippered pouch on her waist and withdrew the requested item. After putting them on, she activated the camera. "How's that?"

William leaned forward when the picture came through on the computer monitor. "Perfect. Clear reception too for now. An added bonus. Now, what's wrong with the stairs?"

"Nothing. Per se. It's me. I feel like I'm being funnelled to a specific route."

"Gut feeling?"

"Yeah. Powerful one."

"Listen to it. If you're not comfortable with the stairs that leaves only one option. The Diamond Exchange."

"William... I don't believe that to be a viable option."

"Because Vargas is always three steps ahead of us." William finished her train of thought. "Well there's another alternative. But I guarantee you're not going to like it."

"I'm all ears." She parroted his earlier phrase back to him.

"Climb up the elevator shaft."

"You're right."

"I am?"

"Yeah. I don't like it."

"I know you're claustrophobic and if there were any other way or more time then we could delve into that. But there isn't and *really* isn't. Vargas undoubtedly knows about your claustrophobia as well. I don't think he'd suspect you to attempt that route." He hated pushing her into this however also knew she'd reach the same conclusion. There was no choice.

"I didn't exactly bring climbing gear with me." Scarlett muttered under her breath.

"You won't need it. Once you're in the shaft you'll see a ladder on one side. All you have to do is climb."

"Security measures?"

"Each level will have a fingerprint and retina scanner you'll have to use for the doors to open."

This was a bad idea. Possibly one of the worst she'd ever considered. A dark elevator shaft, probably zero lighting, and her fear of enclosed spaces. Blowing out a gush of air, Scarlett returned to the elevator doors.

"Do I need to open them with my bare hands?"

Knowing she was trying to make light of things to keep herself distracted, William stifled his chuckle. The harder she tried to make him laugh, the more distracted she'd be. "No. There's a simpler way."

"Will the simpler way trigger any alarms?"

"It's... possible."

"Great cause, you know, what else could possibly go wrong."

"Oy! Are you *trying* to jinx us?" Damon spoke in a whisper. "You *never* say that on a mission!"

"Damon?"

"Yes, William?"

"Shut up."

"Yes sir, Spymaster, sir. Focusing on my assignment. Oh - I found them by the way. They're putting the Eliminator in place and working on securing it."

"Why didn't you say so?" William's astonishment was clear.

"You told me to shut up."

"Since when do you follow orders…"

"How long do we have?" Scarlett interrupted the men before they started into one of their brotherly bickering sessions. "Do you think they'll fire early?"

"Considering I've never see this thing before I… uh… crap…"

"Damon?" Her ears pricked at his turn of phrase.

"I've been spotted. Running on silent for a bit!"

Scarlett swore when his connection cut out. "Okay, William, help me get these doors open. I have a feeling Damon's going to need help but I have to clear this building first."

"Okay - look along the left side of the wall near the doorframe." He wasn't about to tell her he had visuals from Damon like hers and knew what the other agent faced. So far Raynott was managing to elude the guards he'd accidentally alerted to his presence.

"Right…" Scarlett did as requested, looking up and down the left side.

"There." William spotted what he was looking for. "See that symbol that resembles an ancient Roman helmet?"

"Where… okay yeah I see it. Really blends into the paint."

"Definitely on purpose. Place your right index finger over it."

"Are you serious? It's a fingerprint scanner??" Scarlett did as instructed and raised her eyebrows as the doors slid open to reveal an empty elevator car. "Nice." Stepping inside, she reached up to the escape hatch to open it. At least she thought ahead and wore her tallest heels. An advantage for this part but not the next. Even with the heels she wore, Wintyrs still had to jump in order to grab hold of the edges of the opening. Grunting with the effort, she pulled herself up and soon stood on top of the car. Her breath hitched in her throat as the darkness hit her eyes, only enhancing the feeling of the walls closing in.

"I'm right here with you, Scarlett." William's soothing voice entered her ear once more. "Give it another minute. Sensors in the shaft will get a read on your heat signature then activate emergency lighting."

"Okay." Closing her eyes, Scarlett could only whisper the word. Her heart pounded so hard she thought for sure it would burst right out of her chest. Of course, thanks to that fast heart of hers, her breathing grew harsh as well as shallow.

"You've got this."

A red glow pierced her eyelids. With great trepidation, Scarlett opened her eyes to find the shaft bathed in red light just as William promised. Her gaze landed on the ladder, the sight of which caused her to groan softly. The rungs were cylindrical which would make climbing in her heels impossible. She would have to do this barefoot. Sighing softly, she removed the hinderances and held them in her hands for a moment. They could be replaced, of course, but the pair was one she was quite fond of.

"Farewell, dear friends." Scarlett said then tossed them off the edge of the elevator.

"Scarlett? What are you doing?"

"Tossing my shoes."

"Yeah this I can see. Why?"

"Trust me, these heels and that ladder - not a good combination. I'd probably end up falling to my death. Besides, once I'm up there I'll move faster without them. What floor is the Spymaster's main office on? Something tells me it's not the one Amir used."

"Good guess. Top floor."

Shaking her head, Scarlett ruefully looked up at the nine stories above her. "Of course it is. I thought the elevator only had numbers to eight. I'm counting nine levels above me."

"The ninth floor can only be accessed by fingerprint in the elevator. And only I know where the scanner is."

"Well… you can see it's there from the outside of the building. I can't deny I've always been curious as to what's up there."

"And now you get to see for yourself."

Scarlett took hold of the rungs of the ladder and began her ascent. The metal of the bars was cold on her bare feet but she pushed the sensation away. Instead she focused on keeping her breathing slow and even. Exertion such as this could be detrimental to some. She found it nearly exhilarating. Even if she were working up a sweat. Wintyrs maintained a steady pace for the climb. Going too fast would end up with her needing to slow down to recuperate. An even speed was far more beneficial. In fact, she would arrive at the desired floor faster this way.

Continuing her climb, Scarlett heard William quietly muttering to himself. His quirks were becoming clear to Scarlett even though they hadn't known each other very long. This was one she found rather endearing. She doubted he even realized he was doing it. Whenever he did, she knew he was thinking or trying to work out a problem. For her, it was reassuring.

Having his voice in her ear - even if she had no idea what he was saying - helped make her time in the shaft tolerable. Her movements paused when she heard a noise. Feeling as though a fist closed around her gut, Scarlett first looked up then down the way she had come. What she saw made her heart pound.

"Crap." Scarlett said out loud, increasing her rate of climb. Only two floors to go.

"Scarlett?" William caught her glance up then down as well as her now quickened pace. He instinctively knew something wasn't right.

"Someone's activated the elevator." Her words came out in a rush as she tried to ignore the danger now approaching at a steady rate.

"What?!" William swore then proceeded to begin something he promised her he'd avoid. "I'm using the back door. I might be able to override it from here."

"No! Don't use the back door! I'm almost there, I'll be fine!" Not wanting him to risk giving his position away, Scarlett hoped he would listen to her. Even if she didn't quite believe her own words.

"But Scarlett - !"

"Do. Not. Use it! I've only got a few rungs to go…"

"And how close is the elevator car??"

"Do you really want me to stop and look?" Hearing him pause, Wintyrs swore someone was there with him.

"Keep going, Agent Wintyrs." William said, dropping into his Spymaster voice. Cool, calm and unbiased. "Reach your goal."

"Yes, sir!"

A small smile rested on her face while her hands and feet guided her of their own accord. She didn't need to look down to know the lift was rapidly closing the distance between them. There wouldn't be much time for her to escape this shaft. Hopefully the fingerprint scanner would work swiftly when activated.

Hauling herself up the last ladder rung, Scarlett located the needed scanner. She pressed her index finger against the panel, counting each passing second in her head while waiting for first the beep of acknowledgement then for the doors to open. A rush of air from below nearly blew her off the ladder as the lift grew ever nearer at its steady but fast pace. Scarlett began to look for an alternative to being squished like the proverbial bug on a windshield and the only thing that came to mind was jumping onto the roof of the car then flattening herself down on it as much as possible.

Taking a deep breath, Wintyrs prepared to go through with that idea only to hear the doors slide open. Unleashing curse words she was certain William had never heard from her, Scarlett jumped through the now open double doors, rolling to her side on the floor and yanking her feet to safety milliseconds before the elevator would have crushed them. She turned onto her back, chest heaving from both exertion and exhilaration. Cutting things that close always had that effect on her.

Cautiously rising to her feet, Scarlett peered around at her surroundings. The Spymaster's office wasn't what she expected by any means. She'd pictured something similar to how William decorated the one at Dolus. What met her eyes was completely different. Sparse even. There were a couple of paintings on the wall which, given their profession, were undoubtably strategically placed. A large, mahogany desk sat at the other end of the large office with an overstuffed black leather chair behind it. The marshmallow coloured walls made those pieces of furniture along with the oversized television screen hanging on the wall behind them stand out like sore thumbs. As she drew closer, Scarlett noted the chair currently faced away from the elevator. An observance which made her frown.

"Very clever, Agent Wintyrs."

Scarlett froze in her tracks when a voice she easily identified spoke. "Hello, Amir."

The chair swivelled around slowly to reveal the man whom she used to believe was the Spymaster but now knew was only a mouthpiece. She heard a gurgle of astonishment from William in her ear. A sound informing her the man in the chair should not have access to this office let alone look like he'd made himself at home. Narrowing her eyes at the male sharing the room with her, Wintyrs forced her feet to start moving again and had them carry her towards the desk.

Amir slowly clapped his hands, grinning around the fat brown cigar in his mouth. "Well played, Wintyrs. Well played indeed. You know, I bet Vargas you wouldn't show. Told him you'd never be so foolish." He sighed, removing the cigar from his mouth in order to tap some ashes into a crystal dish sitting on top of the desk. "He insisted you would. That you'd never let people you know die if you could help it."

"I guess that's one bet you're regretting." Scarlett stated, sneaking a quick glance around the room.

"Oh don't worry. The only people here are you and me." Amir eyed her, still wearing the same grin. "Then I saw you in the elevator shaft - something I never in a million years thought you'd do. Another bet I shouldn't have taken. And then you managed to outrun the elevator!" He laughed. "I mean, damn! I figured it was a sure thing that that would've killed you!"

"So you're the one who started the elevator while I was climbing."

"But of course. There's only one person besides me who could and you and I both know he's not here right now."

"Amir. Listen to me. You don't need to side with Vargas. Why would you want to? You know what he plans to do here. Do the right thing. The honourable thing. Help me save everyone in the building." Scarlett doubted appealing to his good side would work. Still, she had to try.

Ignoring her words, Amir puffed out a cloud of smoke. "There's one thing I can't figure out though. How on earth did you get your fingerprint added to the database to access this office?"

"Funny. I was about to ask you the same thing. I thought only *one* person could enter this office - and you're not him."

"Now how would you know that unless... oh! Oh, I see. Found the real Spymaster did you? Have him squirrelled away somewhere now to keep him safe? I assume he's on the other end of your glasses camera and probably talking into your ear right now?" Amir's smile turned smug. "We'll find him eventually, you know. And kill him in the most painful way possible. That's from Vargas, by the way, not me. I can't stand the sound of someone screaming in complete agony. So what's he like?"

"You're not going to make me slip up or distract me from my mission, Amir."

"Your mission??" Barking out a laugh, he shook his head at her. "Don't you get it, Wintyrs? There *is* no mission. Because there's no more Centurian Agency. All the other agencies have turned on you. You have no allies. Your mission here was doomed to fail before it even started. Can't you see that? You're done. Everyone in this building will die in just a couple of hours. You can't save them."

"Amir. You know me. Do you honestly think anything you just said will stop me?" A knowing smile wound its way onto her lips when she noted him struggling to remain smug. "You're trying to stall. I'll give you credit - you thought of some interesting techniques to use but they all end with the same result. Me succeeding and you failing. Now - are you going to step aside to let me save everyone both you and I have worked with for years? Or am I going to have to fight you?"

Swallowing visibly, Amir put his cigar in the dish with a hand shaking like a leaf. He'd not expected to have her challenge him. In retrospect, he should have known better. After all, she was right, he knew how she worked, the success rate of her missions, and how good she was in a fight. Then there was the fact he'd never been in the field himself as an agent. There had never been reason for him to be. Which meant if they fought - he'd lose. Rather spectacularly. Watching her, Amir could tell from her eyes alone she'd already arrived at the same conclusion. Hell, she'd probably reached it the second she'd laid eyes on him sitting in the true Spymaster's chair.

"Agent Wintyrs. I am your recognized Spymaster. Your loyalty lives and dies with me. Stand down. Now."

Raising an eyebrow, Scarlett removed one of the two knives she had concealed on her person. She made no move towards him - yet - but allowed him to see the weapon in all its glory so he would understand every word she was about to say next held no hidden meaning and hid no falsehoods.

"You aren't the Spymaster. You were hired as his mouthpiece and nothing more. Continue in your attempts to block me from completing my assignment then I guarantee you *will* be hurt. I won't kill you. I'll hurt you just enough that you won't be able to outrun the Eliminator. The choice is ultimately yours. Me or the Eliminator." Betting his self-preservation instinct would kick in, Scarlett didn't bother tensing her muscles for a fight.

"You…"

"Tick-tock, Amir. I'm kinda on the clock here. Make your choice before I make it for you."

The look on her face ended up being the only incentive needed. Amir grabbed his cigar and ran for the stairwell, beating a hasty retreat. Scarlett shook her head. That man, in her books, was a coward. A weak link. Which meant they'd have an ace in the hole when they made their play for Vargas. Putting her knife away, Wintyrs moved to the large desk, assuming the recently vacated seat.

"You handled Amir beautifully." William said in her ear.

"Thanks." Scarlett responded while reaching under the desk. After a minute's search she located the doorbell-type button William told her was needed. After pressing it, part of the top of the desk lifted up slightly then pulled back out of the way. Once complete, an older-style monitor as well as keyboard rose up out of the depths of the desk to provide the user easy access. "I'm in." She said needlessly since he could see everything for himself.

"Good." William stated, watching through her camera as the monitor in front of her flared to life. After seeing Amir at his desk, a worry settled at the back of his mind that his mouthpiece might have found this unit and tampered with or disabled it. "Proceed with the one-way lockdown. Remember you'll hear an alarm when you activate the procedure."

"Understood." Scarlett followed his orders. True to his word, an alarm sounded followed by an announcement advising those in the building of the partial lockdown. "Lockdown activated."

"Good work. Alright, now for your announcement. You're good with the needed code sequence?"

"William. Photographic memory, remember?"

"Sorry."

"Don't be." While typing in the required codes for making announcements, Scarlett realized seeing Amir alive hadn't been a surprise. In fact, all it did was confirm their suspicions that the head they'd been shown was fake. Now that she thought more about it, there was no way she could see Vargas eliminating someone he considered not only an asset but a most advantageous ally - the supposed Spymaster of a rival agency. A conclusion she berated herself for not reaching sooner.

Just before hitting the final key, Scarlett placed the nearby wired headset on her head ensuring the microphone sat in front of her lips. Once ready, she pressed the button that would allow her to address those in the building.

"Attention employees of the Centurian Agency. You are hearing the voice of Agent Scarlett Wintyrs. I am speaking to you now with the authority of the Spymaster. He sent me here to save your lives. Everyone listening to this knows full-well only the Spymaster can make or approve of announcements of this nature." Scarlett paused momentarily to let her words sink in to those listening. "You all know me. I would never lead you astray. Never lie to you if I knew you were in danger. Which you are. All of you. All of us - I'm in the building with you. Headquarters will soon be the target of a weapon capable of destroying every single living organism within a specific space. The person behind this is intent on the complete destruction of our agency and all we stand for. I have our Spymaster secure and far away from here. He is safe. He sent me back to do the same for all of you. As per our Spymaster's orders, I am enacting protocol Black Tornado. Gather what you can, ensure you have your comms units. Once you're clear of the building and certain you're not being followed, use your backup call-in number to send a written message. That backup will connect you directly to our Spymaster who will respond with rendezvous coordinates."

Scarlett terminated the connection, releasing a deep breath. Another alarm had begun to sound the second she'd mentioned the phrase 'Black Tornado'. She'd known, or thought she had anyway, the reason behind why that particular phrase had been chosen but when William had been instructing her last night, she hadn't stopped him from explaining. According to him the black stood for imminent death and tornado to urge people to understand time was not only crucial but of the essence. Scarlett easily equated the term with 'death comes on swift wings' - and knew she wasn't the only one of that mind.

"Agent Wintyrs? Why aren't you on the move yet?" William asked, a flicker of concern rippled through his voice.

"Sir," she avoided using his name in case Amir had set up any monitoring devices in the office during his stay, "is there a way we can confirm the message has been properly received?"

"Standby."

She could once again hear him speaking with someone on the other end then finally recognized the voice. Myrtle was with him. Good. That reassured her. If he decided to use the back door again then at least Myrtle could stay ahead of anyone attempting to trace the unknown access. There was a bit more debating and she heard a third person whom she quickly identified as Karishma. Which meant William had taken her dead seriously. He'd not only brought in brains - for Karishma was nearly as clever as her husband where Alec was almost as smart as Myrtle - but also skill for protection. Hearing it was Karishma and not Alec surprised her.

"If you're using the back door…"

"Relax. Myrtle is doing a little magic on top of yours to ensure we can't be traced. As soon as she's finished, I can check the camera system to see how your announcement was received."

Scarlett tapped her fingers impatiently on the surface of the desk. She didn't want to leave in case another verbal motivation was needed.

On that same note, she also didn't want to linger much longer. "Well??"

"We're going in now, hang on." William said in response. "Pulling up video feed and... nice. Looks like everyone is heeding your warning and enacting the protocol. Tech teams are wiping our computer systems and any hard copies are being destroyed. This back door will soon be useless. It looks like the elevator is back in operation from what I can see of the building's systems. Recommend beginning your descent as soon as possible. We have..." he paused to check the time, "four hours left. And that's only if Vargas holds to his schedule - which I have trouble believing he will, to be quite frank."

"I'm operating on the same assumption." Wintyrs replied, rising from the desk chair. "Heading for the elevator. Any chance you can tell if someone else is also monitoring the camera feeds?"

"Hang on." Hushed voices filtered through the comms again. It wasn't until she'd called for the elevator that William spoke again. "Sorry, needed Karishma's assistance. To answer your question, yes. There is definitely another party viewing our camera feeds. Externally."

"Ten to one it's Vargas."

"No bet. Karishma's going to see if she can block the transmission —"

"No!" Scarlett exclaimed after a moment's thought. "He's probably enjoying watching the chaos. If we take that from him, I'd bet dollars to doughnuts he'll activate the Eliminator." She stepped into the elevator car the minute the doors opened, pressing the button for the seventh floor. That was where the hard copy files were kept and she wanted to ensure those folks knew how fast they needed to move.

"Okay... that's a really good point. Where are you going?"

"Floor seven. The archives. How's Damon faring?"

"He's successfully eluded the security team he accidentally alerted to his presence. Damon's fine for now. Focus on your assignment, I'll let you know if he needs your help."

"Understood."

Scarlett briefly wondered if William would pick up on what she actually had in mind or not. So far she managed to traverse the building without any of the surveillance cameras seeing her, even managing to evade the one in the elevator car. Which of course meant Vargas wouldn't have any idea she was there. The second she stepped off the elevator, though, all of that would change. It was, in fact, the hidden - and real - reason she'd chosen the seventh floor. Because of all the hard copies, there were far more cameras there than any other level. And she had a very good reason, or so she believed, for allowing him to see her location. The Orion Agency Spymaster had proven to her that he'd only kill her if he felt he had no other choice.

So… she would give him a choice. And hopefully at the same time, buy her colleagues at least a few extra minutes to vacate the building and surrounding area.

31

"How's the evacuation coming, William?" Scarlett asked while the elevator slowly came to a stop at the requested destination.

"Surprisingly well. I've already redirected some assets here. I'm a little shocked that Vargas is letting people go and not activating the Eliminator for maximum casualties." William paused for a brief second. What she was doing must have finally sunk in with the Spymaster. "Scarlett. If he's got eyes inside… floor seven is our most sensitive floor which means also the most cameras being utilized. If you set one foot off that elevator on that level…"

"He'll know I'm here. That's the general idea." Wintyrs responded softly, leaving the lift when the doors slid open.

"Agent Wintyrs… what are you doing."

"Hopefully buying us some time."

"I want an explanation."

"My assignment is to save as many lives as possible, correct?"

"Yes…" His frown could be discerned in his voice.

"That's what I'm doing." Scarlett took her glasses off and placed them on a nearby table which was used for research and some meetings. She angled the lenses towards her then found a thick book to place under them in order to raise the field of vision so William and anyone with him would be able to see events as they unfolded. "How's your view?"

"Good." William answered. "You're going to lure him to you, aren't you."

Even though Scarlett knew the question was rhetorical, she decided to respond anyway. "Yep. If he's in here then we know the Eliminator won't be activated."

"I don't like this…" He sighed, realizing from what he saw on the security cameras she was right. Their people were going to need more time. "Be careful. Remember you nearly died yesterday."

Had it really been only yesterday? Wintyrs snorted a little when she concluded he was right. It felt like a week ago to her. Perhaps because she'd been so busy with everything her concept of time altered. Drawing in a breath, she pushed those thoughts away, instead turning to face the nearest security camera. Knowing Vargas had undoubtedly already spotted her, plus was probably quite aware she was behind the evacuation of the building - the main purpose of her letting Amir flee - Scarlett knew all she'd have to do was encourage him to join her. Which is precisely what she did. Staring at the camera, she put out her right hand then beckoned for whomever was watching to come see her.

"Well, he must've been close by…" William muttered in her ear. "He just moved from level one onto the elevator. You'll be getting company in about a minute."

"Is he alone?"

"Another surprise - yes."

"Interesting. My guess is he was on the way the minute I stepped onto the elevator. Him being alone though…"

"Doesn't feel right, does it?"

"Not in the slightest."

"Greet him at the elevator with your knives in hand then. As a Spymaster, he wouldn't enter a situation he didn't believe he could control or foresee the outcome for."

"Agreed. That tells me he still has someone in here. Probably on this floor with me." Scarlett surreptitiously cast her eyes around her surroundings while moving to face the elevator but remaining in view of the glasses. Nothing had changed. She could see the last three people on the floor scurrying about, destroying sensitive data as fast as they could.

"See anything or anyone acting odd?"

"No. At least no different from when I arrived."

"How many assets are there with you? Elevator is now one floor away."

"Three."

William could be heard instructing Karishma to send coordinates because he needed to focus on this now. "Sorry, gave Karishma my comms so she could copy my other messages to any new ones filtering through. Back to the number. You said three?"

"Yeah... why?"

"Because there should only be two and I can only see two on the cameras."

"Great." Scarlett had no time to compare notes. The light above the lift's doors came to life and a loud ding announced its arrival. "He's here." She said under her breath, her knives appearing in her hands as if called forth by magic.

"Be careful."

"It's me."

"Why do you think I'm saying be careful??"

"Funny man." Scarlett shook her head before evening out her breathing in preparation for anything about to come.

The doors to the elevator slid open, allowing the lone occupant to step out. "Trying to ruin all my fun, Agent Wintyrs?" Mario Vargas asked, his eyes taking in her stature as well as the knives in her hands. "And here I thought you'd be happy to see me. After all, the last time we saw each other you set me up to die. That wasn't very nice of you, was it."

"If I had to do it all over again, I would. Without changing a thing." Scarlett answered with narrowed eyes. "Pretty brazen of you, Vargas. Coming here. On your own."

"Oh, please. After all we've been through together I think you've earned the right to call me Mario." His teeth glinted in the florescent lighting, only adding to his air of ominence. "Although I must admit my surprise at seeing you here. I was certain we managed to eliminate both you and Raynott back at Dolus. See what I did there? Eliminate?" The laugh coming from him sent chills down his audience's spine. "Ah, no matter. I assume if you survived Dolus then Raynott did as well. Honestly I'm not sure if that's a shame or not. Now... how about you put down those knives of yours so we may continue our conversation?"

"You mean the one-sided one you're having?" Scarlett eyed him warily. "My knives stay exactly where they are. I'd love to know why you're risking yourself to confront me."

"Ahh... the crux of the matter. Well, it's quite simple really. You're easily the best agent I've ever seen. Next to myself, of course. I came here to ask you if you'd consider joining the Orion Agency."

Funnily enough, Wintyrs nearly expected him to say precisely that. Which worked out rather well, even with William grousing in her ear about the nerve of Vargas. All she cared about was the fact he wanted to talk. Even if it were merely a ruse, there would be no way the Eliminator would be activated while he was inside the building. "Say I was interested. How would you persuade me?"

The smile on Vargas' face was almost feral in nature when she provided her answer. "You would become my right hand. The highest paid and most sought-after agent. You would be the one all others would turn to for advice, for backup, for help. And you would operate with my authority. Never having to check with me before proceeding with any action. You would have my absolute trust and faith."

Scarlett stared at him. She couldn't deny he just offered her everything she'd ever dreamed of since joining the Centurian Agency. "That... is very tempting..."

"You'll have full immunity and means. Able to do anything you want, whenever you want." Mario felt he was beginning to win her over when her knives lowered slightly. "Anything you've done against Orion would be forgotten and forgiven. You wouldn't just be part of the agency. You would *be* the agency."

Swallowing, Scarlett felt her breath catch in her throat. What he'd offered, everything he said, she wondered how she could say no. Not being held accountable if something went wrong, being able to be fully autonomous while still working for an agency... it was literally every agent's dream come true. And he was willing to hand it to her on a silver platter.

"Scarlett, don't listen to him. You know he's lying. He'd never in a million years stand by what he said." William said in her ear. Vargas hadn't been the only one to notice the knives being lowered. Only William couldn't tell if she was playing along or truly tempted.

"How would that work?" Scarlett wondered, keeping her expression neutral.

"You don't need to worry about that. I'll take care of everything. Including any blowback you might experience. And you'd make significantly more than you do now. Centurian is a sinking ship. Surely you can see that. Why not save yourself? While getting everything you've ever wanted?"

"Everything I've ever wanted, huh? How could you possibly know what I want?"

"Because every agent wants the same thing." Vargas answered without a pause. "The problem is... I can't give you time to think about your answer. I need to know. Right now."

In her mind's eye, Scarlett could picture William sitting forward on his stool. His eyes were probably bugging out of his head at the thought of her being lured away. From the silence, she could tell he was speechless. One of the very few times he'd been rendered such.

"I see…" She said softly. "And if I refuse your offer?"

"I think you already know the answer to that."

"You'll kill me." Shaking her head, Scarlett allowed herself to appear amused. "That's your favourite threat, isn't it."

"I tend to stick with what works." Reaching up, Mario stroked his moustache with his right thumb and forefinger. "My dear, I'm sorry to rush you but I'm afraid I'll need your answer. As I said - right now."

Scarlett eyed him, aware the only people on this floor now were herself, the man in front of her and one other male. Since the other male hadn't departed with the two he'd supposedly been helping, she assumed he was Vargas' backup. "Well… I have to admit - you make a tempting offer…"

"But?"

"My loyalty isn't for sale. It never has been and never will be. I am an agent of the Centurian Agency and I will remain thus until my dying breath." Wintyrs stated, ignoring the quiet, yet jubilant, cheer in her ear.

"You do realize you've signed - and sealed - your death warrant."

"For some reason that doesn't have me quaking in my boots like I'm certain you hoped it would." Scarlett smiled a very little bit when the grin on his face faltered for a brief second. "I mean, think about it. How many times have you tried to kill me? I've lost count. But I'm still standing here. Stronger than ever. Your threats are meaningless. And if you somehow manage to succeed in following through then I assure you - I'll be taking you along for the ride."

Vargas narrowed his eyes at her. "I wish you luck with that, Agent Wintyrs. You won't be leaving this building. At least not while you're breathing."

"Scarlett, behind you!" William saw someone coming at her from behind and realized as she was grabbed in a bear hug with her arms pinned to her sides that his warning came too late.

Scarlett gasped as the arms around her tightened, pressing her against a broad chest and restricting her breathing. Moreso when her feet left the floor. She kicked at Vargas who grinned, retreating into the elevator. When the doors slid shut, Wintyrs knew every second counted. If Damon couldn't deactivate or render the Eliminator useless then she had maybe ten minutes before all bets were off.

"Sorry, sweetheart, but my new boss wants you dead." The Irish male voice was guttural in her ear.

New boss, he'd said. That had to mean he was one of theirs to begin with. Maybe she could reason with him. Scarlett's train of thought was derailed when the arms around her squeezed tighter. Her knives fell from her hands and she struggled to breathe. He was trained well. The attacker ensured she couldn't kick him between the legs by keeping her body angled slightly while still maintaining a firm grip on her. Blackness started to encroach on the edges of her vision. She could hear William trying to tell her something but her ears were ringing so badly she couldn't make it out. The only part that made sense was Alec's name.

"Hey pal, how about picking on someone your own size?" The familiar voice came from behind the pair and was followed by a dull thud then both of them crashing to the floor, her attacker landing on top of her, effectively pinning her down with his size and weight. "Why can they never fall where you want them to...?"

"Alec??" Scarlett gasped his name when the mountain of a man was rolled off her and she could finally see her rescuer.

"The bossman sent me." Reaching down, Storme took her hand to help her to her feet. "He said something about a damsel in distress... my favourite kind of mission."

"How did you..."

"Get here so fast?"

"Yeah."

"I kinda stole your hovercar. And I may have used the emergency thruster option... which may have burned them out but you can yell at me later. I landed on the roof, come on. We need to get the hell outta here. The EMP didn't work, Raynott's already clear just in case. I'll explain everything else once we're in the air." Alec tossed her a pair of white sneakers. "Before I forget - our Spymaster said you were barefoot... I don't think you want to be doing what we need to do without shoes. I found these in your hovercar."

"Thank you!" Bending down, she quickly slipped them on and laced them up. "How did you get down here from the roof so fast?"

"I was hoping you'd ask." Giving her a dashing smile, Storme led her past some rows of shelving which used to house boxes of files - to an open window.

Scarlett peered through the tinted glass and saw a couple of ropes dangling down the side of the building. "You repelled down. Nice. How long are the ropes?"

Alec grinned at her. "They go right to the ground... why?"

"Then we stand a chance of catching Vargas."

"We don't have time! Damon needs our help to wrest control of the Eliminator from them and take it to Myrtle to be destroyed!"

"Then go help Damon. Vargas isn't getting away this time."

"Scarlett, we can get Vargas another day. He has assets from both his agency and ours around the Eliminator. *That* is top priority. I can confirm HQ is clear save for that mountain who attacked you." William quickly lent his support to Storme.

"William, if Vargas gets away now it'll take who knows how long for us to find him again. We can't waste this opportunity!"

"Can we get out of this building and *then* debate this please??"

"Go up and get my hovercar, Alec. I'll meet you on the ground."

Storme eyed her before getting into his harness and starting to climb. Donning the harness he'd brought for her, Wintyrs moved down the outside of the structure as quickly as possible. She wanted to follow William's orders. Knew she was supposed to. But going after Vargas needed to be considered. And her Spymaster was more focused on the short-term not the long-term. If Vargas escaped again who knew what havoc he'd work up next. Which led her to the only conclusion that made a lick of sense. Of course, the consequences would be severe however the chance was one she was willing to take. The second her feet touched the ground, Scarlett looked around then spotted Vargas running towards an abandoned building across from agency HQ. And she followed suite.

Alec brought Wintyrs' hovercar down then frowned when he couldn't see her anywhere. He spoke into his comms, hoping to reach her. "Agent Wintyrs?? I can't see you. Please verify your location." When he received no answer, he swore under his breath. "Spymaster, this is Agent Storme. Do you have eyes on Agent Wintyrs?"

"Negative. Checking local cameras... still negative. Follow primary mission parameters."

"But sir...!"

"You have your orders, Agent Storme. Get away from headquarters and lend aid to Agent Raynott."

Closing his eyes, Alec swore again. "Yes, Spymaster. En route to Agent Raynott now."

Scarlett shadowed Vargas into the vacant building, sticking to the shadows while doing so. The man seemed to be moving with a purpose. Plus he seemed to know exactly where he was going. This structure wasn't that big so he couldn't go far which allowed her a bit of leeway as to how close she needed to follow. If what she saw outside was accurate, then this place had a main floor plus a second level. The only thing she didn't know was if there might be a basement. Not that it mattered for Vargas made a beeline for the stairs heading up. Given there were no doors, only a curtain, to block sound, Scarlett remained at the bottom of the narrow staircase to see if she could get an idea of what might be going on up there. Voices filtered down to her position and she wished she'd grabbed her knives when she and Alec escaped headquarters but she'd been in too much of a hurry.

"What's taking so long?" Vargas' words reached Wintyrs' ears.

"You just want the one building targeted, right?" An unfamiliar male voice answered.

"You know damned well I do."

"Even though it's been thoroughly evacuated? What's the point if no one is going to die?"

"The decoy Eliminator will echo anything the real one does. So anyone around it will also experience the event."

"Some of our own people are down there!"

"Ah, but so are some of theirs. Ours will receive the evac code shortly and the Centurians will move in to try and disable the one there. The second they do... poof. They die."

Eyes growing wide at what she'd overheard, Scarlett made the only choice she could. Leaving the building as stealthily as she'd entered, Wintyrs reactivated her comms. "Spymaster!"

"Scarlett, what the hell..."

"There's no time! Get Raynott and Storme out of there. Now!"

"What?! No. We need to get the Eliminator and permanently disable it."

"We can't know for certain that's the real one! They made a decoy and linked them together. If either of our people touch it, it'll activate! They'll be killed! They need to evac - NOW!!"

32

William stared at the screen in front of him, frozen in shock. They needed to regroup - yet again. First he had to get through to his two male agents. "Agent Raynott, Agent Storme - abandon mission immediately. I repeat, abandon mission! Do you hear me? Please acknowledge!" When the only response he received was static, he growled under his breath. "Wintyrs?"

"I'm here."

"They're not responding. Comms are being jammed."

"Damn it! Send their coordinates to my portable vid!"

"Sending now."

Scarlett took out the small vid screen and looked at the two dots now on the map. Hers was blue, theirs red. From what she saw, they weren't far away. She could get there fairly fast but with no way to send advance warning, the risk of them touching the decoy was great. "I'm already on the move. Is there anything you can do that might make them pause??"

"Maybe. It'll be tricky and I don't even know if I can do what I'm thinking of but I can try."

"Keep talking to me. It'll help me determine where the jamming signal starts." Scarlett ran to the alley where she'd dropped Damon off, knowing he must have found where they were from here. "William - can you tell if the location you sent me is underground?"

"More than likely. Those tunnels Damon used... well there's quite a network of them under where you're standing right now. A perfect location to set up either the real thing or a decoy. Okay, I'm tapped into the city's power grid."

"The power grid? What're you going to do? Turn the lights off?"

Her eyes located the tunnel access Raynott and Storme must have used as the hatch still sat open. Without a second thought Scarlett ran for the entry point.

"Thanks to my history with Damon, I know he knows morse code. I'm going to have the lights in the tunnel send a message for us."

"Wouldn't that also effectively shut down both the Eliminator and the decoy?"

"Unfortunately no. According to the schematics both units are self-sustaining. Vargas would have ensured that so what we're doing, or what I'm about to do I should say, wouldn't interfere with his plans. Which, if I'm being honest, I've got no clue as to what he's hoping for anymore."

"I don't think this was just to showcase the Eliminator to potential buyers." Scarlett's breathing grew slightly laboured as she rushed down the ladder into the tunnels. She tried to keep her claustrophobia at bay by focusing on her fellow agents as well as the conversation with William.

"Tell me what you believe he's up to then." William tried not to sound distracted while he worked on gaining access to the electrical grid. The next question she asked let him know he failed.

"Do you need me to stop distracting you?"

"You're not distracting me."

"I call bullshit on that." Hearing a slight chuckle from his end helped Scarlett ignore the growing sense of walls closing in.

"I'm okay." William said in a soft voice. "I just got into the electrical grid. Are there lights where you are now?"

Scarlett looked at the flimsy wall sconces lining the tunnel in either direction as far as the eye could see. "Calling them lights would be generous." Despite them being LED fluorescents, the bulbs cast a yellow glow on her surroundings. A very faint yellow glow.

"Better than nothing though? I hope?"

"Yeah. So why're you asking about the lights near me?"

"Because you're not too far now from Damon and Alec. Tell me if the lights flicker."

Keeping her one eye on the lighting system as she moved, Scarlett saw them give the briefest of flickers. "Yep. I assume that was you?"

"You got it. Alright, listen, I'm sorry to have to do this to you given how you feel about enclosed spaces…"

"But you don't have a choice. It's okay. Their lives are far more important. Start the flickering. As for what I've been thinking Vargas' ulterior motive is with this test... he succeeded in clearing out our headquarters, gaining entry somehow, and tricked Damon and Alec into going to the second location. Any money he can make on the Eliminator itself would just be icing the proverbial cake at this point." A burst of static hit her ear, causing Scarlett to wince. "William? Can you hear me?"

"Scar... can... arely... you... me?" William's words cut in and out through through more static.

"William, if you can hear me, I think I found the edge of the jamming signal. We're losing contact. I'll reach out once I'm clear again."

"... ger... that... careful..."

Wintyrs was able to fill in the blanks of that transmission and was about to answer when all sound from her comm unit cut out. The device now dead thanks to the interference from the jammer. Not that it mattered. Although he'd provided both a distraction and a comforting presence, she felt confident in battling her demons. When the lights began flickering in an obvious pattern, she smiled. Her Spymaster still had their backs, even if they couldn't talk to him.

Reaching a corner, Scarlett paused upon hearing voices. Definitely more than one. At least three that she could make out. Oddly enough, one of them sounded distinctly like Amir. A fact that made her eyes narrow. Carefully peering around the corner, she silently swore. The decoy was definitely there. And sitting on the ground bracketing it with their backs, tightly restrained together were Damon and Alec.

"Oh this is not good." Scarlett muttered, pulling her head back behind the cover of the wall before being spotted. With Amir were two others - one female, one male - who Wintyrs felt she recognized but couldn't be certain. She'd also made note of about half a dozen others laying unconscious on the floor. The obvious handiwork of the two men who were now restrained. Checking her watch, she unleashed a litany of silent curses. There were less than five minutes before both the Eliminator and the decoy activated.

"Well, gents, it's been fun. Alas, my friends and I must depart. Not only do we want to ensure our survival but these flickering lights are giving me one hell of a headache." Amir's words echoed off the walls. "I'd wish you a long and happy life but... well... you have less than five minutes to live. Ta-ta!"

Scarlett moved deeper into the shadows to remain unseen as Amir along with his conscious cohorts left the area. The second they were out of sight, she ran into where Damon and Alec were bound. "I just can't leave you two alone, can I?"

"Scarlett!" Damon's relief upon seeing her was palpable.

Alec tried to turn his head far enough to see her but his neck wouldn't quite crane that far around. "Don't toy with me... is she really there?"

Cocking her head quizzically, Scarlett noted Damon's 'I'll explain later' expression so she didn't ask the obvious. "Let's get you two out of those ropes."

"Yes, please. My fists have a message for Amir. One I'd really like to deliver myself." Raynott uttered.

"Just... hang tight." She knew she had to get the men loose without jostling the decoy or it would activate prematurely. "I have to be very delicate with this. One wrong move and..."

"Poof?"

"Yeah. I guess you deciphered William's message while sitting here, huh?"

"The parts that made sense, yeah." Damon shook his head. "He needs to brush up on his morse code."

Scarlett snorted at the comment then smiled when the ropes binding the two men fell away. "Come on, we need to clear the blast radius and we only have two minutes until it goes off."

"What about our sleeping friends there? We can't just leave them." The statement came from Alec who'd been rubbing his ears which, Wintyrs noted, had dried blood streaking down from them.

"There's five of them. Scarlett, if you can take one then Alec and I can drag the others out two at a time. Do we know how big a radius we have to clear??"

"I'm going to go out on a limb here. My guess would be we need to get back past the jamming signal."

"Sounds good. Let's go!"

Choosing one of the heavier set males, Scarlett grabbed him under his arms then started dragging. She noted her fellow agents took their charges by the backs of their shirt collars in order to take two at a time. The going was much slower than Scarlett would have liked. Especially with time running against them. Her comms suddenly crackled to life. As soon as the static occurred, she dropped her burden then rushed to help the two men with theirs. They barely crossed out of the jamming signal's zone before they heard what sounded like a muted hurricane force gust of wind approaching. Bracing themselves against the walls of the tunnel for they knew not what to expect, the trio closed their eyes in unison, prepared for the worst. After about a minute, a gentle breeze wafted by carrying with it the smell of death.

"Well… that was anticlimactic." Damon nearly sounded disappointed. "I have to admit I didn't think it'd smell." He crinkled his nose as if attempting to block out the odour.

"Lett… hear me…??" The broken words from William entered Wintyrs' ear.

"Spymaster? I can read you. Assets recovered safely. I'm going back for the decoy." She immediately responded.

"Excellent work. Are you certain it's wise to go back?"

"I don't think there are cameras with it. If there were, I'm hoping the detonation might have short-circuited them."

"I'll leave the decision in your capable hands. Why the Spymaster title, by the way?"

"We have a few of Vargas' folks we rescued from death. What would you like us to do with them?"

William fell silent. The news started him. Given they didn't have the facilities to hold prisoners, he could come up with only one alternative. "Have the guys tie them up. I'll alert the local authorities and send them your current coordinates. They'll come in hot so make sure you're nowhere to be found."

"Timeframe?" Scarlett noted Damon listened intently while Alec covered their unconscious 'guests' with one of their own guns.

"How long do you need?"

"Given I'm not one hundred percent on the decoy being dormant… I don't want to rush this."

"That doesn't answer my question."

"If I knew for certain…" Scarlett sighed, rubbing her brow. "I don't know… twenty minutes for that and for us to get clear?"

"I'll hold off calling for twenty minutes. I'll notify you once contact has been made. When I end comms with them, I'd guess you'd have five to ten minutes to get out of there."

"Understood, Spymaster." Scarlett moved the conversation to the two agents standing with her. "We need something to tie this lot up with."

"These tunnels have utility rooms all over the place. There should be one nearby. With luck there'll be some electrical cords inside." Damon answered, running off without giving the other two time to react or respond. He returned a few minutes later carrying the cords he'd mentioned. "I'll help Alec truss these buggers up then give you a hand with the decoy."

"I can't wait any longer." Wintyrs answered with a shake of her head. "I'm down to eighteen minutes now. Stay here with Alec. I'll be back as soon as I can."

Not interested in, nor willing to wait for, a reply from him, Scarlett jogged back to where the decoy sat waiting for retrieval by either their side or Vargas'. She approached cautiously, not wanting to activate it accidentally. Upon first inspection the weapon didn't look like much. As she grew closer, the complexity became more apparent. Her assumption had been that if this were a decoy then Vargas wouldn't have gone to much trouble creating it. What she saw made Scarlett realize that she really needed to stop forming conclusions based on what she thought Mario Vargas might do. The Orion Agency Spymaster had taken great pains in crafting the decoy. It, in fact, appeared so complex that Scarlett wondered at its intricacies.

"William, can you still hear me?"

"Yeah, I can."

"Interesting. The jamming field must've deactivated the same time this device went off."

"If Vargas thought Alec and Damon dead then he'd have no reason for it anymore."

"True…"

"You don't sound convinced."

"With good reason." Scarlett knelt down next to the metallic object resembling an old-fashioned shoebox. Only not made of cardboard. One side was plexiglass which was what allowed her to see what the inner workings looked like. "Can you hold off on calling the authorities for another ten minutes or so?"

"How about you tell me when I can make the call?" William paused long enough for her to mutter an affirmative. "Now - want to tell me why?"

Eyes never leaving the box-like device, Scarlett used the back of her hand to wipe away some sweat forming on her brow. "Because the longer I look at this, the more I think it might be the real deal."

"Wait… are you sure?"

"No. I wish I still had my glasses. I need confirmation."

"Agent Raynott? Do you still have yours?"

"Yes, Spymaster." Damon interjected himself into the conversation.

"Are the hostiles properly encumbered?"

"Oh they're not going anywhere anytime soon."

"Excellent. Please have Agent Storme remain on guard with them and take your glasses to Agent Wintyrs. Double-time it."

"Understood!"

"Should I proceed, William?" Scarlett crossed her fingers he'd say no. She didn't want to tamper with anything until he had eyes on.

"Don't touch anything yet." William advised. "Myrtle's joining me now. Hopefully we can figure this out."

"William... what if this really is the Eliminator."

"Then we try to ensure it's completely disabled and has no ability to be remotely activated before we start questioning our good luck."

"Luck, yes... not so sure about the good part." Wintyrs muttered under her breath. Like so many other things since Vargas entered the picture, if this *was* the true Eliminator then logic would dictate the scenario in which they found themselves was a setup. Of some kind.

"I'm here." Damon announced, entering the tunnel cross-section where Scarlett knelt on the floor. "Here, love. Our mutual friend wanted you to have these." He handed her the glasses. "If we decide we're taking that with us, maybe double check to make sure it doesn't have some kind of tracking device, yeah? Honestly, I'd be far more comfortable if you just smashed the blasted thing to make sure it can never work again." Giving her a wink, Raynott turned abruptly and headed back the way he'd come.

"Would that work, William? Smashing this thing to pieces?" Scarlett asked, placing the glasses on her face. "Do you have visual?"

"We can see what you see, yes. As for smashing it... while a crude suggestion and method, you probably could... hang on. What, Myrtle? Oh. Oh, yeah, that wouldn't be good. Don't smash it, Scarlett."

"Why? What'd Myrtle say to cause you to do an abrupt about-face?"

"Oh, nothing much. Just that if you were to proceed, even if it's a decoy, the power source is likely the same and has a chance of exploding."

"How big of an explosion?"

"Uh... a city block in a complete radius around your location. Hundreds could be killed. And that's only *if* it's the decoy."

"Okay. No smashing. Got it. Smashing bad."

"Myrtle's wondering if you can see the inside workings?"

"Believe it or not... yeah. Hang on..." Scarlett got down further in order to get the glasses closer to the plexiglass side. "This is the only way without me prying it open."

"Myrtle says what you can see is enough for..." William said something to the lab tech in an aside then came back to Scarlett with a voice coloured in astonishment, "confirmation."

"That it's a decoy?"

"Nope."

"So it *is* the real deal?" Scarlett backed away slowly, eyeing the box with a healthy dose of reverence.

"According to Myrtle - yes."

"That substantiates my suspicions then. What're the chances there's some kind of tracking device so he can keep tabs on it?"

"Very likely. That being said, he wouldn't have been foolish enough to install two different power supplies."

"Foolish? Why would that be foolish? I'd think it'd be smart." Scarlett frowned.

"Hang on." He spoke to Myrtle again then returned. "Sorry, I needed verification. Myrtle says from what she could see, they were able to make the firing mechanism wireless in terms of its connection to the power source. Having a strong second power source could have confused that and resulted in the Eliminator not being able to fire at all. Vargas wouldn't take that chance. And right now that power source is recharging. Which leaves us a small window of opportunity."

"To do what?"

"Get it back here."

"Look, William, I know we want to dismantle it, to prove the Centurian Agency wasn't involved in the construction of such a deadly weapon, but I'm not sure we should risk bringing it back. Vargas will have undoubtedly foreseen us doing exactly that. There has to be another way." Nothing short of the threat of excommunication from the agency would convince Scarlett to take the Eliminator anywhere near her Spymaster's vicinity. And even then, she'd probably accept punishment to ensure his safety.

"Agent Wintyrs." The seriousness with which he now spoke told her she was walking on extremely thin ice.

"Spymaster. The only way you'll get this thing there is over my dead body. I'm through playing into Vargas' hands. I know everything we've been saying is being recorded - as is what you're seeing through these glasses. Use that as evidence."

"Are you refusing a direct order from your Spymaster?"

"To keep you, not to mention our new location - even if it's temporary - safe, yes. I am. How do I permanently disable the Eliminator without bringing it back to our techs? And I mean disable in such a way it can't be ressurected."

A frustrated sigh echoed through the comms. He'd obviously realized he couldn't, or wouldn't be able to, talk her into his way of thinking. "What're the chances of you bringing it back in that state?"

"Zero. Once the power supply is removed I'm going with Damon's suggestion to smash the rest to smithereens. After I ensure there's no kind of tracking on the power source then - and only then - will I bring *that part* back for examination."

William blew out a breath, pushing his annoyance with her to the back of his mind as he realized she made some valid points. "Very well, Agent Wintyrs. I'll trust your judgement."

Scarlett closed her eyes in relief, releasing a deep breath. She'd been wondering, with his long silence, if perhaps he would be telling - no... ordering - her to bring the Eliminator back as is. No matter what. It was at that point she realized she'd never disobeyed an important order before. Not like she just did. Which in turn made her wonder how shocked her Spymaster was when she had done so. Her only hope now? That he understood her reasoning and whatever punishment awaited her wouldn't be severe.

"I'm going to need someone to talk me through this, Spymaster. Are you able to add Myrtle onto this comms channel?"

"Already done. I'm staying on the line as well."

"Understood. Myrtle?"

"I'm here, Agent Wintyrs. And I can see what you're seeing. The Spymaster was kind enough to show me the files you both uncovered regarding this device. I think I can direct you on a walkthrough." Myrtle's voice came through the comms.

"You *think*?" Scarlett raised her eyebrows.

"That's the best I can give you. You guys know as much as I do from viewing the schematics. The only difference is that, as you've told me in the past, I know more of the technical mumbo-jumbo."

Blowing out another gush of air, Scarlett nodded. "Alright. Let's see if we can't do this."

Myrtle allowed herself a momentary smile. She knew from the way Wintyrs spoke that the woman was placing her trust in her. "Okay. First thing's first. We need to get that clear side panel off."

"That's not too obvious?" Scarlett knew she'd question everything if she felt the need. Mainly because she had no desire to accidentally activate the Eliminator.

"No. They'd have needed to be able to see inside while they were encasing it. All of the mechanics and electronics in this particular device are quite complex as well as interconnected."

"That… doesn't sound good."

"Honestly it could go either way. Work in our favour or not. We have a fifty/fifty chance." Myrtle watched the screen as Scarlett pried off the plexiglass with the aid of her fingernails. "Don't touch any of the wiring yet - even accidentally."

Scarlett winced as one corner of the plexiglass nearly did exactly that. "Okay. That's something you should've warned me about *before* I started. We've got to work on our communication." Placing the piece of clear plastic on the ground beside her, she returned her gaze to the objects' internal organs. For some reason considering them thusly helped her focus. Technologically inclined she was not. At least not when it came to putting stuff like this together. Give her a hovercar to fix and she was fine. But this? Truth be told, she'd rather run into enemy fire.

"Sorry." Myrtle responded, genuine remorse in her voice. "Okay, what I want you to do is think of this like a bomb. Not a computer-controlled device which is lethal in nature."

Scarlett paused again, nearly having forgotten the way with words Myrtle seemed to have. On the other hand, after a moment's thought, she realized the suggestion did help. "Alright. I can do that. So what you're saying is as long as I snip the right wire, we're clear?"

"Well, you're going to have to snip all the wires in a specific order but yes, after that, you should be in the clear."

"Hey, Scarlett?"

"Yes, Alec?"

"Please don't blow us all to kingdom-come."

"I'll do my best."

"Not to, right?" Alec met Damon's eyes when she didn't respond. "Right?"

"Sure."

"Not exactly the confidence booster I was hoping for."

"Do you want to come do this??"

"No, no. We're good. I'll shut up now."

With a shake of her head, Scarlett refocused on her task. "Alright, Myrtle, I… don't have a blasted thing to cut these wires with. I dropped my knives back at agency HQ." The silence from Myrtle was unnerving. "Damon, can you or Alec check our friends out there? Maybe one of them has something I can use."

"Gotcha. Hang tight." Damon replied right away and a moment later could be heard muttering to the men who were tied up - even though they were all still unconscious. "Oooh... found a nice one. Bringing it now."

Footsteps echoing off the walls informed Scarlett her partner approached - at a quickened pace. Although glad he took the situation seriously, some part of her feared him tripping and plunging the blade into his own chest. The old adage of 'don't run with scissors' ran through her mind. When he stepped into the room with nary a wound, she hid her relief.

"Sorry for the wait there, love." Raynott went straight to her, handing her the prize he'd ensnared.

"It's alright." Scarlett replied distractedly. The weapon he'd placed in her palm was a work of art. Not a wide or thick blade but Wintyrs could tell from from the weight that it was made of a high-carbon steel. Possibly a 1095 rating - one of the best. Than the hilt. Oh, it was a thing of beauty. A lovely black leather covered with a golden dragon which encircled the hilt in such a way so as to provide a strong grip for the wielder. If she put her fingers in the proper spots, the dragon would lend both support and strength to her grip. "Damon... this is quite literally a work of art..."

"I knew you'd like it. You can thank one of our friends out there. I figured he wouldn't be needing it anymore."

"Thank you." Her voice was a whisper as she caressed the hilt again before wrapping her hand around it.

"But of course." Giving her a sly grin followed by the briefest of bows, Damon backed out of the room in order to rejoin Alec.

"Bet you won't lose that one." William contained the jealousy of Damon giving Wintyrs that gift to the best of his ability. Seeing how she already coveted the item... shaking his head, he concluded said jealousy was, in fact, over the knife itself. An object. He was being ridiculous and he knew it.

When Scarlett heard the tone of his voice, she had to make a conscious effort not to laugh. On the other hand she also hoped no one jumped to any conclusions over what he'd said. Or, rather, how he'd said it. "Definitely not. Whoever crafted it needs to be commended. Anyway, Myrtle, what order am I cutting these bloody wires in?"

"Sorry - your little sidebar there let me have a better look at the schematics."

"If we can believe them." Damon uttered.

"Concerns, Agent Raynott?"

"Just the usual ones, Spymaster. You know, the what-if's."

"And in regards to this?"

"What if Patrick put a bogus schematic on the server at Vargas' request because he knew we'd find it?"

"Damn it." Scarlet inhaled, closing her eyes. "I didn't want to be the one to say…"

"You feel the same, Agent Wintyrs?"

"How can I not, Spymaster? How can any of us not? Mario Vargas seems to think of everything. Which is making us second-guess any decision we make. And that's most assuredly not a good thing." Looking at the wires, Scarlett pursed her lips. "That being said, the colours on the diagram have to be accurate or we'd have known immediately upon seeing this here and now that what we found is fake. Which in turn means…"

"That the correct way to cut them is here but won't be as obvious." Myrtle finished her thought. "Bloody brilliant. Yet another reason I hate Patrick. Give me a couple more minutes with this. There has to be something in here somewhere to give us a clue as to the correct order."

"As quickly as possible please. My legs are falling asleep."

"What colours are there?" The question came from Alec.

"White, blue and red."

"The bastard made it into a riddle. Albeit one I think is easier to answer than any of you realize."

"Elaborate, please, Agent Storme."

"He made the wires white, blue and red."

"Yes, and?"

"He's like you and I, Spymaster. American. And proud of that fact."

"Do you think it could be that easy?" Scarlett quickly caught on to what Storme inferred.

"Patrick isn't Vargas." William said quietly. "Yes, he's an ass and will sell out to the highest bidder but devious he is not. In terms of how his mind works… he hates deviating from his design too much. Alec has a point… he's proud of his heritage. I'm willing to bet the correct cut order is red, white and blue."

In her mind's eye, Scarlett could envision Myrtle staring at William for his reply because he'd dare tread into waters where only she or another tech should be swimming. "Our friends make a valid point. I can't see a hint anywhere to suggest anything different so I'll take a page from our Spymaster's book and instead ask you, Agent Wintyrs, what's your gut telling you?"

"That if I cut the wrong one first we're dead."

"Besides that." Myrtle's eye-roll could be discerned in her words.

"Honestly, I feel like the guys are right."

"Then... what is it you agents always say? Follow your gut."

"Spymaster?"

"If you feel as strongly as Alec and I... then do it."

"Yes, sir." Scarlett placed her knife against the red wire. "Cutting... now."

33

"Well, we're not dead yet." Damon spoke up after making a show for Alec of patting himself down as if to reassure himself he was still alive. The amused grin on the other man's face made the effort worthwhile.

"We're also not out of the woods yet." Scarlett reminded them. "That was only one of three."

"Right. But, if I might point out, you're well on your way to proving Storme's theory, love."

"Damon?"

"Yes?"

"Please shut up and let me focus. Unless you *want* me to make a mistake..."

"Shutting up."

"Cutting white... now." Casting a glance around after doing the cut, Scarlett smiled. It was working. "And blue... now." The hum of the power source shutting down filled the room and the blue glow which had ominously filled the inside of the Eliminator dimmed until eventually vanishing. "Eliminator powered down. Myrtle? Any chance these glasses have a setting to see if there's another, independent power source which might indicate a tracking or communication device of some sort? I know what we said earlier... I want to cover all our bases anyway."

"You know you're the first - and I'd like to point out only - agent to ask or investigate that?" Sounding both pleased as well as impressed, Myrtle continued on. "Yes. The glasses have different filters for many purposes. There's a button on the left hinge for the earpiece. Pressing it will adjust the tint of the glasses. When you do, words will appear in your line of sight to advise you what mode you're in."

"Sweet." Finding out her gadgets had more features than she believed was one thing Scarlett loved about her job. After locating the button Myrtle mentioned, she pressed it once. Immediately the tint changed to red with words popping into her sightline saying 'detecting sources of power'. When she focused on the Eliminator again, a white glow appeared inside albeit faint. "Can you guys see this?"

"Sadly, no." Myrtle responded. "The filter doesn't extend to the camera function unfortunately."

"Okay. I can see a faint white glow in a corner of the wiring grid inside the casing."

"That'd be the power indicator you were hoping not to find. I guess Vargas really is that stupid. Or desperate. If it's faint chances are good it's powering something small."

"So not communications of some kind."

"Definitely not. If that were the case, the light would be bright and unmistakable as comms tend to need a fair bit of juice."

"Okay so I'm probably looking at a tracker."

"That'd be my guess. Any signs there are other sources of power in there?"

"Negative. Only that one faint spot can be seen."

"Good. Removing or disabling it shouldn't affect anything else then."

"Shouldn't? Can't you be a bit more sure?"

"Without seeing what you're seeing? No. On the plus side though - now I know where I need to improve on those glasses."

Scarlett raised an eyebrow, remembering all too well the time she nearly lost her head because of one of Myrtle's devices being enhanced but not thoroughly tested. "And you'll test them, right?"

"Okay, you seriously need to let that go. It was *one* time."

"Yeah. One time which nearly got me killed."

"Think of it this way - your death would've been quick and mostly painless."

Blinking rapidly a few times, Wintyrs was surprised their Spymaster hadn't weighed in yet. "You know, Myrtle… that really doesn't help."

"I've tried the helpful angle. It didn't work. So now I'm trying a different approach."

"Uh, ladies?" William interjected, feeling like they were veering wildly off-course. "Would it be okay with you two if we focused on the mission?"

"Yes, sir." Scarlett couldn't help the smile winding its way onto her face. The banter with Myrtle had had the desired effect. She'd relaxed once more and felt a boost to her confidence. Any lingering doubts she may have had about being able to complete this part of her mission were now tucked away in a darkened corner of her mind. Without thinking about what she was doing, Wintyrs reached in and yanked out the small piece telling her it had power. Pressing the button on the glasses once again caused the lenses to revert to their normal state. "Hey, guys? Any chance there's a sewer or something nearby?"

"Now's not the time to worry about your bladder, Scarlett." Damon stated in a flat voice.

Pursing her lips, Scarlett wished she were in the same area as Damon in order to show him what she thought of his comment. "Not why I'm asking, Raynott."

"Then why?"

"I thought I'd send our friends on a wild goose chase."

"What does one have to do with the other... oh!" A chuckle reverberated through the comms when he'd put the two thoughts together. "Oh, love that idea. Plus it'll keep them out of our hair for awhile."

"Precisely."

"Can one of you please elaborate?" Alec inquired. "I only caught part of that - one of our friends here tried to wake up."

"Scarlett wants to toss that tracker into water with a current."

"Oh... oh, I get it. Let the current carry it where it may and they'll follow. I like it."

"Agreed." The approval came from William. "Make it happen. Let me know once done and I'll contact the authorities about our friends. Don't forget to bring the Eliminator back with you when you load up. I want to have a closer look."

Even though the device was now technically disabled and she'd soon be solving the problem of the tracker, Scarlett still disliked the idea of transporting the weapon to within range of her Spymaster. The man she loved. Even though she really was trying to keep her emotions out of it. "Spymaster..."

"Please don't disobey my orders, Agent Wintyrs."

"I've already voiced my opinion on this matter, *sir*, and I'm not changing my mind."

"It would be in your best interest if you did." William replied in a tightly controlled voice.

The way he said those words made Scarlett feel like she'd been physically slapped in the face. And made her wonder if he'd speak to her the same way if they weren't involved. "Spymaster…"

"You're going to be disposing of the tracking device. Did you see any other power readings?"

"No, sir."

"Then bring it back. Myrtle will ensure there's no other surprises waiting for us once you have arrived and before it's brought inside. Will that satisfy your obvious concern for my safety?"

"Yes, sir." Wintyrs gave in, knowing he would - one way or another - get his way in the matter. Better she brought it to him then when, not if, things went sideways she'd be in a better position to debate the rationalness of the decision he'd made. "Damon, I'm coming to you with both the tracker and the Eliminator."

"Understood. You're in the clear."

Scarlett took the glasses off, placing them in the pouch on her waist. After zipping the pouch up, she took the new-to-her knife back in hand. Examining it closer, she smiled. Doubtless the blade would slide easily into the holster for her old knife for, going from memory, the blades were approximately the same size. Taking a hopeful breath, she slid the blade into the sheath, smiling as she did for it fit like the proverbial glove. Only when her hands were free did Wintyrs pick up the Eliminator and subsequently the tracker. Thankfully the device wasn't as big as some would expect, fitting snugly under her arm. Sure, it was pinching her skin a bit but the discomfort was something she could live with.

After taking one last look at her surroundings, a tickle formed in the back of her mind that she missed something. Some small detail. Yet nothing her gaze landed on rang any alarm bells. Chalking the feeling up to being a tad paranoid given their present circumstances, she headed out to Damon and Alec. Quickly moving from the room, Scarlett ran to where her fellow agents waited.

"Where's that tracker?" Damon moved to her.

"Here." Scarlett opened her left hand to reveal the sought after item sitting in the middle of her palm.

"Tiny bugger, isn't it." Using his thumb and forefinger, Raynott plucked the microchip-sized tracker from her palm.

"Tiny yet sophisticated."

"Allow me." Damon shot her a malicious grin, walking over to a stream of dirty, rancid water in perpetual motion thanks to a current.

Once next to the water source, he held his hand over it thus allowing the tracker to fall into the murky depths. "So... can we get out of here now?"

"Hell yes. I second what Agent Raynott said." Alec spoke up quickly, wanting his opinion on the matter heard.

"Alight boys, let's go." Scarlett smiled at their words. As an afterthought, she passed the message on to William. "Spymaster? We're heading out. Make your call."

"Acknowledged. See you when you get back."

Wintyrs headed out of the area, back towards the ladder she'd used to enter the tunnel system. After handing the Eliminator to Damon, she climbed the rungs back to the surface. When Damon tossed the Eliminator up she caught it easily. Her eyes scanned their surroundings while waiting for her partners to join her. The streets were empty which raised the hairs on the back of her neck. Until she concluded Vargas must have cleared a radius by closing some of the access roads to the area. An interesting thing to note as it meant he didn't want innocents in the area in case the weapon didn't go off as planned. So he had no qualms over killing but if he could avoid collateral damage, it seemed he would.

"Come on, Scarlett. Let's get the hell outta Dodge, yeah?" Damon came up next to her, Alec on his tail.

"Yeah. You guys take the Aston Martin. I'll take mine and the Eliminator. We should take different routes back to the mansion. Just to play it safe. You guys take to the air and use the direct route. I'll come in by land, using defensive driving to shake any tails given I'll have junior here with me."

"Sounds good." Raynott frowned. "'Junior'?"

"Easier to say than Eliminator and far less ominous. See you back at base."

Scarlett knew the pair of them wanted to protest her being on her own. The expression she wore, however, gave them pause and clearly changed their minds. That being said, she didn't argue the point when both men refused to leave until she was safely tucked into her car with the weapon and on her way. Part way down the street, Wintyrs glanced in her rearview mirror to the Aston Martin trailing her just slightly off the ground before flicking its headlights at her then taking to the skies.

Her eyes glanced over at the weapon sitting on the passenger seat next to her. Something still tickled her hackles. Which fit with her plan on taking the land route back to the mansion. The way she chose meant taking twice as long, even with the surprisingly low amount of traffic out and about. Wintyrs held a growing feeling their Spymaster was becoming a man with blinders on where Vargas was concerned. And him having what was tantamount to tunnel-vision was something none of them could afford. Of course, she couldn't tell him any of that. He'd only deny everything. Possibly even sideline her. Playing things close to the vest was the only solution she could come up with. Keeping her Spymaster safe went beyond his physical body. His mind needed the same safeguarding.

Despite knowing William would be tracking her vehicle's movements, Scarlett decided to add a drive by the shoreline to her route. The travel time would be made a little longer than she'd originally planned but that was alright with her. She knew once there that a stop would be an order. Not so much to think as to take it upon herself to do a bit of a deeper dive into the Eliminator. No way would Vargas have made things so easy. Of course, he may not have realized which agent would be in this position. And, sadly, she had to admit there were some whose intelligence needed some work. Perhaps what he'd been counting on.

After all, Vargas seemed genuinely surprised at her appearance at headquarters. He'd thought her dead from his trap at Dolus. Same went for Damon. Therefore why would he go to any extreme lengths to entrap an agent aiming to bring the Eliminator back as a prize for their Spymaster. Vargas' endgame was William. Likely his death, not capture. The idea of which caused an involuntary shudder to run through Scarlett's body.

Pulling into a parking spot, as secluded a one as she could find upon reaching the beach, Scarlett turned off the hovercar. She was semi-surprised William had yet to say anything regarding what she was doing but chalked her good fortune up to him being busy with other things. Even with her windows closed, Wintyrs could hear the thunderous roar of the waves when they crashed onto the beach. Only a few years ago had this place been a bustling nerve centre for shopping. A two-storey mall filled with boutiques. Until part of it collapsed because of erosion. Then the powers that be decided to make the area a beach since it was pretty much unsafe for anything else. A beach in London, though? It decidedly did not get as much use as had been hoped. People like Scarlett, however, would visit if only for some peace and quiet for a little while.

"Scarlett? Why am I showing you as being stopped? And off-course for that matter? Is everything alright?" William finally asked the questions she'd been waiting for.

"Everything's fine." Scarlett's brain moved at warp speed to come up with some kind of plausible reason for her to be where she was. "I won't be here long. My bladder decided to give me a run for my money and it won. I'll be back en route ASAP."

"Do you need me to divert Damon and Alec to your position?"

"What for? You want them to help me pull down my pants?"

"Err… uh…" Stammering at her response, William swallowed at the imagery playing through his head. "No, of course not. I just thought it unwise to leave the weapon unattended."

"Uh-huh." Smirking, for she loved chances to throw curveballs at him, Scarlett continued. "It may be unguarded however I should point out that it's sitting in a car with the best security system on the market. You worry about your end of things and let me worry about mine. Okay?"

"Alright but if you're more than twenty minutes there…"

"Then you have my blessing to send in the calvary."

"Thank you."

When he went quiet again, Scarlett sagged in relief. Hopefully twenty minutes would be all that was needed to erase her doubts about the Eliminator. Not for the first time, Wintyrs was immensely grateful she'd turned down Myrtle's offer to add surveillance to the inside of her hovercar. There were definite advantages to using her private vehicle for Agency business - one of which was being able to refuse tech from the Agency should she choose.

Using the knife obtained with thanks to Damon, Scarlett pried off the clear side of the Eliminator once more. As an afterthought, she darkened the hovercar's windows to ensure no one could look in to witness what she was doing. Seeing the electronic components confirmed she should have taken this directly to Myrtle but even to her untrained eye there seemed to be something there that didn't belong. Like an extra circuit board. Armed with the basic knowledge she had, Scarlett could say one thing for certain. She knew what kind of circuit boards were used in newer forms of technology. Which would definitely be of help now.

With careful and extremely cautious fingers which were far more nimble than what even William had thus far experienced, Scarlett gently perused the guts of the Eliminator. Three quarters of the way through Wintyrs wondered if perhaps her own caution was leading her on a wild goose chase. So far not a single circuit, wire or even connection appeared loose or disconnected in a way that would be conspicuous. The thought of disobeying William's orders for no reason made her feel nauseous. Letting him down would definitely be the worst feeling she'd ever had.

As that thought crossed her mind, however, also happened to be precisely when her fingers brushed against a material which had absolutely no business being in with computer components. The unknown item was fixed into place on the medium-sized circuit board but, holding in line with the run of bad luck they'd all experienced since the very beginning of this series of missions, it sat on the side of the board facing away from her. From what she could feel, it wasn't metal and seemed to be the size of a small bandaid. The composition of the material is what made her frown. Nearly gel-like in nature, she could press her finger into it and a small impression would remain behind. At least until the material bounced back into shape. So to speak. Removing her hand from the insides of the Eliminator, Wintyrs placed her fingers near her nose and cautiously took a sniff. An action serving only one purpose. To confirm her fears.

Which is precisely what it did.

34

"Damn it." Scarlett sat back, away from the box-like device.

"Agent Wintyrs? Your twenty minutes are almost up." William returned to the comms in time to hear her curse. "Why do I have a feeling you haven't been entirely forthcoming with me in regards to stopping where you have?"

"Because I haven't." Scarlett was loathe to make the admission but with her suspicions now confirmed, her hopes lay in his forgiveness.

"Alright. Time to bring me up to speed. Spill. You have my undivided attention."

"I pulled over... well... alright here's the complete truth. I had a strong feeling, possibly the strongest I've ever had, that we missed something. On instinct I pulled into an empty parking lot in order to facilitate a closer look."

"And?" Knowing better than most how Wintyrs' gut feelings saved her in the past, William didn't question her on disobeying his orders - at least not yet.

"I found something."

"Tell me."

"I've uncovered what I believe to be explosive material on the inner workings of the Eliminator." When he didn't respond right away, Scarlett continued. "I can't see it because of its positioning but I recognize the feel of it as well as the smell associated with this type of material."

"How big are we talking?" His voice sounded strained while he processed this latest wrinkle.

"The bomb itself is probably the smallest I've ever seen. Despite its size, however... William, I have no doubt the blast radius could easily

259

take out *at least* five city blocks."

"Just… Scarlett, how do you know so much about this particular explosive?"

"One of my first assignments. The one we talked about not too long ago."

"When you were tortured??"

"Yes. And when I unwittingly met Vargas. That gang was into moving weapons. Big, small, experimental. You name it, they dealt it. And I vividly recall them discussing a bomb that was the size of a bandaid. Mike had to refuse the buyer because it was still in the conception stage. The maker had yet to create one that didn't blow up at the slightest movement. I guess Vargas had Patrick refine and perfect it. I was able to go with Mike to see the inventor who allowed me to examine his creation however I wanted. So I ensured myself a visual and olfactory inspection."

"So… what you can feel as well as smell of this one matches that of the original?"

"They're identical."

"Can you tell if it's armed?"

There was her Spymaster. She could hear his mind working just from listening to his words. "I can't confirm or deny that given where the bomb has been positioned."

"Damn it." William closed his eyes, taking a few deep breaths in order to centre himself. "Alright, we need to operate under the assumption it's armed and ready to blow."

"Agreed."

"Will our comms run the risk of cutting off?"

"No, I don't think so. We should be good."

"How sure are you?"

"On a scale of one to we're screwed?"

"Sure."

"About a seven."

"Great…"

"I could've said we're screwed."

"Very true. Okay, you're the one with boots on the ground. Any thoughts how you want to handle this?"

"You can see my exact location, right?"

"I know your general vicinity."

"Okay… well… I have an idea but it's kinda crazy."

"Unorthodox?"

"Most definitely."

"I'm interested, tell me." Where bombs were concerned, William tended to let his agents work out what needed to be done - as long as they had some kind of past experience with explosive devices. Which he knew Wintyrs did. In abundance."

"You'll owe me a hovercar."

"Let me hear your plan first before I agree to that, darlin'. You tend to have expensive taste."

"Party pooper."

"I haven't said no. Well, not yet anyway. Also, given what you just said, I'm rerouting Damon and Alec to you. I have a feeling you're going to need a ride back if I agree to this."

"You know my hovercar can be controlled by my watch, right?"

"I do now."

"Oh... sorry." Biting her lip, Scarlett winced. She could've sworn she'd mentioned the feature in his presence but let it slide given everything going on. "Anyway... I was thinking of leaving the Eliminator where it is and crashing my hovercar into the deepest part of this body of water, letting it sink along with the explosive."

William leaned back, crossing his arms. The only other option he could think of was sending the vehicle as high as possible into the air and letting it blow up there. "What if you had the hovercar gain altitude instead of making it a submersible?"

"If we did that there's a good chance the general population will see the explosion. Underwater gives us a better chance of concealment."

Cocking his head at her words, William gave the two options open to them more consideration. While true a submerged destination would be less likely to garner unwarranted attention, he wasn't convinced it was the better of the two options. Airborne, at least today, they had the added benefit of some heavy cloud cover swiftly moving inland. If the hovercar went high enough then the explosion should end up being concealed. Not to mention no one had ever tested a hovercar underwater. He didn't think this would be the best time for that to occur. For all they knew, the vehicle could malfunction the second it was completely submerged. Although he did file the thought away for the future to see if, in fact, such a feat could be safely accomplished. Everything that just ran through his head succeeded in making the decision for him.

"We have a storm front moving in - rapidly." William stated after checking the weather radar for confirmation. "Those clouds are pretty dense. If we can get your hovercar above them we should be safe from view."

Looking up, Scarlett saw he was right. A field of thick, incredibly dark grey - almost black - clouds were indeed swiftly approaching her position. Doubtless the beginning of a thunderstorm. And lightning would be quite advantageous for the maneuver she planned to attempt. When she returned to base she'd remember to ask why he'd been almost eager to quash her suggestion.

"How close are Alec and Damon? I don't think they should be airborne when I send this thing up." Scarlett asked almost as an afterthought when she placed her hand on the latch to open the driver's door.

"You should see them any second now. They're already on the ground."

A barely audible click follow by intermittent beeps caused her to look at the Eliminator once more. "Good because I think we just ran out of time."'

"What's happened?"

"Well… it's beeping. In my experience, never a good sound."

"Then get the hell out of the car and put the plan in motion!"

"Already on the move." Scarlett opened the door just as the skies opened up, unleashing a veritable deluge so intense she could barely see two feet in front of her. Only two steps from her hovercar and she was already soaked to the bone.

Wiping water out of her eyes with the back of her hand, Scarlett looked at her watch. Using her right index finger - for she kept the device on her left wrist - she started up her hovercar. The beeping inside grew loud enough the sound could be heard not only through the closed windows but also the driving rain which made her move faster. A flash of lightning managed to elicit a flinch from her. Thunderstorms were not a weather phenomenon she liked. Or could even tolerate. So focused was Scarlett on getting her hovercar into the air, she didn't notice the other vehicle pull up next to her until Damon spoke through the comms to her.

"Get in the front passenger seat, woman! Alec climbed into the back for you. And you look like a drowned rat!"

"Thanks for the compliment." Scarlett raised her voice in order to be hear over the rain and nearly continuous thunder. "I need to be able to see what I'm doing. That means staying out here."

"You can see just as well, actually probably better to be quite frank, from in here. So get your cute ass in gear before you get struck by lightning!"

The second he mentioned the possibility, Wintyrs blinked. It dawned on her that he was quite likely right. Since she had no desire whatsoever to see if his hypothesis would, or could, be proven, Scarlett ran to the passenger door and climbed inside while never once taking her eyes off her hovercar or the precious cargo contained within. In order to properly see what she was doing, Scarlett leaned as far forward in her seat as possible to look out the windshield. The rain fell hard enough now that she couldn't see a thing.

"William? Can you tell where my hovercar is? This weather's too intense. I have no clue where it is!"

"I have it on traffic radar. You need to gain a bit more altitude to be safe."

"Roger that. Thank you." Scarlett continued to instruct her beloved hovercar to go higher even though an alarm began sounding on her watch. She didn't need to read the message being sent. The safety system in her vehicle was providing a warning that the car neared its maximum tested threshold for altitude. "If I go any higher, William, the engine will stall out and the entire kit and caboodle will plummet back to earth."

"Hold her steady there then. I don't think we'll have to wait very long before..."

Their comms cut out without warning, not allowing the Spymaster to conclude the thought he'd begun. Scarlett fixed her gaze on the area she knew her hovercar disappeared into. Through the flashes of lightning she was able to discern a brighter, as well as slightly greener, burst of illumination. If she hadn't been looking for it, she might have missed it completely. Which gave her hope that the general populous may have done exactly that.

"Uh, guys? My comms are dead." Alec broke the silence from his position in the rear of the Aston Martin.

"Same here." Damon looked over to Scarlett, noting water still dripped freely from her hair and clothing. He also saw her shivering though she tried to hide it. Awkwardly slipping out of his black jacket, he gently placed it around her shoulders with the hope she might feel a bit warmer. "Are you able to tell if it worked?"

Wintyrs gave him a smile of thanks when the jacket wrapped around her. She hadn't realized the cold started to seep through her skin until Damon did that. "From what I saw, yeah. The plan worked.

My hovercar, and doubtless the Eliminator along with it, have been destroyed." A tinge of remorse coloured her words. "I'm not quite sure why our comms have been knocked out."

"Well, knowing William, he's probably going nuts trying to find an answer to that very question. Do we need to look for debris, do you think?"

Moving her gaze to the turbulent water in front of them, Scarlett narrowed her eyes to see if she could spot anything floating on the surface. After a minute she sighed. With the amount of rain coming down, the surface of the water was too volatile to see debris - if there even was any.

"Make note of the coordinates we're at right now." Alec suggested. "With this weather there's no way we'd find anything. We need to wait for calmer skies - not to mention water. So if we have the coordinates we can do a sweep later if the big man wants us to."

Scarlett wiped some water droplets from her face while listening to him then nodded agreement. "Good thinking, Alec. That's what we'll do."

"I keep tellin' people. I'm not just a pretty face."

While Damon prepped the Aston Martin for air travel, Wintyrs used her watch to record their precise location as Storme proposed. She'd never worked with the man before this mission but her respect for him was growing. "Alright. Coordinates saved. Let's head for base."

"Your wish is my command, Agent Wintyrs." Damon grabbed the steering yoke and proceeded to take to the airways for a quicker journey. "I'd still love to know what fried our comms. It couldn't have been an EMP since the car's still working."

"You don't like driving in silence, do you?" Scarlett noted, not having realized until now that he'd never really been quiet for any lengthy duration they'd been in a car together for.

"Nah. Time goes by slower when you've got nothing to do."

"You do know that's not actually true, right?" Alec leaned forward in order to be part of the conversation.

"I didn't mean it literally." Raynott glanced in the rearview mirror at his friend. "It was figurative."

"Do you even know what those words mean?"

"If I weren't driving..."

"You'd what? We both know I'm faster than you."

Scarlett looked out her window in an attempt to quell her humour at their conversation. Judging from the nuances in their speech patterns, she felt confident the pair of them were teasing one another. An activity she'd normally love to partake in however the problem of their dead comms continued plaguing her. The fact they went down at precisely the same moment the explosion occurred could only mean the two events were linked. Coincidence wasn't something she liked. Especially in a scenario such as this.

"What do you think, Scarlett?"

"Huh?" Startled by Damon saying her name, she dragged her attention back to the man in the vehicle with her. "I'm sorry, I wasn't listening"

"Yeah, we kinda noticed."

"So what were you asking my opinion on?"

"Nothing." He grinned. "I made a bet with Alec that you were ignoring us. You just won me twenty quid."

"Ha!" Storme snorted. "You only win if she admits she was ignoring us and not just distracted by her thoughts."

"Oy! No changing the rules after I clearly won the bet!"

"We never clarified how you could win."

"My point exactly!"

"Boys!" Scarlett raised her voice in order be heard over the pair. "How about this - I wasn't ignoring anyone, I was thinking about the mission. Which also means technically not distracted. Which then means the only one who may have snagged that twenty quid would be yours truly."

Alec blinked a few times then locked eyes with Damon in the mirror. "Bet? What bet? Do you remember making a bet?"

"Nope. Keep your wallet in your pants."

"You guys really hate losing don't you?" Scarlett raised her eyebrows at their antics.

"We don't hate losing."

"Alec's right. We just can't stand the thought of you outwitting us." Damon clarified quickly.

Scarlett opened her mouth to respond but closed it just as quickly. She knew Raynott tended to use humour after tough missions or when he felt nervous. Apparently Alec employed the same technique. Given what they just went through, she couldn't fault them for that. However she also wasn't about to encourage them. At least, not at the moment.

"Nothing to say, Wintyrs?" Storme's puzzlement over her lack of response echoed in his words.

"Nope. Not a damned thing."

"Really? Well... that sucks."

"Sorry, Alec. I don't really feel like playing big sister to two adolescent boys at the moment."

"I wouldn't have called you our sister after you managed to extinguish our lovely conversation."

"Indeed. What would you have said then?"

"Careful, Alec. This smells like a trap." Damon warned the other man as they approached the mansion.

Looking back and forth at the pair in front of him, Alec eventually shook his head. "Yeah, you're right. I'm not saying a damned thing."

"Are you sure?" Scarlett cast a glance over her shoulder at him, keeping her face as neutral as possible. "I do have experience with extracting information you know."

Alec swallowed involuntarily. With her expression seemingly etched in stone and her voice completely monotone, he couldn't tell if she was kidding or not. "Yeah, I think I'll keep my silence thanks. And no matter how you try, you'll never get me to talk."

"Alec, buddy, quit while you're ahead." Laughing, Damon parked the hovercar in front of the main entrance. "You're already playing right into her hands."

"Well don't *tell* him." Wintyrs complained before grinning at the man in question. "Sorry, Alec. That was me kidding around."

"We need to work on that." He wiped his brow with an exaggerated movement.

Unable to stop the soft chuckle from leaving her lips, Scarlett stepped out of the hovercar. When she turned to face the house, she discovered William on the porch with his arms crossed over his chest and a set expression on his face. Even from this distance she could see he wasn't happy. Looking around the driveway and front lawn, she noted there were quite a few more vehicles parked there. A sight which told her some, if not all, of the remaining loyal agency assets who were in headquarters made their way here. None of the cars appeared to have any damage so she hoped they all arrived unharmed.

"Hey bossman!" Damon called out to William as soon as he cleared the Aston Martin. "You've had someone check over all these cars, right? Make sure they're good to be here?"

"It's been taken care of, Damon, thank you. Why did we lose comms?"

"Well, sir," Alec heard the question as he joined Damon, "we were kind of hoping you could tell us. Comms went off right when the Eliminator detonated."

The silence from their Spymaster suggested to the trio he was either thinking or had absolutely no idea. Scarlett moved towards the porch, concerned as the silence stretched on. Usually he'd say something, even if he didn't know, after a minute or two yet this time seemed different. That's when she noticed his pallor. He'd gone deathly pale, gripping the railing with both hands while obviously using it as a support to remain on his feet.

"William? What is it?" Scarlett asked softly, reaching out to gently touch his arm.

Startled by the touch, William's gaze flicked to her. "It was only your three comms that failed. Myrtle tested other ones we still had here. Damn him. What the hell is he thinking."

"Vargas?"

"Who else?" Taking a deep breath in then slowly releasing it, William chewed the inside of his cheek. Colour returned to his face despite how he remained feeling. Cold inside and out. That was the only way he could describe it. "If he's had Patrick make…" he trailed off, rubbing his brow.

"Make what, William?"

"Not even he could be so… so…" William shook his head as disbelief overcame him.

"William, old boy!" Damon moved up to the porch, snapping his fingers directly in front of his friend's face. "Snap out of it and share with the rest of the class whatever is going through that bloody brilliant mind of yours."

"Besides what could he make that's worse than the Eliminator?" Storme spoke next, eyeing the Spymaster with mounting worry.

"It's not what…" William pressed his lips together. "If what I suspect is right… I think Vargas is creating every device outlawed like the Eliminator was. The most dangerous and deadly. The ones every Agency agreed none of us should ever possess. And I think he's doing it right in our own backyard."

35

"William, why would you think he's making..." Scarlett began, stopping when he started to answer before she finished speaking.

"Because of two very key things. What happened with your comms being the first."

"Okay, what's the other one?"

"No one would have any sort of defence against any of those items."

"And let me guess - most of them were dreamed up by Patrick."

"Yep." William rubbed his eyes. "Which leads us to a larger problem."

"How many restricted or prohibited things has Patrick dreamed up."

"Precisely. I only know about *some* of his creations from his time with our agency. And I'm sure I've only seen the tip of the iceberg."

"So what do you want us to do, boss?" Damon leaned back against the stair railing, crossing his arms as he asked his question.

"For now? Get cleaned up. All three of you. When you're done, come and find me. I hope you don't mind, Scarlett, I've commandeered your office where that secret lab area is."

"That's absolutely fine, William. I'm happy to provide a place for us to fall back to. Have you spoken with the other agencies yet?"

"I've sent messages asking to be heard via a channel Vargas literally has no way to influence."

"Which means the other agencies will listen?"

"Well it means they might read it. I'm hopeful they will as I provided what we had on the Eliminator, Patrick and Vargas."

"So no guarantees they'll bring us in from the cold."

"No. If they did take our agency off their blacklists, it'll be some time before they trust us again. Even if we're technically all rivals, we still hold a modicum of trust for each other and share vital information."

"Like Vargas, Patrick, the Eliminator or an agency going off the books and engaging in activities like what Vargas is doing."

"Exactly. We hold each other accountable."

Scarlett nodded silently, absorbing what he'd told her. "Are you trying to get Orion blacklisted then?"

"In our position, and without physical evidence, there's no way I can go forward with that no matter how badly I want to. That's why I really wanted you to get the Eliminator back here. I'm not sure a picture will be enough."

"You have the schematics too." Damon pointed out. "And, for the record, you do know Scarlett sacrificed her incredible hovercar to save who knows how many lives, right?"

Sighing, William chewed the inside of his cheek again. A habit he knew he really needed to stop. "I'm well aware, Damon. Thank you for reminding me." He met Scarlett's eyes. "Thank you for what you did and the sacrifice you made to save so many lives."

Lips twitching as she fought a smile, Scarlett tilted her head slightly. "That sounded very official."

"Good." He chuckled. "It was meant to."

"Ahh so... gotcha. You fulfilled your official duty... now how do you *really* feel?"

"That's a discussion we'll have in private." William crossed his arms, telling them there was no room for debate on the subject.

"Come on, Alec. Let's get cleaned up like our Spymaster told us to." Damon grabbed Storme's arm and pulled him into the house.

"And for now please call me William! Not the other word!" He called after the two men then looked at the woman still with him. "That goes for you too. I haven't told everyone who I am yet."

"Probably smart." Scarlett leaned back against the porch railing. "You going to ream me out now?"

Pressing his lips together while keeping his arms crossed, William stood silently for a moment. When he felt ready to speak he started pacing back and forth in front of her. "You know I can't treat you any differently just because of..."

"I know, William. Just as you know I don't expect you to."

"Good... good..." He stopped pacing directly in front of her in order to meet her eyes. Rubbing a hand over his mouth and goatee, which was growing in nicely as he worked on changing his facial appearance - albeit slowly. "You knowingly and willfully disobeyed your direct orders."

"If I hadn't, this place would be a crater right now and you and I wouldn't be having this conversation because we'd be dead - like everyone else here."

"That hasn't been lost on me. And if you hadn't lied about why you had stopped then this conversation might have been completely different."

Scarlett winced, bowing her head. "What would you have said if I *had* told you the truth about what I intended?"

With two gentle fingers placed under her chin, William raised her head so they were face to face once more. Searching her eyes, he could see a hint of regret in their depths. "I know you do things for a reason. Always. Even defying orders. You've never lied to me. That's what bothers me the most. If I'm being honest, of course. As for what I would have said - I guess we'll never know. A formal reprimand will be put on your file. We have to decide what to do about the lying. I know it's part of the job…"

Taking a deep breath, Scarlett placed her hand over his fingers which lingered on her chin. "If I need to lie in order to protect you, even from yourself, then you need to understand that's precisely what I'll do."

William narrowed his eyes slightly at the response he received. "I suppose I can't really stop you, can I?"

"Not if you want me to do my job, no." She pulled his fingers down in order to hold his hand. "My, and all of our, main purpose is to keep you alive. And we're all willing to do anything to achieve that goal. What I did today, I did for the greater good and I can only ask your forgiveness for lying to you."

William kept a steady gaze upon her. Eventually he began shaking his head, a smirk on his face. "You want to know the really crazy thing about all of this?" He rubbed one hand over his face.

"What's that?" Sensing she was about to be forgiven, Scarlett let her muscles relax.

"I had this exact same conversation with the last Spymaster when I was an agent. And I swore I'd never subject one of my agents to it."

Grinning at him, Wintyrs nodded slowly. "So what happened?"

"I became Spymaster and started spouting his rhetoric I guess."

"Beer break?"

"Hell yes."

Scarlett grabbed his hand again then dragged him inside to the kitchen. Releasing him once there, she went over to the fridge where she liberated two bottles of beer. Popping the tops off both, she handed him one and watched as he took a good slug while she gently sipped at hers. "I'm going to guess I'm forgiven?"

"Mmmh... yeah. Yeah, you're forgiven." William leaned against the counter, beer bootle in hand. "Why do I feel like that was a leading question?"

"You have killer instincts?"

He sighed. "Alright. Hit me."

"I'm worried about you."

"Uh, okay... why?"

"Because I'm starting to think that - when it comes to Vargas - you have blinders on." The way he looked coupled with his silence disturbed her. "Say something. Please."

Taking another long drink from the bottle in his hand allowed him an excuse to continue his silence while he thought about what she'd said. Eventually, after reviewing everything they'd done in his mind, he could reach only one conclusion. That she had every right to be concerned. "Scarlett... you're right." The only indication he had that he'd startled her with his response was when she quirked her left eyebrow upwards. "I should have seen it. I didn't. If you had blindly followed my orders... damn it." He polished off the beer then shook his head. "My single-mindedness would've gotten us all killed."

"Which is precisely the reason you trust your agents and believe they are doing what they think is in the best interests of the Agency. And you."

William nodded, placing the empty bottle on the counter. "Again. You're right. Thank you. Now..." He cleared his throat, "you should go get cleaned up. I need to talk with Damon and Alec and you look like you're been through the wringer. Literally. When you're ready, please join me in the office?"

"Of course." Scarlett moved to him quickly, pinning him against the counter, and stealing a passionate kiss. "We need some alone time later."

"Damn right we do." William winced when his voice cracked from the feelings she managed to get rushing through his body, causing him to clear his throat again.

Knowing precisely the effect she'd had on him, Scarlett flashed him a smile before sauntering off to follow his instructions. After a warm, slightly longer than normal shower, she went into the wardrobe to get a dry set of clothing. Quickly choosing a loose black sweater and another set of jeans - this time a light blue - she dressed then put her hair back in a braid without drying it. For the first time in awhile she decided to go sans makeup. Not even lipstick. It'd be interesting to see the reactions she received - if any. Lastly, Scarlett put on a pair of close-toed sandals which had no heel. With a soft sigh, Wintyrs closed her eyes to let some of the tension drain from her body.

"Scarlett? You in here, love?"

Shoulders drooping, for she knew her brief respite was already at an end, Scarlett rose to her feet from the cushioned bench at the end of her bed she'd sat on in order to put on the sandals. "Yeah, Damon. And please stop calling me that."

"Nah. Are you decent?"

"Never but I am clothed."

His baritone chuckle penetrated the door while he swung it open in order to gain entry. "You've been hanging around me way too long if you're making comebacks like that."

"Hell, I could've told you that. What's up?"

"You seen Storme anywhere?"

"You're kidding right?" Scarlett allowed a hint of amusement to show. "I've been in here since I finished my meeting with William."

"Well for all I know he could be hiding in here." A mischievous grin came to rest on his face.

Scarlett moved swiftly and tossed a pillow at him. "Shut it, Raynott. Did you check the study? William did say he wanted to do a debrief with each of you after you cleaned up."

Damon snapped his fingers. "The study. Of course. Now why didn't I think of that."

Shaking her head with a small, disbelieving snort, Scarlett eyed him. "Maybe because you're stalling? I have this strong feeling you don't like the idea of debriefs."

"To be fair, the last debrief I had was the first time the previous Spymaster tried to have me killed."

"Oh." Wintyrs felt a wave of shock roll over her. "Yeah, that'd turn me off of one-on-one debriefs as well."

"Right? So, uh..." he scratched his head, revealing the awkwardness he felt, "will you come with me? Please?"

"Damon - William isn't going to kill you."

"You sure about that?"

"I better come with you." How she managed to say that with a straight face boggled her mind.

The pair walked out of the room and down the stairs in a comfortable silence. Scarlett discovered she felt more at ease than she had for awhile. Perhaps due to the Eliminator no longer being in play but she couldn't say for certain. Of course the second she thought of that, she felt herself tense up again. Mainly due to the fact realization dawned that their nemesis had access to the schematics and Patrick which meant he could create another one. Hopefully they had some time before that happened.

"Penny for your thoughts." Damon said when they stepped off the stairs, noting she had a distant look in her eyes.

"Sorry... thinking about Vargas again. Knowing he could create another Eliminator whenever he wants... it's sobering." She answered, leading him towards the office William had commandeered.

"Hey." Taking her hand, Raynott pulled her to a stop then made her face him. "Listen. True, the war isn't over. Not by a long shot. But we - especially you - put a major damper on his plans today. We won this battle. Celebrate the win."

"You're right. You're absolutely right." Scarlett rubbed her face with both hands then gave him a smile.

"And I hope you don't mind me saying this - you look amazing."

"I don't have makeup on..."

"Like I said - you look amazing. Just... don't tell William I said that. I don't need a black eye."

Before Damon made mention of that, Scarlett hadn't considered if the man her heart belonged to was the jealous sort or not. Picturing him as such proved a challenge given how warm and caring she knew him to be. "I didn't know he was the type to be jealous..."

"If you looked in a mirror recently, you wouldn't question it." He smiled wryly. "Shall we?"

With a small nod, Scarlett led him the rest of the way to the office. When she saw the door stood closed, the automatic conclusion she arrived at was Alec beat them there. Wintyrs raised her hand and knocked on the door a couple of times to announce their arrival. No immediate answer came which she'd suspected would happen. She moved to the other side of the hall in order to lean against the wall while being in full view of the door. Damon joining her made her grin. She was about to initiate another conversation with him when the door

273

opened without warning. Alec walked out, giving them the barest of nods before disappearing down the hallway.

"Come on in you two." William called out to them. "And close the door behind you please."

Scarlett preceded Damon into the office, hearing her partner close the door after he entered as well. "Did you want to see us individually?"

"No, it's okay. Thanks though, Scarlett. Agent Storme gave me a very detailed debrief on behalf of the three of you." William looked up from the paperwork he was signing, raising his eyebrows while noting she still carried the new knife she'd acquired in a holster at her hip. "I just wanted to see if you had anything to add to Alec's statement." He reached across the desk and handed the papers to Damon to review first.

After a minute of reading, for he only scanned over the words to see the salient points, Damon shook his head. "This is more thorough than I expected. I've got nothing to add." He let the woman next to him take the sheafs of paper.

Scarlett sat down in one of the chairs across from William while she perused the report. The way it read nearly sounded like Alec recorded everything and played it back during the debrief. "Okay this is... I don't think even I've given reports like this."

"Only Agent Storme is this... shall we say meticulous? While you have a photographic memory, his is eidetic. His mission reports are always like this one."

"I don't think he missed a thing." Scarlett handed the papers back to their Spymaster. "Where'd Alec take off to in such a hurry?"

"Classified." William lessened the harsh impact of the word by giving her a warm smile. "For now, there are no assignments outside of this building. I need everyone's help getting things set up here until we find a new home for our agency. Zaliki and Feiyan have been tasked with researching that. Can you both examine anything they come up with for weaknesses, et cetera? I want our new headquarters even more secure than the last. No matter what it takes."

"You got it, bossman. They in the dining room?"

"Good guess." William watched Damon leave then turned his attention to Scarlett. "Are we okay?"

Standing up and moving behind the desk to where he sat, Wintyrs answered him the only way she could. And when their lips locked, she knew she had truly come home at last.

36

Agent Alec Storme steeled his nerves after climbing out of the Aston Martin he'd 'borrowed' for this trip. The building looming in front of him easily stood ten stories tall. Its exterior was comprised of black brick and the windows were tinted as dark as they could possibly go. Appropriate architecture for Raven's Way. Given the surroundings, this structure blended in with everything else around it. No one would suspect its true purpose. That of being the headquarters for the Orion Agency. Unless, of course, they uncovered the same information he had. Taking a deep breath, Alec moved to the double doors which served as the entrance, pulled one open and proceeded inside.

The second the door closed behind him an alarm blared. Red lights flashed like lights on an old-fashioned police cruiser, penetrating the darkness of the dimly lit lobby. Narrowing his eyes in the hope they would adjust to the ever-changing brightness, Alec realized he was no longer alone in the vast room. He was, in fact, surrounded by darkly clad men and women in what appeared to be full combat gear - including armed rifles. Storme raised his hands in order to appear less threatening.

"I'm looking for Mario Vargas." Alec called into the round. "Is he here?"

"You've got some balls coming here and looking for him. Who's asking?" The answer emanated from the darkest corner of the room.

"My name is Alec Storme. I need to speak with Spymaster Vargas."

"Why is that?"

It dawned on Storme that the man entering the circle of armed guards with him had a striking air of authority about him. There was no doubt in his mind - this was Vargas. "Because I have a question for you."

"For me? You think I'm this Vargas fellow?"

"I don't think. I know. I work for the Centurian Agency."

"Oh, I'm well aware of that. Why do you think there are so many guards here?" Vargas looked the newcomer up and down, appraising him. "I'd advise you to speak quickly. I'm not exactly known for my patience."

Alec's adam's apple bobbed up and down as he swallowed hard. "I overheard the last conversation you had with Agent Wintyrs. Is that offer open to any Centurian Agent?"

"Why do you ask?"

"Well... if it is... then I'd like to accept."

A feral smile crossed Vargas' face upon hearing those words. "Welcome to the Orion Agency, Agent Storme."

To Be Continued...

If you enjoyed this book and series (so far), please leave a review for other readers (and the author) on Amazon and/or Goodreads.

About the Author

About the Author

A. N. Jones lives with her family and two dogs in Ontario, Canada. She has a diploma in Law and Security as well as Cyberspace Security (post-graduate diploma with honours).

She is currently focusing all of her writing energy on this series as it is nearest and dearest to her heart. Writing is her passion and she delves into it whenever she has time. Telling stories is more than just a hobby for her - it's a calling.

If you enjoyed reading this book, and the volumes prior to this in the series, please leave a review on your local Amazon website and / or Goodreads.

You can find the author on Facebook and Twitter ("X") (@authorANJones).

You may also email the author at: anjonesauthor@gmail.com

Thank you for reading The Scarlett Divide!

Manufactured by Amazon.ca
Acheson, AB

12855684R00157